O9-ABE-920

On Ice

Also by David Ramus

Thief of Light
The Gravity of Shadows

On Ice

DAVID RAMUS

POCKET BOOKS
New York London Toronto Sydney Singapore

This book is a work of fiction. Names, characters, places and incidents are products of the author's imagination or are used fictitiously. Any resemblance to actual events or locales or persons, living or dead, is entirely coincidental.

POCKET BOOKS, a division of Simon & Schuster Inc.
1230 Avenue of the Americas, New York, NY 10020

Library of Congress Cataloging-in-Publication Data

Ramus, David.
On ice / David Ramus.
p. cm.
ISBN 0-671-04184-3
1. Government investigators—Georgia—Atlanta—Fiction. 2. Horse breeding—Fiction. 3. Atlanta (Ga.)—Fiction. I. Title.

PS3568.A4745 O5 2000
813'.54—dc21 99-089929

First Pocket Books hardcover printing June 2000

10 9 8 7 6 5 4 3 2 1

Designed by Lisa Stokes

Printed in the U.S.A.

BP/X

For Jessica, Juliana, Nikki, and Sidra

Acknowledgments

Thanks to Jason Kaufman and Ben Kaplan at Pocket for believing in this book, and to Molly Friedrich, Aaron Priest, and Paul Cirone; they know why. For an inside look at horse breeding I am indebted to Priscilla Baldwin, Mimi Parker, Dr. Krista Seltzer, Dr. Ben Schachter, Dr. Dan Sharp at the University of Florida Animal Sciences Department, Dr. Julia McCann at the University of Georgia Equine Program, and Dr. Kit Miller. Thanks to Dr. William Ray, an enthusiastic friend and reader, for his intelligent criticism. Barn building is an art, and Elrick Endersby and his assistant, Cheryl, were kind enough to share a little of their enthusiasm and expertise. For medical advice as it pertains to humans, Dr. Mitchell Hoffman and Dr. Dan Greenwald were more than generous. Thanks to Steve Halsey at Geo. Fowler Welding Supplies for running more than one dicey experiment with liquid nitrogen. Special thanks to Maurice Scharfer, for helping me understand Rollie Shore's misguided identification with his religion. This book would never have been finished without the help and support of Marion Freshman and Connie Kaufman. Finally, I am most grateful to Cathy, for reasons too numerous to list.

Any mistakes are mine.

On Ice

1

Guilty. A tough word to get your tongue around. A bitter mouthful—hard to chew, harder to swallow. I choked on it the first time I heard it used in the same sentence as my name. And time, the one thing I had plenty of, didn't help. It never does in prison.

I'd been down for eighteen months. Eighteen endless months. Half of a thirty-six-month bit I never bargained for. Innocent? Who's not innocent in prison? You tell the judge it was all a terrible mistake, a mistake you deeply regret. Only she's heard it all before. You appeal to a higher court. Everyone appeals. But it's easier to win the lottery than have your case overturned. So you do the time, try your best not to let it do you. Some days it's easy. Other days it's hell. Either way, you just keep breathing. It passes. Slowly, but it passes.

The Bureau of Prisons had designated me to a minimum-security prison camp located in northern Alabama, an unfenced compound cut into the red clay foothills of the Appalachian Mountains. The camp, set hard against the outer fences of a high-security Federal Correctional Institution, was crowded with the FCI's overflow. True, the worst of the violent offenders, the lifers, the serial killers, and head cases were behind the guard towers and concertina wire. But any thoughts that I would do my time rubbing elbows with crooked politicians and bent businessmen went out the window the minute I entered the system.

Eight out of ten of my fellow inmates were drug dealers. Most of the rest were a mix of losers and sociopaths who'd done everything from robbing banks to peddling stolen military hardware. There were murderers and pimps. Gang enforcers lucky enough to have been popped carrying vials of rock instead of their Tec-9's and Mac 10's—the deadly tools of their calling. Tools they handled as skillfully as I handled a finish hammer or a miter saw. Like it or not, these were my neighbors. The men I bunked with. We shared a world of hard surfaces and bright fluorescent lights. A cloistered world where violence was a fact of life—barter the lubricant that kept the place from actually exploding. Even so, after a year and a half inside, I thought I had it wired—that all I had to do was lay low, let the days glide by until it was time to go home.

I was wrong. Nearly dead wrong, as it turned out. I didn't know about real trouble. Not yet. No, the real thing came calling the day Black was explaining the evils of pork. Only at first, I didn't recognize it for what it was.

It was mild that day. The long summer had been wetter than normal. Curtains of rain graying the green humps of the mountains surrounding us—cooling the air and dampening tempers. I didn't complain. When men are crowded into small spaces and there's nowhere to go—no break from the constant friction of strangers rubbing up against each other, the noise, the taste and stink of male sweat, fear, anger, and desperation—it doesn't take much more than a heat wave to set things off. Nothing much had happened lately. But you learn to watch for trouble the way the weatherman on channel 5 watches the Doppler radar scope for tornadoes. That screen lights up, you take cover. Not that I didn't know how to handle myself. You don't bounce around the construction trades for the better part of two decades without learning the hard way that there are times when words just won't get the job done. I knew how to use my fists. But by the ripe old age of thirty-eight, I also should have known enough not to throw my cards on the table without a goddamned good reason. Especially in here.

We were on the rec yard, watching 1-dorm play 3-dorm a half-assed game of softball. Black, my celly, one of the most graceful athletes I'd ever seen, was sitting this one out. Something about the lack of decent pitching—that hitting the crank chemist 3-dorm had put on the mound was too easy to be any fun. A group of us were lounging on the aluminum bleachers between third base and home plate, shirts off, enjoying the gentle Alabama breeze. "It'll kill you," Black was saying. "Pork ain't nothin' but fat and cholesterol. Don't believe me; look at Truck. The man's a walkin', talkin' disaster."

"You hear that, Truck?" Reggie Everett asked. Reggie was like that. An old ponytailed hippie, always seeking the alternative point of view. "The man says you eat too much pork. That true?"

Tony "Tow Truck" Tucker shook his big head and watched the catcher from 1-dorm hit a looping pop-up to short right. "Ain't but one problem with pork," Truck said after the second baseman made the easy out.

"What's that?" Reggie asked.

"Only thing wrong with a pig is it don't get as big as a cow," Truck declared, to Reggie's delight.

Black snorted. "You big as a cow, Truck."

Truck nodded thoughtfully and slapped his ample belly. "More like a bull. Grade A prime black stud. Make them country girls cry for joy."

"What do you think, Ben?" Reggie asked me.

Truck interrupted. "Hemmings's married—he don't know shit about country girls. He the strong silent type—might be he used to know how to live rough, but he a family man now. Wouldn't know what to do with a big ol' wild country booty it smacked him right in the face."

I looked at Truck—all three hundred fifty–plus pounds of him. "Take a damned big booty to smack you in the face."

"Shit! You talkin' like every other skinny white man I know." Truck slapped his belly again. "This right here is a sign of intelligence."

"Intelligence, my ass," Black shot back. "It's the pork, man. You eat the pig, you become the pig."

It went on like this for a while. Easy banter. No one taking anyone else seriously. The afternoon sliding by—soft time. Until an angry buzz started over by the handball courts. Then, the muttering ceased as quickly as it had started. The softball game stopped. So did the rhythmic clank of steel plates coming from the weight pile.

Suddenly the yard was quiet. Dangerously quiet.

"Trouble," Black said, turning his head as though he were sniffing the air to find the source. "Hinchee's on duty, isn't he?"

I nodded. "Saw him earlier. By the weight pile."

"Well, he on the handball court now," Truck said. "Gonna go see what's up." He hopped off the bleachers, surprisingly agile for a man his size.

I stood, too.

Black, having done hard time in three different FCIs, knew better. He shot me a warning look, but I was curious. So I left him sitting on the bleachers and followed Truck.

A silent crowd had gathered on the cracked cement court. In the center of a knot of grim-faced inmates, Corrections Officer Billy Hinchee, a soft-looking hack with a crew cut and a nasty sadistic streak, brandished an aluminum softball bat at Sally. "Fucking mutt bares its teeth at me again, I'm gonna kill it." He waggled the bat. "I'll fucking launch brain matter."

Hinchee's partner, a mellow, older hack named Peterson, stood outside the circle of men, radio in hand, a disgusted look on his face. He might not have liked what Hinchee was doing, but he was trained to back his partner no matter what. If this turned any uglier, it was a good bet he'd call in the SORT goons, a bunch of riot-geared, ready-response hacks who wade into any situation swinging lead-weighted batons. Covered from head to toe in body armor, they hit hard and ask questions later. In prison, there's no such thing as an innocent bystander.

But Sally, a brown-and-white puppy that had somehow found her way onto the compound, didn't know any of this. She shook herself and pranced around on her toes, growling. Maybe she thought it was all a game.

Hinchee didn't look amused. He cocked the bat and swung with all his might.

Sally dodged the blow and barked excitedly. Now the game was getting good.

Someone shouted, "I'll take the dog. Ten to one on the mutt."

Someone else laughed.

The taunts egged Hinchee on. Any chance of his backing down disappeared. He had blood in his eye. A little big man, as long as he wore the uniform.

A nervous ripple went through the crowd; the circle of men a living ring, moving and flowing around Hinchee as he waved the bat at the young dog, who hadn't the sense to get the hell out of there.

For that matter, neither did I.

The puppy, not the first stray to wander onto the compound, had been adopted by Dr. Dave, Rollie Shore's bodyguard and enforcer. I wondered if Hinchee knew. Dr. Dave, once a club fighter, boxing heavyweight out of New Orleans, wasn't a man to fuck with. Despite his nickname, he wasn't a healer. He hadn't earned the name setting bones—he'd earned it breaking them. I'd heard that he toughened his knuckles by punching the concrete wall of his cell a hundred times each day before breakfast—that he once hammered a three-inch nail into a two-by-four with the heel of his hand just to settle a bet. He did his time on the weight pile, training obsessively—his goal to compete as a bodybuilder if and when he ever got out.

But as tough as Dr. Dave's reputation was, it was his association with Rollie Shore that scared even the hardest cons.

No one, not even the hacks, messed with Rollie Shore.

Sally wasn't much of a dog, but Dr. Dave had taken to her. He brought her scraps of food from the chow hall, brushed her coat, spent hours trying to teach her to shake hands and roll over. He showed the little stray more tenderness than he had probably ever shown another human being in his entire sad and brutal life. And now Hinchee was now doing his best to brain her.

He swung again. And again Sally dodged the bat.

My stomach clenched, but there was nothing I could do to stop this spectacle. It could turn out only one way, but not a man in the crowd moved to end it. You could feel the intensity of their hatred, but you don't mess with the hacks. Not unless you're willing to pay the price. A big goddamned price. I wasn't. I wanted to go home—wanted to try and salvage what was left of my marriage. I wanted to be with my daughters. Messing with Hinchee wasn't going to get me closer to home. What it would get me was another charge. More time. Time I couldn't afford. So I stood there like everyone else and swallowed the bitter taste of bile flooding the back of my throat. Helpless, but unable to tear myself away. Silently rooting for the dog, but unwilling to put my ass on the line.

Hinchee's cheeks flushed as he swung and missed a third time.

A voice in my head was screaming, *Do something!* But I pushed the thought away. Making a move would destroy whatever small chance I had to patch things up with Dana. And that was more important to me than a skinny little dog. But for reasons I couldn't explain, the thought shamed me.

The man on my left grunted, and for a second, I thought he could read my mind.

Then I realized it was Dr. Dave.

He had a wedge-shaped head that looked as hard as granite and long curly hair, so blond it appeared white in the afternoon light. I stand six-two, but Dr. Dave had a good three inches on me. He was shirtless, sweating—narrowed muddy eyes the color of creek water, nostrils flared. Crude snake tattoos twined around both of his thick forearms. A vein bulged at his temple, pulsing with every beat of his heart. He held a twenty-five-pound iron plate clutched in his right hand—murder written across the set of his broad shoulders.

If Dr. Dave swung that plate at Hinchee, he'd kill the fat little hack. And I didn't doubt that was exactly what was on his mind.

Part of me wanted to see it happen.

Others in the crowd noticed, too.

A corridor in front of Dr. Dave opened, but Hinchee was too fixated on Sally to see it.

Peterson didn't notice, either.

Hinchee turned his back on the dog. Then, quicker than I would have thought he could move, he pivoted and swung again. This time he caught Sally with a glancing blow to her rump. She backed away, wailing like a baby.

Dr. Dave tensed. He took a step forward.

"Don't," I whispered. "They'll fry you."

If he heard, he ignored me.

Hinchee raised the bat; this time he couldn't miss. But before he could bring it down, Dr. Dave bellowed and lurched toward him, the iron plate held high in his own hand.

Hinchee turned, a horrified look on his doughy face.

Peterson saw. But it was too late. He lifted the radio.

And without thinking, I moved, too. Kicking out with my right foot, I tripped Dr. Dave from behind, dropping him to the ground.

He hit the concrete hard and lay there for a second, stunned. Then he shook his head to clear it and started back up.

"Stay down!" I shouted. But he kept coming, his eyes crazy, the cords in his neck strung as tight as fence wire.

By then, Peterson had grabbed Hinchee and the two of them were moving away from the broken circle of men, Hinchee still clutching the softball bat, Peterson shouting into his radio.

Sally forgotten, Dr. Dave balled his heavy fists and started toward me.

I stood my ground.

A new circle formed around us. My mouth was dry, my heart slamming the walls of my chest. But backing down would only make things worse.

Dr. Dave feinted to his left. I refused the bait.

Someone shouted, "Kill the bastard!"

I was wondering which bastard, when Sally, limping on three legs, came between us and started to whine.

Dr. Dave hesitated. Then he dropped his fists.

"Later, Hemmings," he growled, bending to scoop up the injured puppy.

Then, Black had me by the arm. "You gone crazy?" he shouted, pulling me back toward 1-dorm. "What the fuck were you thinking?"

2

DANA lay beside me. She was long and lean, with a shaggy mop of dark hair, high cheekbones, and flashing eyes that looked right into you and turned from steel gray to pale green depending on her mood. They were green that day. A sure sign she was happy.

A trickle of sweat slid down her chest, a salty track between her breasts. I reached over and traced the line, then touched her nipple.

She sighed. "Again, Ben? Don't start something you can't finish."

"Can't finish what?" I whispered, trailing my hand down the flat plane of her stomach, over the soft, dark triangle of hair, moving my fingers in her wet cleft.

She laughed and pulled me to her.

Spring had come late to Atlanta and the city was blooming—dogwoods, azaleas, forsythia, and tulips, all alive with color. If I'd known what was coming, I might have paid closer attention to how beautiful everything was—I would have spent more time with Dana and our two young daughters. But I didn't see past the nose on my face. I was hell-bent on growing Hemmings Construction, a company I'd started seven years earlier with two hundred dollars in my pocket and a head filled with ambitious dreams.

From the age of eighteen, I'd worked as a carpenter for

other contractors, never knowing when the work would dry up, chasing one general contractor after another for paychecks that bounced almost as often as they cleared. It was a lousy way to make a living, so I started my own renovation business. At first, it wasn't much of a business. I struggled to make ends meet, building decks and turning garages into guest bedrooms, refacing kitchen cabinets, painting houses when there was nothing better—always trying to work my way into better and bigger jobs.

Until a woman named Jackie Longhurst came along and asked if I could build her a barn—on the cheap. I knew as much about building barns as I did about building airplanes. But how hard could it be? I went to the library and discovered *Barn: The Art of a Working Building,* by Elrick Endersby, Alexander Greenwood, and Dave Larkin. I read it, then bought my own copy. Studied that book the way med students approach human anatomy. I kept a notebook, sketching in my own hand the difference between an English- and a German-style barn, between timber frame and balloon frame construction. Learned the logic inherent in designing a building that was basically a tool—a matter of form adapting to function. I copied Endersby and company's illustrations of louvered ventilators and roof lines—designed a compact floor plan combining the best of what the masters had so painstakingly documented with my own sense of scale and proportion. Then I built Jackie a fine little barn complete with a white cupola and a copper weather vane—all on a shoestring budget. People noticed. One thing led to another. Now Hemmings Construction built almost nothing but barns. Over the years, I'd graduated from shoestring budgets to building for owners and breeders who demanded the best and could afford it. I'd built a reputation for delivering on time and under budget. But my reputation came at a cost. I spent long hours on-site, practically ignoring my wife and kids.

That day, after much coaxing from Dana, I'd taken the afternoon off. After a lazy lunch, we spent the afternoon in bed, making love, talking, laughing—enjoying the fact that five years of marriage hadn't dulled the things that had attracted us to each other in the first place.

It was Friday and the girls were with Dana's mother. Which meant pizza and ice cream, *The Little Mermaid* run and rerun on the VCR until even Olivia, three, and her sister Nadine, two, had had enough of Ariel and Prince Eric. Knowing my daughters, Grandma Rose was in for a long weekend. A long weekend my wife and I planned to spend in bed.

We'd made a good start and it was only getting better, when a loud banging on the front door of our house startled us.

"Shit," Dana said, her rhythm broken. "Who the hell is knocking like that?"

"Ignore it," I murmured, pulling her closer, kissing the soft spot on her throat.

The knocking grew even louder. I pulled the covers over our heads.

"Wait." Dana pushed me away. "What if something's happened? The girls . . ." She didn't finish the thought.

I propped myself up on one elbow and shook my head. "You worry too much, Dana. The girls are fine. It's probably some kid selling magazine subscriptions. Ignore him; he'll go away."

I tried to kiss her, but the knocking didn't stop.

"Ben . . . if you won't see who it is, I will."

I could think of a million reasons not to answer that door, but you don't stay married for five years without learning which arguments are worth arguing. This one wasn't. When Dana starts worrying about our children, logic takes a hike. "Okay, I'll go, I'll go. But don't you move—not one inch." I pulled on a pair of boxer shorts. "This won't take a minute. Stay right where you are."

But Dana donned a terry cloth robe and followed me down the stairs, through the living room, and into the front hall anyway, calling, "Wait for me."

"Mr. Hemmings," a deep voice called through the closed door. "This is Agent Partone. I can hear you in there—please open up."

"Ben . . ." Dana was right behind me, her voice tight.

"Just a minute," I said, reaching for the doorknob, wondering if something *had* happened to the children. I turned to reassure Dana as I unlocked the deadbolt.

Then I was flat on my stomach, cheek pressed to the cool hardwood floor, someone's knee between my shoulder blades, the muzzle of a gun held firmly against my head.

"FBI . . . don't move. Don't breathe." The voice was low, not particularly nasty, but the knee in my back and the muzzle of that gun were implacable.

Dana screamed, "Let him alone! What do you want?"

I started to add a few questions of my own, but whoever held the other end of that gun jammed it harder into the side of my skull. Judging from the feet that trampled past me into our house, Dana's protests didn't carry much weight, either.

The rest was a blur. Handcuffs. A uniformed federal marshal holding my arms while a second uniform helped me step into a pair of jeans. Agent Partone, a tall, gray, middle-aged man in a blue windbreaker with the letters *FBI* embroidered on the breast, holstering his weapon and displaying a warrant for my arrest—a second warrant authorizing his men to search the property and seize financial records, business and personal. Partone refusing to say why. The sound of furniture scraping across the floor—contents of drawers being dumped haphazardly. Dana in her robe, hair mussed, eyes blazing—demanding an explanation from Partone. Receiving none. The taller of the marshals reading me my rights in a thick southern drawl.

"This is a mistake," I shouted as the marshals led me barefoot and barechested out of my house. Before they shoved me into their car, I yelled to Dana, "Call Jimmy Grantham; he'll straighten this out!"

I didn't know Grantham well. Neither did Dana. He was a friend of a friend. We'd been introduced at a horse show—he'd talked about buying a pony for his kids, wanted to know how much a barn would cost. I never built anything for him, but we ran into him from time to time, and he'd always ask with a smile if my price had come down. Jimmy was handsome, smooth, charming like only a fourth-generation, big-city southerner can be. More important, he was the only criminal defense lawyer I knew by name. But even as the marshals backed out of my driveway, squad-car lights flashing and sirens howling, I didn't really believe I'd need Grantham to do more than make a phone call or two. I hadn't done anything wrong. This was a simple case of mistaken identity—I'd be home before dinner. With one helluva story to tell my friends.

That was eight months before the trial no one told me I couldn't win.

3

I WAS on my bunk, daydreaming about the first time I'd seen Dana on a horse—confident and relaxed in the saddle, sexy as hell in tight jodhpurs and high boots, smiling at me every time she circled the schooling ring on a big dappled gelding that snorted and tossed his head like the stallion he was born to be but wasn't—when they called count. The dorm's loudspeakers crackling to life, knocking Dana's image out of my head. Corrections Officer Hinchee's shrill voice blaring, "Count time! Count time! The four-o'clock count is a stand-up count. All inmates prepare for count!"

Black was studying the dictionary, Rico picking at his toes with a sliver of wood. Both of them looked up, then shook their heads. "Asshole," Rico muttered.

Closing my eyes, I tried to recreate the daydream, but it wouldn't come.

We were in our cube, our house—a cinder-block enclosure ten feet long by seven feet wide. Originally designed for two men, because of overcrowding it was now home to three: Black, Rico Johnson, and myself.

Black's real name was Herman Glessing, but I never heard anyone call him that. Busted at nineteen, attempting to smuggle two kilos of cocaine into the States from the Bahamas, Black had begun his sentence about the time I started building Jackie Longhurst's barn. The bust was his first arrest; he'd been dealing for years without getting caught. The money he'd made had gone to housing and caring for an extended family. But first offense or not, the judge wasn't impressed. He gave Black the maximum—ten years. And in the federal system, you do the time. He was tall and well put together, his skin so black he looked like he might simply disappear on a dark night. Hence the nickname. While awaiting sentencing in a Fulton County jail, he'd come across a dictionary and, with nothing else to do, he'd read it. Cover to cover, finding comfort in the rhythm and order of the words. He spoke the language of Atlanta's inner-city streets, but Black studied his Webster the way some inmates looked for redemption in the Bible. He was a good celly, quiet and considerate. And somewhere along the way mutual respect had turned into a genuine, if unlikely, friendship. A rare and precious commodity in prison. Even so, after serving eight years in one penitentiary after another, Black was not a man to be taken lightly. The only thing I knew him to be afraid of was bugs. He hated them.

I trusted him completely.

Rico Johnson was a different type altogether. Half black, half Puerto Rican, he was a violent offender with a rap sheet as long as I was tall. Rico worked the system. He was lanky, fidgety—his skinny, café au lait–colored arms dripping with jailhouse ink, three of his front teeth missing. We got along okay, but Rico was a man who kept his options open. If you had something he wanted, he could be your friend. At least for the moment. But trust was out of the question. He didn't talk much about his life on the streets of Jackson, Mississippi, but he moaned and called out warnings in his sleep to someone named *Frog* whenever it rained.

"In the house!" someone shouted. The three of us jumped to our feet, Black still holding his dictionary.

There were four dormitories on the compound, each housing one hundred eighty-six men in sixty-two identical cubes. Every day, at exactly four

P.M., the dorms fell silent. It was the only time you could hear yourself think. Furnished with a steel bunk bed, a matching steel single, and three small lockers, there wasn't room in the cubes for three grown men to stand comfortably at the same time. So you rubbed elbows and hoped it would be over quickly. This wasn't the only daily census—the prison population is counted at least five times a day. But the four-o'clock count is the big one—the only stand-up-in-your-cube census—and I always got a kick out of the way the hacks' lips moved as they counted and recounted until they got it right. Once they were satisfied that no one had escaped, they'd open the chow hall for the evening meal.

Black stood silently until Hinchee and his partner finished counting our dorm and moved on to 2-dorm. Then, he looked up from his dictionary and said, "Ben, you can use the word *frangible* in a sentence?"

Rico grinned a gap-toothed smile. "What the hell *frangible* mean?"

"Black," I said, flopping down on my bunk, "as many times as you've been through that damned dictionary, you ought to know it by heart."

He smiled. "Words . . . they beautiful—they power, you put 'em together in the right order."

Rico snorted. "They so powerful, what you doin' in here?"

Black ignored him. "*Frangible* . . . It means breakable." He fixed me with a hard stare. "Like you, Ben. You don't get this mess with Dr. Dave straightened out, you very seriously frangible."

Three days had gone by since the incident with Sally. Word on the compound was that Dr. Dave had stashed the puppy somewhere while he nursed her back to health. He and I hadn't crossed paths since that day. Which was fine with me. I wasn't looking for a confrontation, but neither was I avoiding one. I couldn't have avoided Dr. Dave if I'd tried; the compound was too small. Sooner or later, we were going to come face-to-face, and I was beginning to think Black was right. Sooner was better than later.

"Stay clear a Dr. Dave," Rico advised. "Less'n you can get behind him in the chow line with a poker." He pumped his right hand in a jabbing motion. "Pop! Pop, pop, pop! Don't give a damn how big the man be—stick him in the right place, he goin' down. All the way down!" He smiled, brown eyes twinkling, obviously pleased with himself.

"Shit!" Black said. "Only time you stick a man with a blade is if he asleep *and* tied up."

Rico glared at Black. "Stick you, you keep on wit them words."

Black laughed, then quickly turned serious. "What you gonna do, Ben?"

Before I could answer, the loudspeaker hummed and Hinchee started screaming again. "Clear count! Clear count! We have a good count. The chow hall is now open for 1-dorm and 3-dorm. One and three *only!* Let's go, assholes. You have fifteen minutes to clear the line." The rest of the announcement was drowned out by the sounds of one hundred eighty-six men shouting and jeering as they thundered out of their cubes and raced to the chow hall where they'd meet up with the one hundred eighty-six men who lived in 3-dorm and have fifteen minutes to clear the line and eat.

When the noise subsided, Black asked again, "What are you going to do about Dr. Dave?"

I wasn't sure. But as I started to say so, Reggie appeared at the door to our cube, out of breath, his face flushed. "Ben," he blurted. "Shit, man, I just ran into Rollie Shore and Dr. Dave outside 3-dorm. Didn't look happy—neither of 'em. Rollie wants to see you. Says to meet him in the Pride Club in one hour."

I looked at Black. The Pride Club was an inmate organization authorized to perform community service—things like painting playground equipment or repairing old bicycles to be given to underprivileged children at Christmas. Rollie Shore had appropriated the storage room the warden had set aside for the Pride Club and had made it his own social club. I'd never been inside, but I'd heard the room was furnished with a television, a small refrigerator, and a hot plate. All the comforts of home. And because Rollie Shore was Rollie Shore, nobody seemed to mind.

Black frowned but kept his thoughts to himself.

Rico grabbed a stack of playing cards, then hesitated. "Ben, listen, man—anything go down, I want your radio."

I just stared at him.

He glanced down at my shoes. "Them Nikes nice, too—they don't get all bloody."

He looked up and flashed his gums, but whatever he saw in my face caused his toothless smile to fade.

"Uhmmm—I g-got to j-jet—got a game," he stammered. "Don't take no offense, Ben. I was just kiddin' you, man. That's all—just jokin'." He backed out of the crowded cube.

"Cold motherfucker," Black muttered.

Reggie waited until Rico was out of earshot, then said, "You gonna meet Rollie, or what?" He looked worried.

I stepped out of the cube and headed for the chow hall.

"Well?" Reggie said, catching up to me. Black was right behind him.

"They've got hot dogs tonight, don't they?" I asked.

Reggie looked at me like I was crazy. "Didn't you hear me, man? Rollie Shore wants to see you in an hour."

"I heard," I said. What else was there to say?

4

THE first time I met Dana was at a party. Not just any party. Augustus Mills Hamilton—Ham to his friends—had invited me to his annual Christmas buffet, an invitation I couldn't refuse. He and his wife, Priscilla, opened their stately Georgian home to the horse set every December. This was their crowd, their people—the lavish party a seasonal event. Men and women far richer than I'll ever be built their social calendars around it. Not to be invited was the kiss of death. At least as far as that crowd was concerned. For me, it was business.

Ham and Babe—nobody called her Priscilla—were members of a strange cult. Horse breeders, wealthy men and women who worshipped speed and strength—qualities measured in inches and fractions of a second—above all else. They memorized stud books, invested fortunes trying to manipulate generations of horseflesh—all their efforts directed at creating a foal who could jump higher, travel seven furlongs or a mile or two miles faster than any of its contemporaries. Ham Hamilton was a duke of this horse-crazed cult, royalty by any standard. I wasn't even a member. I liked horses—thought the good ones were beautiful. But I didn't ride them, didn't own them. I built the buildings that housed the fruit of the kingdom Ham Hamilton wanted to conquer. I'd built his newest barn. Thirty-six stalls, each with arched windows and twenty-foot ceilings set with double-paned skylights and mahogany-bladed ceiling fans, wash racks with hot and cold running water, and a mahogany-paneled tack room with a dozen matching mahogany tack trunks, each mounted with custom-cast brass fixtures and inlaid with the crossed stirrups of the Hamilton Farms logo. There were grooms' quarters above a stable manager's office that boasted state-of-the-art electronics, including a computer that tracked the growth rates, training schedules, and diets of each and every horse Ham had ever owned—ten thousand square feet of barn that smelled more like old money and well-cared-for leather than the animals it was built to house. I'd brought the barn in on budget and on schedule. That's why Ham invited me to his party.

The celebrating traditionally began in the afternoon. Dozens of fine-looking horses frolicked in the white-fenced paddocks and pastures surrounding the house. I supposed the Hamiltons wanted their guests to be able to see what all the fuss was about.

Inside, the enormous house was crowded. Half of the well-dressed guests actually owned horses; the other half wanted to. They all talked a good game. The place was furnished with enough antiques and art to start a museum. A crèche that had been carved by slaves once owned by the Hamilton family was proudly displayed on the garlanded mantel. Even the baby Jesus was black as coal. Other than that tiny son of God, the only blacks at this party were the waiters and waitresses passing drinks and hors d'oeuvres on silver trays decorated with gilded magnolia leaves. I wondered what they thought of the carvings.

I made the rounds, shook hands, and smiled a lot. But it wasn't my type of party, and before long, the forced gaiety started to grate on me. I'd brought a date but soon wished I hadn't. She was blond and frisky and thought the gathering was a little slice of heaven right here on earth. I left her in the study with a group talking hunter jumpers and wandered outside to get a little air.

I was standing on the elevated flagstone terrace, watching the late afternoon light fade across the rolling hills and straight white fences that marked Hamilton's property, when the man himself stepped to my side. He was tall and trim, an elegant man in his early sixties with the erect posture of a born horseman.

"Not a bad-looking farm, is it, Ben?"

"No, Ham. It's a damned fine-looking piece of land."

He nodded, looking pleased by my reaction. Not that my reaction really meant a whit to him. Ham Hamilton's grandfather had owned half the textile mills in Tennessee and Georgia. That money had led to vast real estate and banking holdings. Even so, Hamilton was late on my last invoice—and as usual, my cash flow was hurting.

"You need a drink, Ben," he observed. Turning, he beckoned to the liveried butler who never seemed more than a few steps from his side.

The butler—a walnut-colored man with smooth skin and pure white hair—looked old enough to have been a family retainer back when the crèche had been carved. "Yes, sah?" he said.

"Jasper, bring me a bottle of that Rock Hill bourbon and a couple of glasses—no ice."

"Right away, sah." He scurried off.

"All of this is going to change soon," Ham said matter-of-factly while Jasper went to fetch the booze. "A group of boys are pushing to see that gambling is legalized in Georgia. They want to bring in Thoroughbred racing, build a track. It'll mean big money for some, but too many of the wrong people come with the package. It worries me. What do you think?"

I hadn't thought much about it at all, and I said so. "Give me a good clean site and a clear set of plans, Ham. I know what a two-by-four is going to do when I cut it. Put a lot of money on the table in a room full of politicians, who knows what'll happen. I don't want any part of it."

He laughed. "When you put it that way, neither do I."

After Jasper delivered the whiskey on a silver tray, he stepped back, awaiting further instructions. Ignoring his manservant, Ham poured us each a generous measure, then pointed to a horse standing alone in a paddock. "See that stallion over there—the black Hanoverian with the three white socks? His pedigree is purer than royalty. There aren't two like him in the world."

I nodded. "He's beautiful."

The stallion seemed to know we were watching him. He pricked up his ears and pranced in a tight circle, tossing his handsome head, the muscles of his neck rippling under a coat as black and shiny as obsidian.

"Look at him," Ham said, sipping some bourbon, the pride of ownership shining in his eyes. "It's not just his pedigree. He looks hungry—like he wants to win. Reminds me a little of you. Young, a world beater. A little of that certain something people notice. Especially the ladies. You and I are more alike than you might think, Ben."

"I'll tell that to my banker."

He threw back his head and laughed. "He's just the start. I paid four million for that horse. I wouldn't part with him for eight. He'll be the living cornerstone of my future stable. Someday, we'll clone creatures like him. But that's decades away. In the meantime, I've put together the finest collection of genetic specimens ever assembled. Semen—frozen, preserved—taken from the greatest hunters and jumpers of the last twenty years. I've funded research that'll change the face of horse breeding. A line of champions, Ben. That's what I'm after. Nothing less than champions. That barn you built me is going to house the greatest horseflesh that ever lived. It won't be long before I'll be asking you to build me a second barn, then a third."

"I'd just as soon collect the balance on the first one," I said.

His proud smile froze. "You say that like you're worried, Ben."

"I'm not worried, Ham. Not about you. But I've got overhead, subs to pay."

Just then, a heavyset man wearing woolly tweeds came out onto the terrace. "Ham, you got a minute?" he asked. "I have those numbers."

"Sure, Henry. I'll be right there." Ham clapped me on the shoulder. "I'm glad you came to our party, Ben. Call my office next week; we'll see about a check. Now make sure you say hello to Babe before you leave." Then he joined his heavyset friend, Jasper, as usual, trailing at a discreet distance.

Babe Hamilton was standing alone on the sweeping staircase overlooking the crowded living room of her house. "Hey, Ben, you come up here and say hey," she called, waving a tall glass of clear liquid. Her speech was slightly slurred.

When I climbed the stairs and got close, I saw that she was drunk. Not tipsy but loaded to the gills. She was in her late forties, tall, thin, and as elegant as her husband, even sloshed. Her ash-blond hair was cut short, her jewelry simple but obviously expensive. I'd heard that she once rode as a member of the U.S. Equestrian Team, that she'd helped win the Nations' Cup in '73. She'd retained her athletic figure—she was still beautiful—but something in the lines around her eyes spoke of bitter disappointments.

"I saw you talking to Ham. What's the great man have to say for himself?" she asked, her breath heavy with gin.

"He was telling me about the breeding program he's starting," I answered.

"Looks to me like you could tell him a thing or two about breeding," she said, casually draping one arm around my waist. She measured me with her eyes. "You do know how to breed, don't you?"

"Careful, Babe. You and I start up, we might never stop. Then who'll come out here and build your barns?"

She laughed, a throaty growl. "Did the great man tell you about *her?*" She pointed to woman wearing a dark green silk sheath. She was standing below us, near the Christmas tree on the far side of the living room. A man wearing a blue blazer stood talking to her. She was dark and striking and everything the languid, would-be southern belles surrounding her weren't. She was the most intriguing looking woman I'd ever seen.

"Who is she?" I asked, staring at the woman.

"Nobody!" Babe snapped, removing her arm from my waist. "She used to ride for one of the smaller farms—trained for that woman over on Bethany Road. She's not one of us. Not that Ham gives a hoot; he can't take his eyes off the little tramp."

It was easy to see why. "You said she used to ride. What's she do now?"

Babe flicked her wrist at the question. "She works at that damn lab Ham is funding. He's been after her, Ben. A wife knows these things. But she won't give him the time of day. I don't think I've ever seen my darling husband quite so smitten."

"Is she married?" I asked, pointing at the man in the blazer.

"To Amos Daniels?" She laughed harshly, almost spilling her drink. "Not a chance. He's almost as flaccid as his father."

I turned and stared at her.

"Come on, Ben. You don't think we all know just a little bit too much about each other? It's what we do." She swallowed an inch or so of her drink. "Men aren't so very different than horses—the father tends to be like the son, a little faster, a little slower. God knows Ham and his father turned out alike. I know for a fact that Amos's father is worthless in bed; I also know that Amos doesn't have much to offer, either." She held out her hand, and waggled her little finger. "If you catch my drift."

I wasn't sure what to say.

Babe laughed at my discomfort. "Go ahead. Talk to her, Ben. She's Jewish, but that won't bother *you,* will it? It certainly doesn't seem to bother Ham."

One of the maids approached. Babe turned and started giving orders about the buffet.

I called thanks and escaped while I could.

By the time I crossed the living room, the woman's friend had walked off, either to the bar or the bathroom. I decided not to waste time.

Walking up to her, I said, "You shouldn't stand that close to the tree. It's not fair."

"Not fair? To whom?" she asked.

"To the tree—the poor thing looks hopeless next to you."

She shook her head. "That is absolutely the lamest line I've ever heard."

"I've tried worse," I admitted, laughing.

"Well, I've heard worse, but it ranks right up there." She sipped her drink.

"How about we start over? My name's Ben Hemmings." I offered my hand.

She took it. "I'm Dana Abrams. I understand you're the builder with the golden touch."

I must have looked surprised.

"Don't be modest," she said. "Ham's been showing off your work. He says you're a genius. To hear him tell it, you'd think he discovered you."

"That's nice of him, Dana. But I wouldn't believe most of what Ham says about me."

"I don't believe most of what Ham says about anything."

We locked eyes for a long moment, then she smiled. "Did you come over here just to talk about the Christmas tree?"

"Actually, I came over here to meet the most interesting-looking woman at this party. Now I have."

Her smile grew brighter. "That's a much better line."

I laughed. "It wasn't a line—it was the truth. I know you're here with a date, but are you busy for lunch tomorrow?"

Setting her drink down on a side table, she opened her purse and pulled out a pen. "Give me your hand."

I did.

She pushed up the cuff of my jacket and wrote her name and phone number on my wrist. "One of two things will happen, Ben Hemmings. You'll go wash that off, rather than explain it to the blond you came in with. Or you'll leave it where it is and it'll be there tomorrow at lunch. Call me in the morning and tell me where to meet you. But if my handwriting isn't still there . . . well, I'll know I was right about that first line."

5

BLACK watched, a look of utter disgust etched across his features, as I put away four greasy hot dogs and plate of watery beans doused with ketchup. According to the Bureau of Prisons, this was a healthy and nutritionally balanced meal. At least it was hot.

"Pork, man . . . I talk, but you don't listen," he admonished over the din and clatter of the chow hall. "You know what's in those things? Shit's gonna kill you—"

"If Rollie doesn't get him first," Reggie interrupted. He was sitting on my right, eager to know what I was going to do—how I was going to handle the situation.

I kept chewing. As far as I could tell, there wasn't much to talk about and I was hungry. Tired and hungry. The kind of tired that starts in your hands and tightens the muscles of your forearms and shoulders, aching all the way to the bone. The fatigue that comes from real work.

I'd spent the last two weeks on an inmate construction detail, putting up an addition to one of the administrative buildings that housed offices and training rooms. The building, designed in the early seventies, was a rectangular modern structure, concrete block on a poured slab with little in the way of detail or ornament. Adding to it would be simple.

In theory.

But this was prison. Inmate labor at 18 cents a day. No

incentive to do anything efficiently. No reason to exert more than the minimum effort required to look busy.

Even so, the mess they'd made of the project surprised me.

Chinless Moe, one of the laziest of the hacks, was supervising the detail. But Chinless knew nothing about construction. And judging from what I found when I joined the crew, he had no desire to learn.

They'd already poured a new slab for the addition, only no one had tied it to the old foundation. This had been done a week earlier, and the new slab was already a couple of inches lower than the existing building. How low it would settle was anybody's guess.

I tried to convince Chinless that he had a problem.

"Just do what the fuck you're told," he drawled, ignoring my warnings.

So I followed orders.

Why not? It wasn't my building. Who gave a damn if it fell down?

I kept my mouth shut and humped and stacked a mountain of concrete block. Slung fifty-pound bags of concrete until the muscles in my back burned and salt sweat stung my eyes.

I tried. I really tried, but I couldn't watch them screw up such a simple job. Not even in here.

The afternoon of my second day on the crew, I approached Chinless in the shade by the water cooler.

"Thing's comin' down, C.O.," I observed, then swallowed a cold cup of water.

Chinless glared at me. "I done told you, Hemmings."

"You've got to tie down the new foundation or something's gonna give," I assured him. "The roof, a wall—maybe on the warden's head . . ."

We spent the next two days breaking out the section of new slab where it abutted the old one. We drilled and set rebar dowels into the old foundation and more of them into the remaining section of the new one. Then we repoured the gap, tying the whole thing together.

It was hot, sweaty work under the midday Alabama sun. And no one thanked me for it. But it was clean sweat. I almost forgot where we were. I felt human again. Until it was done and I had to face the hardest part of the job—turning in the prison-issue tools . . .

"You 'bout finished eating that garbage?" Black asked, snapping me out of my daydream. "'Cause Rollie's waiting."

I looked around. The chow hall was almost empty, Hinchee and another hack staring pointedly in our direction.

"Yeah," I said, taking a deep breath. "I'm finished."

■ ■ ■

Rollie Shore's right hand-man, Paul Shapinski, stood blocking the door of the prefab storage hut that served as the Pride Club's office. The hut wasn't far from the handball court, and from where he stood, Shapinski, a burly Russian Jew finishing a fifteen-year bit for hijacking fuel-oil trucks on Long Island, had a commanding view of the rec yard. His nickname was Boris. A few inmates called him the Commissar, but he didn't give a damn what people called him. As a matter of fact, he didn't care about anything or anyone except Rollie Shore, whom he idolized. Boris was short, eligible for release within the next few months, and rumor had it that Rollie had already arranged something sweet for him on the street.

He grunted at me. "Go in, Hemmings." The *in* sounding more like *eeyn.* "Rollie is expectink you." He shifted his wide body out of the doorway so that I could pass, then took up his post again, dark, close-set eyes scanning the rec yard, looking or waiting for someone else.

I didn't ask who. Boris wasn't much on polite conversation.

The office smelled like fried onions and old sweatsocks. A bright bank of fluorescent light fixtures dropped from the ceiling on chains. Out-of-date calendars and faded travel posters hung on the walls. There was a small television sitting on a folding table, and an old refrigerator knocked and hummed against one wall. I didn't see the hot plate, but I didn't doubt there was one.

In the corner nearest the door, Dr. Dave's puppy slept in a cardboard box. When I came in, she lifted her head expectantly. Then she realized I wasn't her master, and she went back to sleep.

Rollie Shore sat at the rear of the office, his feet propped up on a cheap government-issue desk. He watched me as I looked around. I'd seen him on the compound, but this was our first face-to-face meeting. He was in his early sixties, his large head capped with tight gray curls. A big man, gone to fat. But there was nothing soft in his eyes. They were blue and cold and curious. And when he fixed you with his unblinking gaze, you got the feeling that a vast and hungry intelligence lived behind those eyes An intelligence capable of swallowing everything in its path.

"Ben Hemmings," he said without getting up. "I'm glad you stopped by. We should have made a point of meeting a long time ago. Something to drink? Tea? Coffee? A soda?"

"No thanks," I said. I wasn't here to make friends. I was here to try and clear the air with Dr. Dave.

He nodded, as if he had anticipated my rejection.

Pointing to a metal folding chair facing his desk, he said. "Sit down. Tell me about yourself. How do you like prison life?"

"I don't," I said.

He chuckled. "There are worse places than this. Believe me. I've seen some of them. We endure. It's what separates us from the animals."

"Some men endure better than others," I said looking around his little kingdom. "I expected Dr. Dave to be here."

He smiled, but it never reached his eyes. "Dave is a good friend. In here it pays to have the right friends." He shifted his broad bulk in his chair. "I understand you know how to keep your mouth shut. Johnny Forchet should have been more careful—and not just with his telephones. The problem's been dealt with."

"You know Forchet?" I asked.

"Atlanta's a small town, Ben. I know a lot of people. Jimmy Grantham handled your case. Is he handling the appeal?"

"For what it's worth."

"He's a good man—tried to get me to eat grits once." He laughed, a deep rolling sound. Then, he grew serious. "You could do worse than Grantham. When I first moved my operation to Atlanta, he helped me deal with a little problem. It went away and never came back. That's the kind of problem I like."

"Everybody likes that kind of problem," I said, wondering what he wanted—why all the small talk.

"I watched you working on the administrative building. On the street you're a builder, aren't you?"

"I was."

He shrugged. "This is a setback, Ben. A minor delay, not the end of your career. Not from what I saw. You build stables—know your way around the horse crowd, don't you?"

"I've built a couple of barns."

"Barns . . . stables . . . same thing whatever you call 'em, right?" He smiled, then abruptly changed the subject. "I understand your wife is Jewish. So am I. Are the two of you raising your children in the temple?"

There are no secrets in prison. I was surprised but not shocked that Rollie knew as much as he did about me and my case. But I hadn't expected him to know anything about Dana and the girls.

He was looking at me. An appraising look, shrewdly observing my reaction. And I realized he was maneuvering me. It was the oldest trick in the book. Know more than the other guy thinks you know. Make him wonder how you know what you know. Keep him off balance. I understood what he was doing, but not why.

It worked anyway. I felt the blood rise to my face, the hot dogs a heavy lump in my stomach. My life beyond the boundaries of this compound was none of his business. My problems were just that—my problems—and I intended to keep it that way. "Leave my wife out of this, Rollie. My beef with Dr. Dave stays here. It has nothing to do with my family."

He frowned. "Beef? Do you think I asked you here because you and Dave . . ."

Before he could finish, Boris called out from the doorway. "They are comink. Both of them."

Rollie glanced at his watch.

"They're early," he said to me, sounding apologetic. But his eyes didn't match his voice; they were bright with anticipation. "We'll have to finish our discussion later."

He stood.

I stood, too. "I meant what I said about my family, Rollie."

I started toward the door, but he stopped me. "Wait a minute, Ben. Why don't you stick around for a little while." He pointed to a couple of chairs against the far wall. "Sit down. This won't take long. You might learn something."

I doubted it, but I wanted to resolve this thing with Dr. Dave before it went any further. So I took a seat.

As if on cue, Dr. Dave walked in with a skinny black kid from Mobile—a friend of Rico's named T. Sally sat up, wagging her tail. But Dr. Dave ignored her.

It was a pleasant summer evening, but T was sweating, his mahogany face shiny. He hesitated just inside the Pride Club's door.

Dr. Dave took him by the elbow and escorted him to the desk, where Rollie stood, a stern expression on his face.

"You stole from me, T," Rollie said without preamble.

T started to stutter and deny doing any such thing. But Rollie just shook his wizened head. "No use making excuses, T. We both know what happened. The only question is what do we do about it?"

T frowned, the sweat streaming down his face now. "You wrong, Rollie. Didn't take nuthin'. Wouldn't think to take nuthin' belong to you."

Dr. Dave cuffed him on the side of the head. "Don't talk unless Rollie asks you to talk. Understand?" he growled.

T rubbed his head and moaned softly. "You got to unnerstand . . ."

This time Dr. Dave hit him, a short shot to the ribs that dropped T to his knees.

I wanted out of there. But Boris was blocking the door. And where was there to go?

"Easy, Dave," Rollie said.

Then stepping around the desk, he cupped T's chin in his hand and looked down into the kid's wide eyes. "I trusted you, you little piece of shit. I gave you the right to run the game. Hell, I gave you every card game in 4-dorm. Do you think I'm a fool? That I don't know what the house cut should be on a poker table? How much did you pocket?"

I listened as Rollie questioned the terrified kid, wondering how far he would take it. It was a strange sight. Rollie Shore was well known in Atlanta; he'd been written up in the newspapers a number of times. He was the real thing—a player, with interests, legal and otherwise, across the entire southeast. He maintained a Thoroughbred horse farm just north of Alpharetta; he also owned a mansion on Tuxedo Road in Buckhead, a yacht docked somewhere in the islands, apartment buildings and warehouses and nightclubs from Mississippi to South Carolina. If John Forchet was a barracuda, Rollie Shore was a tiger shark. The feds had busted him on tax-evasion charges. He had three years left on a five-year sentence. I wasn't sure how much the house cut on a prison poker table would be, but I doubted it would change Rollie Shore's bottom line.

Still, you don't maintain a reputation by letting kids like T rip you off.

"Do I look stupid?" Rollie demanded.

T mumbled something unintelligible.

Rollie shook his head. "I'm not one of your brothers. Speak English when I'm talking to you."

"I musta counted wrong, Rollie." T's voice was high pitched and shaky.

"Tell me I'm stupid, T."

"Huh?"

Rollie slapped the kid. "I said, 'Tell me I'm stupid.'"

T shook his head, the whites of his eyes showing.

"Goddammit!" Rollie roared. "I tell you to stand on your head, you'll do it. Now say it! Tell me I'm stupid."

"I . . . I cain't." The kid's voice had dropped to a whisper.

Without warning, Dr. Dave backhanded him, knocking him flat on the floor.

Rollie grabbed T by the collar and hauled him back onto his knees. He slapped the kid again, then took him by the ears and shook him like a rag doll.

"Say it!" Rollie screamed, pushing his face at T's. "You got one last chance. Do it! Tell me I'm stupid. Tell me to my face or I'll fucking tear your head off."

T started to cry. "Please . . . I pay you, Rollie. Ten times what I owe."

"Say it!"

"Ten times, Rollie. I swear it . . ." He was crying like a baby now, spittle running down his chin.

Rollie drew back one hand to strike the kid again. Then, disgusted, he let go of him and shook his head. "Stupid, my ass . . ."

T dropped to all fours, trembling like a scared kitten.

Rollie looked down at him for a moment, then walked back around the desk and sat in his chair. His face was flushed, his eyes bright blue chips of ice.

"You'll pay me back tenfold," he repeated softly.

T nodded, wiping at his wet face with the back of his hand. "Ten times what I owe, Rollie. It was a mistake. Didn't mean to take from you. Never . . ." He shook his head violently. "No, sir. It was a mistake."

Dr. Dave glared down at the kid but said nothing.

Rollie looked at me. "What do you think I should do with him, Ben?"

The question startled me. I started to say that it wasn't my problem, but something in Rollie's eyes—maybe it was that cold curiosity—made me want to spite him. "Let him go, Rollie. I think you made your point. Let him pay you what he owes you."

"Fuck that," Dr. Dave grunted. "I say kill the little fucker."

T flinched and made a snuffling sound.

Rollie raised his eyebrows. "You think we should settle this like civilized men?"

"Yeah, Rollie. Like civilized men," I said.

Opening the desk drawer, he brought out a set of four small books bound in red cloth. He beckoned me to his side. "This is the law. It's all here, Ben. Everything."

I stepped over to him and he handed me the books. They were entitled *The Code of Jewish Law.*

"What do you want from me?" I asked, holding the books.

He didn't answer right away.

When he finally spoke, his voice was low. "Those four books are a simplified translation of the Talmud. God's law as handed down over thousands of years to the Jewish people. Look through them. Show me where it says I should let a man steal from me."

I placed the books on top of his desk. T was still snuffling. "He's a kid. I don't care what it says in the books. Give him a chance to pay what he owes."

Rollie sat there for a moment, looking undecided. "Civilized . . ." he said, chewing the thought.

Then he stood and nodded at me. "All right, Ben. I'll do it your way."

T looked from Rollie to me, then back again as though he wasn't sure he had heard correctly.

"Get up, T," Rollie ordered. "Mr. Hemmings is giving you a second chance."

I started to say it was Rollie giving him a second chance, but T blurted, "I pay you, Rollie. Every cent."

Rollie shook his head. "No, T. You won't pay me. You're going to pay Ben."

T had stopped crying. Now he looked confused. "Ben?"

"Yeah," Rollie said. "But not with money. You're to do his laundry once a week, iron his uniforms, keep his cube clean. You'll buff the floor twice a week, and you'll make his bed every morning. You'll do this until I tell you otherwise. Understand?"

I started to object, but T's high-pitched voice drowned me out.

"But Rollie . . . " he whined, " . . . what I gonna tell the brothers? I ain't no white man's house nigger."

Rollie glanced at Dr. Dave, who slapped T on the back of the head.

"You're anyone's nigger I tell you to be. Do you understand?" Rollie asked the kid.

T glanced at me, hatred lighting his eyes. "Yeah, Rollie. I unnerstand."

"Then get the hell out of my sight. Before I change my mind," Rollie ordered.

T hurried out of the Pride Club without a backward glance. Boris followed him out the door.

Rollie stared hard at me. "Satisfied?" Before I could answer, he turned to Dr. Dave and said, "Apologize to Ben."

"What?!"

"You heard me, Dave. Apologize to the man. He did you a favor."

"The hell I will, Rollie. He tripped me from behind, like some pussy-assed punk," Dr. Dave sneered. "I ought to crack his fuckin' skull."

"Fool!" Rollie roared. "Ben kept you from acting as stupid as you look. In doing you a favor, he did me a favor. Apologize and say thank you. Now!"

This was not the way I wanted to handle the situation. But it was too late. Dr. Dave was staring at me; the rage in his eyes made T look warm and fuzzy. My heart started to beat quicker and the fatigue in my shoulders dropped away.

"I apologize," Dr. Dave muttered grudgingly, his big fists flexing and unflexing.

"Good," Rollie said. "And from now on, you'll treat Ben with respect. He's smarter than you are, Dave. Knows how to keep his mouth shut. Treat him as such."

Dr. Dave's face turned bright red. For a moment, it looked as though he were going to explode. Then he stalked over and grabbed his puppy, hauling her into his arms. She yelped in pain.

Rollie watched him, looking strangely satisfied.

Then he grinned at me. "Now, if you'll excuse me, Ben, I have business to take care of."

With that, he sat back down behind his desk and started looking through a stack of letters. Just another senior executive, hard at work.

I'd walked into the Pride Club, reluctant to accept a cup of tea from Rollie Shore. I hadn't wanted to be in his debt. Now, for reasons I didn't understand, he'd manipulated all of us. In the process, I'd gained two new enemies. I wasn't worried about T. I had no intention of letting him become my "house nigger." But prison was no place to have enemies like Dr. Dave. There were too many ways to get hurt.

I started to leave, but Rollie called after me, "You play gin rummy, Ben?"

Turning, I stared at him. "No, Rollie. I don't like games." I couldn't keep the anger out of my voice.

He glanced up from his correspondence and frowned. "Too bad. It's a good way to pass the time. Stop in after count tomorrow anyway. We'll talk. I own a couple of horses. Maybe you can tell me something I don't know about barns. Maybe we can help each other."

He turned his attention back to his mail.

I wanted to tell him to take his gin rummy, his dime-store psychology, and his entire crew straight to hell. But thanks to him, this thing between Dr. Dave and I had turned very personal. I should have let the bastard kill Hinchee. Now, the only thing standing between us was the goodwill of Rollie Shore.

"I'll stop by," I said, the words grating in my throat.

Rollie nodded without looking up. As if there had been any doubt.

6

WITHIN a day of my arrest, Jimmy Grantham had arranged for my release on bail. Three days later, he'd set up a plea-bargain conference with the U.S. attorney.

"Just to see what we're up against," he'd reassured me when I made plain that I'd done nothing to plead guilty to.

While we were waiting in the reception room of Grantham's posh Buckhead offices for the conference to begin, Dana reached for my hand. "That day they took you away, Ben—I tried to imagine what it would be like without you. If they really sent you to prison. But I couldn't do it. None of this seems real to me. It's like it's happening to someone else."

Her eyes were slate gray. Her chin quivered, and for a moment I thought she was going to cry. With a visible effort, she held it in check. In the years we'd been together, I could count on my fingers the number of times she'd cried. Dana was strong, a woman who wasn't afraid to speak her mind or take a position. But now she was as scared as I'd ever seen her. And that scared me. This was no fun for either of us. But it would be over soon, I told myself.

Letting go of her hand, I brushed an errant strand of hair off her cheek. "It's a mistake, Dana. I'm not going anywhere. Someone screwed up—they arrested the wrong guy. I've explained it to Jimmy—he'll get it straightened out this morning."

She nodded, but she didn't look convinced. "I talked to my mother about his fee. She'll help us—not with the whole fifty thousand, but she'll help."

I smiled. "Tell Rose I love her, but we're not going to need anything close to that. I didn't do anything wrong. Jimmy will fix it."

"He's not going to fix it for free, is he?"

"No. But he's not going to charge a fifty thousand–dollar retainer for what I need him to do."

She hesitated, watching Grantham's pretty blond receptionist greet a bearded mountain of a man wearing greasy denims, bikers' colors, and an eye patch. Dana lowered her voice and whispered, "I can't believe we're sitting here talking about legal fees and prison. It's like we've crossed some line and all I want to do is go back to where we started. It's not right. It's just not fair."

"Fair has nothing to do with it," I agreed, watching the biker take a seat, wondering what he'd done.

He looked over at me, nodded, then picked up an *Architectural Digest.*

Suddenly, it dawned on me that he might be wondering the exact same thing about me.

■ ■ ■

Ten minutes into the conference, it became painfully obvious that the government was not at all impressed by my claims of innocence. So far, Grantham and the assistant U.S. attorney in charge of prosecuting my case, a small, sour-looking redhead named Walter Quist, hadn't been able to agree on anything.

Grantham sat at the head of the long, polished walnut table dominating his conference room. In spite of the fact that he was getting nowhere, he looked cool and in control. He was in his midforties, tall, his dark wavy hair graying around the temples and combed straight back from his high forehead. Fingering the knot of his silk tie, he shook his head and said, "This doesn't make sense, Walter. Mr. Hemmings is not now and has never been involved in the drug trade."

Walter Quist smiled condescendingly. "You've seen the indictment. I think it's perfectly clear."

Quist and Special Agent Donald Partone sat on Grantham's right, thick manila case files placed on the table in front of them. This was the first chance I'd had to get a good look at Partone. The last time we'd met, he'd spent most of our time together with his knee planted in the small of my back. He was rangy, much taller than Quist. His craggy face tanned, his large hands calloused. He looked like a graying cowboy, a man who would have been more at home on the back of a horse than in a fancy conference room. Except for his eyes. They were dark beads set deep in his weathered face, shrewd and calculating.

Dana and I sat on Grantham's left, across the table from Quist and Partone. Since entering the room, neither of the two lawmen had addressed me directly. Out of the corner of my eye, I caught Partone stealing glances at Dana. She sat as still as a stone, listening, not saying a word.

Grantham said, "Of course I've read the indictment. But I still don't understand the basis of these money-laundering charges. Ben Hemmings isn't a drug dealer."

Quist searched through the case file in front of him, seeming to ignore Grantham's comments. Grantham waited patiently. For a high-powered criminal defense attorney, he seemed awfully patient and accommodating. I wanted him to breathe fire. But that didn't seem to be his style.

Finally, Quist found what he was looking for and slid several typewritten sheets out of the file. He turned them facedown on the table as though they contained top-secret information. "No one claims your client is a drug dealer, Jimmy. My job is to follow the money—that's the key to these things. The money doesn't lie. That's where Mr. Hemming's scheme came apart. He knew what he was doing. And now either he's going to plead guilty and cooperate or we're going to put him away for a long, long time." He spoke in a nasal whine, managing somehow to sound both indifferent and nasty at the same time.

Grantham nodded calmly, still the southern gentleman. "That sounds pretty harsh, but it doesn't mean anything. Ben Hemmings has operated a legitimate building business in Atlanta for over a decade. He started as a carpenter, Walter. Now he's got his own company. And I can tell you, he's got quite a reputation for building some damned fancy barns for the horse people up in Alpharetta and Crabapple. Hell, he built a barn for Ham Hamilton that cost more money than you and I will make in years of trial work . . ."

"More money than *I'll* make . . ." Quist interrupted, sounding proud of the fact. "Not you, Jimmy."

Grantham smiled patiently. "You're on the wrong side of the table, Walter. I've told you that before. But that's not the point. I want to make sure you understand who were talking about. I know Ben. I've looked over his books. He can account for every dime that's ever gone into or out of Hemmings Construction. It's a clean, well-respected business. No funny stuff—no diversion of funds. It's all there in black and white." He glanced at me.

I nodded on cue.

Quist didn't look the least impressed. "We've got Mr. Hemmings on tape. He's very forthcoming, very convincing. According to the code . . ." Quist started to lecture Grantham about some aspect of the law. I listened for a few minutes, then looked at Dana to see if she was following the conversation.

She met my eye, looking worried.

"It'll be okay," I whispered. But I was beginning to wonder.

Grantham cleared his throat. "Let's cut to the bottom line, Walter. You and I both know the Justice Department hasn't spent time and money wiretapping Ben Hemmings. You're trying to squeeze my client. But I still don't understand what you're trying to squeeze out of him. What's this really about?"

Partone met my eye. I didn't like what I saw there. He nodded, then smiling to himself, he looked down at the closed file in front of him.

"John Jay Forchet," Walter Quist said.

Dana stiffened. I stared at Quist.

"What about John Jay Forchet?" Grantham asked.

Quist sat back in his chair and steepled his fingers. He spoke without emotion. He might have been talking about his grocery list. "Forchet has a piece of everything that's dirty across northern Georgia and Alabama. He's slick, comes across as a *good ol' boy* businessman. But most good ol' boys don't traffic in gambling, prostitution, and drugs. We can tie Forchet to at least three drug-related murders. And drugs are only a part of his operation. Gambling is his real game. We've been investigating him for over a year. So far he's been lucky—keeps slipping the noose. We need someone to get close to him. Your client, Mr. Ben Hemmings, has been laundering money for Forchet. We have him cold. Now he has a choice: help us, or go to prison."

"You've got to be kidding!" I blurted.

Dana was staring at me, her mouth open.

I shook my head. "He's wrong. I never did anything illegal for Forchet."

Grantham looked sharply at me. "I'll handle this, Ben."

The corners of Quist's mouth twisted into a condescending smile. "No. You're the one who is wrong, Mr. Hemmings. You took Forchet's money—over two hundred thousand dollars . . ."

"Of course I took over two hundred thousand dollars. I contracted to build him a dozen stalls, fifteen-foot-high ceilings, custom moldings and solid brass fixtures, white oak, and fourteen-inch heart-pine beams. I'm going to build him a barn—I've known him since grade school. How does that make me a money launderer?" I demanded.

Quist said nothing, supremely confident of his position.

"This is insane!" I shouted. "Tell him, Jimmy! I didn't launder a goddamned penny! Not one penny!"

"Ben!" Grantham said, steel in his voice now. "I don't want you to say another word. If you can't keep quiet, I'm going to end this meeting. Now. Understand?"

My cheeks burned as though I'd been slapped. But I nodded and took a deep breath, trying to get my anger under control.

Dana reached over and squeezed my hand under the table. I looked at her and shook my head. "This is bullshit!"

Then, I looked at Jimmy Grantham. "It's bullshit!"

Ignoring me, he turned his attention back to Quist, who seemed pleased by the reaction he'd prodded out of me. "What do you want, Walter?" Grantham asked.

"Your client as a confidential informant. I want him to help us nail John Forchet."

"You're out of your mind!" I started to elaborate, but a look from Grantham shut me up.

"Are we talking about testifying?" he asked Quist.

Quist nodded. "Wires, videos, whatever the field agents want—including testimony. Hemmings does his job, he won't do any time. Then we can talk about the witness protection program."

As I watched, too stunned to speak, Quist and Partone stood. "Your client has three days to decide," Quist said. "Then the offer is withdrawn."

He turned to me and added, "This is an active investigation, Mr. Hemmings. If I find you've attempted to make contact with Forchet, I'm going to land on you like a ton of bricks."

He handed Grantham the papers he'd taken out of his file, the ones he'd placed facedown on the table. "I've spelled out the case we have against Mr. Hemmings. I wouldn't ordinarily hand it to you on a platter, Jimmy, but in this instance, I thought it might help your client make the right decision." He looked at Dana, then said pointedly, "The right decision for everyone."

Quist and Partone both shook hands with Grantham, then left the room without so much as a backward glance at Dana or me.

■ ■ ■

"Assuming this is true, they have you pretty well boxed in, Ben," Grantham said, after studying the transcripts Quist had handed him.

"I don't understand," Dana said. "How can Ben be held responsible for John Forchet's actions?"

"The minute Forchet told Ben . . . Here, let me quote from the transcript." Grantham shuffled the papers, found what he was looking for, then read: "'You know how it is, Ben . . . a little a this . . . a little a that . . . Long as the right teams keep losin' and the wrong ones keep winnin', I'm happy, man. Listen, I been thinkin' 'bout doin' a little building on that property I own . . . You know, the one we talked about. You ready to put something sweet together for your old buddy?'"

Grantham stopped reading and looked over at us. "Alone, that excerpt is meaningless. Two old friends talking. But according to Quist's notes, just after this conversation was taped, over two hundred thousand dollars changed hands. Quist will make the case that Ben, knowing it was dirty money, put something 'sweet' together for his old friend Forchet—that Ben was going to build Forchet a barn for a grossly inflated price. Doesn't matter how much the barn is actually worth—the government will contend that the price was inflated. It's the oldest trick in the money-laundering business and damned hard to disprove. He'll say Ben was a knowing coconspirator."

"That's insane!" I said, standing and walking to the window. My mind was racing. I'd known John Forchet since grade school. He'd been tough then; he was tough now. He'd always been a wheeler-dealer. Started with nothing—now he owned a couple of restaurants, night clubs, real estate. This barn wasn't the first time he'd asked me to build for him. When I was hungry, just starting out on my own, Forchet hired me to build him a deck. Not because he needed a new deck but because he knew I needed the work. I'd done more than one job like that for him over the years. Sure, he wasn't a gentleman—wasn't smooth like Grantham. He operated in a rough-and-tumble world. I'd heard rumors that he made book. I didn't doubt that he sold a little pot on the side, fooled around with hookers. But a murderer? A big-time gangster? I didn't want to believe it. Even if everything Quist had said about Forchet was true, that didn't make *me* a criminal. Did it?

Dana nodded as though she were reading my mind. "How can it be money laundering? Ben didn't take any cash."

"No," Grantham said. "Ben didn't take any cash. But he took partial payment up front. Over two hundred thousand dollars before there was a contract or any other written agreement." He fixed me with a penetrating look. "That's pretty unusual, isn't it, Ben?"

I looked at Dana. She frowned.

"Forchet and I go back a long ways," I explained. "He knew I had cash-flow problems. It's always been the weakest part of my business. I didn't think getting paid in advance was any big deal."

"What are you saying?" Dana asked.

"I'm saying he offered the money and I accepted. You know how tight things have been."

"Did you know it was dirty money?" she asked.

I hesitated. "It's not like that, Dana." But my voice sounded hollow in my own ears. At some level I'd known who and what Forchet was—you don't know someone for that long without forming an opinion of them—but at the same time, I'd chosen not to know.

"Dammit, Ben! What have you done?" she snapped.

"I kept the business growing, Dana. That's all. I've worked goddamned hard for what we have. You know who I am! No one gave me anything! I never broke any laws. At least not any I knew about. You want to know if I asked Forchet where he got his money? If it was dirty? Hell no! I needed it—and you know goddamn well any one of a thousand other contractors would have been happy to get it, too!"

"Let's all stay calm," Grantham said.

"Yeah—*right.*" I took a deep breath—tried to slow my pounding heart.

Dana refused to meet my eye.

Grantham didn't look at all upset. No one was threatening *him* with prison. "We'll just have to gather all the facts and see if we can make some sense out of this," he said. "But, Ben, the law is very clear: you cannot knowingly accept money derived from a criminal enterprise in return for property or objects of value. It's considered money laundering."

"Forchet owns restaurants, real estate. How the hell am I supposed to know where he got the money for the barn?" I said. "Do you think I ask my clients how they earn their money? They'd think I was crazy!"

Grantham looked again at the papers Quist had given him, then thought for a moment. "Listen, Ben . . . I'm sure you weren't doing anything other than what you say. You're not the problem; it's not you they're after. Ultimately, it's not even Forchet they want. It's like a food chain—the higher they climb, the bigger the fish. You're a minnow, Ben. Forchet's a barracuda. Quist really wants the big sharks—whoever it is that Forchet answers to. The investigation takes on a life of its own. If someone like you gets swallowed in the process, Quist just chalks it up to the cost of justice. It's not pretty, is it?"

Dana looked like she was going to be sick. "That's it? We're the price of justice? What this does to my husband—my family—is meaningless?"

Grantham pressed his lips into a frown. "I'm sorry to say it's true, Dana. They don't care at all about what happens to you or your family. This is how it works: Judging from these transcripts, they've been taping Forchet's conversations for quite some time. They've been looking for a way in. Once Ben took the two hundred thousand dollars, Quist found a chink in Forchet's armor." He turned to me. "They see you as the means of cracking Forchet's operation wide open. Once they're in, they climb the chain until they either get to the top or hit a dead end. Unless you agree to play along, Quist is going to tell a jury that you knew exactly where Forchet's money came from. He paints a terrible picture of Forchet, puts up testimony that significant sums of money changed hands without a contract, then he plays the tapes of the two of you talking about "sweet deals." He keeps it simple, tracks all that money into your account without so much as a letter verifying what it was for. . . . It's going to be damned hard to convince a jury—men and women whose homes probably didn't cost two hundred thousand dollars—that you didn't conspire with Forchet. That you didn't know what he was up to."

"Shit! You make it sound cut and dried. This isn't the first thing I've built him. Forchet's talking about breeding racehorses. Someone gave him the notion he can compete with the big boys. Who am I to argue? He's the client. He owns all kinds of businesses. We didn't discuss where the money came from. He wanted a nice barn—something to impress investors. He didn't ask for a letter, a written agreement—he just wanted my word. My word is enough. The contract would have come later—with the plans, before we started construction. Dammit, Jimmy, can't you just talk some sense into that little redheaded prick?"

"That little prick wants you to testify against Forchet," Grantham said evenly. "He's convinced he can make you do it. We can fight him. But the downside is we lose and you go to jail. Quist is offering an alternative. You need to think about it. I can't decide for you." He paused. "There is the matter of my fee—"

Dana interrupted. "Jimmy, would you excuse us for a minute? I want to talk to my husband."

"Of course." He stood and stepped to the door. "I'll be in my office. Have the receptionist buzz me when you're ready."

After he left, Dana crossed her arms and stared at me. "Did you know?"

"That Forchet was dirty?" I shook my head. "I knew he wasn't a Boy Scout. But I never thought . . ."

"You didn't think it through at all, did you?"

"Dana, I never once even imagined I could be charged with doing anything wrong. You heard Jimmy. It's not even about me. This Quist thinks I can hand him Forchet's head."

"Maybe you need to think about that."

"Think about what?"

She hesitated. "I don't want you to go to prison."

I stared at her. "That makes two of us. Christ, Forchet paid me with a goddamned certified check. Not cash. I wasn't laundering anything. You know that, don't you?"

"I know," she said softly. "But what if you have to choose? What if it's us or him?"

"What are you saying?"

She frowned. "I'm saying I'd rather see him go to prison than you."

I turned away and looked out the window at the traffic moving on

Peachtree Street, twenty floors below. "It's not that simple."

"Is that what you want me to tell the girls when they ask why Daddy doesn't come home? Believe me, I know how that feels!"

I whirled around and stared at her. "It's not the same."

"Maybe not. But this isn't just about you, Ben. Whatever you do is going to affect all of us."

"Dana, didn't you hear what Quist said? He's talking about the witness protection program. Imagine what that would do to our lives."

She drew a deep breath. "But if John Forchet is in jail . . ."

"If what Quist said about Forchet is true, I'd rather take my chances with a jury than cross Forchet."

"You did know—didn't you?"

I didn't answer.

"I don't want my husband to go to prison," Dana repeated. There was more than anger in her voice.

I tried to keep my own voice level. "I don't want us to spend the rest of our lives wondering where John Forchet is—when he's going to get around to looking for us."

A tear slid down her cheek. "What are we supposed to do?" she whispered.

I pulled her to me, but she held herself stiff, refusing to return the embrace.

"We don't have a choice, Dana. We fight."

She didn't say anything.

7

YOU got to do something about T," Black said.

I lowered the *Time* magazine I'd been reading and looked at him. He was lying on his bunk, holding a letter from his big sister, Annalee. His face was impassive, but I got the feeling he'd been thinking about T for a while.

I sat up on my own bunk and tossed the magazine onto my locker. "I told him not to come around anymore; the kid just stares at me. Might as well be talking to the wall. He's got a chip on his shoulder, tell him to take it up with Rollie."

"It's not T I'm worryin' about. It's the brothers in the Nation. Couple of 'em have been complaining. Don't like to see a black man makin' a white man's bed. I told R.C., Abdulla's friend, that it was Rollie Shore, not you, telling T what to do." He shook his head in disgust. "Fool looks at me and says, 'One white man bad as another.' Won't be long before Abdulla decides T's making the brothers look bad."

"That's bullshit! You're as black as Abdulla. What's he say about T doing *your* laundry?"

Black sat up. "Listen up, Ben—if Abdulla thinks I'm dissing his brothers by letting T clean our house, let him come tell me hisself. He can carry his killer shit with him. He's smart; he ain't gonna fuck with me. But not everyone in his crew understands respect. Too many kids doin' too much time. They all be wanting to make a name for themselves—build a reputation. Better to get rid a T than have to deal with every fool in the Nation."

Abdulla's real name was James Davis—a bank robber from St. Louis who'd never managed to score more than a few thousand dollars at a time in his entire professional career. According to the jailhouse rumor mill, they popped him outside Granite City, Missouri, when a dye bomb exploded in his lap, nearly blinding him. Eyes full of red ink, he'd wrapped his van—stolen, too—around a utility pole. Now he was doing fifteen years. It wasn't enough time. Life without parole wouldn't be enough. James Davis might have been an incompetent bank robber, but prison had turned Abdulla Davis into a stone killer. He'd embraced the Nation of Equality, starting out as an enforcer for a crew in an Oklahoma penitentiary. Now he was the leader of his own crew here in Alabama. He was black, bald, angry—and the white man was to blame. Black was right—I didn't need Abdulla Davis and his crew on my case.

I pulled on my running shoes and stood. "Between Dr. Dave, Rollie, T, and the Nation, I'm beginning to not like this place."

Black smiled. "Where else you gonna get three hots and a cot for free?" He laughed at his own joke, then grew serious. "You know what *belabor* means?"

"Yeah, Black. I know what it means."

"Well, I don't mean to belabor the point, but I warned you—this friendship between you and Rollie Shore—it ain't healthy."

I shook my head. "I wouldn't call it a friendship."

"Call it whatever you want. You and the man been walkin' the track every day this week. People shakin' their heads, sayin' you an' Rollie tight."

"The man likes to walk and talk. I listen. He keeps a muzzle on Dr. Dave; I don't mind the conversation."

"Wouldn't have this problem with Dr. Dave if it weren't for Rollie. He's playing you."

I nodded. "Maybe. Maybe not. I'll handle the situation the way I think it should be handled."

Black shrugged. "Just so you deal with it soon. The man wants more than conversation. You're juggling fire. Now you got Abdulla to think about."

His warning was well meant, but I wasn't in the mood to *belabor* the point. I knew who and what Rollie Shore was, and I knew he was after something. But what? Eventually, I was going to have to confront him. On the street, it would have been simple. Thanks but no thanks, walk away. But this wasn't the street.

"How's your sister?" I asked, changing the subject.

Black folded his sister's letter and placed it carefully under his pillow. Then, ignoring my question, he scratched at his stomach and asked, "You and Rollie planning on doing any walking and talking tonight?"

This was getting old. "Yeah. You got a problem with that?"

"Chill, man. I ain't your problem. I was just thinking—if the man likes to talk so much, you ought to have him talk to Abdulla—before this thing with the Nation turns ugly." He got up off his bunk, slipped on his shower slides, and, still scratching, walked out of the cube.

Then, he poked his head back in and added, "After he straightens out Abdulla, have Rollie tell T to quit usin' that cheap-ass soap on the laundry. Givin' me a skin rash. He's gonna do the clothes, tell him to steal some damn *Tide* from someone."

■ ■ ■

The rec yard was crowded with men walking the track, working out on the weight pile, or simply hanging in small groups, making the most of the warm night, shooting the shit and smoking. High-powered sodium vapor lights mounted on tall steel poles cast an alien glare, the hellishly pink light falling across the yard and everything in it with the density of pale fog.

Rollie and Boris were waiting for me in front of the softball bleachers. Boris was shaking his head as his boss spoke sharply, one finger punctuating his words. I couldn't make out what they were saying.

When I got close, Rollie nodded a greeting. He looked irritated, his lined face closed, a white hand towel draped around his neck.

Boris stared at me, a scowl twisting his darkly stubbled Slavic cheeks.

At first, we walked in silence, Boris several paces in front of us. Insects chirped and whirred. In the distant darkness a large truck shifted gears and labored up a hill. Black's words echoed in my head. He was right. Now that Abdulla had become part of the equation, the games had to end. No matter Rollie's mood.

Thinking about Dana and the girls, I told myself to be patient. I circled the track, one eye on Rollie, my mind drifting, imagining Dana circling the schooling ring on that dappled gelding. Smiling . . .

Boris turned and grunted something I didn't catch, then fell silent. He and Rollie were in no mood to talk, both of their sour expressions tinted pink under the rec yard lights, like everything else.

After we'd gone a dozen laps, Rollie turned to me and broke the silence. "I hear you're having trouble at home."

I stopped midstride. "Where the hell did you hear that?"

He kept walking. "What's it matter where I heard it? I'm in the people business. I make it a point to know about my associates. Why didn't you come to me?"

Catching up to him, I said, "Since when are we associates?"

"Careful, Ben," he warned. "I'm not in the mood for jokes. I ask a question, give me an answer. Maybe I can help."

"And if I don't need help?"

He raised one eyebrow. "King Solomon said, 'He that walketh with wise men will become wise.' That's Proverbs. A wise man keeps his friends informed."

He was no friend, and I didn't like the casual way he mentioned my family. "I told you before, Rollie. My family is my business."

"You got a bug up your ass tonight?" His voice was mild, but it managed to hold an edge.

"Yeah—I do. I want to know why you set me up with T and Dr. Dave."

"Set you up?"

"Yeah—set me up."

He compressed his meaty lips into a frown. We walked half a lap in silence. Then his frown inverted itself into a cold smile. "*I* set you up, Ben, and there isn't going to be any doubt about why. I don't know what you're talking about."

I was angry enough to push harder. "I think you do. I don't get it, though. Why? Where's the percentage? I don't want anything to do with your action."

His chilly smile faded into something even colder. "You got squeezed by the feds. Kept your mouth shut. That makes you a mensch. It don't make you tough. You want something from me, ask. I'm in no mood to dance."

I stopped walking and waited until he stopped too. "The bit with T . . . Dr. Dave . . . what are you after?"

His shrewd eyes bored into mine. "What makes you think I'm after anything? A man can't do someone a favor? You think I got nothing better to do than play games with you?"

"You tell me."

He hesitated, his shoulders tight, his eyes blazing.

For a moment, I thought I'd gone too far.

Then the tension went out of him and he smiled again. "The hell with it, Ben. I've got things on my mind; didn't mean to take it out on you. Don't make too much out of a little thing. You were in a bad situation and I thought I could help. No harm done. Right?"

He punched me lightly on the shoulder. "Let it go, kid. I'll make it up to you sometime. Come on—let's pick up the pace. I'll tell you a little story."

I didn't want to hear another of his endless stories, but walking away wasn't going to resolve anything.

So we circled the track faster, Rollie sweating and talking.

"My father, Solomon Schmulowitz, God rest his soul, came to Brooklyn from Odessa in 1922. He had nothing but the clothes on his back. Changed the family name—thought Shore sounded more American." He shook his head, amused at the memory. "America was good to Papa. Opportunity. Freedom. Married a girl in the neighborhood and within five years he was shop foreman for the largest coat manufacturer in Manhattan. He was a little man, small, hairy as hell. But he was hard. Hard as a fuckin' rock. You had to be tough. Within a decade he was the number-two man in the union. How? How did this little fucking yiddle with hairy hands and an accent so thick you could hardly understand him, come over here without two nickels to rub together and become a union boss in a couple a years? How?"

He paused, waiting for me to ask.

"How, Rollie?" I obliged.

"I'll tell you what he used to tell me. There's two things in life got an absolutely clear meaning. Know what they are?"

I waited.

"An offer and a hard-on." He punched me on the shoulder again and laughed. "Think about it. A fuckin' hard-on and an offer. Both got exactly one meaning. Can't misconstrue either of 'em—take it or leave it. Simple as that. The old man used to say every meeting, every conversation's a transaction. It's all business. Life is business. And there's more than one way to structure an offer."

It was a nice story, but I didn't see what Rollie and I were supposed to be transacting. I waited for him to explain, but he marched along, the ends of the hand towel around his neck gripped tightly in either fist. He looked down at the track, focused, I supposed, on memories of past negotiations with hard, little Sol Schmulowitz.

I thought about my own father—Arthur Hemmings. He'd divorced my mother when I was twelve and moved to California. She was dead now, the victim of a heart attack at the too-early age of fifty-three. But as hard as she'd struggled to make a decent life for us after he left, not once do I remember her uttering a negative word about the bastard. Maybe all that pent-up anger is what finally killed her. At first, my father had called once every couple of months. He sent me birthday cards and Christmas presents. Then nothing. No phone calls, no birthday packages, no contact at all. He just disappeared, leaving me nothing more than the memory of how his pipe smelled and a few old snapshots of a tall, gruff-looking man whom I vaguely resembled. I'd tried to track him down once but failed. I didn't know if he were alive or dead. He'd be about Rollie's age now. But it had been so long since I'd thought of him, I wasn't sure how I felt anymore. His memory was a dull pang. A sore that no longer bled but hadn't quite healed. I'd promised myself that my children would never have to spend a single second wondering about me. But I'd broken that promise. Their daddy didn't come home for dinner, either.

"Do you know what it means to be a Jew?" Rollie asked, snapping me out of my own memories.

"In here?"

"Anywhere, Ben. Anywhere in the world. . . . Do you have any concept of it?"

I thought about my wife, her mother, Rose, then shook my head. "I guess not, Rollie."

He nodded. "Of course not. Why should you? He was a small man, my papa. But what he did was big. A very big thing. In the old country, a Jew didn't get up in the morning and wonder how the weather was going to be. He wondered if the Cossacks were going to ride in and burn them out. It was no small thing to escape that kind of oppression. To leave it all behind. Everything but his identity—his religion. But that was enough. He stood up for it—never let anybody take it from him. That's what it means to be a Jew. You learn to fight. When you're surrounded by enemies, you preempt trouble. You don't let anyone fuck you. You take care of yourself, because no one else will."

He was serious, caught up in his own history. It was easy to imagine Sol Schmulowitz pounding these lessons into young Rollie's head. But somehow the message had gone wrong. Rollie was the oppressor, not the oppressed. His father had made it to freedom. He'd survived the pogroms. Maybe that made him a hero. But what had Rollie survived? The mean streets of Brooklyn in the late fifties? Mugging old ladies and making his bones by running numbers and terrorizing neighborhood candy-store owners. I studied him. This was no hero of the Jewish people. All I saw was a bully justifying himself, and I didn't understand why he was bothering to waste it on me.

Then, without waiting for me to react, he changed the subject. "This *tsuris* at home, what are you planning to do?"

The question caught me by surprise.

He was studying me now, that hungry expression I'd grown to despise illuminating his face. "You have to make allowances, Ben. You're inside—she's out there. You're on ice. Hell, we're all on ice. But for them, life goes on. Sometimes they need a shoulder to lean on. You can't take it personally. It means nothing . . ."

"You've got it wrong, Rollie," I snapped, as though he'd prodded me with a sharp spur. "That's not the way it is with Dana and me. Money's tight—we may lose the house. That's all—" I started to say more, then bit it off, wondering why I was defending my marriage to the likes of Rollie Shore.

He was grinning at me. "Sure you will, kid. You'll work it out. What's the name of the bank holding your mortgage?"

I started to tell him it was none of his goddamned business, then realized that it was too late. He'd done it again. Opened me up like a book.

Before I could say anything, a couple of guys from 4-dorm called out to Rollie and headed our way. But Boris, walking a few paces in front of us, waved them off.

"I'll see you fellas later," Rollie shouted. "Come by the Pride Club around eight forty-five."

As they walked off, he turned to me. "I hear Abdulla's been making noise about T."

"You heard right." I was seething.

"Sometimes civilized doesn't work, does it?" He shook his head. "Dave is a child. He's too damned stupid to understand what you did for him. If I hadn't put him in his place, he'd have felt the need to bounce you around a little—prove to the world how tough he is. In another week, he'll forget you exist. This thing with T is another matter. I did what you asked me to do. But it didn't work out so good, did it?"

"No. It didn't."

Resuming his pace, he said, "Okay. Consider your arrangement with T terminated. But remember this: civilized works only with someone who has more to lose than you do. A boy like T has nothing—nothing at all to lose. He doesn't play by the same rules as you or me. You deal with him on his own level. Not yours. Otherwise people get the wrong idea. Understand?"

I just stared at him.

Ignoring my reaction, he asked, "You built some pretty fancy stables, didn't you?"

We'd already had this discussion. "*Barns,* Rollie. I build barns."

"There's a difference?"

When I didn't answer, he frowned at me and said, "Who's playing games now?"

Disgusted with myself, I shook my head. "Barns are working buildings. Stables—I don't know, it just sounds too damned fancy. Why do you want to know all of this?"

"Just curious. How'd you get hooked up with all that old money? Your wife?"

"My wife had nothing to do with it."

"Ease up, Ben. We're just making friendly conversation. Your wife, she worked in that lab, didn't she? The one experimenting with artificially inseminating horses?"

"Yeah, Rollie—she worked there a long time ago. Why?"

"Like I said, just conversation. I own a couple dozen ponies, most of them run at Calder, down in Miami. Ever been there?"

I shook my head.

"One of these days you'll be my guest." He fell quiet for a minute, then he said, "You built Ham Hamilton's . . . *barn,* didn't you? You friendly with him?"

I turned and looked at him. "No, Rollie. We're not friends."

He nodded thoughtfully, seemingly satisfied by the answer. But there was more floating behind that calculating light in his glittering blue eyes. "I've had it, kid. Enough walking for one night."

As far as I was concerned, it had been enough walking for the rest of my sentence.

We stepped off the track and he put a fatherly arm around my shoulders. For a split second I tried to imagined Rollie *Schmulowitz* Shore as Arthur Hemmings.

The image faded as Rollie pushed his big pink face at mine and said, "This problem with the house . . . Don't worry about a thing. You got friends you don't know you got."

Then he joined Boris and the two of them marched off toward the Pride Club.

I shivered in spite of the mild night.

8

THE trial lasted a day and a half—not counting the morning we spent picking a jury. I say *we,* but it was Grantham and his associate, a vaguely pretty blond named Anna Duncan, who selected the eight women and four men who determined my fate.

Before Judge Halstrom, a serious-looking woman in her late forties, ordered the jury to take their seats in the box, Grantham stood and said, "Your Honor, I would like to renew my motion to dismiss the charges against my client. They're nothing more than strong-arm tactics—an attempt to force my client to become an unwilling agent on behalf of the FBI. The government has faifled to meet its burden. There is no credible evidence that Ben Hemmings knowingly and willingly engaged in any kind of a scheme to launder money for anyone. If the court would—"

Quist jumped to his feet, but before he could speak, the judge rapped her gavel twice. "The court," she said, interrupting, "has already spoken on this issue, Mr. Grantham."

Grantham took the interruption in stride. "Your Honor, I've studied the statutes and precedents. In the Ninth Circuit—"

"Judge, we've been through this at pretrial," Quist complained. "It doesn't mater what the Ninth Circuit did or didn't find. The indictment against Mr. Hemmings is perfectly clear."

"I agree with Mr. Quist," the judge stated. "I studied your motion to dismiss very carefully before denying it, Mr. Grantham. The statute is, however, quite clear. If Mr. Hemmings knowingly and willingly agreed to deliver goods or property of value in return for money that was illegally obtained, then he is in violation."

Grantham smiled his best smile. "That's my point, Your Honor. Mr. Hemmings did no such thing. But even if he had suspected Forchet wasn't entirely legitimate, is it incumbent upon a businessman to ascertain the origins of a client's money? Is a tailor who sells a suit to a man who may or may not be a drug dealer guilty of money laundering? A dentist who supplies a gold crown? Where would it stop? According to the Ninth Circuit—"

The judge rapped her gavel again and smiled thinly. "Save it for your rule twenty-nine motion, Mr. Grantham. *After* the prosecution finishes making its case, I'll hear your arguments to dismiss. Not now. Your renewed motion is denied."

"I object, Your Honor," Grantham said, frowning for the first—but not the last—time that day.

"Your objection is noted. Now, if there's nothing else, let's seat the jury." She picked up a sheaf of papers and thumbed through them.

From then on, it went pretty much the way Grantham had said it would. Quist, with Special Agent Partone sitting behind him, made a compelling opening statement, then spent the first afternoon building a circumstantial case against John Jay Forchet. We'd tried to subpoena Forchet to compel him to testify in my defense. But the man had proven to be serviceproof. I hadn't seen or heard from him since my arrest. He'd conveniently disappeared. Which, at least in my mind, seemed to bolster the case against me.

"If they know all this about Forchet, why the hell aren't they trying him instead of me?" I whispered to Grantham as Quist questioned his lead witness. The witness, an FBI forensic accountant, was explaining to the jury a complicated flowchart he'd provided that allegedly tracked Forchet's bookmaking and various other illegal sources of income.

"He's testifying as to the nature of his investigation. Not the results. It's all hearsay—circumstantial—not enough to try a man like Forchet. Wait till they play those tapes," Grantham said, jotting notes on a legal pad. "That's when the fun starts."

"Shit!" I whispered, a little too loudly.

One of the jurors, a heavyset older woman in the front row, looked at me and frowned.

Sitting at the defense table was a damned unnerving experience. You feel every eye in the courtroom watching your every move. And that makes you self-conscious about the simplest things. How you smile. If you should smile. Should you look angry and defiant? Humble? How do you let the jurors know you shouldn't be there in the first place, sitting at the defense table surrounded by lawyers like every rapist and murderer you've ever seen on the evening news? Do you look at the jury? Return their stares? Or do you gaze down at your folded hands, hoping you look as innocent as a choirboy? If you pretend to make notes, can they see that you're really doodling? What will that tell them about you? We had no jury expert. Couldn't afford one. Without my mother-in-law's help—she'd mortgaged her condo—we couldn't have afforded Grantham. And all he said was, "Be yourself."

I turned and looked back at Dana, who sat in the first row of the spectators' section beside her mother, Rose Abrams. Dana's father, an insurance executive, had died suddenly and unexpectedly when she was in her early teens. Growing up fatherless was something we shared—one of the thousand things we understood about each other. Rose, a shorter, heavier, gray-haired version of Dana, also understood the magnitude of that kind of loss. After her husband's death, she'd struggled and sacrificed to make sure that Dana had a home that was safe and solid—a home she could be proud of. But one person, no matter how hard she tries, can't fill that kind of a hole in a young kid's heart. I knew about the loneliness, the fear. You react in any number of ways. I tried to become the man of the house. Dana rebelled. She'd rejected

Rose's efforts to be both father and mother. The two of them had the scars to prove it. But time and love go a long way toward healing even the worst hurts. Now they were as close as any mother and daughter I'd ever known. And that closeness had grown to include me.

Then Grantham was tapping me on the shoulder. "Stand up, Ben. We're taking a recess while the judge deals with another case."

■ ■ ■

It took the jury all of two hours to convict me.

Ninety agonizing days later, Judge Halstrom sentenced me to thirty-six months. Even then it seemed unreal—something that was happening to someone else. At least it seemed that way until the day I self-surrendered. On that day it became all too real.

It was a cold Thursday in January, and although the drive from our home in Atlanta to the prison in northern Alabama to which I had been designated would take less than two hours, it was a drive I knew I couldn't face with Dana. No one had been able to tell me exactly what to expect once I arrived in prison. All I had to go on was Hollywood's version. I wasn't sure how accurate that version was, but I knew better than to arrive with tears in my eyes. Which is exactly what I would have done if my wife had driven me up to the gates and waved good-bye. So I arranged for a friend to drive me. Dana would take me to his house, where we would say our good-byes. Then I'd have the two-hour drive to get myself together.

We'd finalized the practical side of our plans weeks ago. When we'd first met, Dana was just beginning her graduate thesis, studying with her faculty advisor at a research station belonging to the state university. Located near the Hamiltons' farm, the extension lab was perfecting the long-term storage and viability of frozen horse semen, one of Ham's pet projects—a project he funded out of his own pocket. But Dana had put her studies on hold when she got pregnant with Olivia. Now, she was going to go back to work, training show jumpers and giving riding lessons. It wasn't exactly what she wanted to do, but she'd be working with horses and one step closer to resuming her studies. Combining our savings with what she earned, she'd just be able to scrape by until I got home. Money, she'd said, was the least of her worries. But that had been brave talk and we both knew it.

We pulled into my friend's driveway early and sat there for a while. Over the weeks between my trial and my sentencing, I'd explained to Olivia and Nadine what was happening, as best you can explain such things to young children. Now there were only a few minutes left to tell Dana what was in my heart.

"I'm sorry," I said. "If I could undo all of this . . ."

She nodded. "I know . . . I just . . ."

"We're strong enough to survive it," I said, touching her face, my vision blurred with tears.

She reached for my hand, her own cheeks wet. "It won't be that long. We'll come see you, Olivia and Nadine and I. . . . We'll visit . . ." She choked back a sob and closed her eyes. "God, I'm going to miss you. I'm going to miss you so much, Ben."

We sat in the car, holding hands, not saying anything for what seemed a long time. We'd said it all already. We'd said it a thousand times.

After a while, the windshield fogged.

"Like two kids parking," I said, smiling.

Dana wiped at the condensation, then cracked opened her window.

The air that flooded into the car was clean and sharp and carried her scent. I promised myself that I'd carry that scent with me wherever I went—for however long I was away. I closed my eyes and breathed her in.

Then, before I was ready, it was time to go.

Forcing myself to get out of the car, I walked around to the driver's side.

Opening her door, I leaned in and kissed my wife, long and hard. Her lips were salty, and breaking off that kiss was the hardest thing I ever did.

I stood beside the car, my fingers wrapped around the top of her open door, fixing her face in my memory, not knowing how long it would be before I would see it again.

"I'm scared, Ben. Be careful. I want you back in one piece," she said, her voice a raw whisper.

I was afraid, too. My insides were quaking, but I hadn't admitted it to anyone. Not even Dana. "I'll be fine. I promise."

We stared at each other. And in her eyes I could see that I hadn't fooled her at all—that she was more afraid about what might happen to me than about the long and lonely ordeal she was about to face. It almost broke my heart.

"Start the car," I said gently.

She fumbled with the keys, almost flooding the engine. "You'll call as soon as you can?"

"The minute I can get to a phone. Now stop worrying about me. Go home and take care of our girls."

She nodded, but I couldn't bring myself to close the car door. I just stood there staring down at her.

She drew a deep and ragged breath, pulled on her seat belt, then hit the button putting up her window.

Only my fingers were still wrapped around the top of the door frame and the window closed on them. The hard ridge of glass trapping me, cutting painfully into the soft flesh above my fingernails.

"Stop!" I shouted at her.

She froze.

"I love you, Ben," she cried, sure I was at last having some kind of an emotional meltdown.

"My . . . fingers."

She didn't understand.

"Dana! My fingers! Put . . . down . . . the window."

We laughed through our tears as she drove away.

I laughed all the way to prison.

9

THE Wednesday-night line outside the phone room was longer than usual, but I joined it anyway. I'd lied to Rollie. There was more going on between Dana and me than real estate worries. She'd made the two-hour drive to visit me like clockwork, every other week for over a year and a half. Only lately, I found myself wondering about her. About us. What happened was my fault; I carried it with me every day. I'd let her down—then I left her alone. She was angry. Who wouldn't be? But it wasn't the anger that worried me. It was the loneliness. And I was helpless to fight it.

Maybe it was all in my head. But I hadn't been able to reach her in almost a week, and I wanted to hear her voice. Wanted to gauge from what she said, and the way she said it, if we were all right with each other. So I signed the list and walked to the end of the line. Prepared to wait as long as it took for one of the ten pay phones lining the walls of the cramped, cinder-block phone room to come available, more than a little concerned about the way things had gone with Rollie Shore.

"Yo, Ben. What up, man?" Truck shouted from the front of the line.

"Same shit, Truck," I answered, trying to sound cool, untroubled. "Who's the lucky country girl tonight?"

He threw back his melon-shaped head and laughed.

"They all lucky. Every one of 'em. You got a visit? Your wife comin' Saturday?"

"I hope so. This line ever moves, I'll find out."

"You got a beautiful family, man. You lucky they hangin' in with you. Most don't."

"You know it," I said. But Truck was right. Very few relationships survive prison. I desperately wanted mine to be one of them.

The last few times I'd tried to call home, I'd reached the answering machine. But I hadn't been able to leave a message. The pay phones are programmed so you have to call collect. If no one answers, you lose your spot. It's that simple. No one can call you, and there are only ten phones for over seven hundred men. So you wait in line, hoping like hell someone will be there to take your call. If you can't get through, you either give up or go back to the end of the line and try again. When that happens, your imagination can run away with you. The frustration of always being the one to call, and always having to call collect, and never knowing what simple thing might have prevented your wife from answering—a quick stop for milk, a trip to the drugstore or the video store, a late riding lesson—all conspire to set your worst fears howling inside your head. You wonder if everyone is safe. Then you wonder where she is . . .

Then you hate yourself for wondering.

On weeknights the line usually took an hour, sometimes an hour and a half. Once you got to a phone, you had fifteen minutes to complete your conversation, then the connection was automatically cut. Large signs in English and Spanish warned that every conversation was electronically recorded. But those ten phones were the only real-time link to the outside—the voices of those you loved, the only proof that life existed beyond the confines of the compound. So you waited your turn, dreaming about softer places and better days. Wondering how to compress everything you wanted to say into a fifteen-minute burst. Hoping you'd get the chance.

Weekends and holidays were different. The clock slowed cruelly on weekends and holidays. You had time to think—time to realize how isolated you really were. Then the phone line grew to over two hours, sometimes longer. You waited anyway. You get good at waiting in prison.

The line inched forward. Rollie's cryptic advice not to worry about the house or money worried the hell out of me. But I decided not to speak about it on the phone. Assuming I got to a phone before recall at nine-thirty for the ten-o'clock count. I looked at my watch. It was a little past eight-thirty, that gave me an hour.

The last time I'd spoken to Dana, she'd seemed distant, distracted. I rationalized that I understood—that she was scared and lonely. Tired of bearing all the burdens without the partner who'd agreed to be there in good times and bad. She didn't want to lose the house. Who could blame her? It was a fine old Victorian—not large, but well built. Two stories with a wrap-around porch and an enormous ginkgo tree in the front yard. It was the tree, with its wide canopy of fan-shaped leaves that shaded the porch in summer and in autumn reached to the sky in a shimmer of gold, that finally sold us on the house. We'd worked hard restoring the place, put our hearts into it. Now there was nothing I could do to help her hold on to it.

Dana was burning the candle at both ends, struggling to make ends meet—leaving the girls with Rose more often than ever before. For the last month or so, I'd been getting the answering machine more often than I got my wife. And it was getting harder and harder to shut out the ugly voice that chimed inside my head whenever that goddamned machine picked up: *Where is she? Where is she?*

Even now, I had to work to push that voice out of my head.

Ignoring the shouting and jostling around me, I imagined Olivia and Nadine laughing and playing on the swings in Chastain Park. The line advanced at a glacial pace.

Finally, it was my turn.

Dana answered on the third ring. She sounded exhausted.

"You okay?" I asked.

"I'm fine, Ben . . . hold on a sec . . ." She put her hand over the phone, but didn't cover the mouthpiece completely. "Get back in bed. *Olivia* . . . If I have to come in there . . ."

"What's going on? Is everybody okay?" I asked when she came back on the line.

"Everybody's fine. Olivia thinks there's a cat living in the attic. She thinks she hears him at night, meowing. She won't go to sleep; she's afraid he's hungry."

I smiled. "You? Are you okay?"

"Yeah, honey. I'm fine, just a little tired." I could hear her moving around. The clink of dishes, the sound of running water.

"You just get home?" The words came out sounding different than I meant them.

"Dammit, Ben. I'm doing the best I can. I've been in—"

"Hey, I didn't mean anything," I said, interrupting, trying to smooth her ruffled feathers. "I was just worried, that's all."

Silence, the sound of water splashing into the sink. Then, voice hollow, she said, "They're going to put the house into foreclosure next week. I can't stop them."

"Did you see the loan officer in person, take him our financial records?"

"Of course I did," she snapped. "It didn't make a bit of difference. They don't give a shit how much we used to make. We don't have it now. The fact that you're in prison doesn't help."

"Do you want me to call Jimmy?"

"What could he do?"

I shrugged, then realized she couldn't see me. "Have you kept on him about the appeal?"

"I call; sometimes he actually calls back."

"Maybe if you went to see him . . ."

"And when am I supposed to do that? I'm only one person, Ben . . . Dammit, hold on . . . Olivia! *Please* get back in bed. I promise you there's no cat up there. . . ." She put the phone down with a thump and I heard the clomp of her paddock boots on the tiled floor as she walked out of the kitchen.

A few minutes later she came back on the line. "Sorry. She's crying; she thinks the cat has babies. Let me get her settled before she wakes Nadine. We'll talk on Saturday. I'll be there around noon, okay?"

What could I say? *Let Olivia cry—I need you, too?*

"Yeah, Dana. We'll talk Saturday. Give the girls kisses, okay?"

"Ben . . . I'm sorry . . ."

I said I understood, then hung up.

10

SPRINGFIELD, screaming at the top of his lungs, woke me up. "I'll kill the motherfucker touches my shit again! I'm talkin' to all a y'all. Touch my shit and I'll kill ya!"

Answering voices rang out across the dorm—angry threats, pleas for silence, hysterical laughter.

According to my watch, it was a little past two in the morning. Another night in paradise.

I sat up on my bunk and rubbed my eyes.

Springfield was still screaming. "Gonna kill me a fucker! Watch and see. Y'all pretend you ain't 'fraid, but I'll kill a motherfucker soon as look at him." The litany of Springfield's threats sounded like a bad cartoon.

Black sat up, too. Half awake, he looked around, gauging the threat. Then, satisfied that Springfield presented no immediate danger, he fell back onto his bunk with a groan. Rico tossed fitfully but didn't open his eyes.

Someone shouted, "Shut the fuck up, Springfield, or I'll come over there and put my foot down your fucking throat!"

This produced a chorus of cat calls. Springfield started hooting and howling, middle-of-the-night jungle sounds being one of his specialties.

Rolling onto my side, I covered my head with the thin prison-issue pillow and tried to block out the noise. It didn't help. Springfield's screeching penetrated the worn tick-ing and went on and on. Sleep was impossible. I stared at the cinder-block wall by my head for the ten thousandth time. The rough pattern of the concrete blocks as familiar to me as the creases on the palms of my hands. A shiny brown roach scuttled by. I watched him—antlers bobbing, sudden stops and starts—vigilantly following some unseen trail, searching for crumbs, or maybe a girl roach. About then, I seriously considered getting up off my bunk and killing Springfield. I could think of dozens of ways to do it, but I settled on strangling him. Wrapping my hands around his throat until his high-pitched voice went out with one last squeak. I could feel his skin stretched taught under my fingers, see his eyes bulging, his pitiless screaming silenced once and for all.

Only killing Springfield wouldn't do any good. There were twenty or thirty other kids in the dorm just like him. Tough kids, kids you'd cross the street to avoid, the noise their way of coping with the dark and lonely nights.

So I lay there, hoping they'd tire of the game, trying hard not to think about the one thing you try not to think about. Getting out. Going home. Leaving the madness and the filth behind forever.

I imagined Olivia and Nadine, sound asleep in their rooms. I could see myself tiptoeing in to check on them. Pulling the covers up, tucking the blankets around their little bodies. Kissing their foreheads.

Did they dream sweet dreams?

Were they snug and safe?

I fought the memory but lost and found myself thinking about the day I'd told them Daddy had to go away.

■ ■ ■

Dana and I had decided to wait until after Christmas to tell the girls. On December twenty-eighth, not quite a month before I self-surrendered, we all went to Chastain Park to play on the swings. Nadine was three by then, Olivia going on five. They were as different as two sisters could be. Nadine, happy and content, was the more affectionate and generous of the two. Olivia was a sprite, quick to laugh and just as quick to anger, her little mind quicksilver.

Dana held Nadine in her arms while I put Olivia, clutching Silky, the little pink satin bear that she carried everywhere, up onto one of the swings.

"Me swing! Me swing!" Nadine cried. But Dana gave her a bottle of apple juice, which struck Nadine as even better than the swing. Cradled in her mother's arms, she watched, green eyes shining, as her sister swung higher and higher.

It was a sharp, clear day, more like spring than winter, the cloudless sky crisscrossed with contrails. A full, white moon hung low near the horizon. Olivia thought it was a mistake.

"Daddy, does God have a watch?" she asked, staring at the moon as I pushed her higher on the swing.

"I don't think he needs one, honey."

She thought for a moment, her face gravely serious.

I stole a look at Dana, hoping she could hear this exchange. Nadine was sucking on her bottle, one hand tangled in her mother's hair. Dana smiled bravely at me, but she looked on the verge of tears.

"Well, *I* think he's asleep," Olivia said on the next downswing.

"Asleep?" I said.

"You think he's alive, don't you?"

I started to answer, then lost my train of thought. The sky, the bright day, suddenly closed in on me. Time slowed, every detail becoming unbearably vivid. I couldn't stop inhaling—the crisp air too light to fill my lungs. My daughter's red sweater painfully beautiful against the sky as the arc of the swing carried her up and down. The light breeze roared in my ears. I closed my eyes for a second, trying to pull myself together. How was I supposed to tell my children I was going far away for a very long time? Where would I get the strength to leave them? I felt like my heart might simply burst inside my chest.

"Daddy . . . " Olivia said, sounding exasperated. "You aren't listening. Do you think he's alive?"

"Who, honey?"

"God, silly. Do you think God is alive?"

"Of course I do. Do you?"

She took the question seriously. "I think he's alive. Just sleeping. For a long time, asleep."

I stopped pushing and let the swing come to rest.

Olivia was staring at the moon, Silky held tightly under one arm. "I think he's sleeping and we're his dreams," she continued, her eyes focused on the hard white disk she thought shouldn't be hung in the afternoon sky.

I tried to answer her, but I couldn't.

When she turned to look at me, she frowned. "Why are you crying, Daddy?"

■ ■ ■

I pulled the pillow tighter around my head and started to pray. I forgot about Springfield and I prayed long and hard. I screwed my eyes shut and I tried to pray fervently enough to be heard over the din and bedlam of prison. But when I opened my eyes, the cinder-block wall hadn't changed. I was still here, and Springfield was still howling.

And God was still sleeping.

11

THE next morning, T was dead. Beaten to death in the showers of 4-dorm. No one heard or saw a thing. They never do.

The hacks locked the compound down. Standard procedure. All inmates restricted to their cubes—no movement allowed. At first, our dorm buzzed with rumors of an escape.

"Remember them two wanted a beer?" Rico asked Black. He was sitting on the top bunk, swinging his legs, picket-fence smile in place. "Last time they locked us down was on account a them fools. Wonder who done bolted now."

Black had his face in his dictionary, so Rico redirected the question at me.

I remembered, all right. It had happened three weeks earlier. Two men working the outside landscape detail had decided that a cold brew would be just the thing after a long, hot day swinging weed whackers. Being familiar with the general vicinity, they chose a place named the American Road House, a tavern located about three miles from the compound. They put down their weed whackers and walked there. No one saw them leave their detail. No one reported them missing. If they'd made it back in time for recall and count, they might have gotten away with it.

Apparently they sauntered into the Road House just

before three in the afternoon wearing prison blues. Stepped right up to the bar and ordered a couple of Buds like they were regulars. The place was dim and unusually crowded for the hour, Garth Brooks's "Ropin' the Wind" blaring from the jukebox.

But neither of them gave it a second thought. I guess they were thirsty.

The bartender pulled a couple of longnecks out of the cooler, but before he could serve them up, someone unplugged the jukebox. Someone else cranked up the house lights.

The place fell silent.

About then, it must have dawned on them that something was drastically wrong.

The two thirsty cons turned slowly and looked around.

The bar was filled to capacity with off-duty hacks who'd rented the place to throw a retirement bash for one of their own, a balding lieutenant who'd bought a bass boat and a double-wide outside Orlando and had just finished his last duty shift. An hour later and the warden himself would have been there.

The way I'd heard the story, the lieutenant was so goddamned happy to be retiring, he persuaded the other hacks to let the two inmates finish their beers before having them shackled, sent to the hole, and eventually shipped off to a max-security joint in northern Minnesota. The two empty Bud bottles now hung on a specially built shelf in the bar. The two most expensive beers ever served in Alabama.

I was about to tell Rico that I had no idea who might have bolted when the doors at either end of the dorm crashed open and two teams of SORT goons swarmed in.

Banging a lead-weighted baton on a steel locker, the captain screamed, "On your feet, motherfuckers! Now! Hit the floor! Shirts off, hands out. Do it! Do it! Do it!"

The body-armored goons came charging down the aisles separating the cubes, heavy boots pounding the floor, shouting and screaming instructions. Black dropped the dictionary and stood. Rico hopped off his bunk and looked around, eyes wide.

Guards holding riot guns took up positions at either end of the dorm. Helmet visors down, looking more like Darth Vader's cousins than anything human.

They swept through the dorm, inspecting us like so many cattle headed for market.

"Turn around. Let me see your feet . . . Now, fucker! Now!"

"Your hands . . ."

"Move it, asshole! I'm not fucking around."

"Take that goddamned shirt off! Now!"

"Over here, Cap'n. Look at this one!"

It was bedlam. I stood beside my bunk, tensed, ready to hit the floor if they let loose with those riot guns.

Rico, looking like a man with plenty to hide, muttered, "What they want, Black? What they doin'?"

"Chill," Black whispered. "Ain't lookin' for gamblin' slips—they lookin' for marks on your body, some sign you been fightin'. Just do what they say—you cool, man."

It was over almost as quickly as it had started. No one had been shackled and taken away—no sign at all that the violent inspection had turned up any evidence of anything. Prison hacks are strange animals. With few exceptions, men who take jobs caging other men are who you think they would be. Brains and imagination are not job requirements. If Rico had left a hundred gambling slips on his bunk, they'd have ignored them. And conversely, if they'd been out to bust the ever-present card games, they'd have ignored a hundred broken and bleeding knuckles. The rules shift and slide, depending upon who's on duty. We didn't know about T yet. But it all made sense when we found out. Murder would not—could not—be tolerated. It made everyone look bad. Especially the warden. Someone was going to go down for T's killing. But the odds of him being the actual killer were slim to none if he was crewed up.

After the last goon left the dorm, someone shouted: "Out the house."

Voices buzzed angrily—macho complaints about the treatment we'd received, fantasy threats about what would happen the next time a hack looked sideways at anyone. Springfield started with the jungle noises. Calmer voices speculated on what had caused the shakedown.

An hour later, the news about T circulated throughout the dorms.

Sugar Hill, a friend of Rico's, poked his head into our cube and said breathlessly, "Just talked to Wade. They found the motherfucker hanging by the neck on a wire coat hanger wrapped 'round a shower head. Beat his face in. Put a damn nail in his head. Poor fucker didn't even look like T. Looked like a goddamn piece a meat. Blood everywhere."

When Sugar left, Black looked at me. "A nail in his head? That sound like Rollie?" he asked.

I shook my head. "I don't know. Could have been Abdulla."

Everyone had a theory about who did it and what the nail meant. But no one knew for sure.

The hacks kept us locked down all day Thursday and most of Friday. Then, late Friday afternoon, they let us out. But not before throwing ten men from 4-dorm into the hole, pending further investigation.

I didn't know who killed T, or why. But I was painfully aware that I'd had some small part in his death, and I didn't like the way it felt.

Black felt responsible, too. "Need to stick close together," he warned. "Keep your eyes open. Rollie moved on T without Abdulla's blessing, gon' be trouble. They workin' together . . ."—he shrugged—". . . too bad for T, but it takes a load off our asses."

It sounded cold, but he was right. No one had forced T to steal from Rollie—he'd chosen his own foolish course.

I knew all about choosing a foolish course, but I felt sickened just the same by the thought of T hanging, beaten and mutilated, on the end of a wire coat hanger.

"You find out what the brothers are saying," I told Black. "I'll talk to Rollie."

■ ■ ■

By Saturday morning, it became clear that whatever had gone down had gone down with some kind of an agreement in place. After throwing their suspects in the hole, unlucky bastards who had little or no connection to either Rollie or Abdulla, the hacks let the rest of us resume normal schedules.

The compound stayed amazingly quiet. I hadn't been able to speak to Rollie. He'd been locked down like the rest of us until Friday afternoon. Once the lockdown ended, I tried to see him, but he'd retreated to the Pride Club with Boris and Dr. Dave. They'd kept the door locked, refusing entrance to anyone. But not before Rollie and Abdulla had made a show of walking a few laps together. It had been enough to silence any talk of a race riot.

I was in my cube dressing when Black came in with an old con called Chicken Man.

"You got a visit?" Black asked.

"Dana's coming this afternoon." I glanced at my watch. It was almost eleven o'clock, and in spite of everything that had happened, I was excited at the prospect of seeing her—thrilled at the thought of actually touching her. I rolled on some underarm deodorant. Then, ignoring Black and Chicken Man—whatever they had to say couldn't be as pleasant as anticipating Dana's visit—I tried to remember where Reggie kept his aftershave hidden.

Black watched me for a moment, then said, "Chicken says he saw what happened. I thought you might want to hear."

I looked at him.

He shrugged. "You want to know, don't you?"

I closed my eyes and tried to think about the way my wife smelled. But it didn't work. When I opened my eyes, Black and Chicken were still standing there. It was probably safer not to know, but I tucked in my shirt and followed the two of them to the back of the dorm anyway.

When we were alone, Black said, "Go ahead, Chicken. Tell Ben what you saw."

The old man looked around as though he were afraid of being overheard.

He cleared his throat, working his toothless mouth from side to side, as if he needed to warm it up before his voice would function. His eyes were cloudy, the whites yellowed and shot with broken veins. His long hands were calloused, his thin fingers nervously tugging at the buttons of his shirt.

"Go on," Black encouraged him. "Tell him what you told me."

"Ain't young no more," Chicken began, his voice a soft and powdery southern drawl. "Got the prostrate—don't sleep so good. Gots to get up and piss four, five times. Like to make a man not want to sleep at all."

The loudspeaker crackled and paged several men, including Rollie Shore, to the visiting room.

Chicken glanced at Black, then continued, his voice low and slow. "Wednesday night no different than any other. Was up and down, leakin' like a sieve. 'Bout four in the mornin', maybe a little later, I was in the can and I heard voices in the shower." He shook his head. "Been down long as me, you seen it all. Voices in the shower ain't no big thing. Then I hear 'em scufflin'—somebody moanin'. Know better than to go in there. But you knows what they say 'bout curiosity . . . couldn't help wonderin' who was gettin' whupped."

He hesitated. "Nothin' but a boy—got great-granchirren older 'n T. I hates what that man ordered done to that boy. Hates it like hell."

I looked at Black. But he avoided my eye.

Chicken noticed and thought I didn't believe him. "Ain't no rat—Black aks me to tell you what I seen. You don't like it, I be just as happy to go on 'bout my business . . ."

I told him I wanted to hear, that I knew he wasn't a rat.

He nodded, appeased. "Real quiet like, I peeked 'round into the showers. They was two of 'em—leather straps wrapped 'round they hands. Stripped that boy naked, then beat him till his own mama wouldn't know him. They stuffed a piece a rag in his mouth. Knocked him 'round and 'round, back an forth between 'em. Then one of 'em held him down while the other used that boy like a woman. T's eyes like to pop out his skull. Boy start thrashin' and gruntin' 'round that rag in his mouth, but they too much for him. When they finish that business, the big one, he pulls out a rusty ol' nail, must a been six inches long. Boy moanin' through his teeth now—seein' how they 'bout to do him. Start twistin' his head side to side, but they grab him by the throat and pin him down. The big one, he put that nail up under T's chin, then hammered it up into the boy's head with his hand. Took him three, four solid shots. Sounded like a man hittin' a watermelon with a stick. 'Bout threw up all over myself." He stopped and swallowed hard.

When he continued, his dusty old voice was hoarse. "After that, they beat him some more—but I don't think T felt nothin'. One of 'em tried to pull the rag out his mouth, but it must a been stuck on that rusty nail; it wouldn't come. So they left it in there. Then they done hung T on that wire . . ." He stopped.

I waited, but he was through talking.

"Who?" I whispered. "Who were they?"

Chicken looked at Black.

Black put a hand on the old man's shoulder. "Tell him, Chicken."

Then Chicken looked at me with those rheumy eyes, his empty mouth working. "It were Dr. Dave. Him and the Russian."

I just stared at him.

"That ain't all. I turn to leave and see Rollie been watchin' the whole damn show—standin' right behind me. He look me in my eye and wink. I swear to God, he winkin' at me while that boy bleedin' and dyin'."

"He didn't say anything?" I asked. "Didn't threaten you?"

"No. Ain't no need. I unnerstand what that wink mean. Been down as long as me, you best unnerstand. And I ain't tole you—and if anyone aks, I ain't seen nothin'. Nothin'!" Chicken swore.

I nodded, my mind reeling. All I could think of was Rollie's voice telling me that my arrangement with T was terminated.

Terminated . . .

I turned to Black, but before I could say anything, the loudspeaker crackled and hissed and this time my name was one of those called to the VR.

Dana was early.

12

I REPORTED to the hack at the visiting room door, Chicken's words swimming in my head.

A thick-necked officer named McGee had the duty. He sat at a metal desk just outside the VR, the sports pages clutched in his red farmer's hands. He knew who I was, but we went through the ritual anyway.

Lumbering to his feet, he dropped the newspaper onto his desk and reached for his clipboard. "Name?" With his peckerwood accent, he managed to add several syllables to the word.

"Ben Hemmings."

He took his time writing it down, then looked at the watch he wore on the inside of his wrist and noted the time. "Number?"

"45881-019."

"Dorm?"

"One."

"You carryin' anythin'? Comb? Watch? Pens?"

"No."

He finished writing, then set his clipboard on the desk and said, "Turn yourself around—arms up, legs spread."

While he patted me down, looking for any unauthorized combs, pens, or watches I might be trying to smuggle into the visiting room, I thought about what they'd done to T. I felt sick.

When McGee said, "Awright, Hemmings. Report on into the warden's office," I wasn't sure I'd heard correctly.

"I was just paged to the VR. My wife's waiting for me."

McGee looked unimpressed. "Get movin'." He lifted his newspaper and pointed to the door leading to the camp's administrative offices.

When I hesitated and asked again about my wife, he said, "I don't give a good goddamn if the pope hisself is in the VR—do what the fuck you're told, boy. Now."

Before I could ask him what it was all about, he disappeared behind the box scores.

I'd never been to the warden's office, but I knew where it was.

When I got there, the warden wasn't in.

Special Agent Don Partone had taken over the surprisingly plush office. He wore a western style-shirt the color of butter, with mother-of-pearl snaps and a box of Marlboros peeking out of the breast pocket. He sat at the warden's conference table, a thick file open in front of him.

He looked up at me, smiling, almost as if he were happy to see me. Like an old schoolteacher visiting one of his boys who'd made good. "Prison must be agreeing with you, Hemmings. You been working out? Lost a few pounds, huh?"

If it was a question, I didn't bother to answer it. I stood in the doorway, looking at him, sure that he hadn't come here alone on a weekend just to check on my progress and well-being.

"You gonna stand there all afternoon?" he said, finally. "Come in. Sit down." He indicated the chair opposite his own. "We got some talking to do."

I did. On closer inspection, he looked tired. The deeply grooved lines around his eyes were discolored, his skin rough and grainy.

"I thought you guys traveled in packs. Aren't there some abortion clinic bombers running around out there? Some real desperadoes you should be trying to catch?"

He ignored the jibe. Pulling a cigarette from the pack, he lit it and inhaled deeply. "How's the family? Wife and kids surviving without you?"

I bit back the anger. "Everyone's fine, Partone. No thanks to you."

He studied me for a moment, his expression unreadable, then began looking through his file.

I stared at him while he thumbed the pages without saying another word to me. Somewhere, a telephone started ringing, a sound I hadn't heard in over a year and a half. It struck me as a wonderful sound, a beautiful domestic sound. I wondered if Dana was out in the visiting room, waiting for me.

Now that I was here, Partone made a show of ignoring me.

I ignored him back.

I was pretty sure he'd come to talk about T's murder. If that was the case, I was walking through a minefield blindfolded. I tried to stay cool. The more I said, the worse it would be.

Five minutes ticked by. Then he looked up from his file, his bloodshot brown eyes flat. "I've been studying your business records. Turns out you didn't just build John Forchet a barn—you've been dealing with him for years. A whole lot of money changed hands. From where I sit, that constitutes an ongoing criminal enterprise. We're considering reindicting you. Maybe a RICO charge. Ten, fifteen years added onto your sentence."

He paused, waiting for me to say something. But I was too busy trying to digest his words. *Ten years* . . . ten more years! My kids would be teenagers. My marriage a memory. I was struck dumb by the thought.

Partone exhaled a cloud of smoke. "You don't look so good anymore. All that working out for nothing. Ten years . . . It's a goddamn long time, Hemmings. A fucking lifetime. Kids grown. Wife moved on. Nothing left out there to go back to." He shook his rugged head. "A waste, Hemmings. A goddamn waste."

When I didn't answer, he said, "Look at me."

I had trouble focusing.

"You got it in you to do a dime—a ten-year bit?"

I sucked down a deep breath and could no longer keep the anger down. "You can't make it stick. I'm no money launderer. I made a mistake. You think I ought to pay for it by losing my family? Everything I care about? That's insane! It's bullshit! I'm not a criminal, and you know it, Partone."

He shrugged. "Then what the hell are you doing in here?"

It was the question I'd asked myself a million times. Partone knew the answer.

We sat there for a long moment. The room seemed to shrink. I felt like striking out but fought to keep control. I wasn't going to let him do this to me. There had to be a way to fight it.

"Maybe there's an alternative," Partone said softly.

It took a minute to sink in. Then I thought I understood. The stakes had been raised, but it was the same old game. He still wanted me to help him nail Forchet.

He withdrew a newspaper clipping from his file and placed it on top of the table. "You remember this?" he asked.

I looked at the article, then at him. Suddenly too many seemingly unrelated things came together in my mind.

"You remember it, don't you?" Partone repeated.

"What's this have to do with Forchet?" I asked, stalling for time, trying to put the pieces together.

He looked hard at me. Then, using a coffee cup as an ashtray, he stubbed out his cigarette and said, "Forchet is no longer an issue. He's off the board."

"Off the board? What's that supposed to mean?"

He ignored my question, asked one of his own. "You want out of this shithole?"

He knew the answer to that one, too. But I wasn't sure where he was going with this, so I kept my mouth shut.

"Tell me what you know about this," he ordered, pointing to the article again.

I didn't have to read it. The heist had hit close to home, and I knew the details. Staring at Partone, I gave him the condensed version of what I knew.

"About a year ago, three men dressed as police officers walked into the state university's research lab. It was raining, they were in slickers—it was dark, hard to see who was who. They told the guard on duty that they were responding to a distress call. When the guard told them that no such call had been made, they overpowered him—bound him with duct tape and locked him in a utility closet. They went straight to the storage area, lifted what they were after—a collection of frozen horse semen the lab was storing for Ham Hamilton—and were out of there within minutes. They knew exactly what they wanted; nothing else was taken or disturbed. No alarm was sounded. No one knew anything was wrong until the hired hand reported to work early the next morning to feed the horses. That's when they discovered the theft."

Partone glanced down at the clipping. "You forgot to mention that your wife worked there."

"She left the lab a long time ago," I said, thinking about Rollie Shore's sudden interest in the horse world—who I built for, who I knew and how well I knew them . . . where my wife worked . . .

"You know Ham Hamilton," Partone said. "He ever talk to you about this collection of his?"

"You think I had something to do with it?" I asked. "From in here?"

He smiled coldly. "Hell, no. You aren't that smart."

Then his smile faded. "Some pretty important people want Hamilton's property returned. They're making one hell of a fuss over a bunch of frozen horse jizz."

"'Horse jizz . . .'" I repeated, trying gather my thoughts. An alarm was echoing through my head—Rollie Shore's voice asking about Dana, how well I knew Ham Hamilton . . .

"What do you have to say, Hemmings?" Partone was searching my face.

"I don't see what this has to do with me."

"Then listen carefully, 'cause I'm only going to tell you once." He leaned back in his chair and lit another cigarette. "Assuming you don't want to spend the next decade behind bars, you're going to help me recover this missing jizz."

"We've been down this road before, with Forchet. I'm not going to be your snitch."

"Oh, you'll deal, Hemmings. This time you'll deal. You can bet the next ten years of your life on it."

We stared at each other.

Then, I shook my head. "Maybe I'll take that bet—take my chances with a judge and a jury. I don't trust you, Partone. I wouldn't trust you if my life depended upon it."

"Maybe it does," he said cryptically. Then, he added, "I hear you and Rollie Shore have become asshole buddies."

The warning buzzers rang louder. "You heard wrong."

He considered his next words carefully. "A month ago, a lawyer approached Ham Hamilton's people—a real sleazebag—says he represents a man who might be able to help recover some missing property. Says that although his client didn't actually steal anything, he has access to new information that could lead to the safe recovery of certain genetic samples. Unfortunately, his client is currently incarcerated on unrelated charges and unless an early release can be arranged, he won't be able to guarantee their continued safe storage and viability." He paused and shook his head. "I didn't know better, I'd think someone was yanking my chain. But Hamilton has the clout to pull strings that reach all the way to Washington. My people want this thing to happen, so here I am."

Suddenly, the pieces fell into place. I made a show of examining the article, my mind racing.

"You know how much this stuff is worth?" Partone asked.

No one did. The samples, plastic straws filled with frozen horse semen, were priceless and worthless at the same time, assuming they were still viable. Even if they were, it wasn't the type of collection you could list in the local want ads and sell. Dana knew far more than I did. From what she'd told me, Hamilton had been quietly assembling frozen straws of semen from the top European and American show jumpers of the last twenty years. That's why he'd funded the university's lab. He owned semen from stallions that were long dead—irreplaceable genetic material. The proper care and storage of his collection was no simple task. That's where the lab came in. If it remained viable, the collection was remarkable, one of a kind—the generations it represented made the whole worth far more than the sum total of its parts. Ham Hamilton and his insurers had offered a five million–dollar, no-questions-asked reward for the safe return of the straws. But who knew what it was really worth?

"Well?" Partone asked.

I studied him, a senior FBI veteran spending his Saturday afternoon running an errand for a rich man. "I'd say the collection's worth a goddamned big promotion to the man who recovers it."

Partone nodded. "Maybe you're smarter than you look."

He dug through his file again, this time pulling out a single photograph he kept facedown. "What's it going to be? Ten more years in here? Or a shot at helping me find this collection before any kind of a permanent deal is cut with the thieves who took it?"

"You think Rollie Shore has it." It wasn't a question.

He didn't respond right away. Instead, he stared at me, calculating whether or not he had me.

Whatever he saw in my face must have convinced him that he was almost there.

"It was Shore's lawyer who made the offer," he continued. "We'll pretend to go along with it. Cut the bastard an early release predicated on his leading us to Hamilton's collection. But Shore's going to need a go-between—someone who can handle the exchange without implicating himself in the original theft."

"What makes you think he'd choose me?"

"You kidding? You're perfect for the job. You know your way around the horse world—he thinks he can control you. Your wife's an expert. She'll know how to handle the collection safely. Knowing Shore, he spotted you the minute you checked into this pit. You don't think he befriended you because of your sparkling personality, do you?"

I didn't answer.

Partone nodded. "He'll make the first move. All you have to do is go with the flow, follow his lead. You find out where he's hidden the collection before Shore can keep his end of the bargain. Turn the stuff over to me, then I slam him. Hamilton gets his property, Shore gets shipped right back where he belongs, you end up home with the wife and kiddies, and everyone is happy." He paused and frowned at me. "Nothing complicated about it."

Shore had already made the first move, but I kept the fact to myself. "You going to put all of this in writing?"

"It doesn't work that way. We do it quietly. Under the table. The Bureau doesn't want to be seen dealing with convicted criminals. If Hamilton hadn't screamed the right words in the right ears, we wouldn't be having this conversation. You do your part, I'll do mine. No documentation."

I looked around at the warden's beautifully paneled office. "You're forgetting something. I'm stuck in here for the next year and a half. I couldn't be Rollie's go-between if I wanted to."

Partone leaned across the maple wood conference table. "You agree to do what I tell you and your appeal will be granted. You'll be released on bond pending the outcome of a new trial. Only once you get Hamilton's collection back to me, there won't be any trial. The charges will be dropped. You can get your life back—go home to your wife and your children. Build some stables."

"Barns," I said automatically.

He frowned. "Build whatever the fuck you want."

I drew a deep breath. He hadn't bothered to mention the fact that I might not have a life at all if I crossed Rollie Shore. I sat back in my chair, pushing the fear away, thinking hard, trying to figure the angles.

Partone read my reaction as indecision, so he played his trump card.

"If you're sitting there thinking you have a fancy lawyer who can pull your nuts out of the fire . . ." he said, slowly turning over the photograph he'd kept hidden from me, ". . . maybe you ought to ask your wife about that."

The photo was a candid shot of Dana, wearing the short black dress I'd bought her at Neiman Marcus. She was with Jimmy Grantham at Mes Amis, a little Buckhead bistro she loved. She was looking down at her plate, her expression neutral, her face careworn but beautiful. An expensive-looking bottle of wine sat between them on the table. Grantham was staring openly at Dana's cleavage.

My blood ran hot and cold at the same time.

"Ten years . . ." Partone was saying. "A long goddamned time."

But I was past listening to him. In a blind rage, I reached for the photograph and ripped it in two. Then, I stood, my face flushed and hot. "How soon can I be out of here?"

"A couple of weeks. It's got to look real."

"I can't do it alone. I'll need help. Someone to watch my back—someone I can trust."

He narrowed his eyes. "You have someone in mind?"

"My celly, Herman Glessing. You get him an early release, too. Then I'll help you."

He considered it. "And if Glessing refuses?"

I thought about the five million–dollar reward that Partone had failed to mention. "Black won't refuse."

Partone nodded slowly. "I'll look into it. Maybe I can get it done. Sit tight while I work out the details. I'll be back in touch with you in a day or so. I don't have to tell you what'll happen if word of this gets out."

I thought about T and shook my head. "I understand."

He closed his file and pointed to the door. "Get out of here, Hemmings. Your wife is in the visiting room."

I turned to leave, but Partone stopped me. "The details of what we do stay between us. You'll answer directly to me. No one else. Don't tell your wife anything about this until you have the collection—and only tell her then if you need her expertise. For now, let her believe your appeal came through. Women, children . . . men like Rollie Shore draw no distinctions when they feel threatened."

I started to say that men like Special Agent Donald Partone didn't give a damn who they put in harm's way, either. Instead, I turned my back on him and walked out of the warden's office with my mouth shut—thinking about the photo of Grantham and my wife—trying hard to come up with a good explanation. When that failed, I tried to think about the five million–dollar reward.

But the pit in my stomach had filled with ice. It would take more than money to erase from memory the look on Grantham's face while he stared openly at my wife's chest. What else had happened between them?

Nothing, I told myself. But nobody was listening.

13

THE visiting room was crowded. Families and couples sat uncomfortably in stackable plastic chairs gathered around low laminate tables, every move, every embrace, monitored by a pair of VR hacks who patrolled endless circles across the expanse of waxed linoleum delineating their turf. Uniformed men, soured by too many mean hours spent barking orders and watching their backs, all too happy to take their frustrations out on any visiting wife whose skirt they deemed too short or whose kiss they deemed too long. The VR itself looked like a high school cafeteria gone horribly wrong. The smiles forced; the atmosphere poisoned.

I stood there, looking around, no longer sure of anything or anyone. The world was suddenly full of too many once-familiar people colliding in unpredictable ways.

Rocked by the photograph Partone had shown me, I reported to the hack at the desk near the visitor's entrance, fighting hard to keep my composure. After signing in, I scanned the room again but didn't see Dana. Should I confront her? Here? Now? Should I tell her about Partone? What if the deal didn't happen?

Reggie, standing with his wife in front of the vending machines lining the far wall, caught my eye and angled his head toward a table at the back of the room.

Dana sat alone. She wore jeans and a black T-shirt; her hair looked longer than I remembered it. She didn't see me. Her attention was focused on the occupants of the table in the corner nearest her, a concerned look on her face.

But it wasn't Rollie Shore and his friends, a group of large men in flashy clothes, that had Dana looking worried. It was Olivia. Dressed in a bright yellow jumper, Silky squeezed under one arm, she stood in front of Rollie clutching a bag of vending machine popcorn. She was laughing; her little head turning from side to side as Rollie made funny faces, doing his best Don Corleone–in-the-garden impersonation.

It gave me chill bumps.

I hurried over, took Olivia by the hand, and led her back to her mother's table.

Rollie called after me, "You're a lucky man, Ben. That's one *shana punum.* You take care of her; she's a gem."

Someone else at his table muttered something unintelligible. They all laughed.

"He's funny," Olivia said, stuffing a handful of popcorn into her mouth.

Her mother thought otherwise. "He came over here and said hello, like he was an old friend. Then he bought a bag of popcorn for Olivia. . . . I didn't like it. But I let her take the popcorn anyway. I didn't want to make a scene in front of the guards."

Dana looked up at me, her face closed and defensive. Our eyes met and held. But the explanation was unnecessary.

In spite of the icy knot twisting my gut, I wanted to pull her to me, whisper in her ear that I'd be home soon. Hold her so tightly that nothing could ever separate us again. Instead I leaned over and brushed her cheek with my lips.

"It's okay," I said, taking the chair next to hers. "It's not a problem."

Olivia jumped into my lap and gave me a big, sloppy, salty popcorn kiss.

"God! You're getting so grown up I almost didn't recognize you." I held her at arm's length, trying to swallow her with my eyes.

She shook her head gleefully and laughed. "I'm not *that* big, Daddy. Not yet. But I'm strong. Feel this . . ." She handed me Silky, then offered her biceps.

I felt her muscles, then gathered her in my arms and held her against my chest until she'd had enough.

"I want some candy," she said squirming on my lap. "Gimme quarters, Mommy."

Dana fished in her purse and handed Olivia some change. "Come straight back here, honey. I don't want you talking to any more strangers."

But Olivia was already halfway to the vending machines.

"I don't like him," Dana said, glancing at Rollie. "He gives me the creeps."

"He gives a lot of people the creeps. Where's Nadine?"

"She didn't feel well, so I left her with my mother."

"Anything serious?"

"The sniffles—I think she just wanted to watch cartoons and have Grandma Rose all to herself."

We sat there for a moment, looking at each other. A million thoughts sizzled in my head. I didn't know where to start.

"What's happening with the house?" I asked, trying to pick a neutral subject.

Dana frowned. "The bank called; they've extended the grace period by ninety days."

"That's great."

She shook her head. "I don't understand it. I talked myself blue in the face for weeks. They said no! They wouldn't even consider it. Then a couple of days before the house is supposed to actually go into foreclosure, they call and say they're extending the grace period. Why? What changed their minds? It doesn't make sense to me."

I looked past her at Rollie Shore. Then, I said, "Maybe Jimmy Grantham made a few calls . . ."

"If he did, he didn't tell me."

"He would though, wouldn't he?"

"What?"

"Tell you." I hesitated. "The two of you . . . between you and Jimmy—is there anything I should know?"

"Are you asking . . ." she stopped midsentence as one of the hacks walked past us.

I ignored him.

Dana was glaring at me. Once the hack was out of earshot, she continued, her voice low, the anger scalding. "What are you trying to say, Ben? Because if you're implying—"

"I'm not implying anything. I'm asking a goddamned question. I'd like a simple answer."

She started to say something, then bit it off. "I love you, Ben. I made a commitment to you. I stuck with you—through all of this. . . . But that doesn't mean I'm going to drive for two hours so I can sit here and let you accuse me—goddammit! What exactly do you think I do every day? Where do you think I am while you're in here? You think it's easy? That I'm out having a grand old time? Well, I'm not. Between worrying about you and trying to keep a roof over our heads . . . Do you realize that if something goes wrong, I can't even call you? Think about how that feels. I'm tired and lonely and the only ones who care are our children and my mother. And that gets really fucking old. If you think for one moment I'm out there running around—"

Before she could finish, Olivia came skipping back, a Snickers bar clutched in her outstretched hand. "Open it, Daddy. Open it!"

Dana fell silent, her face grim.

Olivia looked at her, then at me. "Are you fighting?" she asked, her voice small.

When neither of us answered, she turned on her mother. "Don't you be mean to Daddy. He's here 'cause you're mean to him. I hate when you're mean. I hate you."

Dana drew a sharp breath. "Olivia!"

Olivia started wailing.

I pulled her onto my lap and took the candy bar out of her hand. Quivering, she grabbed Silky, then buried her face in my chest.

"Mommy's trying hard to take care of everyone," I said, softly stroking her hair. "It's not her fault I'm here. She's not mean and she loves you very much."

Hot tears slid down Dana's cheeks. She reached for Olivia, but I shook my head. "Let me hold her."

Dana nodded without meeting my eye, then searched her purse for a tissue.

After a few moments, Olivia stopped crying. She sat up and wiped her nose on my sleeve.

I tore open the Snickers bar and took a bite. "Mmmmm. This is good. Want some?"

Relaxing a little, she took the candy bar and chewed thoughtfully.

I looked over at Dana, wanting to find some way to breach the distance between us. She'd stopped crying. Her eyes had turned slate gray.

One of the hacks walked by again.

After he passed, I said, "Dana, listen, I didn't mean . . ."

Those gray eyes locked on mine, but a curtain had dropped over them. I couldn't see in, and I realized with a jolt that she knew it. I have an old photograph of her taken before the girls were born. We were at a Halloween party and she was dressed as a Hollywood starlet—blond wig, fake eyelashes, heavy makeup, cigarette holder, the whole nine yards. Her own mother wouldn't have recognized her. The photo's out of focus, Dana's strong features blurred. It was a picture of a stranger, but I kept it anyway. That's how she looked to me now. A stranger—her once-clear outline fuzzy. And all I was doing was pushing her farther away. That voice in my head was telling me to stop, to pull back from the brink. But how?

"I'm sorry," I whispered.

"I've heard that before."

I searched her face, not sure what to think. The distance in her eyes left too many questions unanswered. And suddenly I was torn between loathing myself, loathing the jealousy twisting my insides—and believing the worst of her. I tried to shake it off, but Partone's photograph had burned too deeply into my memory.

There was too much to say and no way to say any of it here.

Olivia was pulling on my sleeve. "I want to tell you something, Daddy . . ." She began a long, convoluted story about a boy who'd found a baby raccoon in his backyard.

I pretended to follow it.

Then, Dana and I made meaningless small talk for another hour—both of our stomachs churning. Trying to smooth it over without touching it—understanding that was impossible.

Then, it was time to leave.

We said good-bye.

Embraced briefly, stiffly.

Olivia jumped into my arms, unable to hold back tears.

Then, I watched them walk away. My wife's back rigid, my daughter's eyes wet.

As I watched them leave, something hard and nameless grew inside me. My mind cleared and one thought filled my head: *No more.* I'd taken all I was going to take. I wasn't going to let anyone destroy the things I held dear. No one was going to stand between me and my family. Not Partone. Not Rollie Shore. No one.

14

I LEFT the VR and walked up to the rec yard, my thoughts focused on what lay in front of me. I found a seat on one end of the bleachers where a couple of dozen cons were already sprawled out, smoking and telling lies, killing time before the hacks announced recall and the four-o'clock count.

Reggie and Truck saw me plop down and wandered over to see what was up. One look at my face convinced them I wasn't in the mood for company. Not that I was alone. In prison, there is no such thing as alone. Privacy is state of mind.

Ignoring the shuck and jive around me, I sat there, trying to work it out. Only there were no good choices. I weighed my options, knowing that whatever I chose to do next, I'd have only one shot at getting it right. By the time the loudspeaker hissed and crackled to life, I'd made up my mind.

■ ■ ■

That night, I explained to Black what I had to do.

At first, he thought I'd gone stir-crazy. But as we walked the track and I laid out the proposal Partone had made to me, talking softly so we wouldn't be overheard, he listened intently.

"Tell me about this reward, again," he said, after I'd finished.

"Five million dollars. No questions asked."

He shook his head. "Let me see if I've got this right. You're gonna waltz in on Rollie's turf and he's gonna hand you this frozen horse sperm. . . . Then he's gonna just sit back and watch you walk off with *his* five million dollars? You got to be hittin' the crack pipe, man. You ain't thinkin' right."

It was hot, the track crowded. Rollie and Boris were among the sweating, pink-tinged walkers, half a lap ahead of us. Pointing to them, I said, "I want out of here. That asshole's holding the ticket."

"You dreamin', man."

"No! It can be done. It's a matter of playing the angles. You just have to cover the angles."

"Hold up a minute. *I* don't have to cover nothin'. Ain't my move."

"Five mill, Black. We'll split it down the middle."

He shot me a funny look. "Can't split what you ain't got."

"I'll get it. I don't have a choice."

"How?" he demanded.

Then, softening his tone, he said, "Ben, you're a good man. You got fucked by the feds, but you're still one a the good guys. You ain't a player. Not in the league Rollie Shore plays in. You want to take him down, you got to be mean. You got to be strong as steel. You a family man, not a killer."

"They're gonna tag me with a dime, Black. Ten years—I'll have no family. The girls will be teenagers; they won't even know who I am. And Dana . . ." I swallowed hard, not willing to put those feelings into words. "You're right, but I don't have to be a killer. I'm going to play Partone against Rollie. I haven't thought it all the way through, but if I do it right, Rollie'll think Partone took him down. He'll never know it was me. I'll do the same with Partone. Let him think Rollie is calling the shots. Neither of them will see the whole picture."

"What whole picture?" Black wiped beads of sweat from his brow with the flat of his hand. Then, he shook his head again. "I hear you talkin', but talk won't take down a man like Rollie Shore. You say you gonna play the angles . . . shit! There isn't an angle out there he don't have covered twice. He knows every fuckin' angle there ever was."

"I want out. If it means taking that collection away from Rollie, that's what I'm going to do. Only to do it right, I need someone I can trust, Black. Someone to watch my back."

"And for some reason you thinkin' I'm that lucky someone, huh?"

"Five million reasons."

"Five million ways to get killed."

"No." I shook my head, drops of sweat burning my eyes. "Shore's flesh and blood. He's not God. He bleeds like everyone else. He can be stung. And he won't be looking for it. Not from us. I'm in the picture because he needs someone to actually make the exchange—a go-between to handle the frozen straws. I'll broker the deal so he can put some distance between himself and the original theft."

"And he told you all this? Rollie told you he's gonna put you in the middle of this thing?"

"It's what he's been after from the beginning. Don't you see? It's what all the bullshit with T and Dr. Dave was about."

Black frowned, but he was listening.

"Think about it," I continued. "Rollie and Partone are both playing me. They both think they've put me between a rock and a hard place, that they're calling the shots. But what if the collection simply disappears? It happened once. The right man in the right place could make it happen again. Hamilton's insurance company will deal with anyone. They don't care what the feds say. All they want to do is minimize the claim they're going to have to pay. And I have access to Hamilton. I know the man. Whoever brokers the deal takes the reward."

"Taking the collection is one thing—keeping it's another." He thought for a moment. "Say you actually pull it off. Say you find Rollie's horse sperm and you manage to boost it. Once you go to collect the reward, the whole world's gonna know who *brokered* the deal. The insurance company will talk. Both Rollie and the feds be all over you like white on rice."

"If we set it up right—"

"Ain't no we!" he growled.

"Okay. Okay. If *I* set it up right, Shore'll think Partone grabbed the collection to queer the deal. That's what he's trying to do anyway. I make Partone think Shore turned the stuff over to Hamilton himself, so he could keep the reward. Play the two of them off each other."

"You still haven't answered my question."

"The money goes to the islands."

"Shit! Every motherfucker and his cousin doin' that. They'll be lookin' for it."

"That's why it'll work. They're going to track the money no matter what we do. So we do the obvious. It's exactly what they'll expect Rollie to do." I was winging it now, but a plan was taking shape in my mind. "We have the insurance company wire the reward money into a numbered account in the Caymans."

"There you go with the *we* again," he growled.

"Just hear me out. We move the money around a few times. Then, let it sit for a while. Sure, the insurance company will tell the feds where they wired the money. But Partone will think Rollie received it. Rollie'll know better. He'll freak—but he'll have the feds all over his back when he fails to turn over the collection. They'll lock his ass up forever. We lay low. Let the dust settle."

"And while you busy layin' low, Partone goes lookin' for that missin' money. Once he gets beat, he'll be hot. Out for get-back. Say you do everything right and he doesn't find the money, doesn't even know it was you who took it. What's to keep him from lockin' you up anyway?"

I thought about it. "Imagine what the papers would do with the story: 'Convicted criminal cons the Justice Department into an early release, then hustles it out of five million dollars.' You think the feds want to read that? No way they'll risk the publicity of a trial."

Black looked skeptical.

Who could blame him? Even as I spoke, I could see holes in the plan the size of Mars. But it was a start. "Listen, I know it's not perfect. But I haven't got a choice. Either I do it Partone's way or I move on Hamilton's collection my way. I have to do something. . . . Otherwise, I spend the next ten years standing count. I can get us both out of here, Black. We do this right, we'll be on the street with a couple million dollars. I think it's worth the risk."

"I think it sound like a good way to get killed."

"Or get rich."

Black's frown deepened, but he kept his thoughts to himself.

We kept walking.

Ahead, Rollie and Boris left the track and sauntered over to the Pride Club. Black followed them with his eyes. A muscle along his jaw twitched, but he remained silent for the next couple of laps, his face shiny with sweat.

"Ain't held a woman in over eight years," he said, finally. "Ain't had a bath in eight years. Not a decent meal . . . no privacy . . . nothin', man. I ain't had nothin' worth havin' in eight fuckin' years. Now you tell me in two weeks' time I can walk out of here. That all I've got to do is set a man up with the feds. Shit! I was willing to rat my people out, I wouldn't be here in the first place. Neither would you."

"Rollie Shore's not your people."

"Yeah. Well, that don't make it right . . ."

"You forgetting T?"

He grunted. "I haven't forgot one thing. Not one thing in eight fuckin' years. Out of the whole dictionary, you know what word I hate the most?"

I shook my head.

"*Incarcerated.* It feels ugly in your mouth when you say it. *In-car-cer-ated.* Make you want to puke. It's the fuckin' ugliest word there is."

"I understand."

Turning on me, he grabbed the front of my shirt. "No, Ben! You don't understand shit! You don't understand one goddamn thing! I got two years left. I could do them two years. Two years ain't nuthin'. Do 'em on my head."

"Easy, Black . . ." I stared at him until he let go of my shirt.

He looked away. "Sorry, man. Didn't mean to grab you."

I took a deep breath. "I'm going after those straws. If you've got my back, I've got a better chance of making it work."

He said nothing.

"You don't see it that way, I understand."

"How I see it don't mean a goddamn thing," he said softly. "I do this thing—I fuck with Rollie and his crew—it ain't for the reasons you think. Look at me. What do you see? You see a nigger got nothin'. No education. No home. No future. I could do the time, easy. Then what? You go back to Atlanta, get yourself a good job—maybe you start right back in the construction business. What you think I'm gonna do? Go back to the projects—back to Herndon Homes? Sit on my ass or get some bullshit thing goin' . . . tote boxes in a warehouse? Load trucks? Cut white folks' lawns with my uncle? What kind a future you think a ex-con like me has?"

I started to argue that he had whatever future he could make for himself, but he interrupted. "I'm twenty-six years old, not some nappy-headed boy think the future all guns and pussy. I'm a man. I'm gonna do this thing with you 'cause when we're through, I'm gonna have something. Two and a half million somethings. And you know what they gonna buy me?"

I shook my head. "What, Black?"

"A real goddamn future."

"After we take Hamilton's collection away from Rollie, we'll both have a future." I started to say *With or without the reward,* then kept the thought to myself. All I wanted was out—out of prison, out from under—but Black needed more. And I needed Black.

He was squinting at me. "You one crazy nigger, Ben."

"Maybe we're both crazy."

He smiled grimly. "I guess we're gonna find out, huh?"

15

THEY released Rollie the first week in September, ten full days before they released me.

Twenty-four hours later, Black was transferred to the penitentiary in Atlanta, pending a compassionate release, ostensibly to care for his ailing grandmother. Boris left the same day Black was transferred, but he'd finished his sentence and I wasn't sure whether he was part of Rollie's deal with the feds.

I was the last to go.

By then, Partone's two weeks had turned into an impossibly long month. The days crawled by so slowly I felt like I was moving under water. But there were things undone, so I sucked it up and did the time as though nothing unusual was happening.

Rollie and I hadn't talked since T's murder. During those last weeks, I saw him in the chow hall or walking the track, but always at a distance. He waved and smiled; his demeanor toward me hadn't changed. And I waited patiently for him to make me some kind of an offer.

When word spread throughout the compound that Rollie's release was imminent, rumors flew faster than the speed of light: Rollie bought the judge . . . he'd paid off the U.S. attorney . . . his Washington connections had whispered directly into the ear of the president . . . he owned a senator, a governor.

There were even more absurd assertions. A twice-convicted arsonist who worked in the prison clinic swore that Rollie was the First Lady's biological father—that he'd seen the DNA tests to prove it. It was ridiculous. But even the most level-headed inmates wanted to believe in the weight of Rollie's connections and his ability to pay off whoever needed paying off.

Hardened men, cons who had cautiously kept their distance from Shore, gathered close around him now. A faithful flock, hoping that if they did or said the right thing, he would use his connections to get them an immediate release, too. He was like a rock star. Everyone wanted a piece of him. Everyone wanted to do something for him.

Black and I just looked at each other. What would these tough guys have thought if they'd known Rollie had no high-powered connections busily twisting the wheels of power behind the scenes—that it was simply a matter of having stolen something important people wanted back more than the government wanted Rollie Shore in custody. It was all a chilling game. But you couldn't play to win unless you knew how to change the rules. And to change the rules, you had to be smart enough to understand them in the first place.

Rollie was plenty smart, a fact Black reminded me of on a daily basis.

Word of my successful appeal spread a day or so before Rollie hit the street. The night before he left, he sent word that he wanted to see me.

We walked the track together one last time.

"Congratulations," he growled, draping his towel around his thick neck. "Grantham must have done a good job."

I nodded. "It took him a while."

"Just be thankful it happened at all. You'll be on the street sooner than you think. You have plans?"

"No. Not yet. I'll make a few calls—something'll turn up."

"You know, Ben, I've been thinking about you, kicking around some of the things we've talked about. I've got a few ideas. . . ." He reached into his shirt pocket, pulled out a folded piece of paper, and pushed it at me. "Put this phone number away—someplace safe. When you get home and get your feet on the ground, call me. The timing couldn't be better. I've got something working that might put you back in business in a hurry."

I took the folded paper without looking at it. "They stopped the foreclosure on my house. . . . You have any idea why the bank would do that, Rollie?"

He smiled broadly. "I told you a while ago, Ben. It pays to have the right friends. You call that number, leave a message for me. We got a lot to talk about."

He punched me on the arm, then walked off the track toward the Pride Club.

I pocketed the phone number and smiled to myself.

It was all falling into place.

16

I DIDN'T tell Dana until after Black was transferred and I was sure it would really happen.

"Oh, God! Is it true, Ben? Are you really coming home? When? How soon?" Then she broke down and began sobbing over the telephone.

When she picked me up over a week later, she started to cry again. One look at her and my eyes filled, too.

We'd fantasized endlessly about this day. But when it finally arrived, it was nothing like I thought it would be. I knew Rollie Shore was out there, waiting for me. But it seemed far off, something someone else should worry about. Not me, not today. Even the September air tasted fresh and new. The morning was mild, but I wouldn't have noticed if it had been twenty below zero. A hot tide of emotion had been building in me for weeks. Now it flowed like a river through my entire body. My hands tingled; my legs vibrated. I felt light, my feet barely brushing the ground as I walked through the front doors of the compound—the same doors I'd seen Dana and the girls depart through after their visits—all of my possessions packed in one small cardboard box.

The hack on the door said something about my wife's having been out there since before first light, but I ignored him. I would have ignored the warden himself. I was free.

And it was the finest feeling I could imagine. I smiled so broadly my lips hurt.

Dana waited by the car, the old GM Suburban I used to use to deliver materials to my construction sites. Now it was the family car. She'd left the girls at home with her mother and come alone. She wore a simple linen sundress and the sight of her struck me dumb.

I tried to call out to her, but my voice was no more than a husky whisper.

She heard anyway.

She ran to me, stopping short, just close enough to touch me. We stared at each other for a moment. Time stopped. There was nothing but the rise and fall of her chest, the jade flash of her eyes. Then I dropped the cardboard box and we were in each other's arms, the tears flowing freely.

"I can't believe it," she whispered.

Before I could answer, she tilted her head up and kissed me. In that one kiss, all my doubts and fears melted away. Whatever the distance we'd traveled, the trip was over. I was almost home.

■ ■ ■

"Do you have any idea how much I love you?" Dana asked. She took one hand off the steering wheel and reached for my hand.

"How much?"

"I'd have waited as long as it took, Ben. Forever, if I had to."

"Well, you don't have to. I'm here." I let go of her hand and reached up, tracing the curve of her neck with my fingers as she drove. "I'm here and I'm not going anywhere. I can't believe how good you smell."

I let my hand trail down to her lap.

She squirmed and grabbed my wrist. "Stop! That tickles. You know I can't drive when you do that."

"I'm going to do more than tickle you when we get home."

She laughed, a warm sound that lit up her face. "You may get more than tickled yourself. But it'll have to wait until we put the girls to bed. They're so excited to see you I didn't have the heart to send them to my mother's house. They're probably standing by the front door. They made you a surprise."

My smile had taken on a life of its own. My cheeks were starting to ache. "Well, we waited this long . . . I guess another couple of hours won't kill us." I settled back in my seat. "What kind of surprise?"

"If I told you, it wouldn't be one."

We drove on for a while in silence, content just being alone together. Breathing the same air. Reaching out to touch each other, as if to prove this was really happening.

The long drive back to Atlanta passed in what seemed a matter of minutes. Before I knew it, we were only a few blocks from the house. But there were things Dana needed to know. Things I didn't want to discuss in front of the girls or her mother. "Stop the car."

"What?"

"Stop the car," I repeated. "I want to tell you something before we get home."

She pulled to the curb and then shifted in her seat so that she was facing me. "Are you okay?"

"I'm fine. There's something you need to know. This business about my appeal . . . it's not—"

She reached out and touched my face. "We'll have plenty of time to talk about all of that. But not today. You're home. That's all I want to know. It's enough. We can deal with everything else tomorrow. Okay?"

"But—"

"No." She shook her head. "Promise me. Not another word about prosecutors or appeals or lawyers. Not one word, right?"

I couldn't help smiling. "Okay," I agreed.

It was a decision I hoped I wouldn't regret.

17

OLIVIA and Nadine had both crawled onto my lap. We were on the couch in the den, the children dozing while their mother walked Grandma Rose out to her car. I looked around, trying to absorb the fact that I was really home. Everything looked just the way I'd pictured it countless times lying in my bunk. I thought about Hemmings Construction, wondered if I'd ever build anything again. Then I pushed the thought away. That part of my life was on hold.

The girls' surprise, a welcome home banner Olivia and Nadine had painted all by themselves, hung on thumbtacks over the desk. It was more beautiful than any building I would ever put up.

The television buzzed meaninglessly. A halo of lamplight fell softly on my children. They were beautiful. I nuzzled their heads and breathed in the sweet, clean scent of them. Home. They smelled like home.

It was early, only about seven-thirty, but the girls were exhausted. It had been a grand homecoming. Dana had been cooking for days; she'd knocked herself out, prepared short ribs braised in dark beer, scalloped potatoes with cream and Parmesan, Caesar salad with big garlicky croutons and her homemade dressing, all my favorite dishes. She'd filled the house with flowers. Rose had thrown herself into the spirit of our celebration, too, welcoming me home as though I were a conquering hero, not her ex-con son-in-law. More than once as the afternoon bled into a fine evening, I'd found myself overwhelmed, clotted with all the emotion I'd kept buried in prison.

"Have a little more, honey," Rose had fussed in her slightly accented English, holding a bowl of Dana's chocolate soufflé or a plate of her white-chocolate chip cookies. "You look too thin to me. Didn't they feed you in there, Ben?"

"Mom, you're going to make him sick if you keep forcing him to eat sweets!" Dana complained.

"Nonsense," Rose said. "I know from hunger—a little chocolate never hurt anyone."

So I took a little more.

Finally, after eating and drinking and laughing and talking ourselves into a near stupor, it was time for the girls to go to bed. Time for us.

Having sent her mother home laden with leftovers, Dana came in smiling. "Rose says you look like the guy in the space war movies."

"The space war movies?"

Dana laughed. "I think it's a compliment."

She stepped over and, with a grunt, lifted Olivia off my lap. "They're getting big," she said. "Big and sleepy."

"Not that sleepy," Olivia said with a yawn.

"It's bedtime," I said, winking at Dana. "No arguments."

Dana nodded, her smile broadening. "Finally."

Holding Nadine, I stood and followed my wife through the living room, then upstairs to the bedroom the two girls shared.

As I tucked her in, Nadine reached up and took my face between her two chubby hands. "Daddy's home," she said, smiling. Then, closing her eyes, she fell instantly, soundly, asleep.

I stroked her hair for a moment.

Then I crossed the room and leaned over Olivia to kiss her good night, too.

Dana checked on Nadine, then whispered, "I'll be in the bedroom. Wait a couple of minutes before you come in."

I promised I would.

After her mother left the room, Olivia opened her eyes and stared up at me. "You forgot to kiss Silky," she said, holding up the little bear. "He missed you, too."

I kissed Silky, then tousled Olivia's hair. "You go to sleep. It's been a big day."

"Are you going to sleep here tonight?" she asked.

"I'm going to sleep here every night, honey."

"Does that mean I can't sleep with Mommy if I get scared?"

"No, honey. You can still sleep with Mommy. But I'll be there, too."

She thought about it. "I guess that's okay . . ." Then, with a sleepy nod, she closed her eyes and fell asleep.

I stood awhile longer in the darkened room, listening to my daughters breathe. The soft, steady rhythm of their life. And suddenly I felt awed by the realization that I had created this—that this was my family and I belonged to them as much as they belonged to me.

■ ■ ■

Dana was waiting in the bedroom.

A dozen candles cast flickering shadows across the walls and ceiling. The bed was turned down, all cool white sheets, my robe draped across the foot. Chris Isaak's voice thrumming from the stereo, singing "Wicked Game," the song we thought of as our own.

She wore a sheer black robe, her skin olive under the soft fabric, the thick thatch of her pubic hair darker.

She stepped to me and began unbuttoning my shirt.

Cupping her face in my hands, I drew her to me and kissed her.

She pulled back and traced the contour of my lips with the tip of her tongue.

She kissed my throat, my chest, and stomach.

Then, disengaging, she unbuckled my pants and found the zipper.

I started to say something, but pressing her fingers to my lips, she shook her head. "Don't speak," she husked. "I've been waiting for this."

Her hands were everywhere and nowhere, her touch light and hard. I wanted her like I'd never wanted anyone in my life.

We lay across the bed, the candlelight a living, breathing thing, our shadows swooping and dancing on the walls and ceiling. How many times had I fantasized this moment?

Dana groaned. I touched and stroked, traced the curves and crevices of her body with my mouth and hands. Her skin taut and silky, her flesh dusky, ripe with desire.

She reached for me, then hesitated. "Is everything all right?" she whispered.

Yes," I murmured. "Do that, harder."

She took me in her mouth. Tried everything that used to work so perfectly.

And I didn't respond.

I wanted her so badly I could scream. But my body wouldn't answer.

"Don't worry," she said, then smiled. "It's been a long day."

"Let's try again," I said, determined.

She did, till her jaw was sore. Then with her hands.

I tried. Pulling, stroking too hard. Wanting too much, too badly. Frustrated to the point of anger.

Nothing.

Falling back against the pillows, Dana took my hand and held it to her chest. I could feel the beat of her heart, the heat of her flesh.

"I love you," she said. "Don't get so intense. It happens. It's nothing to worry about."

"It doesn't happen to me."

"Come on, Ben. Smile. It's nothing. Stress. The homecoming. We have the rest of our lives." She drew me down to her and folded me in her arms.

We lay like that for a few moments, then I started to feel smothered. I rolled over, looked at the ceiling, the candlelight mocking me now. *It's the stress,* I told myself. *Just the stress.* But I felt weak and embarrassed. Betrayed by my own body.

I got up, headed for the bathroom.

"Where are you going," Dana asked, trying to mask the concern in her voice. But I could hear it as clearly as if she were shouting.

"To wash up. I have to wash up."

I closed the door behind me and ran hot water into the sink. I stared at my reflection in the mirror. Tried to see if I looked any different. But it was the same old face staring back at me.

How many times had I imagined this night? How many other nights had I lain awake, counting the days that stood in front of me?

Lonely nights spent on my narrow prison bed, a perfume strip torn from a magazine tucked into my pillow, the perfume not quite the sameas the scent in the hollow of Dana's throat, but better than the locker-room stench of the dorm. Waiting under my blanket until my cellies' breathing sounded regular—until they at least seemed asleep. Grasping myself and thinking about Dana. The way she tasted. The feel of her skin, hot against my own, the gentle curve of her neck. Her breasts riding high, swinging with our rhythm. The thick, throaty groan that preceded her climax. Stroking myself harder. My own climax, silent and secret, spilling hot and sticky into a concealedwad of toilet paper.

"Ben, are you okay?" Her voice startled me.

Steam rose from the sink, clouding the mirror.

"Fine. I'll be out in a minute."

"I'm going to go and check on the girls," she said.

I brushed my teeth, took my time washing my face. I thought about trying again. Surely I hadn't forgotten how. But I was afraid it wouldn't work. Then what?

My stomach twisted itself into a tight knot. I turned out the bathroom light and went to find Dana.

She was sitting on the end of Nadine's bed, her back to me, staring at our youngest. I stood in the hallway, my heart aching, watching her. She touched her mouth, unaware of my presence.

Olivia rolled over, mumbled something in her sleep.

Dana turned to look at her, and as she did, the light from the hall caught the tears streaming silently down her cheeks.

I tiptoed back to the bedroom, my chest full of broken glass.

■ ■ ■

We were pretending to sleep when the phone rang.

Startled, Dana sat up first, reaching for it.

She listened for a minute.

"Who is this?" she asked, her voice pitched low.

Then she held the receiver out to me and shrugged. "He wants you. He won't say who it is."

I took the phone, surprised that anyone would be calling me now.

"Hemmings, welcome home!" Partone's gruff voice unreasonably loud.

"What do you want?" I demanded.

"I want to see you. Now. So get your ass up and dressed and meet me in half an hour at the gas station on the corner of Lindbergh and Piedmont."

I glanced at the clock on the bedside table. It was a little past eleven. "You've got to be kidding. I just got home."

"That's right. You just got home. . . . In that case, I'll give you an hour." He laughed, a coarse smoker's hack of a laugh. "Don't keep me waiting, Hemmings. You want to stay out on the street, you follow my rules. I own your ass. One phone call from me, and you're right back in the joint. Don't ever forget that. Be there—one hour. Make up some excuse for your wife. We've got a lot to talk about."

I started to argue, but he'd already hung up.

Dana was staring at me, looking frightened. "What was that about?"

I reached out to touch her cheek, hesitated, my fingers brushing air. "I have to go out for a while."

"What's going on, Ben?"

I drew a deep breath. "It's a long story . . ."

"I have time."

I looked at her.

Then I told her everything.

18

PARTONE was waiting for me at the gas station. He'd parked his late-model Ford in front of the closed mechanic's bay and stood leaning against the hood, smoking. He wore another western-style shirt—a blue one with silver snaps. I imagined he had a closet full of them.

He had me follow him a couple of miles up the road to the Dunk-N-Dine on Cheshire Bridge. Aside from a couple of tired waitresses working the late shift and two groups of kids eating tuna melts and greasy burgers, we had the diner to ourselves. It was the first time I'd been out in public, and I got the feeling both the kids and the waitresses were staring at me. Like they knew I was fresh out of prison. Another screwed-up ex-con. I tried to shrug it off.

Partone picked a booth toward the rear of the place and ordered coffee. I asked for a glass of water and watched as he lit a fresh Marlboro off the butt of his last one.

"So what's your plan?" he asked, exhaling a thick cloud of smoke.

"I haven't got one yet."

He nodded, his heavily lidded eyes never leaving my own. "What'd you tell the old lady?"

"I told her I had to meet a friend," I lied.

"She bought that shit?"

Before I could answer, the waitress brought his coffee and my water. While he flirted with the girl, I thought about my wife.

■ ■ ■

I'd told her the whole ugly story.

Her first reaction had been anger. She'd grabbed my robe from where it had fallen to the floor at the foot of the bed, pulled it on, and paced the bedroom.

"Why didn't you tell me? No wonder we . . . goddamnit! Why did you hold this in?"

I tried to answer, but she shook her head. "How the hell can they do this to us? Who do they think they are?"

She cursed the FBI for playing dirty, then Rollie Shore, for putting her husband into the middle of his fight with the government.

I let her vent, let her work it out for herself.

"Why?" she demanded, losing steam. "I just don't understand."

There was no good answer.

Eventually, her fury spent, she sat down on the edge of the bed, her back to me, her arms wrapped tightly around herself. "We can't beat them in court, can we?" she asked, her voice thin.

"We've already been to court. You saw how it works."

"All this because John Forchet wanted a barn."

"All this because I was stupid enough to take his money."

She turned and looked at me. "What are you going to do?"

"The only way out is to beat them at their own game. Black and I are going after Ham's collection."

She thought about it. "I want to help."

"I don't want you involved," I said, careful to keep my voice level.

She stood, fists on her hips, and stared defiantly at me. "You're not going back to prison for ten years. I grew up without a father. I'll be goddamned if I'm going to let that happen to Olivia and Nadine."

I wasn't sure what to say. "I know you want to help, but you haven't seen the way Rollie Shore operates. The best thing you can do is stay here and take care of the girls. That way—"

She interrupted, her voice tinged with ice. "Dammit! Don't patronize me."

I held up my hands. "I'm not patronizing you. These people are killers. I want you here—safe—with the girls. That's the help I need."

"Bullshit! I've been here, safe, with the girls. Look how much good that's done us." She took a breath, then softened her voice. "Listen to me, Ben. If you'd talked to me first, maybe none of this would have happened. I'm either your partner or I'm not. Which is it?"

"Dana . . ."

"Don't do that, Ben. You need me. Even if you find Ham's collection, how are you going to keep it safe? What temperature does it need to be stored at?"

"I'm not sure. But . . ."

"Minus a hundred ninety-six Celsius. Do you or Black know how to do that?"

I started to answer, but she cut me off. "Besides, you don't even know what it looks like. Would you know the real thing from a worthless batch of frozen hand cream? Of course not. You need me. It's that simple."

There was no arguing with her. I threw up my hands. "What if it falls apart, Dana? If it all goes to shit? Then what?"

She met my eye. "Together, we won't let it go to shit."

■ ■ ■

Partone was saying something about Black. "They released him three days ago. I expect you to keep track of his whereabouts. He presents a problem to me—it's going to be your problem, too. He fucks up, I fuck you up. Understand?"

"Yeah, I understand," I said, swallowing the bile that clogged my throat.

"When are you going to call Shore?"

"Tomorrow. First I want to meet with Black, make sure we're on the same page."

Partone sipped some coffee. "Exactly what is it that you think the nigger is going to do for you? He know anything about horses?"

I stared at him. He was worse than most of the animals I'd been locked up with. "You want Hamilton's collection?"

He frowned.

Before he could say anything, I added, "You call my partner a nigger again, you might as well send us both back to prison now."

Partone's frown turned into an ugly sneer. "I'm gonna let you have that one, Hemmings. But mind your fucking tongue around me, boy—or I'll tear it out of your goddamned head. I'm gonna give you enough rope to get the job done; try not to hang yourself by the balls."

When I said nothing, he added, "Got a little information for you. They're letting Dr. Dave out tomorrow, part of Shore's deal. Thought you'd want to know."

The news caught me by surprise. But I wasn't sure it changed anything. If it came down to muscle, Rollie Shore had us outgunned. With or without Dr. Dave.

"Don't get hinky on me now," Partone said, smiling, mistaking my silence for nerves.

"I'll keep my part of the bargain—you keep yours."

He studied me, then nodded. "You think this is unfair, don't you? That you caught a raw deal. All of you think that way—doesn't surprise me."

"What I think doesn't matter," I said, trying to decide who I hated more, Partone or Shore. They were cut from different ends of the same cloth.

"A guy like Rollie Shore . . . he's what gets me out of bed in the morning. Keeps it all in perspective."

"Whose perspective?" I shot back.

"You ever watch John Wayne? The one where he rides into the camp, the gang of bad guys is just sittin' around the fire like they got nothing to be afraid of, and in rides the Duke, blazing away. Kills 'em all. No talking, no excuses. Just quick and simple. *Bang!* It's fucking over . . ."

I listened, not believing what I was hearing.

"We lived in a world like that," he continued, "a world where the good guys don't have their hands tied, then men like me wouldn't have to play games with shitheads like Rollie Shore. . . ."

He sat there in his cowboy shirt smoking his Marlboros, comparing himself to John Wayne. I tuned out the words and stared at him, feeling like I might throw up. A few miles away, my wife and kids were in their beds thinking men like Partone were out here making the world a safer place. And I'd invited this crazy son of a bitch into their lives. I shuddered.

He stopped talking and drew on his cigarette. "Relax, Hemmings. As long as you cooperate, you'll be fine. You beat the system. Act like it. The appeal is over; you're out. Go celebrate with that pretty wife of yours. Show yourselves around town. You can bet your sweet ass Shore is watching every move you make."

He shifted in the booth and pulled an envelope out of his hip pocket. Then he wrote a phone number on the flap. Sliding it across the table, he said, "You might need these."

Inside, I found my driver's license and passport. "I'm free to travel?"

He nodded. "You leave the area, let me know in advance."

"How?"

"Call that number; leave me a detailed message."

"What if I need to speak with you?"

"You're not going to need to speak with me till you finish the job," he growled, reaching for his cigarettes. "And I'll know when that happens. Shore isn't the only one going to be watching you."

"All this watching doesn't mean anything if I need some help. I want a way to contact you directly."

"If you need *my* help?" he mocked. "I thought that's what the nigger was for."

I glared at him.

"Use this number and it's not an emergency—I'll sure as hell give you one," he muttered, reaching for the envelope. He wrote down a second number. "That's my pager. You use it only if you're bleeding. Otherwise, I'll initiate contact."

I didn't plan on using it at all. But if there came a time I needed to prove I was working for the good guys, Partone's numbers, written in his handwriting, might be worth having.

"Call Shore in the morning," he ordered "See what he has in mind for you. The sooner you get started, the sooner it's over. And don't go and get cute on me. Remember, I'll be watching."

I stood up. "Keep some distance, Partone. I don't want you riding in and shooting up the wrong campfire."

He lit a fresh cigarette off the butt of the last one. "Join the wrong campfire, I'll turn you into dust, Hemmings. I'll watch you blow away in the wind."

19

THE next day, Black and I met for breakfast at Annie's, a south-side soul food restaurant. I didn't want Rollie to know about Black; Annie's was one place his crew couldn't blend in if they tried.

The morning was bright and warm, summer teetering on the edge of fall. But my mood didn't match the weather. I drove south through Buckhead, parked for ten minutes at one of the countless strip malls dotting the urban landscape and watched as the drive-time traffic passed me by. No one pulled in behind me. No one slowed or swerved to make an unexpected stop.

When I reached midtown, I turned east off Peachtree Street onto Seventeenth—did a quick U-turn in the driveway of an apartment building, then parked and waited. If Rollie's people were following me, they were good enough to stay out of sight.

Pulling back into traffic, I fought the temptation to feel sorry for myself—and lost.

The day had begun badly. I'd woken early, before Dana, painfully aware of how miserably I'd performed on my first night home. Moving quietly, trying not to disturb her, I'd gone downstairs to the kitchen to make coffee. But the coffee wasn't where it used to be. Dana had moved it to the cabinet over the microwave.

A little thing. Meaningless. I'd found the coffee easily enough, but the fact that I had to look was another stark reminder that my family had gone on living without me. Now, they'd have to learn to live with me again. That would mean changes for everyone.

I chewed on that thought as I pulled up in front of Annie's and searched for a parking space.

Black was waiting just inside. Since I'd seen him last, he'd shaved his head. He wore a green and white Fila warm-up suit, a black canvas book bag slung over his shoulder. When he saw me, his face crumpled into a big smile. He greeted me with a hug, then stood back and slapped me on the shoulder. "Hope you're hungry, man. Annie makes the best biscuits in Georgia."

Once we were seated, I studied his face. "What's it like after eight years, Black? Everything okay? You having any kind of problems? Adjusting and all?"

He shook his shiny head, his smile as bright as the sun. "It's sweet, man. Sweeter than hell."

"Sweet." I nodded. But it wasn't exactly the word that popped into my head.

The waitress, a young kid wearing a name tag that read Tamika, brought coffee and menus.

Black ordered eggs over easy with grits and biscuits. I asked for the same, with a side of sausage.

"There you go with the pork, man," he said.

"Last time you started in on the pork, I didn't have a very good day."

"Be big as Truck, you keep on eating that way."

I just shook my head and sipped my coffee. The restaurant, a south-side landmark, was furnished with scarred wooden tables and mismatched chairs. Autographed publicity photos of every rhythm and blues artist you could name covered the walls. Ranks of ceiling fans stirred the air. At this hour, it was crowded with office workers and laborers, catching breakfast before another day in harness. Regulars called greetings to each other, shared the latest gossip. I was the only white face in the crowd, but no one gave me a second glance.

"You called Rollie yet?" Black asked.

"No. I wanted to see you first. I'll call him after we finish breakfast."

I started to tell him about my meeting with Partone, but the waitress came with our food.

"Damn, that's quick," Black told her.

She beamed at him. "More coffee?"

He nodded. "You all that, girl."

She topped off his cup, then lingered, unable to tear herself away from our table. Or, I should say, Black's table.

"You need anything else?" she asked him, staring shyly down at her feet.

"Just that smile. That smile makes me warm all over."

She looked up at him and giggled. "Go on with yourself."

I cleared my throat. "I could use some more coffee."

She held the steaming pot over my cup, but her eyes never left Black's face and a stream of the scalding liquid splashed onto the table.

I jumped out of my chair, knocking it over to avoid the flood.

The girl squealed, then apologized profusely. "I'm so sorry. Just a second, I'll go get a dish towel."

But Black flashed his teeth and told her not to worry about anything. With a flourish, he sopped up most of the spilled coffee with a handful of paper napkins.

The girl almost fainted at his gallantry before gathering herself and heading off to the next table.

I rolled my eyes.

"Got to make up for lost time," he said, watching her rear end as she sashayed away.

"Maybe you could pick someone your own age," I muttered, blotting more coffee off my chair.

He laughed. "You were tellin' me 'bout your meeting with Partone."

As we ate, I went over everything the FBI agent had said, painting a clear picture of how the man acted and thought.

Black's smile faded. "Man's some piece of work, huh?"

I hesitated, a biscuit smeared with Annie's homemade peach preserves halfway to my mouth. "One other thing . . . Dr. Dave is getting out today. They're releasing him as part of Rollie's deal."

Black absorbed the news without blinking. "You think Boris is with Rollie, too?"

"Damn right I do. Boris wouldn't wipe his ass if Rollie didn't tell him when and how hard." I popped the biscuit into my mouth.

Black watched me chew. "Partone, he's probably got a whole team of undercover agents on our ass."

I looked around the restaurant, but no one appeared to be out of place. Turning back to Black, I said, "We're going to need someone who knows how to handle the collection—it has to be kept at minus a hundred ninety-six Celsius—someone Partone and Rollie won't be watching."

He raised his eyebrows. "You got anyone in mind?"

I told him about Dana.

It didn't take much convincing.

After we finished breakfast, Black walked me out to my car.

"You got a gat?" he asked.

"I'm not going to need a gun."

"Time you think you need one, it's too late to go lookin'." He slid into the passenger seat and unzipped his book bag. Inside, wrapped in a towel, were a pair of H&K nine-millimeter automatics.

"Where the hell did you get those?" I asked.

"Lot of things change in eight years. Some don't. Not all a my homeboys dead or in prison. Some of 'em remember they owe me."

He handed over one of the boxy black automatics. "You know how to use it?"

"I know how to shoot," I said.

"Good." He lifted the other pistol and removed the clip, then worked the slide. "Fourteen rounds in a stackable clip. Take you more than fourteen caps to put a man down, you best say your prayers and kiss your ass goodbye."

I started to object, then thought better of it. This was the reason I'd asked him to be my partner. The gun was reassuringly heavy, solid in my hand. I reached past Black and put it in the glove compartment.

"You sure you don't want me to go with you to meet Rollie?" he asked.

"Lay low. I don't want him to know you're around. I'll call you as soon as I know anything."

He put his gun back into his book bag, got out of the car, then leaned back in and said, "Be careful, Ben. Don't make no moves without me."

I promised I wouldn't.

Then, as I put the car into gear, Black called after me, "Yo, Ben. I got one question. These sperm samples—they come from stallions, right?"

"Yeah . . ."

"Well, how do they get a damn stallion to . . . you know . . . put it in a bottle?"

I stared at him for a moment, then said, "Carefully, Black. Very carefully."

20

CONTACTING Rollie Shore was proving to be no easy task.

I called the number he'd given me as soon as I got home from breakfast with Black.

A deep male voice answered on the first ring. "Yeah."

"Is Rollie there?"

Silence, then: "Who's asking?"

"Ben Hemmings. He told me I could reach him at this number."

"He's not here. Try back tomorrow." Click.

I had virtually the same conversation, with the same results, each day for the next four days. Then I gave up. If Rollie wanted me, he knew where to find me.

Part of me hoped he wouldn't bother.

Partone felt otherwise.

He checked in by telephone twice a day, demanding a report. When I had nothing new to tell him, he'd grumble and make reference to the fact that I was on the street for one reason and one reason only, that if anything went wrong, if I couldn't get the job done . . .

Without comment, I listened to him rant and rave and threaten me. What could I say?

In spite of the pressure, Dana and I tried to keep up a normal front. Whatever the hell that is.

We went about our lives. Trips to the grocery store, walks with the girls. Too much television. Dana and I tried to make love. She was patient, unfazed by my dismal performance. I was relentless. Working myself into a lather. This couldn't be happening—not to me. At first, we tried to laugh it off. It was the situation—too much stress. It wasn't important—don't worry. But the more frustrated I got, the worse it seemed to be for both of us. Finally, I just gave up. I found excuses to stay up late at night. When I did come to bed, Dana pretended to be asleep. She'd murmur something soothing, curl next to me, never seeming even slightly concerned. It was an act. We both knew it even though we didn't admit it. Behind her nonchalance, she was worried, plenty worried. But she fought hard not to show it. And for that, I was grateful.

She got up early every morning and went to the stables.

I spent the days with my daughters, trying to make up for lost time. It was the only thing that kept me sane.

Barely.

We went to the park, the movies, shopping, out for ice cream or to Mick's for Oreo cheesecake. But I carried Dana's cell phone wherever we went and I checked our messages often. Then felt guilty that after all this time away from home, I still couldn't focus on my marriage and my children and give both the undivided attention they deserved.

Late one morning Jimmy Grantham called, wanting to take me to lunch at the Cherokee Club. I turned him down, picturing the lewd look on his face as he gawked at Dana in Partone's photograph. One of these days he and I would discuss it. Now wasn't the time.

That afternoon, the girls and I made a trip to ToysRUs. A blatant attempt to soothe my guilt. Olivia and Nadine didn't seem to mind. While we were there, Nadine discovered the talking Teletubbies—Po, to be exact. Olivia, clutching Silky, couldn't make up her mind. Finally, she decided on a *Mulan* Barbie doll, the Little Mermaid having been replaced in her affections by Disney's Chinese warrior princess.

Fifty-five dollars later, we ate an early dinner at McDonald's. The girls munched McNuggets and fries between frequent trips to the bathroom. I resisted the urge to check my messages.

We were pulling into the driveway when Olivia realized she didn't have Silky.

"He's gone!" she screamed from the car seat behind me. I was so startled, I almost hit the garage door.

"Who's gone?" I asked, throwing the car into park, then turning to look at her.

"Silky! Silky's gone!" She started to wail.

Nadine started crying, too.

"Maybe he's on the floor," I suggested.

"I want my Silky!" Olivia shouted, ignoring me. "Get me my Silky back! Now! Nowwww!!!!"

Nadine started crying harder.

Getting out of the car, I opened Olivia's door and searched the area around her car seat. No sign of Silky. "Where do you think you left him?" I asked gently, trying to calm the situation.

"I want Silky!" Olivia shrieked, loud enough for the neighbors to hear. Then she threw her new Mulan doll down on the ground and started screaming at the top of her lungs, as though she were being tortured.

"Stop it," I commanded.

She screamed louder.

"Olivia! We'll find Silky. Just stop screaming."

Nadine, who by this time had stopped crying in order to watch and learn from her older sister, decided to stretch her own lungs.

The two of them sounded like they were being beaten with cattle prods.

It was enough to put me over the edge.

"Stop it!" I screamed. "Both of you—stop it now!"

They ignored me, so I yelled louder.

That was how Dana found us when she came home from work.

"What is going on here?" she shouted.

The three of us stared at her.

Then, within seconds, she had the situation under control, carrying both girls into the house while I stood in the driveway feeling like an overgrown shit.

After frantic calls to the toy store and McDonald's, we were unable to locate Silky.

To Olivia's great sorrow, he had disappeared. And no promises of buying a new bear could console her.

■ ■ ■

At the end of my first week home, Dana and I took Partone's advice and went out to dinner in an effort to show our faces. Neither of us were in the mood to see and be seen, but we chose the Red Barn Inn, a restaurant the horse crowd frequented.

Several local breeders and trainers were camped at the bar loudly rehashing their latest successes, telling tall tales and inflating performances the way fishermen describe the one that got away. As we walked past them, a few looked down at their single malts. There were smug smiles, shouted how-are-ya's. I nodded and waved, my smile glued in place, my arm tight around Dana's waist. But even that was a sham. I didn't belong here. The scene was flabby. Too much posturing. The men in their jeans and cashmere blazers, the women in tweeds and silk scarves, their biggest worry, how fast and how high. Who gave a damn?

I had nothing in common with them. Not even barns.

Not anymore.

I kept walking, my head held high, smiling.

"You okay?" Dana asked.

"I'll make it."

She squeezed my arm. "You're with me—of course you'll make it."

The smile came easier after that.

When we reached the table, a trainer named Greg Gallagher sent over a bottle of expensive Chardonnay and I relaxed a little. If Rollie was having us watched, whoever was doing the watching knew how to blend in perfectly.

We'd just ordered dinner, veal chops with wild mushrooms and roasted vegetables for me, seared salmon with an ancho-chilé glaze for Dana, when Maggie Dennison entered the restaurant.

She scoped the room and saw us. "It's true!" she shouted across the crowded space. "The bastards let you out!" Dragging her husband Matt behind her, she made a beeline to our table.

Maggie was the kind of woman you either loved or hated. There was no middle ground. Intense and outspoken, she'd been Dana's faculty advisor in grad school, and more important, she ran the lab from which Hamilton's collection had been stolen. Over the years, she'd become Dana's friend, always encouraging my wife to pick up her studies where she'd left off, something I wholly approved of. She was in her midfifties, a transplanted New Yorker—brilliant but loud, one of those large women given to wearing brightly colored clothes and oversize jewelry. By contrast, her husband was a thin wisp of a man, an accountant for one of the big firms. They made an odd couple, but if ever a man doted on his wife, Matt Dennison did.

I stood up to greet them.

"You're really out!" Maggie exclaimed, wrapping me in a bear hug. "I knew it was only a matter of time till they came to their senses!"

She turned to Dana. "Congratulations, honey. Everyone knew this handsome lug wasn't laundering dope money. Does this mean you're ready to come back and finish your thesis?"

"Soon, Maggie. First, we have to get our lives back in shape," Dana said. "How's it going at the lab?"

Matt started to say something, but Maggie shushed him. "After what's happened, I can't get funding for half the things I need to do. Even Ham's tightened the purse strings. My budget's eaten up with closed-circuit monitors and a second night watchman. They'd rather spend it on security than science. As if the horse wasn't already out of the barn." She rolled her eyes. "I can't even buy the new motility analyzer we need. Next they'll probably cut my salary. Not that there's much to cut."

"Nonsense, dear," Matt interjected. "Ham depends on you. They wouldn't think of cutting your salary."

Dana glanced at me but said nothing.

"They have no idea who did it?" I asked.

"The big heist?" Maggie shook her head. "At first, they thought it was an inside job. The FBI came through the place like an invading army—acted like we were all guilty. Questioned us for hours . . . searched everyone's home. You should see what they did to my closet. You remember poor Burke Schuster, don't you?"

"Sure," I said. Schuster was a retired genetics professor, a meticulous little autocrat who'd been given the title of lab administrator—which really meant he was supposed to raise funds. Only Ham Hamilton's largesse had rendered Schuster's efforts unnecessary. He was a lifelong bachelor with an old-fashioned brush mustache who cared only for books and baseball. He was an absolute Braves fanatic.

"They don't think he had anything to do with it?" I asked.

"Are you kidding?" Maggie frowned. "It practically killed him, that's all. The day after the robbery, Burke collapsed. He had a heart attack. Do you think that stopped them? Hell, no! They questioned him anyway, right in the hospital. Searched his little town house while he lay helpless. No one was exempt. Not even Ham Hamilton. They searched his house, too. God only knows what they found in *his* closet!"

"Is Burke going to be okay?" Dana asked. She'd always had a soft spot for the old man; she thought he was lonely and misunderstood.

Maggie shook her head. "They put the poor man out to pasture. The university was his life. Who knows what will become of him. For that matter, who knows what will become of any of us."

"Now, now," Matt Dennison said, taking his wife by the elbow. "No one's going to put you out to pasture, Maggie. They wouldn't know what to do with all the peace and quiet." He winked at Dana and me. "Welcome home, Ben. You two enjoy your meal. I'm sure you have a lot to talk about." Then he led his wife toward their own table.

"Damned optimist!" Maggie grumbled, calling over her shoulder, "Come see me when you get a chance, Dana."

After they left, I looked at my wife. "Do you think she would help us?"

Dana shrugged. "Only if it was both legal and ethical. She's an absolute mother bear when it comes to protecting her turf—her lab."

I looked around the restaurant. The clatter and the laughter, the well-fed smiling faces. Then I looked at my wife.

There was fear under her own smile.

I'd put it there.

21

THE next morning I dropped the kids off at Rose's apartment and pointed the car north on GA 400. I had a destination in mind, but I took my time driving along the green, tree-lined corridor linking Atlanta to her northern suburbs, glad for the chance to wrestle quietly with my thoughts. The sky was clear, a stiff breeze out of the northwest holding just a hint of the season to come. But the fresh air did nothing to ease the knot in my chest. I was headed to Alpharetta, my old stomping grounds, for a look at who was building what—a reminder of the life I wanted back.

I stopped by Billy Stegner's hardware store on Cumming Highway for a cup of coffee, but Billy was out and his father was busy loading a landscaper's truck with railroad ties. I didn't know the kid behind the counter, so I took the coffee to go.

After Stegner's, I drove out Bethany to Hagood Road, then turned north on Redd. Even with the gusty breeze, the air smelled more like summer than fall—freshly cut grass and newly turned earth. But in the year and a half I'd been gone, the landscape had been transformed. Half the pastures I'd come to know were now divided with surveyor's stakes into one-acre parcels. Developments with signs announcing DOGWOOD ESTATES and BRIDLE BRIDGE MANOR touted houses starting in the low three hundreds—cluster homes in pastel colors, rising up out of the ground like so many stuccoed toadstools.

There was hardly a horse in sight. Nobody, it seemed, was building barns. At least not on this side of Alpharetta. Here, it was all about estate homes.

I drove north, away from the encroaching suburbs, until I came to the old Cooper place on Dinson Road.

Then, I stopped and got out of the car with my Styrofoam cup of coffee.

Edwina Cooper had inherited eighty-plus acres of prime pasture from her granddaddy. No sign of surveyor's stakes here. The rolling land was waist high with uncut hay. The only building in sight was an enormous old Pennsylvania Dutch–style barn that had been built shortly after Sherman marched through this neck of the woods on his way to Savannah. The original farmhouse was long gone; the present-day Coopers lived in town. But the barn, an old timber frame structure, still stood guard over the property, a graying beauty set near a thick stand of live oaks where once Dana and I had picnicked.

A month before I'd been indicted, I'd been asked by Edwina to give an estimate to restore the barn and put up new fencing along the boundaries of the property, a job I'd jumped at. Unfortunately, I'd never had the chance to present my estimate. The long arm of the law had intervened. But I'd been over the place with a fine-toothed comb. It was a spectacular old building. Fifty feet from the packed earth floor to the top of her peaked hay loft—three cupolas and almost six thousand square feet of covered space. Old buildings have a well-defined personality, and this one was one grand old dame of a barn—in need of a facelift, but strong and elegant in her own way. The structure was supported by thick white oak beams that would bend four out of five modern nails you tried to set into them. The original builder had used chestnut sills and yellow pine siding. The glass of the cupolas and half of the roof shingles were long since gone, admitting moisture and wildlife. But the oak beams were as solid as the day they'd been set. Some of the trunnels, the wooden pegs that held the beams in place, had started to rot, and the lime mortar holding together the original foundation of river stones had dissolved decades ago. The entire barn needed to be lifted and a new foundation poured. The trunnels and the roof needed replacing, but the rest was a matter of good solid carpentry. Nothing I liked better.

A half-dozen barn swallows started and flew circles around my head when I entered the shadowed interior. The place hadn't been touched since the last time I'd been here. Dust motes floated in tight columns of sunlight piercing the ruined roof. Spider webs hung like spun sugar from the rusty tines of the old hay fork, a pair of man-size spiked tongs lying under the hayloft, where they'd once been suspended by thick ropes and pulleys. A small colony of brown bats had taken up residence in the rafters, and every few minutes, one of them squeaked, a soft fussy sound.

I walked over to the hay chute, a wooden ramp used to deliver feed from the hayloft to the floor of the barn, and sat down on the worn surface of the slide, tapping my feet on the trapdoor that opened into the root cellar. It had long ago swollen shut, but it was one of those original details you don't find in modern barns.

I sipped tepid coffee and listened to the old girl creak and groan in the wind. But she wasn't ready to come down. Not yet. Did Edwina still want to restore the place? Would she be willing to give me a shot at the job? I made a mental note to call her as soon as I finished my business with Rollie Shore. Then I swallowed the rest of the coffee, crumpled the cup, and walked out into the sunshine, feeling more optimistic than I had any right to feel.

On the way home, I drove by Ham Hamilton's place. From the street I could see a construction crew, busy working on a new barn not more than fifty yards from the one I'd built. Judging from the lines of the place, they'd copied my plans. I wondered if David Harris, one of my old competitors, had talked Ham into giving him the job I'd always thought would be mine.

I couldn't resist having a look.

Backing up, I turned into the construction entrance, a red dirt track bisecting one of Ham's pristine pastures, and parked next to a jacked-up Chevy truck sporting a small Confederate flag on the antenna.

I hopped out, looking for Dave, but I didn't recognize a soul.

"This Dave Harris's operation?" I shouted to a big man in denim overalls who didn't seem to be doing much of anything.

He sized me up, deciding whether I was a threat to his job.

"Never heard of no Dave Harris," he said after a moment. "I'm workin' for Chattahoochee Construction and Development. Big-ass operation out of Dekalb County. This is their site—and they ain't hirin'."

He turned and sauntered off toward an electrician's truck.

"Yeah—and good luck to you, too," I called after him. If he heard, he didn't respond.

I took a closer look at the job. What I saw didn't impress me. Two big Dumpsters overflowed with scrap; they probably hadn't been emptied in a week. The ground was littered with empty beer cans and fast-food wrappers. Scaffolding stacked precariously against the half-finished wall of the new barn, looking like it might come crashing down at any moment. Tools lying where they'd been dropped. It was sloppy. Worse, it was dangerous, the kind of carelessness that could only mean loose supervision. Most general contractors put more effort into creative bookkeeping than into building. Who gives a damn if the joints aren't square and the flashing isn't tight—just so the estimate is fully padded and the homeowner's checks clear the bank. I got the distinct feeling this was one of those operations.

A commotion by the old barn—my barn—caught my attention. A woman shouted in anger as a large black stallion, a horse that resembled Ham's prized Hanoverian, trotted out of the open barn doors, a loose lead trailing from his halter.

Babe Hamilton, dressed in jodhpurs and a pale blue cashmere sweater, raced out after him. She was followed by a ponytailed young guy, wearing a white lab coat, and two Mexican grooms. I recognized the grooms as longtime employees of the Hamiltons.

You could hear Babe shouting at them from fifty yards away.

"Goddammit, Bobby!" she screamed. "Who taught you to handle a horse?! Catch him, goddammit! Catch him!"

Bobby, the guy in the lab coat, watched helplessly as the two Mexicans moved to corner the horse. But the horse wasn't interested in being caught.

The grooms circled the wily animal, who tossed his head and seemed to be enjoying the game.

Again and again the grooms closed the distance, only to throw up their hands as the horse pranced away.

It was all very amusing until someone on the job site started his truck and it backfired.

At the sound of the explosion, the big stallion panicked and took off at a gallop—only he didn't head for one of the open pastures; he came right at the job site. Right at me.

Without thinking, I moved to intercept him, waving my arms and shouting like a fool.

The closer the stallion got, the larger he looked—his nostrils flared, his eyes wide, his ears pinned to his head.

Someone shouted something I didn't understand. Then the terrified horse was on me.

I shouted one last time, then jumped to the side and grabbed his lead as he thundered past.

Maybe it was my shouting. Maybe it was just chance. But for some reason he threw on the brakes and came to a stop without dragging me to my death.

It took a moment for my heart to stop trying to hammer its way out of my chest.

By then, Babe and the grooms were by my side.

She looked at me, then shook her head. "Ben Hemmings," she said. "I didn't expect to see you here."

Then, she took the stallion's lead from me and headed back to the barn, her hips swaying, diamond rings and earrings flashing in the sunshine.

I followed.

Inside she handed the horse over to one of the grooms and called over her shoulder, "That was a foolish thing to do, Ben."

"You're welcome," I said, still slightly out of breath.

She looked at me then, but whatever she was thinking never registered in those pale blue eyes. "If you're here to see Ham, you're out of luck. He's traveling."

"Actually, I was just—"

"It'll have to wait," she said, interrupting, then turning away to see that the groom properly secured the horse.

"My vet sent this fool"—she shot an angry look at the young man I assumed was Bobby, then continued—"and I've got my hands full. You're welcome to watch. Just stay out of the way until I'm finished."

Without waiting for me to respond, she began examining the horse, who seemed perfectly calm, as if nothing unusual had happened.

I looked around the barn. It had been a while, but the place looked as good as the day I'd finished it. No bats squeaking in these rafters. This was a fully functioning modern barn. It lacked the idiosyncrasies of the old Cooper place, but it more than made up for it with its sheer beauty. Mahogany-bladed fans turned slowly high overhead. The floor, covered in thick rubber matting, was spotless. Expensive horses poked their heads out of a long line of hardwood-faced stalls. The scent of fine leather and old money pervaded the place.

The stallion was tethered to one of the two hot and cold wash racks I'd installed. Babe triple-checked his halter, then turned and examined a group of implements laid out on top of a table set up near the sinks, implements Dana had described to me when she explained how a semen sample was taken from a stallion. Two small buckets—wads of cotton and cleaning solutions. The collection bottle, a small plastic flask about the size and shape the doctor asks you to fill for a urine sample. A leather artificial vagina, shaped like a rifle scabbard, and the rubber liner filled with hot water that fit snugly inside the AV. A large tube of K-Y Jelly sat next to a football helmet. The last two objects seemed oddly juxtaposed.

Babe, satisfied that all was in order, turned back to the horse. Speaking soothingly, she stroked his muscular neck, "It's okay, Ransom. You know what to do, boy. It won't hurt a bit."

The horse seemed to understand. He snickered and tossed his head.

"You have the mare ready?" Babe asked one of the grooms.

The shorter of the two—I couldn't remember his name—nodded.

Bobby filled a bucket with warm water from the sink and added a generous squirt of Betadine solution from a large bottle.

"I'm ready," he announced, tossing a couple of thick wads of cotton into the mixture.

Babe glared at him. "You tell Kit Miller that if he expects to continue working as my vet, he'd damn well better show up himself when I want a sample taken. Understand?"

"Dr. Miller had to perform emergency surgery on Misty, the Calhouns' jumper—" Bobby offered, meekly.

"Emergency, my ass," Babe snapped. "When I want an assistant, I'll ask for one. Raoul! Where the hell is Ron Overton?"

"Señor Overton gone to deliver the mare Señor Hamilton sold last week," the short groom reminded her.

Babe nodded. She examined the artificial vagina and its rubber liner, then pulled up the sleeves of her cashmere sweater and picked up the K-Y. After squeezing a large dollop onto her left hand, she shoved first her bejeweled hand, then her entire arm into the vagina's rubber liner. She moved her arm in and out with a squishing sound, thoroughly lubricating the liner.

I smiled, wondering what her society friends would say.

"Anyone bother to check the temperature?" she asked, removing her arm, her flawless skin now shiny with K-Y Jelly.

Bobby assured her that he had. "Fifty-six degrees Centigrade. On the button."

Babe looked skeptical. "Let's get this finished. I don't have all day."

Turning to the taller groom, she said, "Go and get the mare, Hervé." Then to Raoul, "Ransom gets a little frisky. Better put on the helmet."

Bobby looked confused. "Aren't we going to use the phantom?"

Babe laughed, a hoarse and earthy bark. "Not on Ransom. He's special. Kit and I have him trained to go without it. He knows what to do."

She took a leather lead shank to which a length of brass chain had been attached, looped the chain through Ransom's halter and over his nose, and clipped it to the left side of the halter. Satisfied that it was in place, she took the bucket from Bobby. "You fit the collection bottle onto the AV. I'll scrub Ransom myself."

Raoul, wearing the football helmet, which because it was too big almost covered his eyes, took a tight grip on the lead shank and positioned himself by the horse's head. He muttered something in Spanish that sounded religious.

Ransom lifted one foot then the other, swatted at flies with his tail. Cool as ice.

Babe, holding the bucket, moved to the stallion's side. "Bring the mare, Hervé," she called loudly.

A minute later Hervé entered the barn, leading a mare. He wasn't through the doors before Ransom lifted his beautiful head and snorted from deep within his chest.

The noise reverberated inside the barn.

This was one powerful animal, moved now by the oldest desire of all. It was raw—primal as hell.

As Hervé backed the mare closer to Ransom, the big horse dropped, his penis thick and semihard.

Babe got down on one knee and gripped the dark and fleshy thing in one small white hand, her fingers splayed. She fished a wad of cotton out of the bucket with the other hand and began vigorously scrubbing the stallion's shaft, paying close attention to the mushroom head.

The sight of this wealthy and well-bred doyenne of society on her knees, scrubbing that penis, thick as her forearm, was as strange a thing as I'd ever seen.

The stallion took it in stride. He arched his neck, snorting powerfully again and again. His penis growing to enormous proportions as Babe washed him.

The mare whinnied, driving the stallion to new heights of arousal. He moved against the constraints of the halter, every great muscle in his body tensed, veins standing out in high relief against the obsidian of his coat.

Raoul, hunkered down in his helmet, held onto the lead shank, white-knuckled, as Ransom tossed his head from side to side.

Without letting go of the stallion's shaft, Babe ordered Bobby to bring over the AV. As he turned to get it, she caught my eye and winked.

I stood there, cheeks on fire, painfully conscious of my own recent problems.

Babe instructed Bobby to hold the AV just so, and together they managed to guide Ransom into the ungainly looking thing.

"Back the mare to him," Babe shouted.

Ransom grew frantic as the groom backed the mare's rear to within inches of his face—his neck muscles swelling, bellowing loud enough to rattle the skylights.

Unable to reach the mare, he began humping the AV, grunting and snorting, growing more and more excited while Babe struggled to hold the thing in place without being kicked or stomped.

Less than a minute later, it was over.

Babe handed the AV to Bobby, telling him he'd damned well better be careful with the sample.

Hervé led the mare out of the barn.

Raoul took the lead shank with the chain off of Ransom's halter, then removed the oversized football helmet from his own head.

Babe stepped to the sink and washed her hands.

Ransom lowered his head and looked ready for a nap.

"Am I the only one who needs a cigarette?" I asked, laughing nervously.

Babe looked at me the way a tigress looks at a staked lamb. "I can't visit with you now, Ben. I've got a lunch thing at the club. But call me sometime; we'll smoke that cigarette together."

She strolled out of the barn without looking back.

Raoul, still holding the football helmet, rolled his eyes. "You smoke that cigarette, amigo, you for sure going to get burned."

I couldn't have agreed more.

22

THE call finally came on the second Tuesday after I'd arrived home.

I'd just gotten the girls down for a nap when the phone rang. I picked it up, expecting to hear Dana's voice.

What I got was a burst of static, then Rollie Shore, sounding like he was talking from the bottom of a well.

"Ben, is that you?"

"Where are you? I can barely hear you." I replied.

"It's me, Rollie. How you feeling? Enjoying the good life?"

"It's been an eye opener. I tried calling you . . ."

"I know you did. Excuse the delay, I had a few things come up. Listen, we're down in Nassau on the boat. Why don't you come down for a few days. Catch some sun, burn off that prison smell. While you're here, we'll hit the casino, then we can talk a little business. I've got a proposition for you."

His invitation caught me by surprise. "I don't—"

"No excuses. Delta flies direct out of Atlanta. There's a prepaid ticket waiting for you. Catch the ten-forty flight tomorrow morning and I'll have someone pick you up when you get in. We'll have cold lobsters for lunch."

I didn't like the idea of meeting Rollie that far from familiar territory, but as he spoke, an idea clicked into place. "All right, I'll be there. But Rollie . . ."

"Yeah, kid?"

"Lobster's aren't kosher. They're *traif.*"

For a minute all I heard was static.

Then he laughed, long and hard. "*Traif* . . . I'll be goddamned if you aren't right. You sure you aren't a member of the tribe?"

"Only unofficially," I said.

"Doesn't matter. I got plans for you, Hemmings." Then he hung up.

I stood there looking at the phone for a moment.

"I got plans for you, too," I said, dropping the receiver onto the cradle. "Big plans."

23

YOU just got home," Dana said, when I hung up from Black. "Don't you think this is a little sudden?"

We were sitting in the den, the girls already tucked into their beds. After work, Dana had showered and changed into a loose-fitting cotton sundress. Now she sat next to me on the couch, her long brown legs folded underneath the soft material of her dress. We were both on edge. According to the clock on top of the television, it was almost nine o'clock, but it seemed as though days had passed since Rollie called.

"You having second thoughts?" I asked.

"No. I'm not having second thoughts," she snapped.

She chewed her lower lip for a second, then drew a deep breath. "I thought it was hard when you left. I didn't expect this . . . I didn't know it was going to be even harder when you came back."

Her words stung. But I wasn't in the mood to play the blame game again. "I didn't plan this. You said you wanted to help. Exactly what the hell do you expect me to do?"

"I don't want you to *do* anything. I want you to listen."

"I heard everything you said—"

"No! You hear, but you don't listen. I'm your partner, Ben. That means we make decisions together. That's all I want. It's what I deserve." She stood and stepped to the bookshelf we used as a bar, then poured us both a healthy shot of bourbon.

Handing me my drink, she said, "It just strikes me as damned convenient that within days of Partone returning your passport, Rollie Shore calls and asks you to come down to Nassau. That doesn't strike you as odd?"

"It seems a little convenient," I admitted grudgingly. I took a deep swallow of the smoky-sweet whiskey. "You think Partone knows more than he's saying?"

"If they're watching Rollie, they had to know he was in the Bahamas."

I nodded. "Well, that explains why he gave me my passport, doesn't it?"

Dana met my eye, but she didn't smile. "What did he say when you told him you were going?"

"He wants a full report when I get back."

"That's it? He didn't want to go with you?"

"I can't keep him from following me."

She frowned. "Do you think Ham's collection is down there, on the boat? It would be easy enough to move, as long as the storage canister is kept full of liquid nitrogen."

"No. I don't think it's anywhere near Rollie. Too big a risk. He gets caught with it in his possession and all bets are off. I have a feeling it's hidden right here in Atlanta."

"Why isn't Black going with you? I thought he was supposed to be watching your back."

The tension between us was growing almost unbearable. But there was nothing to do but walk through it. I'd already explained that I didn't want Rollie to know Black was in the picture. I explained it again.

"I have to go," I added. "You know that."

She drained her drink in one swallow. "How do you know this friend of Black's will be there?"

"Black *says* he'll be there. That's good enough for me. The two of them were partners before Black got busted."

"And that's supposed to make me feel better?" She ran a hand up through the still-damp thicket of her hair. "Black's partner in the drug-smuggling business is going to be there if my husband needs him . . . why don't I feel good about that?"

She made it sound so absurd, I almost started laughing. But she was deadly serious.

"Come on, Dana. Rollie is going to make a proposal, that's all. There's not going to be any trouble."

"And if there is . . ."

"If there is . . . Black trusts this guy. And I trust Black. You heard the conversation—it's all set. He'll be there tomorrow."

She shot me a worried look. "How long will you be gone?"

"I don't know."

Lips pressed into a grim frown, she turned away.

Finally, she faced me and said, "I don't like it, but I don't see any other choice."

"There isn't one. Once we return Ham's collection—"

"That's been bothering me, too," Dana said, interrupting. "This reward . . . I don't see how the collection is worth five million dollars. It simply doesn't add up."

"What do you mean?"

"Show jumpers can be worth that kind of money. But not their semen. Not even semen from dead stallions like Galoubet or Zeus, and they're the ones Ham is claiming are worth the most. Assuming the frozen semen is viable—and that's a big assumption—he'll breed some good solid horses. But one foal in a thousand might actually turn out to be really special. The odds suck, and there are too many good living stallions around to pay millions for frozen semen. The math doesn't add up. You just can't freeze the odds."

"Ham thinks you can. The way I heard it, the value is in the collection as a whole."

She tapped her glass against her lower lip. "Maybe. I just don't see it. The reward is out of line. There's something else . . ."

I finished my drink, stood, and set my glass down on the coffee table. "I don't give a damn about the reward. I want our lives back. The way it used to be. That's all I want."

She stared at me. "It's a mess, isn't it? Everything."

I shrugged, unwilling to catalog my failures. "I have to pack."

She started to cry. "Goddammit, Ben. I hate what this is doing to us."

I didn't know what to say.

24

IT was raining in Nassau.

Owing to the bad weather, my flight landed forty minutes late. By the time I cleared customs and exited the restricted area, Boris was pacing impatiently back and forth in front of the rental car stands.

When he saw me, he looked at his watch and shook his head.

His presence here didn't surprise me any more than the fact that a couple of weeks of freedom hadn't mellowed him a bit. It would take more than a tan and a rain-spattered madras sport jacket to soften Shapinski's perpetual scowl.

"How are you, Boris?" I asked.

He grunted and glanced at the canvas carry-on bag I'd slung over my shoulder. "This is all you have?" *This* sounded more like *thees.*

"I'm glad to see you, too. Rollie didn't feel like coming to pick me up himself?"

"Rollie has better things to do."

So did I, but I didn't bother to mention it.

"Where's the men's room?" I asked. "I have to take a leak."

He pointed toward the restrooms, then walked with me in that direction. "Make it quick, Hemmings. I have a car *waitink.*"

"I thought this was a vacation. What's the big rush?"

He marched along beside me without answering. A Russian tank of a man who'd never heard the word *subtle.*

The last thing I wanted was for Boris to come into the men's room with me, but that's exactly what he seemed to have in mind. I glanced at my watch. I was already late. I tried to think of a way to deflect him, but nothing creative came to mind.

So I stopped and tossed my bag at him. "Hold this for a minute. I'll be right out."

He snatched the bag out of the air, then stood there frowning at me.

I turned and walked off without looking back.

■ ■ ■

I was drying my hands when a skinny black man with dreadlocks came out of one of the stalls. He looked around the bathroom, checked under the doors of the other stalls. Then, satisfied that we were alone, he stepped to the sink next to mine.

"You Hemmings?" he asked without a trace of an island accent.

"You Monroe?" I asked, studying him in the mirror. His skin was the color of cured tobacco, his arms all knotty muscle. He wore baggy jeans and a Tommy Hilfiger T-shirt. A thick gold chain hung around his thin neck. Black had described him as smart, reliable, and one hell of a lot meaner than he looked. He'd forgotten to mention ugly.

"*Mon*-roe. Not *Mun*-row. Monroe Moon—I'm Black's cousin."

We shook hands.

"You sure you Black's cellie?" Monroe said, looking me up and down. "Look like a damn civilian to me—and you bigger than he described you."

I grinned. "Been working out with your cousin for the past year and a half. He told you what this is all about?"

"He said to check out this boat you're gonna visit, then keep an eye on you. Says he promised your wife not to let anything happen to you while you're down here. Now I got to make good on that promise." He smiled, and for the first time I could see the family resemblance. "Looks to me like you can take care of your own self. Unless you're expecting some kinda trouble Black didn't tell me about . . . "

"I'm here to do business, not make trouble. What'd you find out about the boat?"

"More like a fuckin' cruise ship." He looked in the mirror and began fooling with his dreads. When he leaned over the sink, the back of his T-shirt hiked up, revealing the slender butt of a small-caliber automatic tucked into his waistband. "It's a flash boat—goddamn floating condominium—name's *Funny Business*—"

"The name fits," I said, interrupting.

He looked at my reflection. "Yeah—if you say so. They got her tied up over on Paradise Island at a fancy marina called Hurricane Hole. Loaded up with pussy, too. Looks like a damn titty bar with radar."

He finished with his hair and admired the look. I didn't notice any difference.

Turning to face me, he said, "Only two ways in or out without getting wet. You either go through the marina office or through the gate on the service road. Uniformed security both places. I don't know what you got planned, but that big-ass boat's no easy target."

"I'm just paying an old friend a visit." I checked my watch. "I've got to get moving. How do I reach you?"

"Some old friend . . ." Monroe muttered. He reached into his jeans pocket and handed me a pack of matches from a place named the Green Room. "I'll be watching the boat as close as I can without putting on a show. You need me, my cell phone number's on the inside cover. It ain't listed, so don't lose the matches. You do, there's some shops just across the service road from the marina. Go in the News Café and leave me a message with Anita Patty. She's the pretty one."

We shook hands again and I left him standing at the sink while I went out to find Boris.

"I don't care how you go! Just take us back to the marina," Boris growled.

"We on the way, boss," Monroe said, slipping the old car into gear.

It took forty-five minutes to drive from the airport to the toll bridge separating Nassau from Paradise Island. We made the trip in a driving rainstorm. Along the way, I noticed that Monroe bore little resemblance to the photograph displayed on the taxi license hanging just above the meter. This wasn't his car. I wondered if it was borrowed—or stolen. Then I stopped wondering and reminded myself that Black trusted the man.

Boris didn't seem to have noticed. He sat huddled against the door of the car in sullen silence. He reminded me of something an old con said when I asked him why he kept coming back: "You can take the man out of prison, but you can't always take prison out of the man."

I'd never been to Nassau, but the island I saw through the streaked and fogged windows of the taxi wasn't the stuff of travelers' dreams. Construction everywhere. Blighted apartment buildings a block or two from glitzy shops that all but screamed, "Tourist trap!" Bars and restaurants with names like Salty Pete's or the Buccaneer Inn, wedged between charming pastel colonial buildings. Row after row of jewelry stores and perfume shops. Palm trees and gumbo-limbos bending under the lash of the storm.

And everywhere, sodden men and women in brightly colored shorts and sandals, carrying cameras and shopping bags. Fresh off the cruise ships, unwilling to give up a day of vacation bargains just because of a pesky little tropical downpour.

Monroe hummed some vaguely familiar reggae tune as he aimed the car through the crowded, narrow streets. Every once in a while he caught my eye in the rearview but gave away nothing.

My stomach growled. I hadn't eaten breakfast, and Rollie's lobsters were starting to sound pretty damned good.

"What the fuck were you *doink* in there?" he demanded
bag back at me.

I caught it, then shrugged. "You gotta go, you gotta go."

■ ■ ■

The car he had waiting for us was a taxi—an old, green Merc
The driver was no where to be found.

"Where the fuck is that lazy black bastard?" Boris snarled, loo
the way we had come, then at his watch.

"You got a date or something?" I asked.

He rubbed his big chin with a hairy hand. "I spent fifteen year
for other people. No more."

A couple of minutes later, Monroe Moon came bopping out of t
gage claim doors. He'd tucked his dreads into an orange-and-green-
cap and now wore a pair of funky yellow shades. "Sorry, mon. I be ch
out the tourists, you know." He spoke with a perfect island patois anc
no sign of recognizing me. "Got plenty a pretty German girls comin'
island today. They love to dance, mon. You like, I'll pick you two
tonight, take you to the island's hottest disco."

Boris snorted in disgust. "Just get in the *fuckink* car!"

All elbows and teeth, Monroe transformed himself into a nervous s
vant.

"Right away, mon," he said, grabbing my bag and throwing it on th
front seat. Then, hurrying around the car, he held the rear door open fo
Boris.

The Russian climbed into the taxi grumbling something in a language
I didn't understand.

I had to bite my tongue to keep from laughing.

Monroe winked at me, then slid behind the wheel. I noticed a fancy-looking camera peeking out from under his seat. The old diesel roared to life.

"Which way, boss?" he asked. "This time a day, the back way be the quickest. Mon be in a hurry, he gone want the back way."

25

THE *Funny Business* was too big to tie up at one of the slips lining the circular marina. One hundred thirty–odd feet of raked decks and shiny chrome, she lay at the end of a pier jutting out into the harbor from Hurricane Hole's protective bulkhead. With her tall radar mast and clusters of communications gadgetry, the yacht looked like something out of a James Bond movie.

One of the marina employees, a kid wearing yellow foul-weather gear, drove Boris and me out to the end of the pier in a covered golf cart. We both got soaked by the rain anyway.

As we climbed the yacht's gangway, a uniformed steward hurried out onto the deck to greet us. He was a thin, anxious man who looked back and forth between Boris and me as if he were waiting for bad news. "The captain's not aboard, Mr. Shapinski, sir. He gave most of the crew the afternoon off. Is there anything I can do for you?"

"Get us a couple of towels," Boris snapped, wiping the rain off his face with his hands.

The steward trotted off to do as he was told.

"Some boat," I observed.

Nodding his agreement, Boris led me into the *Funny Business*'s enormous main cabin. "They call this the saloon," he said. "A *saloon* . . . looks like a *livink* room to me."

We stood just inside the door, dripping all over Rollie's expensive rug until the steward hurried back with a couple of thick white beach towels embroidered with crossed anchors and the yacht's name.

"Anything else, sir?" he asked.

"Any word from Rollie?"

"No, sir. Mr. Shore hasn't been aboard since early this morning."

Boris dismissed the steward, as if he owned the yacht himself. Then he watched my face as I looked around. "You like it, Hemmings?"

I wasn't sure *like* was the right word. The interior of the saloon was almost as big as the entire first floor of my house. There was no sense of being afloat. The yacht was as stable as an island. All plush white carpet, polished marble, and gleaming chrome. A built in wet bar occupied one corner, complete with half a dozen deck-mounted bar stools upholstered in zebra hide. A wide spiral staircase was set in the opposite corner, leading down to the next deck. Rain-streaked picture windows offered views of Nassau, just across the harbor. White leather sofas formed an attractive arrangement at one end of the room. Bad contemporary nudes decorated the walls.

But the tacky art had nothing on the live nudes draped over the sofas and barstools. Every inmate's fantasy. Eight or nine women, in various states of undress, lounged around the saloon doing their nails, thumbing magazines, drinking tropical drinks, and acting bored. They looked up as one from whatever they were doing when Boris led me in. Pretty women, but hard, none of them over twenty-four or -five.

As attractive as they were, there was something disquieting in the uniformly sharp sense of appraisal their sideways glances held. As if they'd sized me up and knew in an instant exactly what I had and how I was likely to spend it.

"Well have a look here! Look what the goddamned cat dragged in."

The deep voice came from behind me.

Draping the towel around my neck, I turned and found Dr. Dave grinning wolfishly at me. He stood at the top of the spiral staircase, his white-blond hair pulled back in a ponytail. He was bare chested and sweating, like he'd just finished working out. "What's up, Hemmings?"

I nodded to him. "Just came to pay a little visit."

He frowned, looking disappointed that I wasn't visibly shocked to find him here. "Shit, man, I thought you'd be happy to see me."

"I am. Can't you tell? But if you're here, who's back at the camp watching Sally?"

His face clouded over. "Didn't think nobody else would take care of her right, so I put her down. I buried her near the track."

I stared at him, too overcome with disgust to say anything. Then I turned to Boris and asked, "Where's Rollie?"

"He's in Bimini on business," Boris said. "He'll be back soon."

"I thought we were having lunch," I said.

"No lunch. Not today." Boris checked his watch.

Dr. Dave shook his head and said, "Someone's gonna take that Rolex off of you, you don't quit staring at it."

Boris glared at him. "It won't be you."

Dr. Dave smirked, then ogled the women. "Shit, Hemmings, there's better things to do around here than fill your damned gut. Even *you* ought to be able to find something to play with till Rollie gets back."

I looked around. Thought about my wife. Then I tried not to think at all.

"You have a room for me?" I asked Boris. "I want to change, then find something to eat."

"Show Hemmings his cabin," Boris told Dr. Dave.

"Show him yourself," Dr. Dave shot back. "I've got a hundred more push-ups to do. Got to get ready for Jailhouse Giants."

"What the hell's Jailhouse Giants?" I asked.

"Body-building contest, man. Up in Daytona, during Bike Week. Only cons can enter—ten grand to the winner. Rollie's gonna sponsor me." He lifted his arms and flexed his swollen muscles. The snake tattoos danced and writhed on his forearms, but if his display was meant to impress the women, it failed.

These women were motivated by a different kind of muscle. It was flat and green and easy to fold.

"Asshole," one of them whispered.

Dr. Dave swiveled his wedge-shaped head. "Who said that?"

"Lay off," Boris growled.

"Fuck you! I don't take shit offa any bitch. Understand?"

Boris locked eyes with him, then shook his head, exasperated. "Go ahead, do your push-ups. I'll deal with Hemmings."

"Fuck'n right," Dr. Dave grunted. He disappeared down the stairs.

Boris pointed at a tall blond sitting at the end of the bar, reading a thick paperback. "Grace, show Hemmings the cabin next to yours. Then find him *somethink* to eat."

"Did you get Lexa a doctor?" she asked, without looking up from her book.

"Do what I'm telling you, Grace!" Boris ordered. "Or maybe you'd rather discuss it with Dave."

Placing the book facedown on the bar, the woman stood and walked slowly, deliberately to the spiral staircase without so much as glancing at Boris or me. She was one of the few fully clothed women, but even in baggy sweatpants and a halter top, you could see that she was light on her feet, like a dancer or an athlete.

She started down the stairs, then hesitated when she realized I wasn't following her.

Only then did she look at me.

She was pretty, almost beautiful, her thick blond hair shiny, her skin milky white, her pert nose almost too small for her almond-shaped face. But her eyes were her most striking feature.

They were deep blue and as old as the world.

"You coming?" she asked.

■ ■ ■

Grace showed me to a small cabin on the lowest deck, then left me alone.

The cabin was furnished with mahogany bunk beds. There was no window or porthole—no view of the harbor. Shallow steel shelves had been built into one wall; a chest of drawers and a small matching desk were mounted across from the bunk beds. The entire cabin was about ten feet by twelve feet. Bigger than the cube I'd shared with Black and Rico, but not exactly luxurious. There was no sink or toilet; the head was at the end of the hall.

I stripped off my wet clothes and pulled dry jeans and a polo shirt out of my bag. Then I went down the hall to wash up.

On the way back, I noticed the door to the cabin across from mine was cracked open. Inside, someone whimpered.

A female voice whispered words of encouragement.

Curious, I peeked through the crack.

The cabin was a mirror image of my own. Grace knelt next to the bottom bunk, whispering to someone huddled in a fetal position. Reaching into an open duffel on the floor beside her, she pulled out a vial of white powder. Then she turned quickly, as if she'd sensed me standing there.

"What do you want?" she demanded, dropping the vial back into the duffel.

"I heard you . . . sounded like you might need some help."

She studied me with those ancient blue eyes, then said, "Come in and shut the door behind you."

I did.

She stood and I could see that the bunk was occupied by a woman about Grace's size, but even younger. I couldn't tell if she was pretty or not. What I could see of her skin was elaborately tattooed. A dozen steel rings pierced one ear. But that wasn't all. Someone had beaten her savagely about the face and head. Her eyes were nearly swollen shut, her mouth a ragged mess, her nose badly broken. What I took to be dried blood crusted her cheeks and matted her dark brown hair.

I looked at Grace. The surprise must have registered on my face.

"The freak with the tattoos did this to her," she said, flatly. "I think a couple of ribs are broken. They won't get her to a doctor."

"When did it happen?"

"Yesterday. The asshole gets off on pain—other people's pain. He beat the crap out of her and laughed. Sick fuck."

The girl groaned, then whispered, "I have to pee. Help me up."

"Can you sit?" Grace asked, bending over the girl, touching her shoulder.

I started toward the two of them, intending to help Grace get Lexa up on her feet, when the door behind me opened and Dr. Dave poked his head into the cabin.

"What the hell are you doing in here, Hemmings?"

"You fucking freak!" Grace shouted. "Touch her again and I'll kill you."

Lexa made a frightened, strangled noise.

"Get out of here, Hemmings," Dr. Dave said, ignoring the two girls.

I stared at him. "You did this?"

"I said get out!" He pushed the door all the way open.

"She needs a doctor."

"You don't get out of here now, you're going to need one, too."

I shook my head. "This kid needs help and she needs it now."

Dr. Dave's bulk blocked the doorway.

"Careful of him," Grace warned. "He's a faggot. They hit from behind."

"Faggot," Lexa echoed.

The big man's face colored. "Yeah? Didn't think I was a faggot yesterday, did you, you little cunt?"

He stepped through the door, balling his heavy fists.

I glanced around the cabin, but the only thing resembling a weapon was a half-empty bottle of rum sitting on one of the steel shelves.

A broken bottle might be enough.

I edged toward it, but Dr. Dave saw what I had in mind.

He took a step closer to me, smiling now. "Go ahead, Hemmings. I've been wanting a piece of you. I'll even give you the first shot."

I could smell him, a rank animal odor.

There was no room to maneuver. Nothing to even the odds.

My heart was racing, the blood roaring in my ears. I was back on the rec yard, but this time it was just Dr. Dave and me—no crowd, no hacks.

Behind me, I heard Grace working the zipper of her duffel. Then a metallic snap.

"Take this," she said, pushing an open switchblade into my hand.

Dr. Dave backed up half a step, then smiled crazily. "You gonna stick me, Hemmings?"

He crouched and moved warily to his left, both hands open now, arms extended in front of him. "Come on. Take your shot."

"Back off, Dave. We don't have to do this," I said, gauging the distance between us.

"You gonna talk me to death or you gonna do something?" He sneered.

"What the hell is going on?" It was Rollie, suddenly filling the space behind Dr. Dave.

"Stop it!" he roared. "Both of you! Now!"

Slowly, Dr. Dave relaxed and drew himself up to his full height. He glared at me. "One of these days, Hemmings . . ."

"One of these days nothing! Now come with me—both of you!" Rollie ordered, backing out of the crowded cabin. "And put away that knife, Ben. Before someone gets hurt."

"What about her?" I said, pointing to Lexa, my heart still pounding like mad.

"What *about* her?" he said.

I followed Rollie and Dr. Dave up the yacht's spiral staircase into the saloon. Rollie had gained weight since I'd last seen him. He was fat, but he took the stairs two at a time with the vigor of a much fitter man.

"Donny, I won't be a minute. The girls taking good care of you?" Rollie called to a well-dressed middle-aged man sitting on one of the white leather sofas.

"Take your time, Rollie," the man answered in that slow southern drawl I associated with old money and bad manners. "It's a charming boat you have here. I quite like what you've done with it."

There was an edge of sarcasm in his praise, but if Rollie took offense, he didn't show it. "What's mine is yours, Donny."

The man smiled. He looked like a banker or a white-shoe lawyer with his tan, his prematurely gray hair cut short and combed neatly and his cashmere blazer just old enough to look comfortable but not worn. His manner evidence of the fact that he found waiting for Rollie Shore to be nothing unusual or particularly scary.

Four of Rollie's in-house women fluttered around him. They'd miraculously transformed themselves into charming hostesses—laughing and chattering, seemingly unaware of their near nakedness, no longer bored by the rainy afternoon's lack of activity. A bottle of iced champagne sat on the cocktail table beside a platter of cold seafood—shrimp and the lobster tails that were supposed to have been my lunch.

One of the women giggled at something old Donny said.

Another bent over him to fill his champagne flute.

The afternoon was quickly becoming evening, the light fading from the charcoal sky. All of the saloon's lamps were lit, casting a golden glow over everything and everyone. Someone had put a Frank Sinatra disk on the yacht's elaborate stereo system.

I wondered if his crooning penetrated all the way down to Lexa's cabin.

Rollie put a heavy hand on my shoulder. "Pour yourself something to drink at the bar, Ben. Give me a few minutes with Dave, then we'll talk."

Without waiting for an answer, he and Dr. Dave walked the length of the saloon and exited through a door just beyond the sofas.

26

I WASN'T thirsty.

And I wasn't in the mood to watch the four women compete for Donny's favor. So I let myself out of the saloon and explored the exterior of the yacht until I found a set of outside stairs leading to the upper deck.

The rain had stopped, but the dark waters of the harbor roiled with wind-driven chop. I walked toward the bow of the *Funny Business,* the beginnings of a serious headache spreading behind my eyes.

A sport fishing boat idled past, green and red running lights on. She was some two hundred yards out in the channel, but by a trick of the wind and water, the captain's voice carried to where I stood.

"*Damn thing went three-fifty if it went a pound . . .*"

A couple of brown pelicans swooped low overhead. Somewhere in the distance, a calypso band was tuning up.

I was leaning over the railing, staring down at the water, trying to decide the quickest way out of this insanity, when a female voice behind me said, "Thanks."

Turning, I found Grace standing near the top of the stairs. I'd been so wrapped up in my thoughts, I hadn't heard her approach.

"You startled me," I said.

"Sorry." She stepped to the rail. "For what you did . . . thanks. But you shouldn't have gotten in his face. He's a freak. A certifiable fucking freak."

"I know. I did time with Dr. Dave."

She gave me a reappraising glance, some of the hardness in her eyes softening. "You don't look like a con . . ."

"No? What do I look like?"

"I'm not sure . . . maybe an undercover cop. More like a cop than a crook. But one of the good ones. The kind who'd give a poor kid an even break."

I'd been called a lot of things, but never a cop. Not even a good one. I couldn't help smiling. "I used to build barns. My name's Ben Hemmings." I offered my hand.

She took it and we shook. Her grip was strong and dry. "I'm Grace Money."

"That's your real name?"

"Who could make up a name like that?"

Reaching into my pocket, I pulled out the switchblade and returned it to her. "What else do you carry in that bag?"

She laughed. "Believe me, you don't want to know. Where'd you build barns?"

"Atlanta."

"Oh yeah . . . I work in Atlanta—dance at the Top Hat Club. You ever been there?" She started to say more when someone on the deck below us slid open one of those picture windows. It made a heavy grating sound, then a fragrant cloud of rich cigar smoke drifted up to where Grace and I stood.

Rollie's muffled voice floated up with the smoke, only I couldn't make out what he was saying.

I looked around; Grace and I had the upper deck to ourselves.

"Let me know if you see anyone headed this way," I whispered.

Then I climbed over the railing and stepped out onto the narrow outer ledge of the top deck. Gripping one of the chrome stanchions supporting the railing, I crouched and leaned out over the water to get a better look.

Rollie stood with his broad back to the window. I could hear him clearly now.

"I've told you a hundred times, Dave . . . I need Hemmings. When this is over, you can do what you want with him. But not till I say so. Understand?"

Grace leaned over the railing and looked down at me. She started to say something, but I shook my head.

"I want your word . . ." Dr. Dave was saying. He sounded like a sulking child.

"I sent Shapinski over to Lyford Cay. Bring him these papers, then take the night off. Go into town, have some fun," Rollie ordered. "On your way out, tell Donny I'm ready to see him."

"About Hemmings . . . I have your word?" Dr. Dave grumbled.

"Get the hell out of here, Dave," Rollie barked. "I say something, I damn well mean it."

A door clicked opened, then closed with a bang.

As the full meaning behind Rollie's promise to Dr. Dave sank in, I nearly slipped off my perch. The bastard was going to give me up like a bone to his favorite dog. Cursing silently, I tightened my grip on the stanchion, but my arms were starting to ache from holding myself cantilevered out over the water. I wanted to hear what Rollie had to say to his friend Donny, but if I stayed where I was, I'd end up in the bay.

The deck below me was empty.

Moving carefully along the narrow ledge, I inched away from Rollie's open window. Then, I lowered myself over the side of the yacht, legs dangling, feeling with my feet for the railing on the deck below. For a moment, I hung suspended over the bay, breathing hard, my legs churning air. Then my left foot bumped the rail and I scrambled down—flattening myself against the wall six inches from the window.

"Have a cigar, Donny," Rollie was saying.

"Gave 'em up, my friend. Doctor's orders."

"None of us live forever," Rollie observed. "I wasn't expecting you till tomorrow. Why all the pressure? Have I ever let you people down?"

"That's not the point, Rollie. We're concerned about our deal. No. No, just hear me out. Nobody's denying you've been a big help to us. I've got three state senators on the way down here tomorrow. With this setup of yours, we're sure to get their backing."

"Damn right," Rollie grumbled.

"Point is, we've spent nearly fifteen mill to push this referendum through. God knows what it'll be worth once we actually have a track up and running. One thing's for sure, pari-mutuel betting's coming to Georgia. But how do we justify taking the next step with you? I hear the feds are buzzin' 'round you like flies on rotten meat—that's why you're holed up down here in the Bahamas."

Rollie didn't deny it.

"What about it, Rollie? You hiding from the feds?"

"Let's just say I'm waiting." Rollie's voice was flat now. "I've made a deal. Once it's closed, the feds are no longer an issue."

"So you say. Just remember, we didn't offer you a piece of the action to be an absentee partner. We're about ready to push this thing to the House floor. These boys we're entertaining tomorrow, they'll be the swing vote. Once we pass the referendum, we don't want the wrong people deciding they can wet their beaks in our glass. That's where you come in. But I don't see you're much use to us locked up in prison."

"I've given my word, Donny. What more do your people want?"

"Now, that's a delicate subject. We're asking a lot of good God-fearing Christians, state representatives from all over Georgia, to back us on this thing. It wouldn't do for a man . . . uhh . . . in your circumstances to be too visible. This deal you cut with the feds, it worries me. You see any chance of it going south on you?"

A cloud of cigar smoke hovered near the window. I could picture Rollie fixing his guest with his most sincere gaze as he puffed away on a stogie the size of a canoe.

When he spoke, his voice was loud, full of confidence. "None, Donny. Tell your people everything is on track. Johnny Forchet hurt me personally. What he did, he did on his own. But you can rest assured that I'll put it straight. And I'll do it quietly . . ."

Someone opened a door five feet from where I stood. Light flooded that portion of the deck. I held my breath and tried to shrink. Whoever had opened the door hawked, then spit out over the railing. Cold sweat ran down my spine. I waited. He cleared his throat, spat again.

A moment later the door closed.

When my pulse slowed, Rollie was laughing at something I must have missed.

Then Donny asked, "These girls of yours, you're sure they're clean? You've had a doctor examine them?"

"Donny . . . what do you take me for? Of course the girls are clean. Come on, I'll introduce you to my favorite. This kid has an ass you'd think . . ."

I'd heard enough. Walking quietly back toward the stern of the yacht, I wondered who Donny was and what role Forchet had played in his plan. One thing was obvious, Rollie had more than the feds on his mind.

Grace met me at the bottom of the stairs. "Jeez! What the hell were you doing? I thought you were gonna fall in the water."

"Probably safer in the bay," I said softly. "All the damned sharks are on the boat."

She didn't look amused. "I heard part of what they were saying. Were they talking about Johnny Forchet from Atlanta?" she whispered.

"You know him?"

"He owns the Top Hat Club. Only he's dropped out of sight. No one knows where he is."

I wasn't sure what to make of that, but someone was coming and now wasn't the time to think about it. We hurried across the stern to the opposite side of the yacht.

"Rollie won't let you and Lexa leave, will he?" I asked.

She shook her head. "The Russian has our passports. We aren't allowed to go farther than the marina pool without permission." She pointed across the docks to a lit-up swimming pool and sundeck bar. Beyond the pool, I could see the service road Monroe had mentioned, then a small shopping plaza.

"You have your wallet? Your Georgia driver's license?" I asked.

"Yeah. Why?"

"Lexa, too."

"I'm pretty sure she does."

"Go back to your cabin and get Lexa cleaned up," I said. "I may be able to help you."

"How?" she asked, grabbing my arm. "You're in as much trouble as we are."

"Wait for me below. I'll be down after I talk to Rollie."

■ ■ ■

I was standing at the bar when Rollie walked his friend Donny back into the saloon.

The two of them shared a private laugh, then Rollie waved me over.

"Ben, this is Donald Devore. Donny, this is the best builder in the South."

Devore offered his hand, but he didn't look particularly pleased to have been introduced by name.

"Don't worry, Donny. Ben here knows how to keep his mouth shut," Rollie boasted. "Don't you?"

I didn't answer.

"He'd better," Devore said coldly.

One of the women called, "More champagne, Donny?"

Without another glance at me, he clapped Rollie on the shoulder, then rejoined the group of women on the sofa.

Taking me by the elbow, Rollie said, "Come on into my office."

To Devore , he called, "I'll only be a few minutes. Then we'll go over to the casino, see if our luck is any good."

Rollie's office was a spacious mahogany-paneled cabin set just behind the bridge. One wall of the office held floor-to-ceiling built-in bookshelves. Half the space on the shelves was taken up by an enormous saltwater aquarium, filled with tropical fish. The rest of the shelves were lined with leather-bound volumes, many of whose pristine spines were marked with Hebrew lettering. I doubted any of them had ever been opened. The wall across from the bookcase held a sofa above which hung dozens of framed photographs, including one of Rollie in Jerusalem, wearing a yarmulke and a prayer shawl, standing in front of the Wailing Wall. I wondered if this was what he thought it meant to be a Jew. I hadn't overheard any religious philosophy when he was promising my ass to Dr. Dave or offering his women to Donny Devore.

Rollie took a seat behind a large, modern glass-and-chrome desk, his back to the open window. The top of the desk was empty except for a brass clock, a heavy crystal ashtray with a matching lighter, and a complicated looking phone set.

He motioned me to the sofa, then picked up a partially smoked cigar and relit it. He didn't offer me one.

When he had the cigar going, the smile he'd shown his friend Devore faded. "What the hell is wrong with you, Ben? You're not here an hour and you're ready to go at it with Dave. Are you crazy, or just plain stupid?"

"What are you going to do with the girl he beat up?" I asked.

He waved the question away. "She'll be fine. They had a thing. It got rough. These things happen, but it's not your problem."

"She needs a doctor."

"It's not your problem," he repeated emphatically, fixing me with a hard stare.

Reluctantly, I nodded.

He held my eye for another long minute, then he settled his broad behind deeper into his black leather executive chair. It creaked under his weight. "You ready to talk a little business?"

"That's why I'm here."

"Good. It's important we understand each other. Before the feds came along, you knew your way around the horse crowd, right?"

"Yeah, Rollie. I guess I did."

"Well, I want to hire you. You remember the lab heist a year or so ago.

The one where they took Ham Hamilton's collection of frozen horse semen?"

"I remember."

"Some job, huh? Like clockwork—in and out before the cops could respond . . . Not a shred of evidence left behind . . ."

I listened while he waxed on, patting himself on the back for a job so cunningly well done.

"The collection they took," he was saying, "it's worth big bucks, isn't it?"

I nodded, waiting for him to get to the heart of the matter.

"But you couldn't put it on the market, not without calling unwanted attention to yourself ." He hesitated, then smiled even more broadly at me. "What do you usually charge for your services?"

"I don't usually charge anything for my services. I build buildings."

"Say I wanted you to do something else for me . . . would five thou a week get you motivated?"

I shrugged. "It would depend on—"

"You're right," he said, interrupting. "Five thou is chump change for what I want. I'll pay you a flat fee of a hundred grand. Cash. It shouldn't take you long to do what I have in mind. What do you say?"

Here it comes, I thought. I wondered if I should pretend to bargain for a bigger cut. Then I decided against it. "A hundred thousand is a good round number, Rollie."

"Damn right it is." He looked pleased. "A hundred grand it is. I'm going to point you in the right direction, then I want you to find that collection of horse semen for me."

"What?" I said, not sure I'd heard him correctly.

He sat behind his desk, hands folded across his big belly, grinning like a Jewish Buddha. "The horse semen—Ham Hamilton's collection—I want you to find it for me."

"You don't have it?"

He shot me a funny look. "If I had the goddamn stuff, what the hell would I need you for?"

27

I SAT on Rollie's sofa, stunned by what I'd just heard. A long time seemed to pass with nothing being said. It was probably less than a minute. Looking down, I noticed that my hands were gripping my knees hard enough to turn my knuckles white. Taking a deep breath, I told myself to think—forced myself to relax. If Rollie didn't have Ham Hamilton's collection, who did?

I looked up, forming the question in my mind.

Rollie was staring at me. He drew on his cigar, the weathered pleats of his face wreathed in blue smoke. "You all right? You don't look so good."

I nodded. "I'm fine. I'm not sure I understand, that's all."

"What's to understand? I'm making a simple proposition. A quick hundred thou . . . a couple of days . . . a week's work at most."

"If it's that simple, why pay me anything?"

"Maybe *simple* isn't the right word . . . "

I waited for him to explain.

His hale and hearty demeanor faded. He pursed his lips, looking as though he was uncomfortable with what he was about to say. Then he spoke haltingly, as if the words left a bad taste in his mouth. "Dammit, Ben. I don't like to admit this. See . . . I know who took the stuff. I have a couple of ideas about what he might have done with it. Ordinarily, I'd deal with the problem myself, but right now . . . well, I'm needed here. My people already screwed this up once. I need someone outside the loop, someone who can move about freely without drawing attention to himself. Someone I can trust to find out who's holding Ham Hamilton's horse semen."

This was not the in-your-face, all-seeing, all-powerful Rollie Shore I thought I knew. He was off balance. A man used to giving orders, not asking for help. Someone was squeezing him, and they were squeezing hard. Donny Devore? The feds? Both?

I thought about what Devore had said about Rollie lying low in the Bahamas to avoid the feds. If that were true . . . if Rollie had promised the feds that he'd return Ham Hamilton's collection and then he couldn't deliver . . . couldn't even enter the country . . .

Maybe my position was stronger than I thought.

"Well . . ." Rollie was staring at me. "What's it gonna be, Ben?"

I met his eye, feeling a sudden surge of confidence. "A hundred thou is a lot of money, Rollie. What if I can't find the stuff? I'm not even sure where to start looking."

"I'll point you in the right direction. The semen didn't disappear. It's up there . . . I just need someone to root it out."

"And if I say no?"

His eyes narrowed. "Are you? Saying no?"

We stared at each other.

"A hundred thousand, Rollie. Half now, half when I find the collection. If I can't find it, I keep the down payment. Deal?"

He stood up and came around his desk. Looming over me, he pointed the glowing end of his cigar at my face. There was nothing hesitant about him now. "Done. We have a deal. I'll tell you what I know, start you in the right direction. But understand one thing: once I do, you're in, Ben. No quitting on me. No bullshit. You and I become partners; you don't stop till you find the stuff. You need money, muscle, I'll provide it. You answer to me, no one else. We're partners, and in my business, there's no such thing as ex-partners. I can't afford them. You understand me?"

His face was grave, his meaning clear. But he didn't know that I'd overheard his conversations with Dr. Dave and Donny Devore. I knew exactly where I stood with Rollie, *my new partner.* And I knew what was on the line if he couldn't put his hands on Ham Hamilton's collection. Until he had the stuff, he needed me.

I smiled at him. Not just a little twist of the lips. I turned on the high beams, and it took everything I had to make it look real. "Okay, Rollie. I'm your man. As long as we're going to be partners, how about offering me one of those cigars? They Cuban?"

The wattage of my smile must have caught him by surprise. For a moment, he said nothing.

Then he laughed. At first, softly. But it rose up in him from his big gut to his thick throat, until it filled his office. A great earthy, rolling laugh. And while I lit the cigar he handed me, I tried to decide which was scarier: Rollie Shore's menacing threats about permanent partnership or his laughter, which bounced off the walls but never touched his eyes.

"All of this," he began, after the sound of his laughter died. "Everything." He waved his arm in a gesture I took to mean the yacht, the women, the entire setup. "It's all business. Like I told you, everything is a negotiation. There are big things in the works. Negotiations that required my presence. The goddamned feds had other ideas of where I should be spending my time, so I had to come up with a compelling argument to change their focus."

I twirled the cigar in my fingers, watching Rollie's face as he spoke.

"It was your old friend Johnny Forchet who gave me the idea, Ben. He loved the ponies. Got himself involved with a couple of breeders—not the kind who like to see their names in the stud books. I'm talking guys on the fringe. Guys old Ham Hamilton wouldn't be caught dead with. But you know all of this. It was Johnny's barn that landed you in prison, wasn't it?"

"Yeah," I said through the cigar smoke. "If not for that barn—"

Rollie cut me short. "You know anything about Thoroughbreds? The Jockey Club? What Johnny was planning to put in that barn he paid you to build?"

"Not much," I admitted.

"The Jockey Club . . . a bunch of goddamned old-money hypocrites in tweed. Fucking bluebloods. But racing's their game. It's been their game for over three hundred years. They own it—control it. And they work goddamned hard to keep riff-raff like Johnny Forchet out. Only it doesn't work. There's too much money involved.

"They've got a rule. No artificial insemination. Not of racehorses. You do whatever the hell you want to breed hunters and jumpers. But no artificial breeding practices with a horse you want accredited by the Jockey Club. And without their approval, you can't race. It's that simple. You want to win the Derby, the Preakness, you breed the old-fashioned way. Live cover. But our boy Johnny, he wasn't going to let a few silly rules stop him." Rollie paused, and for a moment his face was suffused with pride.

"I inherited Forchet," he explained. "Before I moved my operation south from Jersey, Atlanta was wide open. Guys like Johnny Forchet were all over the map. No one thought in terms of the big picture. I put a little order into things. Made it a little easier to do business. Some of the locals understood. They didn't fight the inevitable—they went with the flow. Johnny was one of them. He had talent. He was smarter than most—had his finger in a lot of pies. Made a bundle running a numbers game. I helped him grow the business. Taught him to run book out of one of his clubs, place called the Top Hat. Forchet didn't make a move without considering his options, doing the research. I liked the kid. He played straight and we both made a lot of money." He shook his head sadly. "Then he got a little too smart. Greed. It'll kill you . . ."

"This greed—it's got a name?" I asked.

Rollie raised his eyebrows, then went on like I hadn't said anything. "So Johnny gets hooked up with some guys trading frozen horse semen. Illegal stuff. Samples from some of the greatest thoroughbreds racing ever produced. Stuff you wouldn't advertise in *Horse and Rider Magazine* . . ."

"How?" I said, interrupting. "I thought you said it was illegal."

"It's illegal to breed Thoroughbred race horses artificially. But if you're going to pay a huge stud fee, you want proof that the stud is fertile, that the semen is viable. It's all high tech as hell. They take blood and semen samples from the stud to analyze—medically. But some of these vets and some of these labs are bent. Not all the semen ends up on little glass slides, if you catch my drift."

I thought about Dana—wondered what she would think about what Rollie was saying. "So Forchet bought illegal samples of frozen semen from some great racer—I don't see the connection to Ham Hamilton."

"Some great racer?" Rollie snorted. "How about Northern Dancer, Secretariat, Nijinsky . . . For the right money, you can buy almost anything—frozen in little plastic straws. Just like the straws you get at McDonald's. Is the stuff what it's supposed to be? Is it viable? Who the fuck knows? But with all the crooked vets and breeders out there, you can bet some of it's the real thing. Forchet thought he found a shortcut—spent a goddamned fortune on this stuff. Even tried to get me involved, Crazy bastard . . . He came across an article about Ham Hamilton when he was researching the hows and whys of equine artificial insemination. A mouthful, huh? *Equine artificial insemination* . . . Johnny used to like to toss it around, like saying it made him a big-time breeder. Hell, he even managed to meet Hamilton; the two of them talked about it. I'd like to have seen that meeting—Ham Hamilton and Johnny Forchet making polite chitchat about horse breeding." Rollie shook his head. "Forchet knew a mark when he saw one. Had his people case the breeding lab Hamilton funds. Johnny learned as much about the science as he could. See . . . Johnny was under orders to find a bargaining chip for me to offer the feds. I'm sitting on my ass in prison waiting for the right thing to present itself when Johnny fingers Ham Hamilton's collection of horse semen. I knew he'd hit gold. Better than gold. It was a brilliant idea. Nothing much in the way of security protecting it; high dollar value, fragile, rare, irreplaceable . . . And most important of all, the stuff's owned by someone with the clout to make sure things would happen if he were properly motivated." He paused again to let the words sink in. "And Hamilton was . . . properly motivated."

I tried to see Johnny Forchet through Rollie's eyes. Johnny was smart. Smart and tough. I could see how the two of them would be attracted to each other.

"So what went wrong?" I asked.

"Human nature." Rollie shrugged his meaty shoulders. "I gave the go-ahead and Forchet set it up. He used his own people. It went off like clockwork. The setup was perfect. Perfect . . . until Hamilton offered a goddamned five million–dollar reward. I hadn't figured on that. Half a mill . . . maybe a million—but five fucking million dollars?! Who the fuck knew?" Rollie fell silent, his face cloudy, his eyes hot.

"And . . ." I prompted him.

"Forchet got greedy. Figured I was on ice, decided to go into business for himself. Thought he'd pocket the reward, then find me another pigeon. But it's a goddamned small town, Atlanta is. And I got word. Yeah . . . I got word before he could make his move."

"And now Forchet is missing. Where'd he go? Did he take Ham's collection with him?"

"Not exactly." Rollie watched a tendril of smoke rise and spread out across the ceiling. "My people picked him up as soon as I heard what he was planning. He was questioned. At first he wasn't talking. He was a hard kid. Came up hard and stayed hard. But even hard nuts crack. Only our friend Johnny Forchet had to be persuaded more than most. The collection didn't go far—it's stashed up in Alpharetta. Johnny had someone working with him. Someone outside his organization. Someone who knows horses and horse breeding. Someone local. My people got that much out of him . . . before he stopped breathing."

"Stopped breathing?" I asked.

"Yeah, goddammit. The rat fuck stopped breathing before he told us where he'd stashed the collection. It goes to show you, you want something done right, you gotta do it yourself. Only I wasn't in the vicinity."

Rollie didn't seem to think it at all odd that in his mind Forchet had gone from being a smart, tough, kid to being a rat fuck in the space of a few seconds. But the fact chilled me.

Rollie shook his head sadly, then drew on his cigar and smiled at me. "No use crying over spilled milk, eh? All we have to do is find out who Johnny was working with, then persuade him or her to give up the collection. That's where you come in."

He looked at his watch, a thick gold Rolex. "I've got people waiting. Finish your cigar. Make yourself comfortable. Think about what I've told you. Sleep on it. We'll talk more in the morning, over a decent breakfast. I'm a breakfast man. You, Ben?"

I didn't say anything. I was still thinking about Johnny Forchet—and how he'd *stopped breathing.* I looked up into Rollie's smiling face. There was a cold light in his hooded eyes, a predatory hunger that unnerved me. And I realized with a start that his moment of indecision—when he'd seemed off-balance, reluctant to ask for my help—had been an act. It wasn't a matter of negotiation. It was about control.

Rollie nodded as though he could hear my thoughts. "You'll get it done, Ben. It's a small world up there in Alpharetta. A guy like Johnny Forchet gets noticed. Someone knew what he was up to. Tomorrow you'll go back to Atlanta. I'll arrange the fifty thou; then it's up to you."

He started toward the door, then turned and added, "Ben, don't go getting any high-flying ideas about that reward. Forchet was smarter and tougher than you. And look what happened to him. Remember, crime doesn't pay."

He laughed at his joke, winked at me, then walked out of the office.

A sudden image of Rollie winking at Chicken Man as Dr. Dave and Boris raped and murdered T chilled me to the marrow.

I sat there on his sofa for a long time, the surge of confidence I'd been feeling long since gone.

28

BY the time I got up off Rollie's sofa and propelled myself out of his office, the main saloon was empty except for a man I hadn't seen in a long time. He sat on one of the zebra-striped bar stools—a whip-thin, raw-boned north-Georgia cracker. He was fifty, give or take a decade, wearing a pistol the size of a small canon in a black leather shoulder rig. His name was Luther Culbertson, and he was about the last person in the world I expected to find here.

Culbertson sat at the bar, pawing through a worn copy of *Road & Track* magazine, slugging away at a bottle of St. Pauli Girl beer every time he flipped a page. Half a dozen empties stood on the bar in front of him, all in a neat rank. When I drew nearer, he looked up from his magazine and studied me with yellowish brown eyes that were as coldly impersonal as a lizard's. A wad of chewing tobacco bulged in his left cheek. One of Rollie's heavy crystal goblets sat on the bar near his elbow, a convenient spittoon. Luther had sallow skin, bad teeth, and wrists as thick as pine boughs. Attached to those thick wrists were a pair of grossly oversized hands, hands that looked like they could take and twist a length of number six steel rebar into a pretzel-shaped knot.

I'd known Culbertson for years. Not well. But I knew his kind. Knew them well enough to know it was best to treat him like a dozing rattlesnake. He came from a long line of shit-poor Smoky Mountains tenant farmers. Farmers who grew corn to feed their stills, not their livestock. Hard men brought up with a sense of honor that had nothing to do with wealth or poverty and everything to do with unyielding pride. He'd been one of Johnny Forchet's sidekicks. One of his construction supervisors, or so I'd thought.

"Luther," I said, nodding a greeting. "You working for Rollie now?"

His flat eyes never registered the question. Shifting the plug of tobacco from his left to his right cheek, he lifted the beer to his thin lips and swallowed, his big Adam's apple bobbing as he drained the bottle. Then, lining the empty up on the bar with the others, he almost smiled. "Ain't you heard? Ever'body works fer Rollie. Some jes don't know it."

He turned back to the magazine.

■ ■ ■

Lexa was dressed. She was sitting on her bunk, propped up by a pile of pillows, when I walked into the cabin she and Grace shared. Her eyes were feverish, glassy, and pinned. Her face a mess. Most of the dried blood had been washed away. Her thick brown hair was combed forward over her brow. Sunglasses and a floppy hat might hide some of the damage, at least in the dark.

"Where's Grace?" I asked her.

She stared blankly at me. Then she mumbled through her ruined lips, "Bahhroo . . ."

It took a minute . . . Then I realized she was saying *bathroom.*

I glanced at my watch. It was a little past seven in the evening. Tomorrow this time, I'd be home—searching for Ham Hamilton's collection. How I was supposed to find it was a mystery to me, but there was something I wanted to do here before I got back on a plane.

Lexa moaned, lifted one hand, and let it fall limply back on the bunk.

"You okay?" I asked.

She fought to focus on me, and even in her sorry state I could see that she thought it to be about the stupidest question she'd ever heard.

I didn't take it personally. I didn't know her well enough to be insulted. The only thing I knew was that she needed help, and she needed it now.

The timing couldn't have been better. Dr. Dave and Boris were in town; Rollie and Devore were at the casino with the other women. The only security I'd seen aboard the yacht was Luther Culbertson.

He was the wild card . . .

Only Lexa didn't look capable of making it onto her feet, much less off this yacht.

I was trying to decide how best to move her without doing further damage to her injuries when Grace walked into the tiny cabin, a wet towel wrapped turban fashion around her head, otherwise as naked as the day she was born.

She stood blocking the doorway. I couldn't leave. And although I tried, I couldn't not look.

Her body was without blemish, her milky skin damp and flushed from the shower. Grace was as light as Dana was dark. And in the middle of this insanity, I reacted to her. The familiar tightening between my legs. That smoky lick of heat where I'd felt nothing. Now. With a complete stranger. When I least wanted it.

She laughed at the expression on my face. "Don't sweat it, Ben. You're not the first to stare. Hand me my underwear." She pointed to a pile of clothing on the top bunk.

I reached for the sheerest pair of silk panties I'd ever seen, and a bra to match. Then I didn't even try not to watch while she slipped them on.

Lexa made a soft, wet, snickering sound.

"You okay, baby?" Grace asked, leaning down to touch the injured girl's shoulder.

Lexa exhaled. "Suhhh—jes fahhh." *Sure, just fine.*

"What did you give her? Will she be able to walk?" I asked, as Grace pulled on jeans and a man's dress shirt.

"You know what a speedball is?"

"No. I don't."

"A mixture of coke and heroin. I've hit her twice since you and I talked. There's more if she needs it. She'll walk—slowly, but she'll walk. You planning to tell us where the hell we're supposed to be walking to?"

"Not too far," I said, thinking Grace didn't look like any junkie I'd ever seen. Maybe the dope was Lexa's.

I started to tell Grace to leave the drugs here on the yacht, but Lexa snickered again. "Noh wahh—floooo . . . "

I looked at Grace.

"She says she'll float. But she won't float far." She finished buttoning her shirt, then hesitated. "What are you doing here? With these people? You aren't one of them."

"I'm trying to get home."

"Home?"

"Yeah . . . back to my family."

"Well, you sure picked the long way, didn't you?"

I took a deep breath. "It's the only way I could find."

Grace didn't say anything for a moment. Her blue eyes locked on mine and I could see how afraid she was.

We stood there, looking at each other. The sound of Lexa's labored breathing filled the cramped cabin.

Suddenly Grace's fear was contagious. A twist of panic traveled up my spine and lodged in my throat. An unwanted chorus in my head started screaming at me. Things like: *What the hell are you doing? You're a fucking builder . . . People stop breathing . . .*

I pushed the panic down, tried to focus on the problem. But I kept seeing Rollie's face, the web of wrinkles spreading across his cheek and forehead when he winked at me.

"Where are we going?" Grace was staring at me—waiting for an answer.

"Off the yacht—off the island," I said, trying to sound more sure of myself than I felt. "Somewhere safe, then a hospital. We need to do it now, while everybody's gone. You both have your driver's licenses?"

She nodded. "Why?"

"You don't need a passport to get in and out of the Bahamas, just proof of residency."

"I hope you know what you're doing," she said, turning to look down at Lexa.

I didn't say anything.

Bending, Grace took Lexa's hand and gently tried to coax the injured girl onto her feet. But the effort was too much for Lexa's cracked ribs. Gasping, she collapsed back on her pillows.

Grace knelt at her side, whispering encouragement.

This is a mistake! the chorus in my head shouted.

Lexa moaned pitifully.

I pictured Dr. Dave's ham-hock fists thudding against the slender girl's torso, her face. Breaking, brutal force—a sickening image. Anger swelled inside me, shutting down the goddamned choir, pushing me into gear.

"Lexa . . . this is going to hurt," I explained, taking one of her arms. "But we have to get you out of here. Now."

She looked up at me and nodded, not quite as out of it as she had been.

Grace took her other arm and together we hauled Lexa to her feet as carefully as we could. She drew a sharp breath, then her knees buckled.

"Try, Lexa," Grace urged.

She did. Leaning hard on us, she struggled to stay upright, then took a couple of tentative steps toward the door.

"We'll walk out to the pool, get some air," I said. "Think you can make it that far?"

"She'll make it, if I have to carry her." Grace promised. Then she asked, "Why are you doing this? Helping us?"

"It's not a big deal. Rollie needs me more than he needs you two. He won't be happy. But he won't do anything—not yet. Not until I've finished a job for him. Then . . ."

"Then what?"

I didn't know the answer to that one. "Come on, let's get going before I change my mind."

"You won't change your mind . . . you don't know how," Grace said.

Lexa snuffled.

■ ■ ■

Luther looked up from his magazine when Grace and I reached the top of the stairs, Lexa supported between us. She was limp, teetering on the edge of consciousness.

The line of empty beer bottles on the bar had grown. Luther had a fresh one wrapped in one large paw.

"You three planin' on goin' somewhere?" he asked.

"Just out by the pool for some air," Grace blurted before I could say anything.

Culbertson's opaque eyes traveled from Grace to me, then settled on Lexa. He put down his beer, reached for the crystal goblet, and let fly a thick stream of tobacco juice. "She don't look so hot," he observed, wiping his lips with the back of his hand.

"She'll be fine," I said.

He raised his eyebrows. "The hell she will."

"Come on, Luther. You've seen her in worse shape at the club," Grace said.

"Not lookin' beat to hell like that, I ain't." He scratched at a smear of tobacco juice on his chin.

"Luther . . ." Grace said, a coy note creeping into her voice, "what could happen to us by the pool? You can shout if you need us. And I'll owe you one."

He thought about it. Took a slug of beer, then nodded. "But don't go no further. Y'all stay right by the pool. Don't wanta have to come searchin'."

Then, he flashed me a strange look before turning back to his magazine. A look I couldn't decipher.

29

THE rain had stopped, but the night was damp, the air heavy with humidity. A pale haze formed bright halos around the dock lights and settled wet on the skin of my arms and face as we moved slowly down the dock, Grace and I taking most of Lexa's weight. A calypso band played full tilt somewhere across the harbor. A flotilla of pleasure and sport fishing boats filled almost every one of the marina's slips. Snippets of conversation and music, the tinkle of ice-filled cocktail glasses carrying across the water, boisterous laughter from a large catamaran, the thrum of the breeze against wire rigging. We caught a few odd stares. But it was the dinner hour, and most people were too busy partying to pay us much attention.

Halfway to the pool area, Lexa's eyes fluttered open and she began to cough. Blood-flecked spittle ran down her chin as the spasms contracted her torso and damaged ribs. She cried out. Then her eyes rolled back in her head and she went limp.

Grace and I carried her to a chaise by the pool and gently laid her down.

The poolside bar was closed due to the weather. We had the area to ourselves.

Lexa looked gray and waxy. I reached for her wrist. Her pulse was fast but regular. I couldn't tell if she was bleeding internally or if the flecks of blood came from her cut and swollen mouth.

Grace gently wiped the girl's chin with her own trembling fingers. "I'm going to kill that bastard. I swear to God I'll fucking kill him."

She didn't have to say who.

While she tried to make Lexa comfortable, I thought about what she'd said to Culbertson as we were leaving the yacht.

"You knew Luther in Atlanta?" I asked. "At the Top Hat Club?"

"I told you, Johnny Forchet owns the place. You do business with Johnny, sooner or later you end up at the club. Luther was there all the time. Even Rollie came in, before he got busted. That's how he and Luther met."

Johnny didn't own the club anymore, but I kept the observation to myself. "Is that where you met Lexa?"

Grace stared defiantly at me. "No. She's my. . . my partner. We've been together a long time."

I met her gaze without comment.

Then she looked down at Lexa, and her tone softened. "We ran away together when we were fifteen. Thought we were hot shit. I've been looking out for her ever since. If anything happens to her . . ."

At that moment, one of the parties on one of the boats broke up and a noisy crowd of drunken revelers came marching down the docks.

I pointed to the shopping plaza on the other side of the marina's service road. "I'm going to go see someone at the News Café. Wait here. I won't be gone long."

■ ■ ■

Forty-five minutes later, Monroe Moon pulled onto the marina's service road in his borrowed taxi.

He wasn't alone. An enormous black man wearing an African dashiki got out of the passenger seat and leaned against the hood of the old Mercedes. He watched intently as Monroe, still wearing his orange-and-green-striped cap, walked up to the small guardhouse and chatted for a minute or two with the guard.

He came out laughing, then sauntered casually over to where Grace, Lexa, and I waited by the pool.

"Yo! What up, man? Anita Patty tracked me and T-Bone down—said you needed me," Monroe called, eyeing the two girls as he approached.

When I explained the situation, he scratched the back of his skinny neck, looking from where Lexa lay to me, then back at Lexa again.

"What happened to her?" he asked. "Or should I ask who?"

"Better that you don't know," I said.

"A fucking freak took his bullshit out on her," Grace growled.

Monroe studied at her, then grinned. "You got it goin' on, girl. This *fuckin' freak*—he got a name?"

"Doesn't matter," I said, interrupting. "We aren't looking for get-back. I want you to help the two of them get off the island, then to a hospital."

"Shit, mon. You don't be askin' much, do you?" he said, lapsing momentarily into his "native" patois.

"Black said—"

He cut me short. "Ain't no heavy thing. I'll do it—get these two as far as Jackson Memorial in Miami. But I promised Black to be lookin' out for you. Once I drive outta here, you best be hittin' the road your own self. In a hurry. You mess with a man's string a pussy, you messin' with more than his pocketbook. Understand?"

Grace started to say something, but I shook my head.

"Don't worry about me," I said to Monroe. "How much will this cost?"

He frowned at me. "Cost? It ain't cost you nothin'. I told you once . . . me and Black, we go way back."

He pulled off his cap and shook his dreads loose.

It must have been some kind of signal. As soon as the cap came off, the man in the dashiki hurried over.

"T-Bone, put that girl in the back a the car," Monroe told him. "Then hustle on over to the café and tell Anita she ain't seen me or talked to me in a long damn time. A month . . . maybe longer. Tell her I make it up to her. That I'll be by to see her mama next week."

T-Bone bent and gently lifted Lexa in his huge arms. He carried her like a sleeping baby to the car.

Grace put her hand on my arm. "I owe you. I know Forchet—how he operates. I know things . . . Back in Atlanta, you need anything, you call me. I'm in the book under *G. Money.*"

Standing on her toes, she kissed me quickly on the cheek. Then, she followed T-Bone and Lexa to the taxi.

Monroe was stuffing his dreads back under his cap. "You do what I tell you," he said. "Don't be fuckin' 'round with this thing, 'cause you sure as hell just shit on someone's dinner plate."

He turned and strolled back to the guardhouse. Before he went in, I saw a flash of green as he pulled something out of his pocket.

A moment later he stepped out of the guardhouse and headed for his car. I could hear him whistling.

He looked back at me once, and called over his shoulder, "You tell Black that Monroe Moon don't ever forget his blood."

Then the old taxi sped off into the damp Bahamian night.

30

ONCE Grace and Lexa had been safely delivered into Monroe Moon's protection, I realized I was hungry. Not hungry—starved. I couldn't remember the last time I'd eaten. Nothing had been offered aboard the *Funny Business,* so I walked back to the News Café.

A smiling young waitress with processed hair and skin the color of milk chocolate seated me. Anita Patty was nowhere to be seen. I assumed she'd left work in a hurry after T-Bone's warning. Not that she had anything to worry about. Rollie would be pissed, but his anger would be directed at me. He wouldn't press the issue—not too hard. No matter how bent out of shape he got, Rollie Shore was a businessman first. He needed me. I had a job to do.

And after . . .

Now wasn't the time to think about that. Once I had my hands on Ham Hamilton's collection, everything was up for grabs anyway.

My stomach rumbled.

The waitress suggested the special. Who could say no to that smile?

I packed away a fried-grouper sandwich with extra tartar sauce, coleslaw, a double order of fries, and two pieces of Key lime pie. The waitress looked pleased when I paid the bill. Another satisfied customer. Or was it the tip? I'm a fool for good service. Don't mind paying when it's done right.

Outside, the mist had lifted and a dusting of stars shone through the broken cloud cover. I wasn't ready to go back to the yacht. A long walk on the beach seemed like a much better idea.

Dodging mopeds, I crossed the main street of Paradise Island, took off my shoes, and walked out onto the damp sand. It was cool on my bare feet, the light breeze soft on my face. To my right, an enormous pink resort scattered light and noise across the calm surface of the Caribbean.

I turned left.

A gentle swell rolled up and then retreated from the sloped beach. Somewhere in the distance, the calypso band was playing louder than ever. Couples and groups of vacationers strolled hand in hand, arm in arm. Talking, joking, laughing. Wednesday night in tourist heaven—no work tomorrow, just the beach, the sun, and a glass or two of rum. I shared none of their joy. I thought about Dana and the girls. They were a million miles away. The beach was beautiful, but I might as well have been back in prison. Home . . . that familiar hollow ache in my chest. I didn't want to mess with Rollie or Special Agent Partone—I didn't want any of this. I just wanted things to be right with my wife, to wake up and make pancakes for my daughters then strap on my tools and frame out a building. I wanted a thick ham-and-onion sandwich with a cold beer for lunch. The smell of fresh-cut lumber, the grind and whirr of power tools, the jokes and curses and laughter men make when the job is going well. Quitting time, dinner, television, bed . . . then another day.

Would I ever get my life back? Nagging doubt started to eat at me. The chorus in my head began tuning up.

Stop! I screamed silently.

Just focus on finding Ham's collection. Then make your move . . .

What move?

I drew in deep drafts of sea air, waiting for my heart to slow. Then I thought about the conversation I'd overheard between Rollie and Donald Devore. Tried to put the pieces together in some kind of a pattern that could be used to my advantage. But it was a complicated puzzle and nothing fit neatly. I was tired—exhausted. My thoughts as scattered as the clouds. I wanted this nightmare to be over.

■ ■ ■

No one challenged me when I stepped aboard the *Funny Business.* The main saloon was empty except for a uniformed steward, the one who earlier in the day had brought Boris and me towels. Luther Culbertson had either taken his beer drinking elsewhere or called it a night. I didn't mind; it saved me having to explain what happened to Grace and Lexa. But the lack of security surprised me. Obviously, Rollie didn't lie awake nights worrying about it—which struck me as arrogant.

Then again, the biggest sharks don't fear anything in the sea. Why should they?

At first, the steward didn't notice me. He was busy setting out platters of cold meats and seafood on top of the bar. Sliced tenderloin and cold roasted chickens, huge stone-crab claws, split lobsters and tiny little clams, some kind of dip with generous dollops of caviar mounded on top. Half a dozen bottles of Dom Perignon champagne sweating on ice in silver buckets.

The poor guy was fussing over the lavish buffet like an artist painting an edible still life. And I'd settled for a grouper sandwich and French fries . . .

"What's going on?" I asked when he'd finished arranging the crab just so.

He nearly dropped the mustard sauce.

Looking up at me, he blinked nervously. "Oh God, I'm going as quickly as I can. . . . Just give me a minute. I won't be another minute."

He was frightened half out of his wits. Maybe waiting hand and foot on the likes of Rollie Shore and his crew of miscreants did that to you. "It's okay," I reassured him, "I just wondered where everyone was."

"I—I'm not sure, sir. They usually come in for a late supper around midnight. The other steward is off. I'm alone, and I'm running behind. I still have to get the desserts ready. But if you need anything . . ."

"No thanks. I've already eaten," I said.

He looked relieved.

I walked past him, headed for the spiral staircase and my cabin, wanting to catch a few hours' sleep. When I reached the stairs, I stopped and asked, "What time do they get up for breakfast around here?"

The steward wiped his shiny forehead with a white linen napkin. "Whenever they feel like it, sir."

■ ■ ■

It took a while, but lulled by the faint sound of water lapping the hull of the yacht, I finally fell asleep. I dreamed I was chasing Dana; she was naked, riding a wild, dappled gray mare. I was laughing, running after her with a hard-on, the endless green pasture a blur under my bare feet, when the mattress on my bunk came to life. It heaved upward, dumping me onto the floor of my cabin in a dazed heap.

"The fuck you think you are? Asshole!"

I squinted up into the enraged face of Dr. Dave. He stank of rum and cigarette smoke.

Behind him stood Boris. In the door of the cabin, I could see Luther.

No one looked happy.

I made it to my feet before Dr. Dave swung. But he telegraphed the blow and I caught it on my left shoulder. The force of the impact shocked me. It was like being kicked by a mule. My shoulder went numb, my left arm a heavy, sluggish thing. If he hadn't been so drunk, the one punch, well placed, would have been enough.

"Where are they, asshole?" he screamed.

"Who?" I shot back, edging to his left, away from that heavy right hand.

"The two dykes, Hemmings. Where the fuck are they?"

A tremendous bloom of pain spread outward from my shoulder. I looked around for a weapon. Nothing . . .

Then he was coming at me, lobbing a left at my chin.

He was powerful, but slow. I ducked and his fist barely grazed the top of my head.

It was enough to make my eyes water, but I landed a hard right of my own just under his rib cage.

He grunted, backed up a couple of steps.

Then he laughed. "Come on, Hemmings. Take another shot," he taunted, motioning me in. "Go ahead, a free one."

Dropping his hands, he stood straight up, inviting me to hit him. He was grinning madly, red faced, slurring. But I wasn't about to fight his fight. Not unless I had to.

"Talk to Rollie," I said, circling to stay out of range. "This isn't between you and me."

"The fuck it's not." He stuck out a wild jab and missed.

"You're making a mistake," I warned.

But Dr. Dave wasn't listening. He had an audience and he wanted to put on a show.

Deliberately, he took his eyes off me and grinned at Boris. "Check this out, Commissar." He waved his right fist over his head, the snake tattoos on his forearm dancing over bunched muscle. "I'm gonna introduce Hemmings to this—to Mr. Pain."

It was an opening, the only chance I was likely to get . . .

"You forgot something . . ." I said, slipping a step closer.

"What?" He turned, a sneer on his lips.

"This!" I said, lashing out with my foot, catching him square in the balls. It was a trick that shouldn't have fooled any self-respecting eighth grader on the playground, but Dr. Dave, overconfident and drunk, walked right into it.

For a fraction of a second he didn't react. He just looked at me, his sneer fading. Then he clutched at his crotch and fell to the floor.

He lay there, curled in a tight fetal position, gasping for air.

Boris shook his head.

Luther laughed out loud.

I sat down hard on my bunk, the top of my head aching, my shoulder throbbing, surprised I was still in one piece.

"Now what y'all gonna do?" Luther asked Boris. "Challenge him to *wrassle?*"

"Shut up!" Boris spat.

Dr. Dave didn't move for what seemed a long time. His breath came in ragged gasps, his long blond hair matted to his skull with sweat.

I kept one eye on the door, but there was no way around Boris and Luther.

"When Rollie gets here, you better have a *fuckink* good story," Boris growled at me.

Then he and Luther hauled Dr. Dave to his feet.

"He suckered me," Dr. Dave complained. "Fucking suckered me . . ."

"You can walk?" Boris asked him.

Instead of answering, Dr. Dave's hand snaked under Boris's madras sport coat and jerked a fat chrome-plated automatic out of the Russian's waist-band.

"Think you're smart?" he hissed, pointing the thing at me. "How smart you feel now?"

"No!" Boris shouted, grabbing for the gun. "Rollie has plans."

The two of them grappled, light glinting off the shiny automatic as they twisted and turned. I didn't know where to put myself. There was no way out, nothing to duck behind.

Boris had one hand on Dr. Dave's neck and one hand on the gun when there was a deafening explosion.

The two of them stood there, eyeball to eyeball.

Boris said something in Russian, then collapsed on the deck, a bright red slick of blood staining his chest.

Dr. Dave stared down at him for a long moment.

Then he looked at me, his flushed face contorted with anger and fear. "You did this . . . you and your smart-ass bullshit. He's fucking dead."

He brought the gun up slowly—pointed it at my face.

"Don't," I whispered.

Time stopped. A roaring noise filled my head. The stink of burned cordite . . . My vision narrowed to a small cone of light centered on the gun. I could see Dr. Dave's finger tighten on the trigger. Part of me didn't believe—couldn't accept—that this was happening. Minutes earlier, I'd been asleep, dreaming. What about Dana—Nadine and Olivia? *I'm sorry,* I wanted to tell them. *So sorry . . .*

Then Dr. Dave was facedown on the floor next to Boris. Luther stood over him, holding his own pistol by the barrel.

"Dumb fuck has a head like a hickory nut," he said, holstering his gun. "Didn't think the boy was gonna go down. Fer a minute there, thought I might have to shoot him."

I didn't say anything. My body belonged to someone else. Time passed. A minute? An hour? The roaring faded. I could hear the sound of water against the yacht's hull, distant strands of music. But I couldn't speak. My hands were shaking. I breathed deeply.

"Got us a little mess, huh?" Luther was saying.

I nodded.

"Don't much like all that blond hair," he observed, aiming a thick string of tobacco juice at the center of Dr. Dave's back. "Boy looks like a sissy, you ask me."

I felt myself smile, but there was nothing funny here.

Luther shook his head.

"Guess I best go and find the boss," he said, pocketing Boris's gun and starting out of the cabin.

I didn't see any way around it.

31

ROLLIE paced the length of the main saloon, a scowl on his face. His late-night supper had been postponed, the women and Donald Devore hustled back to the casino.

"What the fuck went on here?" he asked.

He wasn't speaking directly to anyone, and Luther had already recited the facts. So no one answered.

"Goddamned inconvenient," he muttered.

I stood by the piano, waiting for the explosion. A trickle of sweat ran down the back of my neck. I'd helped Grace and Lexa thinking Rollie needed me, that he wouldn't overreact. I hadn't planned on anything as inconvenient as Dr. Dave's shooting Boris.

Rollie paced, back and forth.

Back and forth . . .

Dr. Dave sat on one of the white leather couches, an ice-filled towel held to the back of his head. Once in a while he looked up and glared at me. But for the most part he just sat there looking at nothing. Silent, sulking.

Luther had helped himself to a plate of food from the buffet. While Rollie paced, the skinny redneck ate with gusto, sucking down one lobster tail after another.

Boris's body lay wrapped in a bloody sheet, laid out on top of some cardboard Luther had placed on the saloon's white carpet.

Nobody paid it much attention.

Finally, Rollie stopped his pacing. "You shit on my hospitality, Ben. Goddammit! I treated you like a friend. *This* is how you repay me?"

"I warned him . . ." Dr. Dave began . . .

"And you, you stupid fuck," Rollie roared, "what the hell did you have to go and shoot Boris for?"

"It wasn't like that, Rollie . . ."

"'It wasn't like that, Rollie.'" Rollie mimicked. "So exactly what was it like?"

Dr. Dave didn't answer.

"I'll tell you what it was like," Rollie continued. "It was like amateur night, the blind leading the fucking blind. Boris was a brother to me. We had a bond . . . I think about the time we did together. The trust . . . Christ! I leave you two alone for a couple of hours and you blow a fucking hole in him."

"It wasn't my fault—it was an accident," Dr. Dave complained.

"An accident . . ." Rollie glanced at the shrouded body, then looked over at Luther. "You think that cardboard is thick enough? You can't get blood out of a white carpet. I've tried."

Luther's mouth was stuffed with lobster, so he nodded.

Frowning, Rollie pointed at Dr. Dave. "You . . . get your sorry ass up off my couch and go see our friends on Lyford Cay. Tell them I need some people to clean this up . . . the Jamaicans. Tell them to send Tosh and his crew. And try not to shoot any of them on the way back, okay?"

Dr. Dave pushed himself up off the couch. As he turned and started out of the saloon, Rollie did a double take. "Jesus fucking Christ!" he bellowed. "What the hell is all over your back?"

He looked from Dr. Dave to the couch. "What'd you do to my leather?"

Confused, Dr. Dave stared at the shit-brown stain he'd left on the back of Rollie's couch. Then he craned his neck, trying to get a look at the back of his shirt.

Luther was grinning into his plate of seafood.

"What is this?" Rollie demanded, getting down on one knee, examining the stain.

Then, he fixed Dr. Dave with a look that would loosen the bowels of any normal person. "This is Italian leather, you moron!"

Dr. Dave mumbled something unintelligible.

Rollie shook his head in disgust. "Get the fuck out of here! Clean yourself up and get over to Lyford Cay. And send the goddamn steward in here with some leather cleaner. I have guests—I want this mess cleaned up!"

Then he turned on me. "What the fuck is wrong with you? You go against my wishes right under my nose. Why? For a couple of cunts? Are you crazy?"

"She might have died . . ." I said.

He stepped closer, poking a fat finger at my chest. "*She* might have died." He pointed at Boris's body. "*That's* not dead? If that's not dead, then what the fuck is it? You tell me!"

I started to say something, but he cut me off.

"You put me in a bad position, Ben. Made me look weak . . ." He paused, scratched his nose, and looked at me the way an angry pit bull looks at fresh meat.

I thought about the last person who'd made Rollie look bad. Dr. Dave had hammered a spike into his head. Tears and begging hadn't helped T.

Rollie seemed to sense what I was thinking. "Wipe that tough-guy look off your face, kid. One word and Luther over there will take you out fishing, only you'll be the bait."

"That would be bad business, Rollie."

"Ahhh, you've been listening to the things I've been trying to teach you. Business . . . it's all business. That what you're thinking?"

I nodded. "Like you said, it's all a negotiation. You want Ham Hamilton's collection. Turn your man Luther loose and I won't be much help, will I?"

Rollie smiled, a frosty little grin. Then, without warning, his fist shot out, catching me squarely on my right eye. More a poke than a knockout punch, but he was a big man. It stung like hell.

I raised my fists, ready to defend myself if he tried it again.

"Unn-unhh." Luther had his gun out, a smear of cocktail sauce on his pointy chin. "Simmer down, boy. Just as easy for them Jamaicans to dump two bodies as it is one."

Taking a deep breath, I dropped my arms. Luther lowered his gun.

My eye was already starting to swell, but I resisted the urge to touch it.

Rollie was smiling broadly now. "Smarts, huh? Call it an advanced lesson in negotiation. There's good faith, and then there's business. Wait here."

He stalked off toward his office.

A moment later he returned, holding something hidden behind his back. "A deal is a deal, but you ever cross me again, I'll take that eye. I'll take the eye and anything else I want. Including your family. Understand?"

He took his hand from behind his back. He was holding a small stuffed animal. Grinning, he twisted it in his hands until it tore in half. Then he tossed me the head.

As it spun through the air, I recognized it.

My heart froze.

It was Olivia's Silky.

"How?" I asked, my mind spinning back to the day it had disappeared.

Rollie was studying me, his blue eyes blazing. "She's a cute kid—Olivia, right? Likes popcorn. I remember her from the visiting room. We live in a fucked-up world, Ben. It'd be a mistake to take your children's safety for granted. No matter how cute they are."

I just stared at him.

"You're always where I can reach out and touch you, Ben. Never forget that."

I clutched my daughter's stuffed bear in both hands, his threat echoing in my ears. A thousand images and regrets flashed through my head, none worth repeating. One thought, however, stuck.

"Go near my family, Rollie, and I'll kill you or die trying." I said it simply, my voice a distant, shaky thing. But I'd never been more serious in my life.

His face turned red. "Get out of here before I change my mind! Find that goddamned collection. Call the number I gave you and leave a message for me the second you have a line on it. I'll be waiting."

"About my family—I meant what I said. Stay away from them."

But Rollie had turned his back on me. "Luther!" he shouted. "Get him off my boat. Take him to the goddamned airport. Sit on him all night. I don't want him out of your sight until he's on the next flight to Atlanta."

Then Luther was by my side, one of his big hands clamped around my arm. "You heard the man. Let's get a move on."

32

THE flight back to Atlanta lasted an eternity. I spent most of it kicking myself in the ass for being a fool. Black had said it best, back when the whole thing started: "There isn't an angle Rollie Shore hasn't got covered twice." Only I hadn't thought of my children as angles.

Before boarding the plane, I'd persuaded Luther to let me call Dana. He'd stood breathing down the back of my neck as I spoke, prepared to stop me if I made a break for it. Maybe he was worried I'd run to the airport bar and drown myself. Not that the thought hadn't crossed my mind . . . I'd given Dana my flight number, told her I was fine, then managed to end the conversation without getting into what had happened onboard the *Funny Business.*

She was waiting for me when I cleared customs, wearing jeans and a striped shirt, her thick hair pushed up and back by a tortoiseshell headband. The sight of her made my heart jump.

After embracing me, she held me at arm's length and stared hard at me. "What happened to your face?"

I had a pretty good shiner where Rollie had hit me, but that was the least of my worries. The man had threatened my family, my children. I wanted them safely out of his reach—today.

"Where are the girls?" I asked, trying to sound calm. Failing.

"They're with Rose," Dana answered, her eyes digging holes in my face. "Why? What's wrong?"

"Where did she take them?"

"To lunch. I don't know where . . . What's the matter, Ben? What happened?"

A uniformed customs agent stood a few yards away. He seemed to be watching us.

"Let's get out of here. We'll talk in the car." Taking Dana by the elbow, I shouldered my carry-on and steered her toward the exit.

She started to argue, wanting an explanation, but something in my face silenced her.

We hurried through the crowded terminal, which was busy for a Thursday morning—loudspeakers blaring announcements, tour groups, families off for a long weekend trailing sullen teenagers, business travelers whispering into cell phones. Dana's frown grew deeper with every step we took.

By the time we reached the car, she'd had enough. Stopping in front of the old Suburban, she said, "What is going on?!"

"Let's go get the girls. You drive—I'll explain on the way."

"I told you, I don't know where they are." She stood in the parking lot, her arms crossed, not moving an inch. "Now, are you going to tell me what this about or are we going to stand here all day?"

"We don't have time for this!" I exploded. "Get in the goddamned car!"

She glared at me for a second, then slid behind the wheel, fumbling with the keys.

"What's happened to you?" she asked. "You're there in front of me, but it's not you. Like something's gotten twisted up—turned inside out."

"It's not me I'm worried about. Head home; we'll wait for the girls there."

"Tell me what happened? Why are you so worried about the girls?"

"Drive—I'll explain on the way."

It was bright and sunny, the air crisp with approaching autumn—a startling contrast to the tropical weather I'd left behind in Nassau. The story came tumbling out of me as she drove north toward the city, sounding bizarre, almost unbelievable on such a beautiful day.

As I spoke, Dana's knuckles turned white on the steering wheel. But she listened silently, her eyes glued to the road.

"We don't have a choice," I said, when I finished.

Dana didn't respond. Maybe it hadn't sunk in.

"Until this is over, I want you and the kids to go somewhere," I repeated. "Somewhere Rollie can't find you."

She shook her head. "It's too crazy. This just isn't happening."

I pulled Silky's head out of my carry-on bag and propped it up on the dashboard. "Rollie had this, Dana. Like it or not, it's happening."

At the sight of the little bear's head, she drew a sharp breath, as though she'd been slapped. The car swerved, nearly sideswiping a Toyota.

"Watch out!" I grabbed for the steering wheel.

"Goddamnit, Ben!" Dana shouted, slapping my hand away.

Once she had the car under control, I put my hand on her shoulder. She shrank from my touch.

"I'm sorry, Dana," I offered. But we both knew the words carried no comfort, no safety.

She drove on, refusing me even a glance.

I sat there, feeling sick in my heart.

After a few miles, she spoke, her voice strained, "I told you, I'm not going to watch the girls grow up without a father."

"Nothing's going to happen to me."

"It already has."

I started to argue—to tell her she was wrong—then realized it was pointless. Maybe I had changed. But the only thing that mattered now was getting her and the girls out of Rollie's reach.

"We have to find someplace safe for you until this is over," I said. "Then we can sort things out."

"Oh, that's brilliant! Just fucking brilliant. Like a goddamned movie.

Only this isn't a movie, is it? This is our lives . . . our children's lives. For Christ's sake, Ben! You have to—"

"Dana . . ."

"Don't *Dana* me. I'm not a child."

"Then listen to me! There isn't any other way!"

"Yeah? And exactly where the hell would you have us hide? Where is this safe place? Have you even thought that one through?"

"What about your aunt, the one in Fort Lauderdale?"

"Great idea," she said. "We'll pack our bathing suits and run down to Aunt Carol's. We'll go to the beach while you play games with Rollie Shore! He'd *never* think to track us down through my family, would he?"

"Then come up with a better idea. I didn't plan on any of this, but I'll be damned if I'm going to sit back and pretend it hasn't happened."

"Nobody's pretending anything," she snapped. "You've got to go see Agent Partone. You can't hide from people like Rollie Shore. Tell Partone it's over—we want to call the whole thing off. If he tries to send you back to prison, let him. We'll fight."

"If it would protect you, I'd go back. I'd do it in a second. But it's not that simple. It's gone too far. I know too much. The only way out is to finish it."

"What's that supposed to mean?"

"I'm going to find Hamilton's collection."

She shook her head defiantly. "Go and see Partone, before it's too late."

"You're not listening!" I said, my voice rising. "It's already too late. Pack a couple of bags and go away. If not your aunt's place—we'll find someplace else. There's no other way to protect the girls."

She turned and looked at me, her face tight. "How do you know? When did you become the expert on all this? I think we need to talk to someone. If not Partone, we can talk to Jimmy Grantham."

"I don't trust Jimmy," I said, my voice flat.

She hesitated. "But I'm supposed to trust you? We wouldn't have this problem if you hadn't . . ."

"If I hadn't what?"

The blood had drained from her face and all I could see was the fear in her eyes. "You're the one who went to jail. Not me. Not the girls."

■ ■ ■

When we got home, Dana stormed into the kitchen and got on the phone, trying to track Rose down. I went into the den and called Black. He promised he'd be over within the hour.

It was a little past noon, but I poured a stiff whiskey anyway. I slugged it back, then went upstairs and showered.

As I dried off, the face that greeted me through the fog on the bathroom mirror, was haggard, the purplish swelling around my eye an ugly reminder of exactly what I'd gotten us into.

Us . . .

The steamy bathroom shrank around me. My head throbbed with every beat of my heart. I could barely breathe. I kept hearing the terrified anger that had colored Dana's voice on the way home from the airport. My self-loathing grew teeth and claws, became a matted and stinking thing trying to rip its way out of my gut. I closed my eyes, turned away from the mirror, tried to calm myself. But Dana's voice, full of fear and revulsion, reverberated inside my head. Whirling around, I balled my fist and drove it into my own reflection, shattering the glass.

The noise drew Dana at a run. She flung the door open, then gaped at me, her face pale, her eyes full of horror.

Blood dripped to the tile floor from a gash on the back of my hand.

I stood there, wet, naked and bleeding. "I . . . I . . ." My mouth refused to form any words. I was locked inside myself.

We stared at each other.

Dana drew a breath; the ice in her eyes melted. Then she was beside me, her arms around me.

We sank down onto our knees and held each other.

If I'd been more of a man, I'd have cried.

33

BLACK pulled up to the house a little before two o'clock, driving a beaten-up old pickup truck loaded with gardening equipment. He came to the door wearing faded coveralls and a big straw hat. "My uncle's truck . . ." he said, doffing his hat and grinning when I opened the door. "Anybody watchin' the house, they're gonna think I'm your damn yard man."

His grin faded when he got a closer look at my face and my bandaged hand.

"Shit! I turn my back on you for five minutes, and look at you." He shook his head. "I thought Monroe had your back. What the hell happened down there?"

"Nice disguise," I said, looking up and down the street behind him. If anyone *was* watching, I couldn't tell. "Come in. We've got a lot to talk about."

I moved back and held the door open.

He stepped inside the house and looked around.

"I thought I heard the doorbell." Dana stood behind me in the entrance hall. She'd been in the kitchen, working the phone, still trying to find Rose. I hadn't heard her approach. She forced a smile for Black. The two of them had met in the prison VR, but he'd never been in our home. It felt awkward.

"Thanks for coming," she said. "I'm starting to think you'd be better off without us."

Black shook his head. "You'd be wrong if you thought that. I'm here 'cause I want to be. All the nights I had to listen to Ben talkin' 'bout you . . . hell, I figure we're almost family."

She smiled. It wasn't much of a smile, but it was genuine, and some of the tension drained out of my neck and shoulders.

I showed Black into the den. "You hungry? Thirsty?" I asked.

"No, man. Tell me everything that went down."

"It's a long story." I pointed to one of the easy chairs, then sat myself down on the couch.

Dana joined me there.

Black settled into the chair, balancing his hat on his knee. "Well . . ."

"Boris is dead—" I began.

"The fuck, you say!" he said, interrupting. "You capped his Russian ass?"

I shook my head. "Not me . . ."

It came easier the second time. Black listening carefully as I spoke, asking me to repeat a detail here and there, his face growing grimmer as the words spilled out.

When I finished, he sat back and whistled through his teeth. "Got the tiger by the tail, don't we?"

I didn't answer.

He looked at Dana. "Ben's right. Rollie's stone cold. You and the girls need to lay low—disappear till this is over."

Her pale face grew even paler. When she spoke, her voice was steady, but barely above a whisper. "I don't like it. I don't like any of this."

"There's nothing *to* like," I said. "But it's happening and we have to do something about it."

"I know," she snapped, staring hard at me. "But then I'm coming back here to help you finish this thing."

"Dana . . ."

"Stop it, Ben! We've been through it already. This is my fight, too. They made sure of that when they took Olivia's Silky. They fucked with my husband, that was bad enough. But they shouldn't have fucked with my children. You and Black want to find Ham's collection, I can help. You need me."

I glanced at Black.

He shrugged, as if to say, "This is your call, not mine."

"Let's just focus on finding a place for the girls," I said, changing the subject.

She didn't react. As far as she was concerned, the decision had been made.

"I told you 'bout my sister Annalee, didn't I?" Black asked.

"Yeah," I said. "About twice a day. Why?"

He frowned at me, then addressed his answer to Dana. "Annalee's been like a second mother to me. Got grown kids of her own now. When her husband ran off, the girl taught herself to cook. Now she's workin' at one a the smaller plantations down south, near Albany. You know, where they hunt them little birds—quail and shit. Only the owner had to have heart surgery and his doctor won't let him go near the place till after the new year. Annalee says it's nice and quiet down there. Got a couple a guest cottages, and with the owner laid up, they all empty. She's tight with the caretaker and his wife. I'll call her. See if she can take you in for a week or so. No one gonna look for your girls down there."

Dana didn't say anything.

Black caught my eye.

"Sounds worth a look," I offered.

"Y'all could come down to meet Annalee," he suggested. "See if you think the place would be okay . . ."

"You don't like it, you don't have to stay," I added quickly.

"Maybe . . ." Dana said slowly. "But don't expect me to leave Olivia and Nadine unless I'm goddamned comfortable with the situation. And then, only if my mother agrees to stay there with them."

"Understood," I agreed, thinking that when the time came she wouldn't be able to leave the girls at all—that she'd stay with them, safe and out of Rollie's reach. "It's your decision. You don't like the situation, we'll find something else."

Dana held my eye for a moment, then looked at Black. "Go ahead. Set it up."

"I'll call her now," he said, pulling a tiny cell phone out of one of the pockets in his coveralls. He flicked it open and dialed.

It didn't take Black long to convince his sister.

Once we had Annalee's blessing, the three of us sat in the den trying to figure out how to get the girls out of town without being followed. Only all our fancy plans were either ridiculously complicated or way too dependent on luck to have a better than even chance at success.

I thought about what Rollie had said about reaching out to touch me whenever he wanted. Someone *was* out there—seemingly invisible—waiting, watching every move I made. It dawned on me that I needed to stay behind and make myself very visible. I didn't want to give Rollie any reason to reach out—not yet.

Black got up and started to pace. As I watched him move around the den, my eye fell on a stack of newspapers that had piled up near the desk. Yesterday's Living section was on top. There was a story about a new Disney feature on the front page. I stared at it, thinking the girls would love to see it . . . and suddenly I knew what we had to do.

Twenty minutes later, Dana had located her mother, explained the situation, and we were ready to move.

She packed a week's worth of clothing and toys for the girls into several brown paper grocery bags that Black carried out to his truck. With his straw hat jammed low on his head, it looked like he was carting off some junk we no longer wanted. He waved, then drove off, the pickup spewing smoke as it rattled down the road.

Shortly after Black left, at around three o'clock, Dana, carrying only her purse, followed me out to the Suburban and we drove to the Lenox Square Mall, where I dropped her at the front entrance. It was silly to think that anyone was close enough to hear, but I called out to Dana as she walked away from the car, "I'll pick you up at four-thirty."

"Make it five," she shouted back.

I smiled to myself as I pulled out of the parking lot.

I didn't see the rest of our plan unfold, but later Dana told me it went smoothly.

While she was waving good-bye to me, Rose and the girls were buying tickets to the Disney movie at the multiplex theater located at the other end of the mall.

Dana took her time browsing through Macy's, trying on clothes, testing various perfumes, making it plain to anyone who might be watching that she was out to do a little shopping, nothing more. After Macy's, she made her way toward the food court, which happened to be located adjacent to the multiplex.

At four o'clock sharp, Rose stood up in the darkened theater to take the girls to the restroom. "But I don't have to pee, Nana!" Olivia argued loudly. Rose got a firm grip on her little hand and said, "*I* have to, and you are coming with me."

By that time, Black was waiting in a borrowed car, parked just outside the theater's rear exit. Within seconds of leaving the restroom, the startled girls were being led out to Black's car by one very strong-willed grandmother.

Dana was close on their heels.

Three minutes later, the five of them were speeding down the interstate.

While all of this was going on, I drove slowly home. Once there, I opened the hood of the car, pretended to check the oil. After that, I walked out to the curb and made a show of retrieving and examining the mail.

Then I sat in one of the porch chairs, propped my feet up on the railing, and watched traffic go by, serenaded by a family of squirrels chattering in my ginkgo tree.

After a few minutes, I closed my eyes, took a deep breath.

There wasn't a more visible man east of the Mississippi.

34

I CAME awake with a start, sitting on my front porch. Night had fallen. There was a chill in the air, but my watch had stopped and I had no way of knowing how long I'd been asleep. Rubbing my eyes, I took a deep breath and forced myself up and out of the chair. Somewhere down the block a car door slammed.

Inside the house, I lit all the downstairs lamps and checked the kitchen clock. It was just past seven o'clock. The girls and Black would be getting close to their destination. I'd promised to call them from a pay phone at nine—that gave me a couple of hours to kill. I reset my watch, then turned the television to CNN. Images of bombed-out buildings, talk of terrorist attacks here, in America. I'd heard it all a thousand times before, but now it seemed distant, irrelevant. I had terrorist problems of my own.

My mind wandered. I was tired but too edgy to sit still. When my stomach started growling, I realized that the last meal I could remember was at the News Café in Nassau. I threw together a ham sandwich and washed it down with a glass of milk. Then I made a second sandwich. By then, the weather was on. According to the CNN meteorologist, the first cold front of the season was settling over Georgia and the southeast—temperatures were expected to dip into the forties overnight. Cold enough to make this old Victorian house uncomfortable.

I looked around the kitchen at the black and white tile, the glass-fronted cabinets, the woodblock island, and the big Viking range . . . it hadn't looked this way when we'd bought her. The place had been a disaster. But that hadn't deterred us. I'd done most of the renovation myself. And I'd done it right. But the thing about owning an old house is that it requires constant upkeep. I hadn't put my hands on the old girl for over a year and a half and it showed. Paint flaking in the upstairs hallway, water stains on the ceiling of the master bath . . .

I'd installed central air, but Dana had wanted to keep the old radiators. She thought they were charming. They leaked and clanked and clanged and were either too hot or not hot enough, but they *were* charming. Usually I didn't fire up the system until sometime in late November, but I needed something to do now, so I went down into the basement to light the boiler. Once I had it going, I went around the house adjusting the valves on each of the radiators to their lowest setting—except for the ones in the girls' room and the den. Both of those were broken, stuck on high. More proof of my neglect.

It was still too early to call Albany . . .

I poured a drink and sat down in the living room. Only I wasn't thirsty and the smell of bourbon got me thinking about Ham Hamilton. Was he entertaining tonight? Pouring fancy whiskey for his fancy friends while my family ran and hid like scared rabbits? The thought pissed me off. What next? Where did I start? Johnny Forchet was the logical place to begin, but my thoughts kept coming back to good old Ham Hamilton. Why was he offering such a big reward? How had his collection come to the attention of Forchet? Who had it now?

The more I thought about it, the angrier I got. Hamilton knew some of the answers, but as far as I could tell, no one had bothered to ask him the questions.

Why not?

I put down my drink and got a thick pea coat out of the hall closet.

This nightmare wasn't going to end until I ended it.

■ ■ ■

The Hamilton house was a good forty-minute drive from my own. I started my car thinking I'd drive evasively—try to lose anyone who might be tailing me. Then I decided not to bother. Ham Hamilton didn't need protection. He was the deep pocket. No one was reaching out for him.

Except me.

Halfway there, I stopped at a gas station to use the pay phone.

A woman with a deep voice answered on the second ring. "Fallen Oaks Plantation."

"Is this Annalee?"

"Depends on who's doin' the askin'."

"It's Ben Hemmings—Black's friend."

"Ahhhh. You the husband. Got you some fine-lookin' girls—I'm glad Black brought 'em to me. But listen here—I got to question your taste in friends. Why a family man like you hangin' out with a player like my baby brother?" At this, she laughed, a hearty booming sound.

In the background I could hear Black pretending hurt feelings. "Why you do me like that, sis?"

Annalee ignored him. "You just hold on a sec, Ben. I'll go get your wife."

Then Dana was on the line.

"You okay?" I asked.

"Tired . . . but Annalee is great. The girls are already in love with her."

"Good. It won't be for long."

"I hope not."

I could hear Nadine laughing hysterically and Olivia shouting something about Black's being too big to tickle. I closed my eyes.

"You there, Ben?"

"Yeah . . . I just called to see that you're safe. I'll call again in the morning. Give the girls a kiss, okay?"

"Wait! Where are you? Why the big hurry?"

"At a gas station. I'm on the way to Ham's place. I want to ask him a few questions."

"Does he know you're coming?"

"Not yet."

"Do you think that's smart?"

"I have to start somewhere. Now's as good a time as any."

She hesitated. "You're just going to show up? He's a powerful man, Ben . . ."

"I don't have time to make an appointment."

"Yeah . . . but maybe you should talk to someone else first."

"Stop it, Dana. This is hard enough without having to justify every move I make. No one said this would be easy. Either you're with me or you're not."

Silence.

Then she said, "I'm sorry. Just be careful, huh?"

I promised I would.

35

THE Hamilton house was almost as dark as the pastures and paddocks surrounding it. Only a handful of lights showed in the windows of the sprawling mansion. The half mile of twisting, dogwood-lined driveway leading up to the house was illuminated by flickering antique gas lamps placed precisely twenty yards apart. I know I measured them once. A spur of the driveway led off to the right, toward the barn I'd built and the new construction site.

Jasper, Hamilton's butler, opened the door as soon as I rang the bell. I'd probably tripped some kind of alarm the second I'd turned onto the drive. He stood profiled in the spill of light falling through the open doorway, wearing black trousers and a starched shirt as white as his hair. No livery tonight.

"What can I do for you, Mistah Hemmings?" he asked, his voice so deep and mournful he sounded like a preacher on the cusp of a eulogy. He stared at my black eye, then looked away, a hint of a smile on his dry lips. "Missus Hamilton isn't home tonight."

"You've had your ear against too many keyholes, Jasper. I came to see *Mr.* Hamilton. Is he home?" I asked.

He shook his head. "No, sah. He's not."

"Is he back in town?"

"I'm afraid I can't say, Mistah Hemmings."

"Why not, Jasper?"

We looked at each other for a few seconds and something odd glimmered behind his old yellow eyes. It was like talking to someone from another world, another time. He was the very picture of civility, but there was a condescending air about him. As though he were a house servant and I belonged in the fields. I shifted my weight from one foot to the other, wondering what Black would think of this throwback to the slave days.

Jasper didn't move, didn't even seem to be breathing. Finally he said, "Is there anything else, sah?"

"Yeah . . . maybe there is. You mind if I go speak with Overton?" Ron Overton was Hamilton's stud manager, a big, blustery South Carolinian. He'd been out delivering a mare when Babe had collected the semen sample, but he lived in one of the apartments above the barn. The horses were his responsibility. Surely he knew about Ham's collection.

Jasper shrugged his thin shoulders. "Well, sah, you aren't the first to ask me about Mistah Overton. I suppose he's over to his apartment, but I heard he's not been . . . feelin' well. It would be better if you waited and talked with Mistah Hamilton."

"I don't have time to wait."

Jasper shook his grizzled head. "Don't you go takin' advantage of Mistah Overton's condition. Sometimes a man forgets his place."

■ ■ ■

The only car parked in front of the barn was a flashy new BMW. Ham Hamilton wasn't known for paying his people big money. I wasn't too sure exactly what Ron Overton's *place* was, but judging from the new wheels, he must have been doing something right.

We'd met during the construction of Ham's dream barn. Overton had been gruff, not the easiest man to deal with. But he was competent and hardworking—knew his stuff forward and backward. He was a bull of a man in his midforties, red faced and freckled, arms as thick as fence rails. But Jasper was right—I'd never seen Overton looking quite like this. His eyes were bloodshot, his breath foul when he opened the door of his apartment wearing a pair of riding breeches and a T-shirt dappled with ketchup stains. He was holding a half-empty bottle of Jack Daniel's in one hand, tugging with the other at the waist of his breeches, which strained against his bloated gut.

He squinted at me for a moment, then frowned when he recognized me. "Hemmings! What'd they do? Let you out for good behavior?"

"Nahh. They let me out 'cause I'm a menace. Thought the prison would be safer without me."

He laughed drunkenly, pointed the bottle at my eye, and said, "Next, you're gonna tell me the other guy looks worse, huh?"

"No. The other guy is on a yacht in the Bahamas—partying with a bunch of strippers."

He looked confused for a moment. "Say what?"

"Nothing. Forget it. Listen, I drove out here to talk to Ham, but he's not home. Thought you might be able to help me."

"Help you with what?" he muttered suspiciously. He raised the bottle, took a slug of whiskey, then wiped his mouth with the back of one calloused hand. "Already tol' that other guy . . . I got nothing to say."

"What other guy?" I asked carefully.

He stared at me with glazed eyes. Then, without another word, he shut the door of his apartment in my face.

I stood there for a moment. Who else had come to see Overton? Why? Was *he* Forchet's contact in the horse world? I pushed the door open and stepped inside.

Overton's back was to me, the bottle glued to his mouth.

"Ron, who else has been out here asking questions?"

My voice startled him. He spun around and nearly fell on his ass.

"Tol' you, I got nothin' to say." he said angrily, slurring his words. "So get the hell outta here!"

"Take it easy . . . I just want to talk for a few minutes, that's all. It's important."

"Important to who . . ." he muttered.

"Important to me. They've threatened my family."

He stared at me in surprise, then shook his head. Moving with exaggerated deliberation, he carefully placed the whiskey bottle down on top of the coffee table, then collapsed onto a couch that had seen better days. Closing his eyes, he took several deep breaths. When he spoke he no longer sounded angry, just exhausted. "What do you want from me? Who sent you?"

"Nobody . . ." I sat down on the arm of an old recliner facing the couch. "I came on my own. Nobody sent me, Ron. I want to talk. That's all. You know a man named Johnny Forchet?"

He looked blankly at me. "Who?"

"Forchet . . . a slick guy, owns nightclubs and real estate—got interested in horses, started breeding. You ever do any business with him?"

"Never heard of him."

I stared at him. If he was lying, he was doing a pretty good job of it. "You know anything about the collection—the missing semen?"

At the mention of the collection, his face closed like a fist. "Don't know what you're talking about."

"Come on, Ron. You have to know something."

He shook his head vehemently.

"*You* didn't steal it, did you?" I prodded.

He glared at me, reached for the bottle, and took a deep pull.

My heart started to pound—I'd hit a nerve. I decided to press harder. "Ham trusts you, doesn't he? You've worked for him for a long time. I hear he's tight with a buck—but you got yourself a new BMW. How'd you buy it on what Ham's paying you?"

He swallowed hard, his face burning. But he said nothing.

I stood up, pointed a finger at him. "He doesn't know how you paid for the car, does he? I can tell by the look on your face. Did you set him up, Ron? Did you steal the collection? Did you finger it for Forchet?"

He erupted up off the couch. "You calling me a thief?!" he shouted, spittle flying from his lips. "You don't know anything! I didn't fuck this up—not the dates—none of it! I got a reputation. A goddamned reputation."

He took a half step toward me, staggered, and fell back on the couch breathing hard. Closing his eyes, he mumbled, "Gotta name . . . a good name. Ask anyone . . ."

Then his face collapsed and he started snoring.

"Wait!" I leaned over him, shook him. Slapping him on the cheek, I shouted: "Overton! Talk to me! Wake up! Come on, man, wake up!"

He was past listening—or talking. He was out cold. A big man, frightened deep into the bottle. Why? Judging from the way he'd reacted to my accusation, I was pretty sure he wasn't Forchet's man. But he knew something. What? Who did he think had sent me? What dates were fucked up? Where'd he get the money for a flash car? My mind was racing. I'd come looking for answers. All I'd found were more questions.

I left him where he lay and I looked around.

The small apartment was a pigsty. Empty beer and whiskey bottles, dirty clothes, and grimy dishes. Overton had been at it for days—maybe weeks. The man was in charge of millions of dollars' worth of horseflesh. Did Hamilton know what was going on with his stud manager? The butler knew—how could Hamilton not know?

The bedroom was worse than the living room. Overton's desk was the only relatively clean spot in the place. I rifled through the drawers, moved empty beer bottles, and scanned the stack of papers on his blotter: receipts for feed and tack repairs, a fencing estimate, vet bills and medical charts concerning a jumper named Gravity's Shadow. Under a pile of dirty socks, I found a breeding ledger. But when I opened it, the neatly penned entries meant nothing to me.

I turned on his computer, scanned the files. Overton ran straightforward livestock management programs, nothing exotic, nothing that looked the least bit suspicious. There were records of Ham's artificial-insemination efforts and a shorter listing of his live-cover breeding attempts over the last several years. It was Greek to me, but I printed it out anyway. Maybe it would make sense to Dana.

In the living room, Overton groaned and muttered something about rain. Then he began snoring even louder.

I checked my watch. It was almost midnight.

Until Overton was able to talk coherently—and that wasn't going to happen anytime soon—there was nothing else I could learn here.

I shut down the computer, grabbed the pages I'd printed for Dana, threw a dirty blanket onto Overton, then left the way I had come in.

I was getting into my car when it dawned on me that Dana might want to see the breeding ledger, too. So I went back in and borrowed it.

36

FRIDAY morning I was up before dawn, sitting at the kitchen table, drinking coffee, and trying to make sense out of the printouts and the breeding ledger I'd borrowed from Overton. Maybe Dana would be able to make something out of them, but I was kidding myself if I thought I'd discovered some direct link to the collection.

I was about to give it up and take a shower when someone began knocking on my front door. The noise startled me. I sat perfectly still for a moment. I wasn't expecting anyone. Why answer it?

You're afraid, I thought. *Scared to answer your own front door.* The realization sickened me.

Tightening the belt on my old bathrobe, I threw back my shoulders and went to face whoever was there.

Randy McBride was raising his fist to knock again when I opened the door a little too aggressively.

"Jesus! You startled the crap out of me," he said, jumping back a step.

I couldn't help smiling. "Thought the only thing that scared you was your wife."

"Yeah . . . well that ain't the first time you been wrong, is it?"

He flashed a shy grin, then looked down at his well-worn work boots. I'd known him for over a decade—he and his younger brother, Jerry, ran a small construction company —and I was damned surprised to find him standing on my front porch. He was a small, leathery man in his early forties, with a sharp face and thin dark hair—quiet, except when it came to hustling for jobs.

"What's going on?" I asked. "You get lost or something?"

He fiddled with the flap on the pocket of his red flannel work shirt. "Hell, Ben . . . I shoulda come by sooner. Tommi-Jo, she saw Dana over at the Parker place—she helps out there with the ponies, you know—well, Dana told her you was back in town, and me and Jerry, we got three houses up out of the ground and Smitty hurt his back haulin' trusses, and we could use a man like you."

"You trying to hire me?"

"It was Jerry's idea." He threw a thumb over his shoulder.

I looked past Randy and waved to Jerry, who sat in the cab of a blue pickup idling in front of the house.

Jerry grinned through the windshield and toasted me with a cup of Dunkin' Donuts coffee.

The sun had just cleared the horizon, the morning sharp and clear. White plumes of exhaust rose from the rear of the pickup. And suddenly I wanted to forget all about Rollie and Partone and the horse semen and every lousy thing that went along with it and hop into the cab of that truck, shoulder to shoulder with the McBride brothers, off to do an honest day's work.

"Pay's gonna be a little less than you're used to, runnin' your own operation and all," Randy was saying. "But the work's steady and there's more on the books than we can handle without Smitty."

I clapped him on the shoulder. "It's the best damn offer I've heard in a long time, Randy. But I'm in the middle of something . . . I can't help you out just now."

He sucked his teeth, then looked pointedly at my ratty robe. "No reason to be proud, Ben. We all been there once or twice. Me and Jerry have always got a place for you. Just give a call if you change your mind."

I watched the two of them drive off, wanting to explain that pride had nothing to do with it, wishing I could tell them the truth about what was going on. Knowing I couldn't.

Back in the kitchen, I glanced at my tool belt, hanging on a peg by the back door. I wouldn't need it today. I cracked some eggs into a pan and started stirring. Only by the time they were scrambled, my stomach had soured and I couldn't eat. It wasn't quite seven o'clock, but I had to do something. I carried the printouts and the breeding ledger into the den and stashed them in the top drawer of my desk. Then I went upstairs to shower and dress.

I was pulling on a flannel jacket, planning to head back out to the Hamilton place to finish my conversation with Overton, when someone knocked politely on the front door. I smiled, thinking McBride had come back to try and talk me into working for him. At least I was dressed this time.

When I opened the door, I found two plainclothes detectives standing on my porch. I didn't need to see the gold shields displayed on their belts—spend a little time in prison and you learn to recognize a cop blindfolded.

"You Ben Hemmings?" the taller of the two asked. He was a middle-aged black man, wiry, with a fade haircut and pale brown eyes that looked right through you.

His partner, a young white guy wearing a good suit, didn't speak.

"I'm Hemmings. Who are you?"

I made them show their IDs. They were from the Fulton County Police Department. The black detective was named Jackson—Lieutenant Charles Jackson. His partner was Hank Cray. Neither of them looked happy.

"What's the Fulton County Police Department want with me?" I asked.

"We've got a few questions we'd like answered," Jackson said. "You mind riding down to the precinct with us?"

"Yeah . . . I do mind. I've got plans this morning."

"Cancel 'em," Cray snapped.

"You're arresting me?"

"Is there a reason we should arrest you?" Jackson asked.

"No, there isn't. You mind telling me what this is about?" I said, determined not to be intimidated.

We locked eyes.

"I think you know why we're here," Jackson said.

I didn't respond.

He frowned. "Mr. Hemmings, we're asking you to come with us willingly. All we want is a statement. It would be in your best interest to cooperate."

"A statement about what?"

Cray shook his head and smiled menacingly. He had expensive-looking teeth. "I'm beat, Charlie. Let's just read this asshole his rights and get this over with."

Jackson closed his eyes and pinched the bridge of his nose. When he spoke, he sounded like a man trying to be reasonable in a world gone crazy. "I've been up all night. I don't feel like playing games, so I'm going to make this easy. We pulled your sheet, Hemmings. You're out on an appeal bond. . . . How much effort do you think it would take to have that bond revoked?"

"Fuck the bond—let's just book him," Cray grumbled.

Jackson shrugged. "It's up to you, Hemmings."

The two of them stared at me, knowing full well how it was going to end.

Cray patted me down, but he didn't bother to cuff me before escorting me to the unmarked car.

Jackson drove. Neither of them said a word until we reached our destination.

■ ■ ■

The Fulton County Criminal Division occupied a converted grocery warehouse off Fulton Industrial Boulevard. The two detectives flanked me as we walked into the precinct through a side door. We passed through a large, partitioned bullpen, then down a short hall.

"In here," Jackson ordered, opening a door marked INTERVIEW-1.

"Make yourself comfortable," Cray added.

Then the two of them left me alone to stew in my juices.

Except for the mirrored panel set into one wall and the solid click of the lock as Jackson closed the door on his way out, the room looked more like an office break room than my idea of an interrogation cell. It was clean, well lit and well ventilated. The only furnishings were a round black table surrounded by four comfortably upholstered chairs. But I recognized the smell—the animal stink of anger and fear that seeps like greasy poison out of the pores of caged men, contaminating everything it touches.

I took a seat and waited, wondering what the hell these cops could possibly want with me.

Forty-five minutes later, Jackson came back into the room carrying a manila file. Cray was close on his heels, carrying his own file. All cops carry files. Files, not guns, are the most important weapon in law enforcement.

"Where were you last night between midnight and two A.M.?" Jackson asked, taking the seat across from my own.

"I've got nothing to say until I see a lawyer."

Jackson nodded. So did Cray.

"You sure that's how you want to play it?" Jackson asked, sitting back in his chair. "See, the way I figure it, it won't make much difference to us whether or not you talk. Once the crime-scene techs are through, I think we'll have enough to nail you cold. I'll bet we find your prints all over that apartment. The butler puts you at the scene at the right time. No . . . I don't much care what you say. I just thought you might want to try to help yourself . . . clear up a few questions. Murder one is a tough rap."

"Murder?" I repeated, my stomach folding in on itself.

Jackson closed his file. He sat there looking at me without saying a word.

Cray moved around behind me. I couldn't see him, but I could feel him hovering there, and it made my skin crawl. Suddenly there wasn't enough air in the room.

I fought to keep calm—tried to remember everything Jackson had said. I knew one butler in the entire world, and that was Jasper.

"Who was murdered?" I asked struggling to keep my voice level.

Cray snorted. "He's good, Jimmy. A goddamned Academy Award actor. You gotta give him that."

I twisted in my chair and stared at him. "Are you out of your fucking mind?"

His smile disappeared. "Watch your mouth, you piece of shit."

I started out of my chair.

Jackson shook his head. "Take it easy, Ben. You don't need to go digging yourself a deeper hole."

He was right. I forced myself to calm down. "I don't understand. Who's dead? Who do you think I killed?"

"You tell me," Jackson said. "Where were you last night after midnight?"

"I was home by then."

"Anyone there with you?"

"No."

"You make or receive any phone calls?"

"No."

"He doesn't sound so cocky now," Cray said.

"Shut up, Hank," Jackson snapped. "Mr. Hemmings is trying to cooperate. Maybe we got this wrong. Let's give him a chance."

I nodded at Jackson, found myself feeling grateful. Then I realized how easily their good cop–bad cop routine had sucked me in. "I want to call my lawyer, and I want to call him now!" I demanded.

Jackson shrugged. "That's your right . . . once we've finished."

"*You're* claiming your rights?" Cray exploded. He stepped in front of me and leaned over so that his face was inches from mine. "What fucking rights did you give Ron Overton? Did you let that poor bastard use the phone to call *his* lawyer before you split his head with that goddamned shovel? Did you? Tell me that, Hemmings."

Jackson stood and put a restraining hand on Cray's arm. "Back off, Hank. The man wants a lawyer. That's his right. Won't change anything."

"Overton's dead?" I said, Cray's voice still echoing in my ears.

Jackson looked at me sympathetically. "He's dead, all right. And unless you have a damned good story to tell me, you're going down for it."

I stared at him, but I was seeing Overton's flushed features. He'd been dead drunk, but definitely alive when I'd last seen him. I never touched him. The thought hadn't occurred to me. Why would I kill him? I started to tell these cops I was a builder, not a killer. A goddamned builder . . . barns . . . nobody did them better . . . . *builder!* I formed the word in my mind but couldn't say it out loud. I looked into Jackson's impassive face. I sucked in a deep breath and forced myself to focus. Who and what I used to be didn't matter—not anymore. Overton was dead. I couldn't quite get my mind around the thought. Why? It was a setup, and I'd walked right into it. But how? Who would gain anything by killing Overton and implicating me? Who knew I'd been there? It made no sense. Nothing made any sense.

Jackson and his partner were waiting to see if I had anything to say.

What could I tell them?

Someone knocked on the door.

"Yeah . . ." Jackson called.

A uniformed cop poked his head into the room. "Commander wants to see you, Lieutenant Jackson. Right away."

Jackson glanced at Cray, raised his eyebrows.

Then the two of them walked out of the room.

I closed my eyes—then snapped them open.

The inside of my head was a terrifying place to wander around in alone.

37

HALF an hour later, Special Agent Partone walked into the interview room and sat in the chair Jackson had vacated. No western garb today. He'd dressed for the occasion—a white shirt, striped tie, and a rumpled blue blazer, the lapels flecked with cigarette ash. An unlit Marlboro dangled from the corner of his mouth. Fixing me with a baleful stare, he shook his head but didn't say anything.

"How did you know?" I asked, almost, but not quite, relieved to see him.

"They ran your prints through NCIC. Your file is flagged; I was notified," he said dryly.

"Where'd they get my prints?"

"Off a corpse, from what I hear."

"They've got it wrong."

He shrugged. "Maybe. But the locals see it different. They've got you pegged as their man, Hemmings. They say you brained one of Ham Hamilton's employees. Used a shovel—did a goddamn messy job of it, too. Crime techs are still out at the scene—on their hands and knees, pickin' pieces of skull out of the carpet with tweezers." He shook his head again. "They aren't happy."

I started to say something, but he held up his hands. "Don't say another word. I don't want to know. Whatever you did or didn't do is between you and your God. Understand?"

"No! I don't fucking understand! I told you—"

"Stop!" he interrupted. "Unless things change in a hurry, you aren't going to be charged. You're working for me; that means you're under my umbrella. As long as we're reading off the same page."

I must have looked confused.

He cut his eyes toward the mirrored panel. "You are being recorded—audio- and videotape. Anything you say in here can and will be used against you."

I nodded uncomfortably.

A sardonic smile twisted his lips. When he spoke, his words were strictly for the video camera. "Now, they tell me you deny any knowledge of the crime in question. They can place you at the scene some time before the murder, but they have nothing else to tie you to the actual killing. I choose to believe you had nothing to do with Overton's death. That your presence at the scene was an unfortunate happenstance. That's what my report will reflect. And since you're part of an active and important federal investigation, the state is going to release you into my custody."

"Are they looking for the real killer?" I asked.

He ignored the question. "Let's get out of here. I'll give you a ride home."

■ ■ ■

As we pulled out of the precinct's parking lot, Partone growled, "What the fuck where you doing out at Hamilton's place?"

"It was an unfortunate happenstance," I said.

He hit the brakes. "The fuck it was. Tell me what you were doing. Was Overton involved with Rollie Shore?"

"No. I went to see him because we're old friends. We talked about old times . . . had a couple of drinks," I lied.

"And after you left, someone popped in and splattered his brains on the carpet. You expect me to believe that shit?"

This time, I told him the truth. "I don't know why anyone would want to kill Overton."

"You didn't?"

"Of course I didn't."

Partone nodded, then put the car back into gear. He hadn't bought a word I'd said. But he had other things on his mind.

"We'll talk about your visit with Overton later," he said. "What happened in the Bahamas? Why didn't you report in?"

I told him I was about to call when the Fulton County detectives showed up. Then I gave him an edited version of my trip to Nassau. I left out the fact that Rollie Shore didn't have Ham Hamilton's collection—that he didn't even know where it was. I said nothing about Boris's death or the conversation I'd overheard between Rollie and Devore. I also forgot to mention that I'd borrowed some records from Overton's apartment. Otherwise, I told him pretty much everything.

Partone listened carefully. He wanted to know about the connection between Rollie and Johnny Forchet. How they'd met. What businesses they had in common. How they were structured. I told him what Rollie had told me. Then I asked him again about Overton—what the police were going to do to track down the real killer. But Partone didn't seem interested. His focus was on the collection and my dealings with Rollie Shore. He seemed perfectly willing to overlook the fact that I might be a cold-blooded killer, as long as I did my part to help him reach his objective.

"Shore was testing you," Partone said, one hand on the steering wheel, the other shaking a fresh cigarette out of the box. "He'll be in touch again to make you an offer. I want to know about it when he does."

"Who do you think killed Overton?" I asked, unwilling to let it go.

"Assuming you didn't, it's not your problem," he shot back.

"The hell it's not. What's Ham Hamilton going to think? What if he makes it his business?"

"I'll worry about the locals—and Hamilton. You've got other fish to fry."

He pulled his government sedan to a stop in front of the Peachtree Center MARTA station. "Listen to me, and listen good. You've got one concern—one thing that ought to be filling your head. One problem. That's convincing Rollie Shore to let you be his go-between. Nothing else matters. Nothing!"

I stared at him. "Did you have anything to do with Overton's death?"

He looked at me like I was crazy. "Get the hell out of my car. Take the train home—I don't want to be seen with you. And Hemmings, stay away from Hamilton. You go near the man again and the locals are gonna make me look like your fairy godmother."

I started to protest, but he cut me short. "Overton is dead. As long as it doesn't affect my operation, who the fuck besides his mother cares? Maybe he pissed someone off. Maybe he was just in the wrong place at the wrong time. Maybe it was God's will." He hesitated. "But if I find out you're playing me, that Overton *was* part of Shore's scam . . ."

"He wasn't," I said.

"God help you if I find out you're wrong . . ."

"I said he wasn't involved with Rollie. I'm sure of it."

"Then I don't want to hear another fucking word about it."

"You've got a heart as big as the outdoors, Partone."

"Don't be stupid, Hemmings. I've had enough stupid to last me the rest of my life. I've given you a chance to start over. Grab it. Quit worrying about Overton and do your job. And one other thing . . . while you're working for me, try not to leave your prints all over any more homicide scenes. It doesn't look good on my report."

38

IT took twenty minutes to walk home from the Lindbergh MARTA station. I was cold and I was empty and I was goddamned angry. To hell with Partone and his warnings! Who the hell did he think he was? I slammed the front door behind me, thinking I'd put something hot in my stomach, then go out and force Jasper to tell me who else had visited Overton. But it was a fool's mission, and I knew better.

"Where have you been?!" Dana called angrily from the den. She stepped into the front hall, her arms crossed stiffly over her chest. "The car was here . . . the door was unlocked, but you were gone. I thought something had happened to you."

I was so startled that at first I didn't know how to respond.

"Well?" she demanded.

"I'm fine. I wasn't expecting you, that's all."

We stood there staring at each other.

Black poked his head out of the den, looked from me to Dana, started to say something, then thought better of it and withdrew.

"You scared the shit out of me, Ben," Dana said. "I didn't want to do it, but I left the girls in Albany anyway—rushed back. When you weren't here and the house was open . . ."

"I'm okay," I said, stepping closer. "Everything's okay."

I held her by the shoulders and tried to read her face.

She met my gaze, her eyes the color of cracked ice.

I might as well have been holding a hostile stranger; two people sharing the same nightmare, anger and fear an impenetrable wall between us. I let go of her and stepped back.

"I called Maggie Dennison at the lab," she said, her voice gone flat. "I told her I wanted to talk about a job—we're supposed to meet at four o'clock."

My head was spinning. "How did Maggie react?"

"She's looking for a lab assistant—said she could use me right away. It would give me a chance to sniff around and see what they know about Ham's collection."

"Good," I mumbled. I turned and took my time locking the front door, trying desperately to think of something to say, something I could do to bridge the distance between us.

When I turned back, still racking my brain for the right word, the right gesture, she hadn't moved.

"You think anyone followed you and Black?" I asked.

It was the wrong thing to say.

She shook her head, looking hurt and more distant than ever. "You haven't even asked about your daughters."

I opened my mouth, then closed it. Nothing I said was going to help.

A long moment passed, my marriage disintegrating before my eyes.

I spoke to fill the silence. "How are they?"

"The girls are fine," Dana said, suffering as much as I was.

"They like Annalee?"

She nodded. "They think it's all a great adventure."

She started to say more, then blinked back tears and changed the subject. "I don't know if we were followed. Black parked a block over. I didn't think it mattered if anyone saw me coming home, so I walked around the corner to the front door. He cut through John and Lee Sloan's yard, climbed the fence, and came in through the back."

"Lucky John wasn't home," I said. "He'd have thought Black was there to rape and pillage."

She didn't smile. "Are you going to tell me where you were?"

"Yeah . . . I am. Let's get Black. I want him to hear this, too."

The three of us went into the kitchen. I put on a pot of coffee and we sat around the kitchen table while I explained all that had happened.

Black listened silently.

Dana looked like she was going to be sick. "I can't believe anyone would kill Ron Overton like that," she whispered.

"Someone else had been out there asking questions. He was scared. Drunk out of his mind. Raving that it wasn't his fault—not the dates, none of it. I didn't know what he was talking about."

"If he was drunk, maybe he was making things up," she said.

I looked at her. "Then why kill him?"

She thought about it. "You think it was to set you up?"

"No one knew I was coming."

"Rollie?" Black asked. "Could his people have followed you?"

"I don't know," I said. "What would be the point?"

Black frowned. "You're right. Makes no sense—not if this Overton knew something."

"None of this makes sense," I agreed. "But if it wasn't Rollie . . ." I left the unfinished thought hanging in the air like a dark cloud.

It was a crisp, fall afternoon, the sun shining, the trees just starting to show some color. But I felt like I'd been dragged into some gray world where the things I'd always believed in no longer meant anything. Not even my marriage. I swallowed some coffee. It tasted like ashes. Dana was sitting next to me, still as a stone. Who was she? A stranger with a familiar face? Hell, I didn't even know who I was anymore. I used to be a builder—the McBrides still thought of me that way. But they were in the minority. Partone thought I was his snitch. Rollie had me setup as his fall guy and Detective Jackson had me pegged as a killer. How had it gone this far? I looked at my wife, but she was staring down at the cup of coffee she hadn't touched, probably wondering the same thing.

I stood up, banging the chair halfway across the room with the back of my knees. "I've had it! I've had enough! I want my life back!"

Dana started, nearly spilling her coffee. She stared up at me.

"This is destroying us! I don't care what it takes—I'm going to get my life back!" I repeated.

Black glanced at Dana, then stood up, too. "I got your back, man. Let's settle this damn thing before it settles us."

Dana hesitated, looking back and forth between Black and I.

A hard lump formed in my throat. I looked at her, hoping my voice wouldn't betray me. "Help me, Dana. I need you."

A single tear slid down her pale cheek, as if I'd stumbled across the key to unlocking her.

"I'm here," she whispered.

I stared at her for a moment, afraid to speak.

Then I cleared my throat. "All right. This whole thing began with Forchet. That's where we start looking. He was a gambler—made book out of the Top Hat Club. Whatever connection he had to horses probably began with betting. We'll go down there and see if anyone knows anything about it."

"Might not be that simple." Black shook his head. "You say they wasted Forchet. Might be a whole new crew down there. Gonna be suspicious we show up askin' questions 'bout horses."

"Maybe," I shot back. "But we won't know until we try."

"I think it might be better if you and Black went without me," Dana said, rising slowly to her feet. "I have to meet Maggie in an hour."

"Before you do, will you take a look at the stuff I took from Overton?" I asked.

I pulled the printouts and the breeding ledger out of the desk drawer in the den and brought them to her. She spread them out on the kitchen table.

Black and I looked over her shoulder as she sat and thumbed first through the breeding ledger, then the printouts. After a minute or two, she shook her head. "It'll take time to go through these."

"Do whatever you have to do. We need to know if they mean anything. I'll call you as soon as Black and I are finished—and good luck with Maggie."

She looked up at me, opened her mouth to say something, but I quickly cut her off.

"I know," I said. "We'll be careful . . ."

39

THE Top Hat Club was one of a dozen strip bars located along a blighted two-mile stretch of Cheshire Bridge Road in midtown. We pulled up to the place a little past three in Black's car, having cut through my neighbor's yard so we wouldn't be seen leaving the house together. Brittle sunlight bounced off the chrome and glass of the dozen or so cars and pickup trucks already parked in the club's lot. Temperatures had been falling all afternoon; the day had gone from cool to cold. Usually I loved the fall. But the chill in the air on this day seemed to go all the way through me. Before leaving the house, I'd gone out to the Suburban and retrieved the nine-millimeter I'd stashed in the glovebox the morning Black and I had eaten breakfast at Annie's. I hadn't told Dana about the gun. I doubted I'd need it—even felt a little silly carrying it. The solid weight of the automatic in the pocket of my pea coat was reassuring just the same.

There were fancier clubs in Atlanta, but the Top Hat was one of the oldest and it had a reputation for being one of the wildest. I'd been here before, as Johnny Forchet's guest. He'd bragged about how he'd picked the place up for a song after the original owner fled the country two steps ahead of the law. He'd had to fight to get the club licensed—promising city officials that he would clean the place up and run a straight operation. To Johnny that had meant a fresh coat of paint for the exterior and a gaudy new marquee shaped like a woman in a top hat outlined with hundreds of blinking lightbulbs. Then it was back to business as usual. According to Rollie, the bookmaking operation had come later. But it was a natural progression. Johnny rarely missed an opportunity to turn a buck.

That's what killed him, I reminded myself as we walked in.

The interior of the club was all plush velour and polished brass, dark and cool, the smell of cigarette smoke and stale beer competing with the scent of perfume and musk. Aside from a couple of well-dressed bouncers near the front door, the place was staffed entirely by scantily clad women, another of Johnny's touches.

Black and I found seats at the bar. A driving techno beat throbbed through hidden speakers, the bass so powerful it shook my insides.

"Got to be a white DJ," Black yelled. "Ain't no brother playin' lame shit like this."

"What can I get you guys?" the barmaid, a young brunette wearing a short black baby-doll negligee shouted over the music.

"A Heineken," I shouted back.

"I'll have one, too," Black said, staring as the girl turned around and bent over to reach into the cooler. He shook his head. "Music ain't everything . . ."

When our beers came, we swiveled on our stools to face the mirror-backed stage, which ran the length of the room opposite the bar.

Harsh spotlights fell on a tall woman wearing a black lace camisole, a black G-string, high heels, and a garter from which peeked a lonely couple of dollar bills. Either stoned or so bored she looked stoned, she twirled lazily around a brass pole set in the center of the stage.

"Take it off," someone shouted.

If the girl heard, she didn't respond.

"All right, gentlemen. That's Brandi up on stage," the DJ announced over the music. "Let's pump it up—give her what she deserves."

"She deserves a damn kick in the ass," another heckler, this one seated near the stage, shouted.

Brandi glared into the spotlights and flipped him a finger.

I turned to Black. "This is a class operation."

He smiled. "It's early, man. The afternoon shift's just gettin' it together."

I raised my eyebrows. "You a regular or something?"

"Not here. But these clubs all the same. The girls work for tips, man. You want 'em to take it off, you got to tip." With that, he stood, walked to the stage and slid a folded bill into the woman's garter.

She almost smiled.

By four o'clock, the place began filling with men who'd knocked off early, their Friday paychecks burning holes in their pockets. Soon the bar was doing a brisk business and the women onstage were naked by their second number, their garters bristling with sweaty bills.

I couldn't help thinking about Grace Money, Lexa, and the other women I'd seen onboard the *Funny Business.* Somehow the club looked smaller and meaner, as if I were seeing it through their eyes.

Black didn't seem to notice. He was a regular charmer, ordering table dances, buying drinks, throwing money around.

A tiny blond named Lilly staked us out as her patrons of the moment. Black ordered her drink after drink—Tanqueray and tonic, no lime. She laughed at his jokes. Smiled enticingly at me. If you didn't look too deeply into her hard eyes, she was pretty. Her skin was flawless, her small figure as lithe and flexible as a gymnast's.

"You been working here long?" I asked, after she finished her third table dance.

She slipped the ten-dollar bill Black offered into her garter, pulled a sheer camisole over her head, then plopped onto a bar stool she'd placed between Black's and mine. "Used to dance at the Gold Club. I guess I've been here a year, year and a half. Why?"

"You know Johnny Forchet?" I asked.

"Everyone knows Johnny." She took a sip of her drink.

"I heard he'd take a bet now and then. Who would I speak to about that?"

She frowned, took another sip of her gin and tonic, then waved to someone across the room. "Listen, if you guys don't want another dance, one of my regulars just came in."

Without waiting for an answer, she abandoned us as quickly as she'd adopted us.

Black shook his head. "Ain't gonna learn shit with you sittin' there like you made of wood. You want these girls to talk, smile. Throw down some green. You got to loosen up."

"I've been accused of murder, my kids are in hiding, my wife's barely talking to me, I've got the feds squeezing one way, a boatload of freaks squeezing the other way. How fucking loose do you want me to get?"

He punched me lightly on the shoulder. "We all got our troubles, Ben. Just smile a little—try not to scare these girls away before they start talking."

I thought about killing him . . .

A succession of women sat with us, took off what little they wore, and danced for us. I smiled myself silly, bought more drinks than I could count. Then watched each one of them walk away as soon as the conversation turned to Forchet or gambling.

Black wasn't faring any better than me. Between us, we spent two hundred dollars over the next hour or so and learned nothing more crucial than the fact that every one of these girls had shaved her pubic hair into an identical little mohawk. I thought Dana might have something to say about the lack of diversity, but I kept the thought to myself.

Black tried talking to one of the bouncers and got nowhere.

Either gambling was a thing of the past or Black and I were simply too much of an unknown quantity to be trusted.

We'd hit a dead end. There wasn't much reason to stick around.

"Let's get out of here," I said.

Black, looking slightly disappointed, drained the last of his beer and stood. "You know what *fecund* means?"

"Yeah, Black," I said, remembering a stallion named Ransom. "I know what it means."

"Prolific and fertile. That's what it means." He eyed the brunette on stage. "And Atlanta fecund, man. It's fecund as hell."

"I don't think that's how they meant the word to . . ." But he'd already turned and started out of the club.

I followed.

As we crossed the parking lot, he asked, "You got a plan B, don't you?"

"Jasper's plan B. We go see him, find out who else was talking to Overton."

He looked dubious but said nothing.

We were pulling out of the parking lot when I looked up and shouted, "Wait!"

"What?" Black yelled, slamming on the brakes.

"There!" I pointed to an old man on a ladder replacing the handful of burned-out bulbs in Johnny's marquee. "Pull closer to the sign. I think I recognize him."

Black did as I asked, muttering something about scaring the shit out of him.

I rolled down the window and called, "Huey! Is that you?"

Startled, the old man looked down at me, a week's worth of grizzled stubble on a sunken face I'd known for years. The last time I'd seen Huey Abbott, he'd been an electrician on one of Johnny Forchet's construction crews. I thought he'd retired long ago.

"Who's that, wants to know?" he asked suspiciously.

"Ben . . . Ben Hemmings. What are you doing up there, Huey?"

"You say Ben Hemmings? Thought you was in prison." He climbed down from the ladder, moving slowly, carefully, like he'd fallen a time or two.

Then he approached the car, squinting into my face.

"I was in prison, Huey. I'm out now. I thought you'd retired."

He shook his head, then pulled off his work gloves and rubbed one claw of a hand over his liver-spotted pate. "Don't carry an electrician's card no more. But I ain't quit work—need the money too much for that. Can't move the way I used to—too slow to keep up with you youngsters. Johnny kept me on anyway—has me lookin' after a few of his properties. You know, like a handyman and such."

I glanced at Black.

He shrugged.

"You seen Johnny lately?" I asked Huey.

Huey hawked, then spit on the blacktop. "Johnny's done vanished. Ain't seen a trace of him in months. From what I hear, that's the way Rollie Shore and his crew operate. You cross 'em, and you're disappeared. Like you never existed. Johnny wouldn't be the first. Ain't likely he'll be the last."

I nodded. "Shore's crew took over here?"

"Couple a know-nuthin' goons from up north took over the day-to-day. Ain't seen Shore since they locked him up. But these boys keep payin' me, so I ain't complaining."

"What happened to Johnny's people?" I asked.

A wary light appeared in his eyes. "Why you so interested?"

"I'm looking for something Johnny had. It's pretty important."

"Never figured you for the type to be involved in anything wasn't square, Ben."

"I'm not. But I'm in a hard place. If you know anything . . ."

He studied me. "I heard how you took the fall—wasn't your fault, but you kept your mouth shut. Johnny thought pretty highly of you."

"Yeah—but he isn't around to help me. Can you?"

Huey pressed his lips into a frown. "You get to be my age, folks don't pay you no mind. Treat you like a piece of furniture—or worse. But I seen plenty. Believe me. Ain't nothin' wrong with my eyes."

"What kind of things have you seen?" I coaxed.

The old man smiled to himself. "I seen them come in after Johnny disappeared and like to tear this place apart looking for something. Only whatever they was looking for, they didn't find it. No sir, they sure didn't."

"Do you know what they were looking for?" I asked, trying not to sound too interested.

"Hell no. Made it my business not to know half of what Johnny was into. But I got a good idea who would know. Only no one's ever bothered to ask me."

"I'm asking, Huey."

He squinted at me for a moment, then spat again. "I was lookin' for something Johnny had—and it was important—I'd track down Manny Sharp. He ran Johnny's action—paid out the winners and collected from the losers. Knew what was what. Things 'round here ain't quite the same without him."

He moved back toward his ladder.

"Where would I find Manny?" I called.

Huey looked over his shoulder. "Got no idea."

I hesitated. "They threatened my kids, Huey."

He stopped in his tracks, then walked back to the car and eyed me. "You and Johnny—you two came up together, went to school, played ball, didn't you?"

I returned his unblinking gaze, then nodded.

"Johnny's been good to me. He broke all the rules, laughed while he done it. But I never ever heard of him threatening a man's family. He wouldn'ta stood still for crap like that . . . but I don't think he's comin' back." He pulled on his gloves and walked away again.

Halfway up the ladder he turned and looked down at me. "No one was supposed to know—the two of 'em were real hush-hush. But you can't keep secrets from the guy that fixes your toilet. Manny used to play games with a dancer named Ruby. Find her, you got a good shot at finding him."

40

HOW the hell are we supposed to find a dancer named Ruby?" Black said as he pulled out into traffic. "Must be a thousand strippers in Atlanta. Maybe more."

"Let me borrow your cell phone."

He frowned. "Ain't gonna have her listed in the book as Ruby the Stripper."

"Drive the car," I said. "I'll find Ruby."

While he drove, muttering to himself, I dialed information.

There were three G. Moneys listed in the metropolitan Atlanta directory. I reached the one I wanted on the second try.

Only it was an answering machine that picked up: "Hi. Grace and Lexa aren't here at the moment, but your call's important to us. If you're calling for an appointment or an out call, please try our beeper number . . ."

I did, punching in Black's cell phone number followed by a 911, hoping she'd understand that the message was urgent.

"You think she's back from Miami?" Black asked.

I shrugged. "Maybe she has one of those pagers that works anywhere."

Then I tried to reach Dana at home. It was nearly six o'clock, but I got no answer there either.

"Dana's out," I said, handing Black his phone.

"Probably still meeting with that woman at the lab. You hungry?"

"Nahh. I'll sit with you."

"Good. All that beer and skin gives a man an appetite—I could eat something spicy. Something got a little kick to it."

He turned onto Piedmont, then parked in front of a Cajun joint called Lenox's.

While he ordered a shrimp po'boy and a large order of rice and beans, I went into the restroom to wash up.

He was smiling, chatting with the waitress when I came out. She giggled at something he said.

"Can I get you anything?" she asked, looking up when I joined Black in the booth.

"Yeah. How about a new identity?"

She stared at me for a second, then scurried off to take care of another customer.

"Man, you're startin' to scare people," he said, stirring about ten packets of sugar into a glass of iced tea.

"That sweet enough?" I asked.

"Maybe you drink some of this, you'll sweeten up."

"I've got a few things on my mind."

He tasted his tea, added another packet of sugar. "Hang in there, man. Dana loves you. Ain't a doubt about it. She's just scared half to death—that's all. Between Rollie and Partone, she forgot which way is up. The girl turned upside down."

"I'll be goddamned if it's going to stay that way."

"These hard people, Ben. I told you before we got into this—we gonna have to be hard, too."

I grit my teeth. "If they go near my family, I swear . . ."

Black jumped up out of his seat before I could finish the thought.

"What?" I said, jumping up, too.

Eyes bulging, he pointed to the seam where the table of our booth joined the wall. A large roach was crawling along, minding his own business.

Black made a sound in the back of his throat but stood there, frozen.

If I'd been in a better mood, I'd have laughed. Instead, I took a napkin and crushed the thing.

The cell phone rang as I threw the wadded napkin into the ashtray.

Black answered it, raised his eyebrows, and handed it to me. "I think it's your friend," he said, sliding back into the booth.

"Grace. It's me—Ben Hemmings."

"Ben . . . I got your page—didn't recognize the number. I wouldn't have called if not for the 911. Neat trick. I'll remember it."

"Where are you?"

"In Miami, thanks to you. If you hadn't helped us, Lexa might have died. The bastard ruptured her spleen—she's still in Jackson Memorial. They operated on her, took it out. She's got three cracked ribs and a fractured cheekbone."

"Is she going to be okay?"

Silence.

When she finally spoke, the bitterness in her voice was as sharp as a blade. "Lexa's a tough kid. She'll make it. I don't think we can come back to Atlanta for a while. Maybe we'll head to Dallas—someplace out west."

"I called because I need to find a girl named Ruby. She used to work at the Top Hat Club."

"Yeah, I know Ruby. Ruby Santoro. Why you looking for her?"

"It's Manny Sharp I want. I heard they hang out together."

She thought about it, then laughed. "Manny and Ruby . . . that explains a few things. I can't believe I didn't see it. Hold on; I'll go get my book."

A minute passed. She came back on the line and gave me an address and phone number. "Ben, you watch yourself. Manny has some moves. Johnny trusted him, but you be careful."

I jotted the information she gave me on a napkin. "Is there anything I can do for you and Lexa?"

"You already did it. Don't let those bastards take you down—that's all." Then she broke the connection.

"That's the address? For Ruby?" Black was staring at me, looking impressed.

Flicking his cell phone closed, I tossed it to him and got up out of the booth. "Even a garbage can catches a steak bone now and again. Saddle up—let's get moving."

"My food . . ."

"You can eat later."

He glanced at the wadded napkin in the ashtray. "Didn't really want to eat here, anyway."

41

RUBY Santoro lived on the third floor of the Parker House, a rambling old brick apartment building in the Morningside section of town. Black and I drove slowly past the place, then parked a block over and walked back. Night had fallen early, and although the wind had died down, the air held a keen edge. We were getting closer to the collection. I could feel it. A shudder ran down my spine, as much from anticipation as the cold.

The three-story building, a U-shaped structure with wooden columns and trim, faced a quiet residential street. Two wings formed a kind of central courtyard with facing balconies and low boxwood hedges. It was the kind of building favored by young couples and single women. Cozy. High-ceilinged charm for a quarter of what you'd pay in Buckhead or midtown. Warm lights showed in most of the windows. The muted blare of half a dozen television sets tuned to as many stations. Cooking smells filled the courtyard—roasting meat and something yeasty, almost ready to come out of the oven. It wasn't the kind of building I imagined someone like Ruby choosing. Then again, I'd never met her.

A security intercom was attached to the wall outside the only entrance, a heavy glass and oak door. Apartment 3G was marked with the carefully lettered initials *R.S.* I hesitated, trying to decide whether to use Grace's name when I buzzed Ruby for admittance. But Black pushed against the door and it swung open on well-oiled hinges.

The last person in or out of the building had carelessly left it slightly ajar. A mistake, even in the quiet backwater of Morningside.

I stepped into the building. "Let's go see if Ruby's home."

Black grabbed my arm before we reached the stairs. "How you want to play this?"

"No games. Let's just go in and speak to her."

"And if she doesn't feel like talking?"

"We play it by ear."

We stopped outside the door of apartment 3G. Inside a stereo was playing—classical music, a complicated violin solo.

Raising my fist, I knocked politely.

Nothing.

I knocked louder.

The stereo went silent. "The door's open, baby. I've got a surprise for you." Ruby's voice was low and throaty.

I glanced at Black.

He shrugged.

We walked into a tidy little living room with a glowing fireplace. In front of the fireplace someone had placed a small round table set for two. Flowers. China, crystal, a couple of candles and a bottle of wine in an ice-filled bucket. Salad in a wooden salad bowl, ready to be tossed.

Posing beside this picture of domesticity, her back to us, was a tall, slender woman wearing a pale green silk kimono. She had long red hair and fingernails to match.

"Ruby?" I said.

At the sound of my voice, she whipped around.

"Who the fuck are you two?" she snarled, ruining the effect.

I stared. Black started to laugh.

Either Ruby was a man, or this wasn't Ruby. He had a long, fine-boned face that might have been handsome, the tall thin body and muscular legs of a distance runner or biker. Except for a garter and a pair of silk hose, he was obviously naked under the kimono. He wore high-heeled feathered mules; a string of pearls dangled on his hairless chest. Lipstick, heavy makeup, and big hoop earrings completed the ridiculous ensemble. But there was nothing girlish or silly about the anger burning in his dark eyes.

"Who the fuck are *you?*" I shot back.

He sized us up without the slightest hint of embarrassment. "That fat fuck Rollie Shore sent you, didn't he?"

"You're Manny Sharp, aren't you?" Black said.

"How'd he know I was here?" No attempt at the throaty falsetto we'd heard through the door. "How did that fat fuck find me?"

Black and I looked at each other. This was not the bag man I'd expected. The image of Johnny Forchet, the rough-and-tumble wheeler-dealer I'd known most of my life, trusting this tough-talking transvestite to collect his book was beyond funny.

But Manny wasn't amused. "I asked you a question."

"Nobody sent us," I explained. "I was a friend of Johnny's. He had something I need to find."

Manny looked me over, then reached up and plucked off his red wig, revealing a close cropped head of black hair. "The builder . . . you're the guy who went to prison over the barn."

"It wasn't part of the plan. I didn't implicate Johnny. Now I need some payback."

"Don't we all," he said, scratching his scalp. The fake fingernails made a rough scraping noise. "Well, you're too late. Whatever Johnny had to pay you back with, he doesn't have anymore."

Dropping the wig on the table next to the salad bowl, Manny stalked across the room on his high heels and poured himself a stiff drink from a bar set up on a tray table. In spite of his getup, there was nothing feminine about the way he moved.

"I'd offer you one, but you won't be here that long," he said, knocking back half a glass of whiskey.

"Where did Johnny hide the collection?" I asked.

He glared at me. "I don't know what you're talking about."

"Sure you do. Who helped him?"

Manny tossed off the rest of his drink and poured another. "You're wasting your time. Why don't you and Moses over there get the fuck out of here."

"Moses?" Black said.

Manny put down his drink and planted himself in front of Black. "Moses. Leroy. Abdul. I don't give a fuck what they call you—I just want you out."

Without seeming to move, Black slapped him, knocking Johnny's bag man to the floor. One feathered mule flew straight up in the air like a mutant bird.

"I don't care how you dress—don't give a damn if you're a man or a woman—but don't ever talk that way to me again. Understand?" Black demanded.

Manny dabbed with the back of his hand at the corner of his mouth. He inspected the drop of blood he'd blotted. Then he smiled. "You'll regret that."

"Yeah," Black said. "I already do. Now how about you talk to us, so we can leave and you can get back to whatever the hell it is you're doing here."

Manny scooted across the floor on his rear end until he was able to lean his back against the couch. "I told you, I don't know anything."

Black glanced at me.

In that split second, Manny's hand shot under the couch and came out holding a small nickel-plated revolver. He pulled back the hammer. "Both of you . . . get over next to the fireplace."

We did as he ordered.

He stood and kicked off the other mule. Then he paced in front of us, the gun continually pointed in our direction.

"Sorry . . . I shoulda seen that comin'," Black whispered.

"Shut up!" Manny shouted. "What the hell am I gonna do with you assholes?"

I watched him carefully, my heart pounding like a triphammer, the nine-millimeter heavy in my coat pocket.

He muttered something, then resumed his pacing.

I waited until he turned, then slipped my hand into my pocket and gripped the automatic. But I didn't pull it. Manny was agitated. Angry as hell, but he didn't look any happier about this than we were. Exchanging gunfire would make us all losers.

"This doesn't need to go any further," I said. "Just tell us about the collection. Then we're out of here."

"Sure. Straight to Rollie Shore. How much did he pay you to find me?"

"You got it wrong, Manny. We don't work for Rollie."

"So you say. . . . He took Johnny down the hard way. That was no easy thing to do. Now you show up, waltz in here, talking like I owe you something on Johnny's behalf. What's your angle—how'd you get involved in this?"

"I did time with Rollie in Alabama."

"So did a thousand other guys. You know how his people did Johnny—what they did to my friend? Rollie talk about *that* in prison?"

"No," I said. "But I know what he's capable of."

Manny nodded. "Rollie thinks I was in on it. That I helped Johnny try to scam him."

"You didn't?" I asked.

He looked at me like I was crazy. "Johnny stole that shit to give Rollie a bargaining chip—wasn't till the reward was announced that he changed his mind. Far as I know, he was working alone. If he had help, it wasn't from anyone I knew. But you can't tell that to Rollie. He wants to clean house—surround himself with new faces."

"They're not all new faces. He's got Luther Culbertson with him."

"No fuckin' way! Luther was closer to Johnny than me. That fat fuck must want me out cause he thinks I'm a faggot. Can you believe this shit? He thinks I'm a faggot."

"You're not?" Black asked.

"Of course not!" Manny shouted indignantly. "I dress up now and again. Doesn't make me a cocksucker."

"How long have you been hiding from Rollie?" I asked.

"What is this? Twenty questions? We got a situation here, in case you didn't notice."

"I noticed. Let's deal with it."

He looked hard at me, then seemed to make a decision. "I've kept my head down since they capped Johnny. Over three months now."

"You know a man named Overton?"

"Should I?"

"No. He's dead. Why don't you put the gun away," I suggested. "Johnny and I were friends. Maybe we can work together."

He looked doubtful.

"If we were with Rollie, we'd have come in here shooting, asked questions later."

"Maybe . . ."

Black cleared his throat. "You're sayin' you ain't a sissy?"

Manny waved the gun. "What kinda stupid question is that?"

"Take it easy," I said, sensing a way out of this. "We don't like Rollie; you don't like Rollie. Doesn't make any sense to do anything rash—bring the police in on this."

Manny stared at me. "I should trust you?"

"What's the alternative? You start shooting, you're gonna make it harder to lay low."

He looked at me a moment longer, then lowered his gun and started to laugh. "What the fuck . . . Rollie knew where I was, he wouldn't have sent a couple of talkers like you two."

"No," I admitted, breathing a sigh of relief. I took my hand out of my pocket.

Black wasn't satisfied. "That Moses shit . . ."

Manny shrugged. "I was trying to piss you off—get you to swing so I could land near the couch without your pulling a gun first."

"Well, it worked," Black grudgingly admitted.

"Like I said, Rollie would have sent a couple of pros." Manny pointed to the bar. "Fix yourselves a drink. I'm gonna put on some clothes. Ruby comes home, tell her I'm in the bedroom."

Ten minutes later, he was back, dressed in jeans and a black leather jacket. The fake nails and the makeup were gone and he looked like a normal guy.

"What's your proposition?" he asked.

Black was staring at him. "I can't believe the difference."

"Believe it," Manny said. "Now tell me the deal."

"We need to know everything you can tell us about who was betting on the horses. How Johnny made contacts in the horse world."

"You're going after the shit? You think you can scam Rollie?"

I didn't say anything.

He looked from me to Black. "You guys are crazy."

When neither of us responded, he shook his head. "I don't want any part of it. I never met you two—never heard of you."

"Same with us. We never met you, never heard of you. But about the horses . . ."

He shook his head again. "We never booked bets on the ponies."

"Never?" I asked.

"We stuck to the ball games. College, the pros. Made a bundle on the World Series . . ." He stopped, thought for a moment. "There was one guy—up in Alpharetta—gambled big on the series. That's horse country, isn't it?"

I told him it was.

He nodded. "A professor type—real freak for the Braves. Lost large a couple of years ago when the Yankees blew the first two games, then swept the next four. The guy was in deep, but Johnny told me not to collect. Said he'd work something out."

The story rang a bell. "This professor type have a name?"

"Nah. Not that I remember." He scratched a spot on his wrist. "A mustache! The old guy had a mustache like a fat caterpillar. I remember thinking it looked silly as hell."

I asked a few more questions, trying to keep the rising excitement out of my voice.

A couple of minutes later we were out of there.

As we hurried back to the car, Black turned to me. "You know what *quixotic* means?"

"No, Black."

"It means romantically absurd."

"Your point?"

He shrugged. "A guy like that. What makes him tick?"

I didn't try to answer.

As he started the engine, he said with some disappointment, "We never met Ruby."

42

I WAS sitting in the den channel surfing when Dana finally came home a little before eight o'clock. "Long meeting," I said, turning off the television and standing to greet her. "I was worried."

She put her bag down on the desk and gave a tired nod. "This was on the porch." She held out a thick manila envelope, the front of which was blank—no address, no postage, no return.

I took it, turned it over in my hands. "What happened with Maggie?" I asked, careful to keep my voice neutral.

"It went fine, I guess. She's on her way to a conference in Denver, but she set everything up. I start at the lab on Monday as her assistant. Not a soul there I recognized—not one of the old faces. But I'll have run of the place. If anyone there knows anything, I'll find out."

I stood there, holding the envelope, staring at my wife. But she avoided my eyes, made a careful study of one of her cuticles.

"I tried to call you at the lab—it was getting late. I got a machine that said they closed at five."

"Oh . . . I went for a drive," she explained a little too smoothly. "I needed some air, some space."

"Did it help?"

She hesitated. "I don't know . . ."

We locked eyes.

"Are you going to open that?" she asked.

I did.

Inside were two fat stacks of bills and a short note:

Here's the down payment on our deal—the carrot . . . you've seen the stick. Get busy, Ben. I want results and I want them fast.

My stomach twisted. The note was unsigned, but I recognized Rollie's handwriting. I shuffled the bills—fifty thousand dollars in used hundreds.

Dana was staring at the money, her eyes wide.

"Where'd you find this?" I asked. "I came in through the back door."

"It was right at the top of the steps," she said. "I'll show you."

We went out onto the porch and she pointed to the spot where she'd found the envelope. "There. Right there."

Whoever delivered it hadn't left a calling card.

I walked down the front steps and stood in front of the house, looking out into the night.

Dana stepped to my side, her anxiety a palpable thing.

The neighborhood was quiet. A station wagon full of kids cruised by, their car stereo thumping. Someone was grilling steaks in spite of the cold. Life went on. Dinner, homework, television, a fire in the fireplace. Some of our neighbors would make love tonight.

But not us.

They were out there—Rollie's people—invisible, watching.

Dana looked back at the house. "The gingko tree is going to turn soon."

It seemed a funny thing to notice. But for some reason it eased my heart a little. Maybe because we'd always considered it to be *our* tree—one of the reasons we bought the house. I pushed Rollie out of my mind and tried to remember better days. It wasn't easy . . .

"What's that mess?" Dana said, snapping me back into the now.

She pointed to a glistening splatter of brown gunk running down the trunk of the gingko.

I took a closer look. It was tobacco juice.

The hair on the back of my neck stood up. I scanned the street.

There was no sign of Luther Culbertson. But he was out there. I could feel his presence.

"Let's go back inside," I said, trying to sound calm. "I could use a drink. I've got something to tell you."

She stood near the desk, staring at the money while I poured us a healthy measure of whiskey.

"What are we going to do with this?" she asked.

"That's the least of our problems. Black and I found out who acted as Johnny Forchet's contact. It was Burke Schuster."

It took a moment to sink in, then she shook her head. "No way. It couldn't be. You heard what Maggie said. The poor guy had a heart attack—the break-in nearly killed him. They even searched his town house while he was in the hospital. He was a tenured professor. He had no reason to do anything criminal."

"Baseball," I said, handing her a glass.

"What are you talking about?"

"Sit down, I'll explain."

We sat on opposite ends of the couch while I told her everything Black and I had learned. She listened silently, her disbelief turning to sadness as I spoke.

When I finished, she got up and freshened her glass. I stared at her stiff back, wanting to climb into her head and learn what thoughts were spinning inside.

There were a thousand things I wanted to tell her, but she would have heard none of it. So I waited, expecting the familiar pang of guilt that had settled deep inside my chest, finding instead that it had turned into anger. Anger so intense I was afraid to turn it loose.

Finally she stepped to the desk, lifted a stack of hundreds, and let them slip through her fingers to the floor. "Everything this touches turns to shit. Now it's Burke Schuster . . ."

I fought to control my voice. "We didn't start it, Dana. We didn't ask for any of it."

She shook her head. "Doesn't matter. It's such a sordid little story. Burke was always so proper. Made such a fuss about getting the details right. How did he get himself in so deep?"

"Gambling, greed. I don't know."

"What are you going to do?"

"Confront him. Find out what he knows."

"I want to be there."

"Then come. Black went to get something to eat. He's meeting me in front of the Sloans' house at eight-thirty. I don't want anyone following us, especially now."

"Tonight?" She walked over and put a cool hand on my cheek. The tender gesture surprised me. "You look exhausted, Ben."

The anger in my chest dimmed but didn't go out. I covered her hand with my own and looked into her gray eyes, trying as hard as I could to penetrate their depths. But she was a mystery to me. Her story about needing space—going for a long ride—had struck me as false. But what could I do? Accuse her of lying? To what end? No, whatever demons she was wrestling, I could only stand back and watch.

I had a few battles of my own to fight.

■ ■ ■

Burke Schuster's town house was the last in a row of eight identical two-story brick units. Part of a new development of townhomes that stood on what had recently been rolling green pasture. One of a hundred such developments with horsey names and flimsy sheetrock walls not quite thick enough to keep the neighbors' personal quirks personal.

Schuster came to the door in his pajamas, trailing a small green canister of oxygen on a little chrome hand truck. He was pale and thin, a tiny stick figure wrapped in a faded blue silk robe. But his eyes were hard brown buttons.

The clear tubes feeding oxygen from the tank to his nose had dug a furrow in his cherished mustache. He fingered it as he greeted us in a dry, wheezy voice. "Dana, Ben, to what do I owe this honor?" He took a raspy breath, then looked past me, noticing Black. "I'm afraid I don't know you, young man. But come in—all of you."

We followed him into the dusty town house, through the living room, which had been converted into a bedroom complete with a hospital bed and much larger oxygen tanks, then down a short hall that led to a book-lined study.

The room smelled musty; it needed a good airing out.

"Get off of there, Balthazar." Schuster shooed a fat black cat off the couch and motioned for us to sit. Then, moving slowly, he dragged his little oxygen tank to an oversize wingback chair and carefully lowered himself into it.

"Excuse the new decor," he said, once he'd settled into the big chair and caught his breath. "I don't get upstairs much these days, so I've been forced to convert the living room. But such are the slings and arrows of life, no matter how well spent. Ben, you look no worse for the wear. But you've always been a rough and eager young fellow. I hear prison isn't a bit like they portray it in the movies. I'm sure you fit right in."

I stared at this pompous little man. Tried to find pity in my heart, but all I found was anger. "No, Burke. I didn't fit in, and it's not like the movies."

"Well, at least you're out," he observed, not looking particularly pleased by the fact. Then he turned his attention to Dana. "Have you been well, dear? It can't have been easy, left alone with two small children."

She glanced at me. "I'm fine, but we didn't come out here to talk about me—"

"Of course not," he said, interrupting. "This isn't a mere social call, is it? What can I do for the three of you?"

"Johnny Forchet," I said, studying his reaction.

He gazed calmly at me, nothing at all registering on his face. "I'm afraid I don't understand."

"I think you do," I shot back.

"Well, my boy, you think wrong." He shook his head, those brown eyes flashing. "But that's nothing new, is it? Wrong thinking—or should I say no thinking—is what landed you in jail, right?"

He turned to Dana. "I warned you, back when you married him. Stay with your studies, I told you. You had a brilliant academic career in front of you. Now this . . . prison, disgrace. A future, wasted. For what? You could have done better, Dana. Much better."

"Burke!" she gasped. "You have no right—"

"I have every right to speak my mind in my own home. You made a mistake marrying this one. Everyone but you saw it coming."

"You're wrong," she said. "Ben is the best thing that ever happened to me."

"No doubt," he sneered, "if being a felon's wife is your idea of achievement. I thought you had bigger plans."

Dana inhaled sharply. "Who do you think you are? If you weren't a sick old man, I'd knock you off that high pedestal of yours. Don't you dare talk about Ben that way. Don't think for one minute I'm a victim in this. I have my eyes open—I saw what happened. I'm with him because I choose to be."

I looked at her, too surprised to speak.

Schuster shook his head. "In that case, I wish you two well. Perhaps I've overestimated you, Dana. Water seeks its own level, they say. So, apparently, does trash."

Black started up off the couch.

I put a hand on his arm, wondering if Schuster was goading us on purpose—if he suspected our reason for coming and was trying to end the conversation before it began. There was a chance that I was wrong—that Burke Schuster had never placed a bet in his life. That Manny Sharp had been talking about some other professor type with a mustache. In that case, we were back to square one.

But there was only one way to find out.

"We met with Forchet's bag man, Manny Sharp," I said. "He told us what happened, Burke. All of it. So why don't you cut the bullshit. It's time to come clean. Tell us what you know about Johnny Forchet."

"Who?" he asked innocently. But something else, something sharp and ugly, was working behind his eyes.

I pressed harder. "Gambling debts. The theft of Ham Hamilton's collection. You were the guiding light, weren't you? You fingered the collection for Johnny Forchet in return for his letting you off the hook. You were the inside man."

He waved away the accusation. "You're a fool, Ben. Stick to working with your hands, building your barns. It suits you."

I pointed a finger at his chest, then tried to bluff. "You can talk to us, Schuster, or you can talk with the FBI. Your choice—I don't give a damn. You're going down either way."

He rose to the bait, sucking in a deep rasping breath, pink spots flaring on his sunken gray cheeks. "Have you gone out of your mind? Do you know who I am? Do you know my reputation? You're out of your league, boy. Way over your head. What right have you to come into my home and start accusing me of being involved with Jewish gangsters? I've already spoken with the FBI. I'd be happy to speak with them again. But as you don't represent them, I suggest you leave. Now! Before I call the local police and have you arrested for trespassing."

I smiled at him. "I'm right, aren't I, Schuster?"

He glared at me, breathing hard now. "Out! Get out of my home."

Dana took my hand. "Let's leave, Ben. He's not going to help us."

I stood. "He'll talk. He hasn't got a choice. He just doesn't know it yet."

"Out! Out!" he stammered.

We showed ourselves to the door. I could hear Schuster, still sitting in his chair in the study, struggling to catch his breath as we left.

In the car, Dana took my hand. "He's a miserable, old man, Ben. Don't listen to the things he said."

I looked at her. "Some of it was true."

"Bullshit! Nobody can talk that way about you—about us. I didn't give up anything to marry you." She squeezed my hand. "This thing with Rollie—we won't let it destroy us. We can't."

"Yo—I'm in on this, too," Black said.

"Lucky you," I said, Dana's words echoing in my ears.

He caught my eye in the rearview. "Damn right. Come time to count that reward, we all be lucky."

"I almost forgot about that," Dana said.

"Ain't no forgettin' five million dollars, girl," Black said.

He drove on in silence.

Dana and I holding hands, sitting close in the backseat. Something she'd said niggled at the corners of my mind, but I couldn't bring it into focus.

■ ■ ■

The dots didn't connect until much later.

Then I sat bolt upright in bed knowing what I had to do.

According to the clock on the night table, it was after midnight, but I got out of bed, found the number, and picked up the telephone, anyway.

It took a little convincing—I had to promise a chunk of the money Rollie had had delivered to my door. But by the time I hung up, it was set.

First thing in the morning, we'd find out exactly what Burke Schuster was made of.

And if I was right, we'd learn what he knew about the collection.

43

BY eight o'clock the next morning, the three of us were back on Schuster's doorstep. This time he was slow answering my knock, even slower to invite us in.

"Didn't I make myself perfectly plain yesterday?" he grumbled, his thinning hair mussed, his red-rimmed eyes hard and cold.

He attempted to close the door in our faces, but I stuck my foot into the opening. "We need to talk, Burke."

"Remove your foot," he snapped. "Or I'll call the police. If you aren't gone in one minute, so help me God, I'll call the police."

"You do that," I said. "But first you might want to take a look out here."

He hesitated. Peeked around the door.

I pointed to a black Mustang parked in front of his townhouse.

He opened the door wider, came out onto the stoop, and squinted into the raw, clear morning.

As he did, Manny Sharp climbed out of the Mustang and waved. "Hey, Doc," he called. "How 'bout them Braves?"

Schuster's face blanched.

"Go ahead, Burke. Call the police," I urged.

"You're a true bastard, Hemmings," he spit. But there was no real heat in him.

"You're right. A bastard in more ways than one."

He pointed a bony finger at my face. "Don't trifle with me. I'm not as helpless as I look."

If I hadn't felt so desperate, I would have laughed in his face. But I wanted him to know he was in, and in deep. "It's over, Burke. You as good as told me yourself. Laid it out on a platter last night. Manny pointed me in the right direction, but I had doubts. At least until you started talking about Jewish gangsters. I never said a word about Rollie Shore—but you were goddamned quick to point out that you had nothing to do with *Jewish* gangsters. You're going to help me, or we'll call the police together."

Without responding, he turned and retreated slowly back into the shadowed quiet of his townhouse, the door wide open behind him.

Sharp climbed back into his car. He held up the envelope full of hundreds I'd handed him earlier and called, "I'd have done this for free—just to see the expression on that prick's face."

Then he sped off.

■ ■ ■

Schuster sat in his wingback chair, glaring silently at us.

"Start at the beginning," I suggested.

He didn't say anything. A muscle in his jaw twitched.

"You have no choice, Burke. Talk to us or talk to the authorities."

Dana and I sat on the couch, waiting for him to make up his mind, while Black prowled around the study, looking at Schuster's books and mementos. He lifted a crystal paperweight off the desk, put it down.

Then he pulled a framed certificate off the wall. Studied it. "This old fool graduated summa cum laude. Ain't that somethin'?"

"Put it back," Schuster ordered. "It's from Johns Hopkins."

"Well, old John Hopkins gonna have to send you another, isn't he?" Black said, dropping the certificate to the floor and grinding the glass under his heel.

Schuster closed his eyes. His breath came faster. "Why? Why are you here? Are you trying to kill me?"

"No, Burke," Dana said gently. "We don't want to kill you. We need your help. Talk to us, then we'll leave you alone. No one else will ever know."

He stared at her. "Why should I trust you?"

"I give you my word," she said. "Help us and no one will know."

Black lifted another framed certificate. "Where's Oxford?"

Schuster raised his hand, started to say something. Then his frail shoulders sagged and he looked up at me, those hard brown eyes splintering like broken mirrors. "Please, don't . . . tell him to wait. It's as you say—I knew Johnny Forchet."

"Gambling?" I asked.

"Yes." Barely a whisper.

"How, Burke? How did you get involved in something like this?" Dana asked.

He looked at her, his face tinged with shame. "How does anyone fall from grace?"

"She asked a question. Answer it," I said.

He looked down at his hands. "I won at first. It seemed easy. I've always loved baseball—came to love the Braves. I bet in pools. Nothing big. But I developed a taste for it, the way some men like a drink. An acquaintance introduced me to Johnny Forchet. I still won, but the numbers got bigger and bigger. Then, my luck changed."

He stopped to catch his breath. Our presence—the reason we were here—was taking a toll.

Black returned the Oxford diploma to the wall, then joined Dana and me on the couch.

"Are you okay?" she asked Schuster.

He fumbled with the valve on his portable oxygen tank. "Fine—I'm fine. Just a minute—give me a moment."

The tank made a hissing sound. Schuster sucked air—in and out like a creaky bellows—his face damp, looking like he might expire at any moment.

Black glanced at me.

I shrugged, hoping the old man wasn't having another heart attack.

Dana got up and knelt next to his chair.

"Relax, Burke." She spoke softly, reassuringly. "Everything is going to be okay. Take slow, easy breaths—like that. Nice and easy."

He tried to smile, a ghastly grimace.

"Burke," I urged. "Just tell us about Ham Hamilton's collection, what Johnny Forchet did with it."

He shook his head from side to side. "That's just it—Johnny didn't do . . . anything with Ham's collection."

I wasn't sure he'd understood the question. "What do you mean Johnny didn't do anything with the collection?"

Schuster opened his mouth to answer, then started to cough. Dry, wracking coughs that shook his delicate frame. His face turned the color of wet cement and his lips were tinged blue.

He looked imploringly at Dana. "Pills by my bed . . . small bottle—now."

Dana jumped up and ran into the living room. She was back in seconds with a vial of small white tablets and a glass of water.

"Two . . ." Schuster gasped.

He swallowed the pills dry, then sipped some water.

Black, Dana, and I watched him closely. Six wide eyes, staring.

"Do you need an ambulance?" I asked, praying that he didn't—not yet.

He shook his head. "Just . . . catching . . . my breath."

There was nothing to gain by pressing him, so we waited.

The minutes dragged on.

His color slowly improved. He drank more of the water while his black cat wove back and forth between his bony ankles.

After what seemed an eternity, he felt well enough to continue speaking, gulping air every few words. "It was my dirty little secret. . . . I bet everything—baseball, football, basketball. . . . Started losing . . . bet more to make it up . . . and lost more. . . . Couldn't pay . . . it grew so fast . . . became too much."

I leaned forward on the couch. "Easy, Burke. Don't get all worked up again. Just tell us what happened."

He nodded anxiously, took several shallow breaths.

Then it all came pouring out of him, as though the story had been dammed up for too long and we'd breached the dike. "I stole, padded accounts, siphoned funds belonging to the university . . . and was still behind on my debts to Forchet. He found out about the lab, what we did there . . . said he'd expose me to my colleagues, unless I helped him." The old man hesitated, tears welling. "I couldn't bear the thought—after a lifetime—disgrace, prison . . . I couldn't give it all up."

"Hamilton's collection," I reminded him.

"It's there—in the lab—hidden in plain sight."

"How?" I exploded, my voice too loud in the musty confines of his study.

Schuster flinched.

"In the freezer—there are dozens of canisters. . . ." He paused and then raised the water glass to his thin lips, sloshing some onto the front of his robe. He swallowed, then closed his eyes, the act of confession a greater strain than any of us had expected. "Dozens . . ."

"Ham's collection," I repeated. "Where did Johnny hide the collection?"

Schuster mouthed something, struggling to catch his breath.

I was beside myself.

"Calm down, Ben. He's doing the best he can," Dana said.

"It's not good enough! What canisters? What the hell is he talking about?"

"You've seen them," she said. "In the lab. Steel canisters—filled with liquid nitrogen. They look a little like beer kegs, only with wider mouths and two handles. That's where they store the semen."

"They got beer kegs full of horse semen?" Black asked.

"No," Dana said. "Little plastic straws full of semen. They're placed in racks suspended on rods that hang down inside the canisters. It's a fairly efficient storage system, but every time you open a canister to extract a straw, the liquid nitrogen is exposed to warm air and it expands—builds pressure and bleeds off. That's why the canisters are stored in the lab's walk-in freezer—to keep the nitrogen stable."

Schuster was nodding. "Exactly. Dozens of canisters, each marked for contents."

"I understand," I told him. "But what's it got to do with Ham's collection?"

"Do you think . . . I'll go to prison?" he asked, a new note of fear in his quavering voice.

I wanted to lift him up out of his chair and shake the information out of him. Instead, I looked him in the eye. "If you go to prison, it won't be because I sent you there."

"No—I will have sent myself. A death sentence."

"Tell us what happened, Burke," Dana coaxed. "Maybe we can help you."

"It was simple—so simple. . . . The lab keeps a canister full of . . . bull semen. Easier to store bovine samples than equine samples . . . a baseline for research. My idea . . . to put Ham's collection . . . in with the bovine samples. Johnny took Ham's canister, but it was empty. . . . He'd already hidden the straws."

Dana shook her head. "That can't be, Burke. After the robbery, they inventoried the entire contents of the lab. Each semen straw is marked. If someone had switched the bovine samples, it would have been obvious."

He looked at her, a slightly triumphant light back in his eyes. "They didn't empty the canisters . . . too dangerous . . . too much work to empty liquid nitrogen, then replace it. . . . Didn't need to . . . just checked the racks . . . inventory proved only Hamilton's collection missing."

Her eyes grew wide as she comprehended what he was telling her. "My God! He dumped Ham's straws directly into the bottom of the canister. They're still there—submerged in the nitrogen—under the rack of bovine samples. That's right, isn't it?"

Schuster frowned. "Quite the thief . . . aren't I?"

I jumped off the couch and started pacing in front of his chair, my mind on fire. "So it's there. It's sitting right where Johnny left it."

Black was nodding, a smile forming. "It was stolen, but not stolen . . ."

"Exactly!" I said. "Do you see what Johnny did? He needed the theft to be discovered—otherwise Ham wouldn't have been motivated to pull strings and Rollie wouldn't have had anything to offer the feds for his freedom. So Johnny takes the empty canister. Makes it seem like the collection has been removed from the lab. But it was like a kidnapping—if everything worked out, someone was going to have to return the victim once the ransom was paid. That's where these things always go wrong. In the exchange. But Johnny set it up so he didn't have to make an exchange. If things had gone according to plan, he never would have set foot within miles of the stuff. Once Rollie was out, all Johnny had to do was place an anonymous call and tell them where to look."

"Eloquent," Black agreed. "A goddamned eloquent plan . . . if Johnny hadn't gotten greedy."

"*Eloquent?*" Dana asked.

"He means *elegant,*" I explained.

Black glared at me. "That's what I said. It's a damn elegant plan. Till Hamilton offered that reward."

I turned to Schuster. "Does anyone else know about this? Anyone?"

"Johnny—that's all."

"What about the people who helped him break into the lab?"

"They wouldn't know . . . Johnny planned carefully . . . went into the freezer alone. The others watched the doors . . . drove. Helped him carry out a canister of nitrogen . . . no semen."

"One thing I don't understand . . . what makes Ham's collection so damned valuable?" I asked.

Schuster shrugged his narrow shoulders. "My expertise is . . . reproductive theory . . . not practice. . . . Ask Hamilton."

"Ron Overton's dead. Murdered. Did you know?" I asked.

He stiffened. "Hamilton's man?"

"Yeah. Someone brained him with a shovel. Any idea why anyone would want him dead?"

Schuster shook his head, speechless.

I stepped closer and knelt in front of his chair. We were face-to-face, eyeball to eyeball. "No one knows you were involved in this, Burke. No one but us and Johnny. And Johnny's not talking. It has to stay that way. Otherwise we can't protect you."

He hesitated. "I wish to die here . . . at home. Not . . . in prison."

"No one is going to lock you up—as long as you don't tell another soul what we've just discussed."

"Of course," he whispered.

"We'll find a way out of this, Burke," Dana promised.

He patted her hand. "I pray you do."

"Do you need anything before we leave?" she asked.

He looked at me. "The things I said . . . last night. I knew I'd be exposed—eventually. But I expected the FBI . . . someone from Washington. Not . . ."

"Not a goddamned carpenter!" I said, finishing the thought for him.

He shook his head. "A builder, Ben. A builder."

I met his eye. "Understood, Burke. I'll come see you when we get this straightened out. You can apologize formally."

"It will be . . . my pleasure." He nodded, looking strangely relieved—of a private hell he no longer faced alone. "Now go. I'm fine. Just tired. Very tired . . . want to rest."

■ ■ ■

In the car, I looked at Black. "You know what we have to do?"

"Ain't lookin' forward to it."

"What are you two talking about?" Dana asked.

I turned to face her. "We're going to steal Ham's collection—for the second time."

She stared at me. "Are you kidding? Why not just tell Partone where it is? We can leave Burke out of it. Partone doesn't have to know how we found the collection—it won't matter. He'll pick up Rollie and this will all be over."

I shook my head. "Even if I trusted Partone, which I don't, Rollie's no fool. He's down there on his yacht, waiting to hear from me. You think it's a coincidence that he's in the Bahamas, out of Partone's reach? Hell no! If Partone put out a warrant for Rollie, how long do you think it would take that fat son of a bitch to hear about it? How long before his yacht puts out to sea and Rollie turns up in South America? or Mexico? or the South Pacific? One phone call from anywhere in the world and his people are on our doorstep."

She looked shaken. "Why the hell did they let him out of the country in the first place?"

"I'm wonderin' the same thing," Black said.

"I can't answer that," I admitted. "Maybe he told them the collection was stored offshore—that he had to go and get it. Maybe he negotiated an unconditional release and they had no grounds to stop him. Who knows why the feds do what they do? The only thing that matters to us is that Rollie's out there . . . until we reel him in."

"And to do that, we need to steal the collection," Dana said.

I reached for her hand. "Exactly! It's the only thing we have to trade. We have to have it in our possession; otherwise, we're no longer needed. We're expendable."

She thought about it.

"I don't want to be expendable," she said, after a while.

"That makes two of us," Black chimed in.

We drove a few more miles in silence, then Dana asked, "How much did you give Manny Sharp?"

"Five thousand," I answered.

"That leaves forty-five. That would be more than enough."

"For what?" Black said.

She wasn't listening.

"I wonder how long it's been since they topped off the liquid nitrogen in the canisters," she said.

Black and I looked at each other.

"Why?" I asked.

She explained.

44

THERE was a lot to do and time was short. We had a pretty good idea of how, but we still didn't know why. So Dana elected to stay home and study Ham Hamilton's breeding ledger while Black and I went truck hunting.

Only finding someone willing to paint a logo onto a rental truck on a Saturday afternoon isn't as easy as it sounds. We were standing on the lot of the U-Haul center on Buford Highway, trying to decide what to do next, when Black said, "Maybe we need to do this the old-fashioned way."

"What's the old-fashioned way?" I asked, watching a young couple fit a towing hitch onto the back of a jeep.

"Forget Hertz and U-Haul—all that yellow and orange shit. Nobody wants to paint over one a them. Let's just borrow a truck from someone who doesn't need it. Fella I know over on Stewart Avenue'll paint it for us. Won't cost much at all."

I raised my eyebrows. "Borrow?"

"Sure. We return it when we're finished."

"You got a lender in mind?"

"Let me make a couple of calls." He flicked open his cell phone.

A few minutes later he hung up on someone named L.L., dialed another number, and spoke with someone named Maurice. Then he pocketed the phone and smiled at me.

"Done. I got us an eighteen-footer with a lift gate, almost new. I'm supposed to pick it up at three-thirty. I'll take it over to Maurice, my paint man—be dry and ready early Monday morning."

I looked at my watch, not quite noon. The day was bright and cool, but I didn't feel up to waiting around for Black's friends. All I wanted to do was go home and get some sleep. "Why can't we just pick it up now? Get this over with?"

Black frowned. "That'd be a problem."

"Why?"

"Well, it's like this—the truck we're borrowing, it's in use right now. But my man L.L. is gonna go and get it as soon as all the meat and shit is delivered."

"Meat and shit?"

"Don't worry, Ben," he said, putting an arm around my shoulder and steering me toward his car. "No big thing. It's a large company—won't even miss the damn truck till sometime Monday morning. And by then, we're almost through with it."

I stopped, stared at him. But he pulled me along in his wake.

"Don't sweat this, Ben. I got it covered. Let's get you home. Dana can sketch out that logo for me, and you can lay your ass down and get some shut-eye. Gonna need you rested and ready to go."

I started to argue, but in the face of our present circumstances, grand theft auto seemed like the least of our worries.

45

THE telephone woke me at four in the afternoon. I'd fallen asleep on the couch in the den to the rattle of the radiator and the muted sounds of kids laughing and playing out in the street.

It was Partone, sounding angry.

"What the fuck do you mean he hasn't called you?" he shouted. "You want me to come over there and call him myself? You think this is a fucking game?"

I held the receiver a few inches from my ear. "I meant what I said. Rollie hasn't called yet."

"I swear to God, Hemmings, I'm this close to putting you away. Don't mess with me, 'cause I'm in the mood to do it. You reading me?"

I took a deep breath, tried to slow my racing heart. "You want me to call him—try to get him to make me an offer?"

"You do that. And you do it right. 'Cause I've about had it with you—you and your goddamned nigger. I'm ready to wrap this up. I want results. I want that collection. You get it for me now or say good-bye to everyone you care about, 'cause you're going away."

He hung up, but not before a spreading pain took root behind my eyes.

Dana came into the den. "Who was that?"

"Partone. He wants this thing wrapped up."

"He just might get what he wants. Look at this." She

plopped down on the couch, pushing the breeding ledger at me. "Take a look. Ron Overton was right—these dates are screwy."

I glanced at the ledger entries, then rubbed my eyes.

"Don't you see it? Here's the problem. This column lists the date of each live cover in Ham's breeding program. Here's the sire's name, the mare's, the foal's." She ran her finger down the page. "Something's not right with these dates."

"What exactly is a live cover?" I asked, my mind still on Partone.

She rolled her eyes. "It's a polite way of describing what happens when a stallion covers a mare. Sounds better than—"

"I get the picture," I said, interrupting. "What's wrong with the dates?"

"The dates are wrong. Not all of them. There are twelve pregnancies. Not bad, for eighteen covers. But four of the twelve, a third of the mares, delivered late. Statistically, that's a lot."

"Why would it matter?" I asked, my headache growing tentacles, squeezing.

"Normal gestation for a horse is around three hundred thirty-three days, not quite a year," she said. "For a Thoroughbred racer, when you're born matters a lot. Breeders want a January or February foal, so they plan cover for mid-February through early March."

"Okay." I shrugged. "But what's it got to do with Ham?"

"Everything. The Jockey Club rules are based on the calendar year, not the date of a foal's birth—so you race as a yearling after your first January. If you're born in February, that means you're eleven months old when you start racing as a yearling, almost two years old when you finish. If you're born in October, you're only three months old when your yearling season begins. A January foal has a huge advantage. More time to grow and train. A better chance to win."

"And Ham was screwing around with the dates? Trying to claim January foals that were born earlier?"

"No." She shook her head. "It's more complicated than that. These four foals that dropped late, they were born at the end of February, only four weeks late. They still would have been January foals. But for four out of twelve foals to drop late, and all of them almost exactly a month late, that's odd. Damned odd."

"How often do mares come into season?" I asked, trying to work out the numbers.

"Every twenty-one to twenty-eight days."

We sat and thought about it, then Dana looked at me. "That's it! That's why they're all a month late. It's hard to believe, but I'd bet anything that's what Ham was up to. No wonder Ron Overton was upset about his reputation. If anyone found out . . ."

"Wait! Slow down. Explain."

"You can pinch off a pregnant mare—abort the fetus—she'll be ready to conceive again a month later. If you covered a mare live but didn't want her to carry that sire's foal, you could pinch it off. Then four weeks later, you could artificially inseminate her. The records would show a live cover, so the foal would be eligible to race. The foal would drop a month late, but that's no big deal; it happens. No one would question the sire unless there was a reason to look. Even then, all the records would show is an unusual pattern. Unless whoever was asking knew about the connection to Johnny Forchet."

I drew a deep breath, not understanding a thing she was saying. "Why would someone like Ham Hamilton breed a horse, then not want it to drop a foal?"

"Listen, Ben. It's simple—like Black said, it's elegant. Racehorses can be conceived only by live cover, no artificial insemination. But if you had access to the right semen samples—stuff like Johnny Forchet was buying—and you wanted to start a great stable and you didn't care that the listed sires of your stable were average horses, that's what you'd do. You'd record the live covers, pinch off the fetuses, then artificially inseminate using the illegal semen samples. Didn't you tell me Johnny Forchet had samples from Northern Lights, Secretariat?"

I nodded. "And according to Rollie, Johnny knew Ham. They'd met, talked about breeding."

"That's what I'm saying, Ben." Her face was flushed with excitement. "Maybe Ham was buying this stuff from Johnny Forchet, storing it at the lab, but telling everyone it was a collection of samples from show horses, hunters, jumpers . . . Who would argue with him? But if the samples really came from racehorses, and Ham was worried he'd be exposed . . . no wonder he's offering such a big reward for the return of the collection. If news of what he was doing got out, he'd be blacklisted. Completely disgraced."

This was pure speculation, but Dana was right—there was a certain elegance to the whole scenario. "If it's true, wouldn't there be a record of semen samples from Ham's collection leaving the lab? Wouldn't the dates correspond to the breeding ledger?"

She nodded enthusiastically. "Of course. I'll check it out."

There was another catch. "If Ham can't claim the real sires of his foals, what good does all this do him?"

"Winning!" she exclaimed. "It's all that matters to a man like Ham Hamilton. If he produces winners from matching average mares with average studs, he looks that much smarter than everyone else. A great judge of horseflesh—able to see possibilities that others overlooked. If he wins big, he starts a new dynasty."

"We're talking about Augustus Mills Hamilton—a goddamned pillar of the community. The man's above reproach."

She shook her head, her eyes a fierce shade of green. "Give me one other good reason he'd offer a five million–dollar reward for a collection that could only be worth a fraction of that amount."

I thought about it. There were too many points that converged at Ham's feet, too many opportunities to believe it was all a coincidence. And Overton's murder . . . would Ham go that far?

Live cover . . . a goddamned fancy term for screwing. And that was exactly what Ham Hamilton had set out to do—screw the entire racing establishment. His greed had set all of this in motion—his vast arrogance. And now my family was paying the price. I felt the anger rise slowly up into my belly, a cold hard knot.

"If we're right about this—if Ham did what you say he did—he might be easier to deal with than I'd thought," I said.

Dana nodded. "*If* we're right, Ham will do just about anything to get his collection back."

I settled deeper into the couch, my headache a throbbing symptom of the anger I barely held at bay. I hadn't thought much about the reward—hadn't wanted to think about it. This wasn't my game. All I wanted was out.

But they were the ones making up the rules . . .

"Ben," Dana said. "The other night, after I met with Maggie . . ."

I shushed her. "It's okay. You needed space. That's good enough for me."

"That's not what . . ." She started to say something, then stopped, looking more than a little worried.

"Let it go," I insisted, thinking I was doing her a favor. "We'll deal with it when this is over."

Then I closed my eyes, visions of the five million dollars swimming inside my head.

Why not?

We knew where the collection was . . .

We knew what it was . . .

All we had to do was go and get it.

46

FROST lay heavy on the front lawn Monday morning when Dana left for the lab.

I watched her drive off in the Suburban, then wandered around the empty house, nervous and irritable, Partone's threats still echoing through my head. Drinking too much coffee, I paced while the hands on the clock took their own sweet time crawling closer to nine.

Then I cut through the Sloans' yard without incident and met Black.

True to his word, he pulled to the curb in a truck, the sides freshly painted with an official-looking logo that read, UNIVERSITY OF GEORGIA—DEPARTMENT OF ANIMAL SCIENCES.

He had on blue coveralls, a baseball cap pulled low on his head.

"Brought you a pair of coveralls and a clipboard," he said, pointing to a brown paper bag on the passenger seat of the truck. "You can be the supervisor."

"Thanks," I said. "Just what I always wanted to be—your supervisor."

He laughed. "The white man's curse—always gotta be the boss."

While he drove, I slipped on the coveralls. "You know where we're going?"

"Yup. Got the map Dana drew us—and the diagram of the lab," he said, indicating the clipboard. "First we pick up the tank. Traffic's not too bad, we should hit the lab around ten."

I checked my watch, and nodded.

He pointed the truck west and we drove cross town to the North Georgia Bottled Gas Company depot on Howell Mill Road. The loading dock foreman, a big, bald guy named Steve, showed us where to park. "New truck, huh? You guys new, too? They usually send Ethan or Frank."

"Ethan's off today," I explained, "and Frank's got the flu."

"Goin' around this time of year, I guess. Wait here. I'll get your order." He disappeared into the warehouse.

A few minutes later he wheeled out a fat silver cylinder bolted to a steel dolly. "Here you go, a GP-45. Filled her myself; tops off a little over forty-five hundred cubic feet. Got the order this morning—some new chick at the lab called it in. Name's Dana. Sounded kinda hot."

"She's jiggy, man," Black agreed. "She da' bomb."

He caught my eye and winked.

"How much does this thing weigh?" I asked Steve, doing my best to ignore Black.

"Better than three hundred and fifty pounds—try not to drop it." He patted the side of the tank. "And keep her away from direct heat. The liquid nitrogen warms up, it'll build pressure."

"This thing could explode?" Black asked.

"Nah. Nothin' like that. Long as you don't get any on you, it's just a matter of bleedin' off the excess pressure. Pain in the ass."

"You mind showing us how to work it?" I said.

"Nothin' to it." He demonstrated the pressure valve, the safety valve, and the transfill valve that connected to the transfill hose, a braided stainless-steel tube through which the liquid nitrogen was dispensed.

I glanced at Black to make sure he was following all of this.

He nodded. "Nothin' to it."

"Make sure you have the hose pointed where you want the nitrogen to go, then turn this," he said, cracking the transfill valve. The tank made a spooky wailing sound as the stainless-steel hose contracted until it was cold enough for the liquid gas to flow through. Thick white vapor spewed out, followed by a trickle of clear liquid that evaporated into an even thicker cloud as soon as it hit the concrete floor of the dock.

"Will it flow faster if the valve is all the way open?" I asked him.

"It'll take a couple of minutes for the transfill hose to cool down, then it'll flow plenty fast."

"Looks simple, you ask me," Black observed.

"Simple, as long as you take your time," Steve warned, closing the valve and handing Black a thick pair of insulated mittens. "Get this stuff on your skin, it'll burn hotter than fire. Exposure for a second, maybe two, it'll freeze the skin all the way through. Dip your hand in for four seconds, then hit it with a hammer, it'll shatter."

"Who the hell is gonna try something like that?" Black asked, shaking his head.

The foreman shrugged. "Just be careful, huh?"

"Let's get her loaded," I said.

Once the tank was secured in the back of the truck, we headed for the lab.

"These gloves somethin' else," Black observed, holding up one of the thick mittens.

"Watch where you're going," I said. "Last thing we need is an accident."

"Chill, Ben. We under control. This thing gonna be like takin' candy from a baby."

47

THE lab was located in Alpharetta, not far from Ham Hamilton's farm. Ham actually owned the secluded property, three acres of wooded land fronting Hopewell Road. The building itself wasn't much to look at: a sprawling one-story yellow brick structure the size of a big ranch house, a covered walkway connecting the lab to a functional barn behind which stood two fenced paddocks.

The paddocks were empty today, a cold breeze stirring the oaks. Our Suburban was parked at the side of the lab next to an old station wagon and a red Jeep. A white van sat in the shadow of the barn. According to Dana, three lab techs, all grad students, would be working inside the main building. The night watchmen didn't report for work until late in the afternoon. That gave us plenty of time to top off the storage canisters. We'd work under Dana's direct supervision. If asked, she'd say Maggie Dennison had given the order before leaving town. Once we were in the freezer, we planned to fish Ham's collection out of the bovine canister—segregate his straws and place them in one of the smaller shipping canisters the lab routinely used for out-of-state clients. The shipping canister would leave with Black and me. Dana would handle any questions. A simple plan. Nothing complicated about it.

Black pulled the truck into the asphalt driveway and parked in front of the main entrance. "Ready?"

I picked up the clipboard, studied the diagram Dana had drawn of the lab's interior, took a deep breath. "Let's do it."

We unloaded the silver tank, wheeled it right through the front doors of the lab. Moving purposefully, we pushed it across the cracked linoleum floor of the reception area toward the swinging doors that led to the actual laboratory and the walk-in freezer.

A young kid sitting behind the front desk, shouted, "Hey! Where do you think you're going?"

Black and I stopped, the tank between us.

"We got a delivery," I explained.

The kid hustled around the desk. He was pale and lanky, wearing a white lab coat, his glasses thick, his beard thin. "You can't just come through here with that."

"No?" Black said.

I lifted the clipboard, made a show of studying it. "I got the order right here."

"Well, something's wrong. I topped off the tanks last week," the kid said.

I looked at the clipboard again. "I dunno—it says here I'm supposed to deliver today. You in charge?"

The kid hesitated.

I shrugged. "Someone named Maggie Dennison placed the order last Friday. Can't leave without her authorization."

"*Dr.* Dennison?" the kid asked. "She knows I filled the tanks. She saw me do it."

"Beats the hell out of me," I said. "Why don't you check with her?"

"She's out of town—I'll tell her assistant. But this isn't *my* mistake." Shaking his head, the kid stepped back around the desk and picked up the phone.

We hadn't planned on this.

Black looked at me.

"We're going to have to improvise," I whispered.

While the kid made his phone call, hopefully to Dana, I checked out the reception area. A couple of vinyl couches facing each other; half a dozen scientific journals strewn across a glass-topped coffee table. Not much in the way of comfort. Aside from a security camera mounted over the swinging doors—a tiny red light blinking on and off—the place hadn't changed much in the years since I'd come calling on Dana after we met at Ham's Christmas party.

A lifetime ago.

The kid hung up the phone and a minute later, the blinking red light on the security camera went out. Dana's job was to turn off the system.

Then she strode through the swinging doors, wearing her own lab coat, looking official as hell. "Ethan, what seems to be the problem?" she called to the kid behind the desk.

Ethan smiled at her, a loopy, infatuated grin. "I don't know whose fault it is, Dana. But the tanks are full. I did it myself. Come on, I'll show you."

She stopped him. "That's okay. I'm sure you're right."

"Of course I am," he said.

Turning to face me, she rolled her eyes. "There's obviously been a mistake, gentlemen. I'm afraid we'll have to make other arrangements."

"We don't have time to make other arrangements," I said emphatically. "We've got a schedule to keep. Look, I got the order right here." I held out the clipboard, thinking we were going to have to wing it—create some kind of diversion.

She took it, studied it carefully. "Well, whoever placed the order was wrong. The tanks don't need topping off."

Black frowned. "Somebody 'round here need to get themselves together. This damn tank no easy load."

"There's no reason to be rude to her," Ethan said, bravely sticking up for my wife.

"You'll have to leave," Dana ordered.

"Leave? Awww, for chrissake!" I said, raising my voice. "What the hell is wrong with you eggheads? Do this . . . don't do that . . . it's always somebody else's mistake. . . . We've been all over town this morning. You know how heavy that goddamn tank is?"

Dana picked up on what I was doing. Placing her hands on her hips, she raised her voice, too. "I don't give a damn if it weighs a ton. I want it out of here. Now!"

"I'm union, lady! You can't talk to me that way!"

"I'll talk to you any way I want. Get it out of here, now!"

Two more lab-coated technicians, a young man and a girl who looked no older than twenty-one, came through the swinging doors to see what was going on.

That made four of them, including Dana. The entire full-time staff of the lab.

I glared at her, then backed down. "Let's get this damned thing back on the truck," I told Black.

Under my breath, I whispered, "Spill it."

He nodded.

Together, we spun the tank around on its dolly. Only we pushed a little too hard, somehow managing to tip it onto its side. Our luck being bad, I accidentally opened the transfill valve at the same time.

"Goddamit!" I yelled, jumping back. "Look what you did!"

"Ain't my fault," Black shouted, as the tank started to make that wailing sound.

The eerie noise grew louder.

The stainless-steel hose coughed cold white vapor, then began writhing like a copperhead on hot pavement. Liquid nitrogen spurting, all smoke and noise, missing Dana's legs by inches.

I shoved her out of the way, snatched one of the gloves from Black and tried to grab the moving hose, nearly getting sprayed myself.

Then we all backed away, my brilliant diversion quickly spinning out of control as frigid white vapor obscured the reception area.

"Jesus Christ!" Dana shouted. "Someone help them."

"Gimme the glove," Black hissed.

e without getting doused, and tucked it into
at the liquid nitrogen flowed onto the floor

d.
e valve's stuck."
her techs instructed as Black pretended to
get too close."
ment," Ethan yelled.
ed behind the reception desk.
hickened to a roiling fog as liquid nitrogen
med a quickly evaporating puddle on the

ack.
see if they got another pair of gloves," he

her hand and said quietly, "The canister—

through the swinging doors, back to the

re stacked on steel shelves.
the back of the freezer.
lf was marked BOVINE/UGA.
We'll sort it out later," she said.
led it out of the freezer. The thing weighed
ds, but the adrenaline was pumping and it

area was shouting that the fire department

me to the back door, threw it open.

"After we leave, tell them you're sick—get home
said.

"I'll be there within the hour." She closed the door

I lifted the canister and trotted around to the corne
heart pounding like crazy.

I was about to head for the truck when a brown va
veway and pulled up in front of lab.

Cursing, I lowered the canister to the ground and
in a UPS uniform got out of the van and consulted her

She stretched, then walked around to the rear of th
doors. She rummaged around in there for what seem
oblivious to what was going on inside the building.

In the distance, a siren began screaming.

My heart started pounding even faster.

The woman lifted a small package and carried it to
lab.

As soon as she opened them, a chill river of nitrog

She backed away.

The siren was joined by a second one in a distant

It had to be now.

Lifting the canister, I ran around the building as f
that much weight and made a beeline for the back of

The UPS woman stared at me. "What's going on?

"Accident! Chemical spill. We're evacuating th
now!"

"Shit!" She looked at the package in her hands, th
van, jumped in, and sped away, tires squealing.

Within seconds, I had the canister stowed in the

Then I ran back into the lab to help Black stabili
tank.

As soon as he saw me, he twisted the transfill va
long enough," he whispered. "Probably get cancer fro

I did.

He managed to grab the hose without getting doused, and tucked it into the steel frame of the dolly so that the liquid nitrogen flowed onto the floor in a directed stream.

"Turn it off!" Ethan screamed.

"Stuck!" Black shouted. "The valve's stuck."

"Watch out!" one of the other techs instructed as Black pretended to struggle with the valve. "Don't get too close."

"Someone call the fire department," Ethan yelled.

All three of the techs retreated behind the reception desk.

Within minutes, the vapor thickened to a roiling fog as liquid nitrogen spewed out of the hose and formed a quickly evaporating puddle on the reception area's floor.

"You okay?" I shouted to Black.

"Can't turn this valve. Go see if they got another pair of gloves," he shouted back.

"I'll get them," Dana called.

The fog rose higher.

In the confusion, I grabbed her hand and said quietly, "The canister—where is it?"

She hesitated, then led me through the swinging doors, back to the walk-in freezer.

Inside, dozens of canisters were stacked on steel shelves.

"There!" She was pointing to the back of the freezer.

A canister on the bottom shelf was marked BOVINE/UGA.

"Just take the whole thing. We'll sort it out later," she said.

I grabbed the canister, wrestled it out of the freezer. The thing weighed seventy-five, maybe eighty pounds, but the adrenaline was pumping and it felt lighter.

Someone out in the reception area was shouting that the fire department was on the way.

"Hurry!" Dana urged. She led me to the back door, threw it open.

"After we leave, tell them you're sick—get home as soon as you can," I said.

"I'll be there within the hour." She closed the door behind her.

I lifted the canister and trotted around to the corner of the building, my heart pounding like crazy.

I was about to head for the truck when a brown van turned into the driveway and pulled up in front of lab.

Cursing, I lowered the canister to the ground and watched as a woman in a UPS uniform got out of the van and consulted her watch.

She stretched, then walked around to the rear of the van and opened the doors. She rummaged around in there for what seemed like a long time, oblivious to what was going on inside the building.

In the distance, a siren began screaming.

My heart started pounding even faster.

The woman lifted a small package and carried it to the front doors of the lab.

As soon as she opened them, a chill river of nitrogen vapor flowed out.

She backed away.

The siren was joined by a second one in a distant chorus.

It had to be now.

Lifting the canister, I ran around the building as fast as I could carrying that much weight and made a beeline for the back of the truck.

The UPS woman stared at me. "What's going on?" she called.

"Accident! Chemical spill. We're evacuating the lab. Better get out now!"

"Shit!" She looked at the package in her hands, then hurried back to her van, jumped in, and sped away, tires squealing.

Within seconds, I had the canister stowed in the rear of the truck.

Then I ran back into the lab to help Black stabilize the liquid nitrogen tank.

As soon as he saw me, he twisted the transfill valve closed. "Took you long enough," he whispered. "Probably get cancer from breathin' this shit."

"You'll be fine. Just help me get it out of here."

The fog started to clear as the last of the liquid nitrogen on the floor evaporated.

"That was close," the female tech complained indignantly, while Black and I struggled to right the heavy tank. "Someone could have been seriously injured."

"An accident. It wasn't our fault," I said, wheeling the tank towards the doors. "The thing is busted. No harm done."

"Your supervisor is going to hear about this," Dana threatened.

The four of them followed us outside into the bright fall morning, glaring angrily while Black and I pushed the tank onto the truck's lift gate.

We were pulling out of the driveway as the first fire truck appeared on the scene.

Then we were out of there, headed for home.

Like taking candy from a baby . . .

48

TWO hours later, Dana wasn't home and I was getting goddamned worried.

"Try the lab again," Black suggested.

I dialed the phone number, then hung up. "Still busy. I'm telling you, something's wrong—she should have been home by now."

He frowned. "What do you want to do?"

"I'm not sure."

We were sitting at my kitchen table, the bovine canister on the floor by the refrigerator. Our next move was critical. We'd been over it step by step, without the benefit of Dana's input. I checked my watch for the hundredth time in what seemed as many minutes. Not quite one o'clock. Black had had time to return the tank of liquid nitrogen, wipe down the truck for prints, get it back to his friend L.L., then drive his own car back here. But Dana hadn't shown, and she hadn't called. What the hell was keeping her?

"Try the operator; see if the phone's out of order," Black said.

"It's not out of order. They used it to call the fire department."

"Call," he insisted. "Ask for verification."

I did.

A clammy finger twisted down my spine as the Bell

South operator matter-of-factly said that there was indeed trouble on the line and that she would report it.

I slammed down the phone and headed for the hall closet. "We're going back out there."

"What about the canister?" Black asked.

"Put it in the den," I called, "out of sight."

Then I pulled my pea coat out of the closet, checking to see that the nine millimeter was still in the pocket.

■ ■ ■

The front doors of the lab were locked. I cupped my hands around my face and tried to peer through the glass, but nothing inside was moving—nothing looked disturbed.

Black followed me around the building to the back door. It stood slightly ajar.

We looked at each other.

"I don't like it," he whispered, his face set in a grim frown. A gun appeared in his right hand. I hadn't realized he was carrying one.

I pulled my own gun and jacked a round into the chamber. My heart was banging around inside my chest.

"Let's go in," I said, pulling open the door, every instinct I had screaming that something was wrong, very wrong.

Stepping quickly through the deserted lab, we checked the walk-in freezer, the reception area, the small offices. The place was empty—silent. Nothing stirred. No sign of violence, no evidence that anything bad had happened here.

"Fuckin' spooky," Black said. "Where the hell did everyone go?"

"I don't know."

Outside, we circled the buildings.

Dana's Suburban was still parked on the south side of the lab next to the Jeep and the station wagon.

"You think they left together in the van?" Black asked.

I was about to say it beat the shit out of me when a muffled bang startled us.

It came from the barn.

We ran in that direction.

Without hesistating, Black shoved the door open and darted inside, his gun extended in front of him.

I was half a step behind him, nerves stretched tight, expecting the worst.

Only the barn was empty.

Almost . . .

A large bay kicked the side of his stall, the same bang we'd heard a minute earlier. The big stallion, the only horse in the barn, was spooked. He snorted, kicking out again.

"Easy, boy," I said softly, checking the unoccupied stalls around him.

Black moved toward the opposite end of the barn.

"Ben!" he shouted a few seconds later. "Get over here. Quick!"

My stomach lurched at the tone of his voice.

He was standing upright outside the last stall, staring inside. Before I reached him, he pocketed his gun.

The three lab techs lay on the floor of the stall. Two of them were bound with duct tape and gagged—they were wide eyed and terrified. The third, the young girl, hadn't been bound or gagged. They hadn't needed to restrain her. She'd been shot in the chest. Her blouse was torn to the waist, her small breasts stained with blood. The tip of her tongue protruded from her mouth, a look of surprise etched forever on her unblemished face.

Dana wasn't with them.

Ethan made a strangled grunt.

I pocketed my gun and tore off his gag. "Who did this?"

"Thank God!" he spluttered, sucking deep draughts of air. "They killed Anna—I didn't think anyone was coming."

"Dana! Where's Dana?" I asked.

He looked up at me, recognition dawning. "You're—"

"Never mind that! My wife—where's my wife?"

"Dana—your wife? They took her. They tied us up and—"

"Who?" I roared. "Who took her?"

"There were three of them. A fat older guy, another one with tattoos on his arms, he shot Anna—and—"

"When? How long ago?" I ripped the tape off his wrists.

He grimaced. "An hour, maybe less. They came in as soon as the firefighters left. Why? Why'd they do this?"

I started for the barn door. "We've got to hurry," I shouted over my shoulder at Black.

He was already moving.

"What about us?" Ethan cried.

"Finish untying yourselves and call the police."

Then we were in Black's car, headed for the highway.

"Faster!" I said. "We have to get back to the house. Give me your cell phone."

He tossed it to me.

While he drove, I dialed Partone's number. Got a machine.

"Partone! This is an emergency! I've got the collection, but Rollie has my wife. I need help. Now! Get over to my house as soon as you can."

"Hurry!" I urged Black, breaking the connection. "Drive faster."

I dialed information, found the local number for the FBI, but the woman who answered refused to patch me through to Special Agent Partone, connecting me instead to his voice mail.

I left a similar message, hung up, dialed the house.

No answer.

My chest felt like it was wrapped in steel bands; I could barely breathe. So smart . . . I'd been so goddamn smart about not being followed. For all the good it had done.

I clenched my fist and pounded the dashboard in frustration.

"It's gonna be all right, Ben. We'll give up the collection. That's what he wants—he can have it."

I glanced over at Black, knowing what the reward represented to him.

He laid on the horn, weaving back and forth through the congested lanes of GA 400.

I forced myself to think. When had Rollie returned from Nassau? Did he know we had the collection? Of course he did. But how? How the hell could he have found out so quickly? My mind was spinning. If he hurt Dana . . .

"She'll be okay," Black said, as though he were reading my thoughts. "Nothin's gonna happen till we give up the collection. They don't know where it is and Dana can't tell 'em."

"Where'd you hide it?" I asked.

"In the den, like you said. Stashed it under the skirt of that table by the window."

"They'll beat us there," I said, trying to keep the panic down. "If they find it first . . ."

"They won't," Black said, not sounding so sure. "When we get there, we deal. Rollie can have the shit. All we want to do is walk away."

"Right," I whispered.

Fifteen minutes later, we were there.

Black screeched to halt in the empty driveway and we ran inside.

No one was home.

49

BLACK and I searched the house to be sure.

The house was silent, empty. We were alone, the canister sitting exactly where Black had stashed it.

I dug out the phone number Rollie had given me and frantically dialed it.

No answer.

I tried again. Still no answer.

Then I paced the den like a caged animal.

"They'll call," Black assured me. "They got to call. We got what they want."

We had what they wanted, all right. But how would that keep Dana safe?

I wracked my brain for a plan, pacing back and forth, the panic bubbling up inside me. If nothing else, I had to get Dana out of this safely. But how? I thought about the female lab tech. They'd shown her no mercy.

Dana could expect the same—or worse.

A thousand horrifying images flooded my brain, most having to do with Dr. Dave. I could hardly breathe, much less think. I fought to get a grip on myself. *Slow down. Think it through. Rollie is calling the shots. How do I motivate him? What makes him tick? How can I get to him?*

There had to be something . . .

Suddenly, the answer seemed as clear as day.

The rough outline of a plan started to take shape in my head.

It wasn't a good plan. It wouldn't set things right. But maybe, just maybe, I could get Dana out of this. First, I had to convince Rollie that I was desperate enough to do anything. I had to control the exchange—Dana for the collection. And it had to be on my ground, a location that gave us an advantage. At least a fighting chance. The old barn at Edwina Cooper's place came to mind.

The longest half hour of my life passed, then the phone rang.

It was him.

"Ben!" Rollie began, sounding like it was a social call. "You did it. I never doubted you, kid. Great work. I guess it's time for you and me to have a heart-to-heart talk."

"Cut the crap, Rollie. I want Dana. And I want her in one piece."

"Sure you do. And you have something I want. Let's arrange a trade. Nothing complicated. Bring the collection and meet me at—"

"No," I said, interrupting. "I've seen your people in action. We're going to do this my way."

"Your way?" He was silent for a moment.

I could hear myself breathing.

Then Rollie laughed. "You fucking kidding me? You're going to dictate terms? Get real, kid. You aren't in a position to dictate anything. You want your wife, you do what I tell you. Understand?"

"Remember what happened to T, Rollie?"

He hesitated. "What about it?"

"You told me never to deal with someone who's got nothing to lose. They don't play by the same rules. You remember that?"

He didn't answer.

"I've been pushed as far as I'm gonna be pushed. I've got nothing left, Rollie. Nothing to lose. You hold all the cards, and I don't trust you. That cuts down on my options."

"You got no options," he growled.

"Oh, I've got options, Rollie. The way I see it, I could turn Ham's collection over to the feds. You might kill my wife. Hell, you might let Dr. Dave do that anyway. Only once the feds have Ham's collection, your deal is dead, too. They'll issue an arrest warrant. You can run, but for how long? What'll that do to your arrangement with Donny Devore? Those good ol' God-fearin' boys don't need an absentee partner, do they? Think about it . . . all that money down the drain . . . millions . . . for what? I'm willing to give you the collection. But we do it my way. If you want to deal, let me talk to my wife. I want to hear Dana's voice. Otherwise, we've got nothing more to talk about."

"Don't push me, Hemmings. You're in way over your head."

"Yeah. I'm fucking drowning, Rollie. But if I go down, I'm gonna take you with me."

He started to say something, then covered the phone with his hand and shouted to someone. His voice was muffled. I couldn't understand his words, but the anger was clear enough.

A moment later, Dana was on the line.

"Ben . . ."

"You okay?" I asked.

A sob caught in her throat. "Yes . . . I'm—I'm okay."

"Is anyone listening on another line?"

"I don't think so."

"Good. I'm going to give Rollie what he wants. It may not be enough. If it gets ugly, I want you to run. Run to the trees where we had that picnic. You'll understand when you get there. Don't look back, just run like hell. Promise me."

"Ben . . ."

"We don't have time, Dana. Promise me."

"Okay," she whispered, her voice soft and small.

"I love you, Dana. No matter what happens, I love you. Now put Rollie back on."

There was the sound of the phone being passed, then Rollie came back on the line. "You got some onions on you, kid. I'll give you that. Your wife's fine—you heard her. But if this goes wrong, she won't stay that way."

"It won't go wrong. You can have the collection—but we'll do it my way or we won't do it at all."

"I heard you the first time. What do you have in mind?"

"You know Dinson Road, out in Alpharetta?"

"I can find it."

"Bring Dana to the old Cooper place—she knows where it is. Meet me inside the barn. I'll be there with the collection in one hour."

I started to tell him to keep a short leash on Dr. Dave, but he'd already hung up.

Black was staring at me. "He agreed?"

I placed the phone back on its cradle. "He's overconfident—probably thinks it doesn't matter where we meet."

"He's probably right. You trust him to play it straight?"

"Not for a second."

"How do you want to handle it?"

"This isn't your battle, Black. Maybe it's time you got out of here."

"Bullshit! Rollie wants my ass, he damn well gonna have to take it."

I stared at him. "You sure?"

"I'm sure."

"Then we've got one shot at doing this right. There'll be three of them—Rollie, Dr. Dave, and Luther. Dana will be close to Rollie; that's how he operates. As long as he's got her under control, he figures we won't do anything. He'll use the other two to muscle us. We've got to make it a little more difficult than that, give Rollie an easy choice: take the collection and let Dana go . . . or chance losing it all."

"I got something in the trunk of my car might catch all their attention," Black said.

I grabbed him by the shoulders, wanting to tell him how I felt. All I managed was a hoarse "Thank you." It sounded hollow and inadequate and I promised myself that if we managed to pull this off, I'd somehow thank him properly. But *if* was too big a word, and there were too many things that could go wrong.

Together, we retrieved the canister from where Black had hidden it under the skirt of the table next to the radiator. I grabbed my tool belt from the peg by the back door and we hurried out to Black's car.

Then we were headed north, racing through the autumn afternoon to beat Rollie and his crew to the old Cooper place.

As Black drove, I called Partone's machine again—left another message, this time telling him where I was meeting Rollie and why. "We'll be at the barn in ninety minutes," I added. "Bring help."

"We'll be there a lot sooner than that," Black said when I hung up.

I nodded. "Once Partone gets there, any chance we have of cutting a deal with Rollie goes out the window. But if we can't deal with the bastard, I want Partone there with plenty of backup."

"You think ninety minutes is enough time?"

"Unless Partone knows where the Cooper place is, it'll take him that long to find it," I said, hoping I was doing the right thing, that I hadn't cut things too close.

50

BLACK and I beat Rollie to the Cooper place by a good twenty minutes, long enough for us to wrestle the canister up the rickety ladder to the hayloft and hide it under a loose pile of damp hay. Then, I walked Black through the barn, giving him a rough idea of how it would go down, assuming Rollie took the bait—namely, me.

Black pointed at the tool belt slung over my shoulder. "You planning on doing something to these?" he asked, pushing against one of the barn's central beams. "'Cause you knock this place down, it's gonna fall on us, too."

"No time to rig anything fancy. Besides, it would take a lot more than these tools to knock this old place down," I said. "I've got something simpler in mind. First, let's move your car out of sight."

He glanced up at the ruined roof, spikes of sunlight piercing jagged holes like golden prison bars. "Good thing it ain't rainin'."

We moved his car into the thicket of live oaks, leaving the keys dangling in the ignition. If Dana got that far, I wanted her to have the means to get out fast.

Then Black produced a twelve-gauge riot gun from under a blanket in the trunk.

"This bad boy ain't nothin' nice," he commented, racking the slide as we hurried back into the barn, leaving the big double doors open behind us.

The sight of him holding that fat, blacked-out gun gave me a little confidence. But not much. We were on a fool's mission—our goal, to free Dana without getting killed in the process. Overconfidence was one mistake I didn't intend to make.

We went over the plan, if you could call it a plan, one more time.

"Say a little prayer," Black suggested, laying down the riot gun and checking the clip of his nine-millimeter. He jacked a round into the chamber before sticking the gun in his waistband. "Ask God to make sure we don't shoot no blanks today."

"Just wait for my signal," I said, my mouth dry. I stashed my own gun behind the nearest beam; I needed to appear unarmed, an easy target.

Black picked up his riot gun. "When this shit starts, stay low, Ben. This fucker'll knock down a damn tree."

I promised I would.

Then I took a hammer and a short pry bar out of my tool belt and started on the trapdoor of the root cellar.

It wouldn't budge.

Using the hammer, I pounded the pry bar deeper into the groove of the door and put all of my weight on it.

The trapdoor groaned, gave an inch—then stuck. The wood was swollen after years of exposure.

"Help me," I said.

Black lent his weight to the bar.

Together, we leaned into it. With a loud crack, it gave, swinging up and open, the rusty hinges shrieking.

We stood there, looking down into the dank space under the hay chute.

The biggest spider I've ever seen scuttled out. Something we couldn't see rustled in the shadows.

Black stared at me, his face as pale as a man that dark could turn.

I dropped my tools into the root cellar, and waited—not knowing what to say. Our plan depended upon this.

After a long moment, Black drew a deep breath. Then, without uttering a sound, he took up a position in the dark with the bugs, leaving the trapdoor barely cracked—invisible in the shadows, unless you knew exactly where to look—and ready to pop out the moment he was needed.

Courage isn't the absence of fear; it's doing what has to be done in spite of the fear. At that moment, I loved Black like a brother. I hoped I would be half as brave.

I looked around the hushed interior of the barn. One of the bats in the rafters squeaked, then settled down. The place felt strangely peaceful. Quiet. Still as an old graveyard. A good spot, marked by hard work and careful craftsmanship. I swallowed hard.

As good a place to die as any . . .

I thought about Olivia and Nadine—the day I'd told them I was going away, far way. Would I ever see them again? Taking Black's advice, I said a prayer, but it had nothing to do with shooting blanks. I closed my eyes and whispered a fervent prayer for my daughters and their mother—hoping just this once, that God was awake.

The rest was up to Rollie.

■ ■ ■

I didn't hear them arrive.

Luther simply appeared inside those big double doors, silent as a cat.

He blinked as his eyes adjusted to the light.

Standing in the center of the cavernous barn, well away from the hayloft and the hay chute, I faced him—heart pounding, unarmed, my hands held out from my sides.

"Turn around," he ordered, gesturing with his long-barreled revolver, his face impassive.

I did, a full three-sixty, my arms held high so that he could see I wasn't carrying a gun.

Then, seemingly satisfied that all was in order, he shouted, "Come on in!"

Dr. Dave marched into the barn first, brandishing a baseball bat, his eyes glowing hungrily. He was wearing Boris's cherished Rolex—a cannibal, happy to eat his own kind.

He was followed by Rollie and my wife. They stepped out of the sunlight together, a large automatic pressed against Dana's side.

"Check up there," Rollie ordered, pointing to the hayloft.

Dr. Dave climbed the ladder without letting go of his bat.

I held my breath.

"Nothing up here but a little hay. Not enough to cover a man," Dr. Dave called, starting back down the ladder.

Rollie looked at me. "You're alone, Hemmings?"

Ignoring him, I studied Dana. "You all right?"

Her eyes were swollen, her lower lip quivered. "They were waiting at the lab—they came in and . . . I'm so sorry, Ben."

I held her eyes. "You did fine. They want Ham's collection, that's all. We'll give it to them. There's nothing to be afraid of."

"Goddamned right you'll give it up," Dr. Dave growled, stepping in my direction.

Rollie waved him back. "You should have kept me informed, kid."

"She's got nothing to do with this, Rollie. Let her leave and I'll tell you where the collection is."

"It's not here?" he asked, that big automatic jammed hard against Dana's ribs.

"Do I look that big a fool?" I said.

"A fool? I'm not sure what you are, Hemmings. Why didn't you call me?" he demanded.

"We found the collection this morning—I haven't had a chance to call."

Rollie just stared at me, his blue eyes as cold and distant as the autumn sky. "I don't think so. I don't think you intended to call me at all."

I started to deny it, but he cut me off. "Why didn't you tell me about this Burke Schuster? Or Ron Overton?"

"Did you kill Overton?" I shot back, wanting to keep him talking, knowing instinctively that the longer Rollie kept his mouth moving, the better chance we stood of getting out of this alive.

"Why the hell would I kill Overton?" he was saying. "We had a conversation—only he didn't tell us anything we didn't already know. Besides, I was depending on you to find the collection. And you did. You did a damned good job. If the fire department hadn't shown up at the lab, we could have handled this without involving your lovely wife. But they were there as soon as you took off—lazy bastards sat around for nearly two hours. We couldn't leave until they did. By then, you were long gone. I thought your wife might come in handy when we caught up with you, so we took her."

"You killed an innocent girl in the process, Rollie."

He shrugged. "Collateral damage. I told you before—Dave doesn't think before he acts. Sometimes that's not such a bad thing. So far, I've kept him off your wife. How long that lasts depends on you."

I didn't rise to the bait. "How did you know about the lab in the first place?"

He laughed. "All that coming and going through your neighbor's yard—that was inspired. Foolish, but inspired."

"You followed me anyway?"

"Of course not. I just listened, Hemmings. That's all."

I must have looked confused.

"This is the age of electronics, kid. Your house is wired. Nothing to it. Took my people an hour while you were at the park with the kiddies. . . . Speaking of the children, how are they? Having fun in Albany?" His voice changed, became a low and threatening rumble. "Did you think for one minute I didn't know—that I couldn't reach out and crush you? All of you? Anytime I wanted? Who the hell do you think you're dealing with?! I know everything, you rat fuck! Every little detail! Now where's your partner? Where's old Black?"

Dana gasped. She'd been silent, but now she looked like she was about to scream.

I stared at Rollie, a hard lump forming under my breastbone, the blood roaring through my ears. He knew about Partone—the deal with the feds. There was no way this was going to end peacefully. I tried to keep the sudden surge of fear in check.

"Where's Black?" Rollie repeated, his voice a menacing growl.

I met his eye. "He went to dump the truck we used at the lab. Let's get this over with, Rollie—let Dana go and I'll give you the collection before the police come." I glanced at my watch, praying he'd buy what I was saying. "We've got about ten minutes."

He squinted at me, weighing the odds. "What police?"

"If you've been listening, you know," I said.

"Where's the collection?"

"Let her go," I repeated.

"Fuck that!" Dr. Dave shouted. "Let me get it out of him."

Rollie nodded. "Go ahead."

"No!" Dana cried.

Dr. Dave raised the baseball bat and moved toward me, followed by Luther.

This was it.

I stood my ground. They came on, grouped as close together as a covey of quail.

I waited . . . staring directly into Rollie's frigid eyes.

This time, he didn't wink.

When his men were within ten yards of me, I turned to Dr. Dave and shouted, "Count time!"

A command he couldn't ignore. He hesitated.

In that fraction of a second, Black was out of the root cellar, the riot gun leveled. At that range, he'd take both Dr. Dave and Luther down with one blast.

The balance had shifted. Not decisively, but now it was a stalemate.

"Let her go, Rollie," I said. "I'll get you the collection after she walks out that door."

"Kill the cunt," Dr. Dave muttered, dropping the bat.

I could smell the sweat on him from ten yards away. I looked into his muddy eyes, thinking of Lexa and the young girl at the lab—of my wife. Cold sweat ran down the back of my neck, the blood pounding hot and thick in my head.

I turned to Rollie. "Do it, and so help me God, you'll never find the collection."

Rollie's eyes locked on mine, his fist tightening on the gun.

I met his gaze.

Time seemed to stop.

"We've got a few more minutes, Rollie. Don't let this slip away. The collection's yours. The cops get here and it's out of my hands."

He hesitated.

"Business, Rollie. It's all business," I whispered.

He shook his big head, then took the gun away from Dana's side. "You surprise me, Hemmings. Maybe I underestimated you. But you're right, business before pleasure."

My knees felt weak, but I fought not to show it.

"You know what to do, Dana," I said, my voice not my own. "Go to where we picnicked."

She took a step away from Rollie.

"Go!" I shouted.

She hesitated.

"Get out of here!"

As she backed slowly away, Rollie called. "Now what, Hemmings?"

"I'll tell you what! Drop your weapons and hit the floor! All of you!"

It was Partone, standing framed in the barn doors—his gun drawn, pointed at Rollie. His arrival couldn't have been more poorly timed. Behind him stood Ham Hamilton—not exactly the backup I'd expected.

Everyone froze.

Except Dr. Dave. Moving faster than I could react, he grabbed me and spun me around. Holding me in front of him like a shield, he drew a gun from the small of his back and pointed it at Partone, his breath sour against my cheek, his knuckle white on the trigger.

Rollie reached for Dana and pulled her back to his side.

"On the floor!" Partone screamed, his gun aimed at Rollie's head. "All of you—now! You're under arrest." He was John Wayne, riding single-handed into the outlaws' camp. Only this wasn't the movies and he'd come in talking, not shooting.

"Mr. Hamilton . . . Agent Partone, I presume," Rollie said calmly, holding Dana between him and Partone, his own human shield.

Luther took a few quick steps to his right, putting some space between him and Black. Partone tracked him with his eyes, but his gun stayed trained on Rollie and my wife.

I stood rooted to the spot.

We'd been close. So goddamned close . . .

Now it was falling apart before my eyes and there was nothing I could do.

"Let's all take this slowly," Rollie said. "No one has to get hurt."

"Drop your weapons and get on the floor!" Partone screamed, moving closer to Rollie. "You've got ten seconds—then you're dead!"

Rollie didn't move, didn't even acknowledge Partone. "Ham—you don't mind if I call you Ham? You and Agent Partone are obviously working together, am I right?" When Ham didn't answer, Rollie continued. "Of course you are. Why else would you be here now? Did he promise to keep you informed, or was it more than that? Does he know about the collection? Is he going to make sure no one else ever has the chance to examine it? How much does an FBI man cost these days?"

"Shut up, asshole!" Partone shouted, a vein throbbing at his temple. "Five seconds!"

Rollie still ignored him, speaking only to Ham. "Whatever your arrangement, why don't you have a word with him? Explain that this is business. Maybe we can settle it without bloodshed—like gentlemen."

Ham looked back and forth between Rollie and Partone. But before he could speak, Partone shouted, "I have twenty federal agents on the way here. Give it up, Shore. Now. Before I blow a fucking hole in your fat face."

Rollie raised his eyebrows. "Ham?"

It was enough.

"Stop!" Hamilton commanded, stepping to Partone's side. "We don't want a bloodbath."

"I'll handle this!" Partone barked.

"No, Agent Partone, you won't," Ham said, reaching for Partone's gun arm, his voice now full of stern authority. "We have an arrangement. I want my collection back—quietly. The rest of this can be settled later. I'll see that you're properly rewarded."

"Rewarded how?" It was Black's voice, coming from the shadows to my left. He'd moved away from the root cellar while all the talking was going on.

Partone hesitated, glancing over to see who was speaking.

As he did, Dr. Dave shoved me out of the way and fired, catching Partone in the throat.

The agent crumpled to the floor, blood spurting.

The rest fragmented into slow motion.

Dana screaming. Rollie pushing her away, crouching, moving. Dr. Dave's face contorted with rage, his automatic sweeping at me in a slow arc.

My own gun hidden behind the beam.

Everything slowed.

That shiny automatic tracking from my chest to my face.

I stopped breathing.

The riot gun went off like a canon.

Dr. Dave flew back, his gun dropping out of his hand, a gaping wound where his chest had been.

The room exploded. Gunfire, punctuated by the heavy roar of Black's riot gun. Screams of anger and pain.

I tried to get to Dana, but something heavy slammed into my right shoulder, knocking me to the floor, my arm suddenly numb.

Then it was over as quickly as it had started.

A sudden ringing silence.

I struggled to my knees, searching desperately for Dana.

She was curled in a fetal position in front of the hay chute.

I crawled over to her, afraid to look. "Dana," I gasped.

She lifted her head—then sat up. "I'm okay," she said. But her eyes grew wide when she realized I'd been hit.

"It's not as bad as it looks," I said, praying I was right.

"Luther, over here!" Rollie shouted. He stood across the room, looking down at Partone's body, his big automatic in his hand.

Ham Hamilton stood near him, unscathed.

"Black!" I called, suddenly feeling sick, leaning back against the hay chute.

He didn't answer.

"By the ladder," Dana whispered. "They shot him."

My breath caught in my throat. "Bad? Is it bad?"

Then Rollie was standing over me, his gun pointed at my face. "Ham, we have a problem," he said, his voice strained.

Hamilton looked at him, shaken, but under control. "Yes. We do."

I didn't say anything. Blood ran hot down my right arm. The edges of the barn curled up on themselves, but I fought it.

Dana sat next to me, perfectly still, one hand clutching my leg.

Rollie pointed his gun at her head now. "Where's the collection, Hemmings?"

It was over, no plan, no angles. Nothing left to bargain with.

"In the loft," I whispered. "In the hay. Take it and go."

He turned to Luther, who was bleeding from a wound in his side. "Get it."

Then Rollie looked at Ham. "What do you think the boys at the Jockey Club will say when they hear the truth about what you've been doing? No way to keep it quiet. Not after this."

"You said we could settle it," Ham said. "What do you propose?"

Rollie smiled. "I propose we get the hell out of here. We can work out the details later. I don't care how well connected you are—you don't want to have to try to explain a dead FBI agent."

"What do we do about them?" Ham asked, indicating Dana and me. His eyes were flat, his voice emotionless. He might as well have been talking about a couple of nags that were no longer worth feeding.

"We kill them," Rollie said. "No witnesses."

Dana gasped.

Ham shook his head. "No more. I want my collection back. I don't want it badly enough to kill anyone. And without me, it's worthless to you."

"Don't be a fool!" Rollie snapped. "We can't leave them talking."

"No more killing," Ham repeated.

They faced each other, two men used to getting their own way.

Then, Rollie nodded. "Okay. We take *her.* Dana comes with us—an incentive to Ben to keep his mouth shut until we've established an alibi."

Ham said nothing.

Dana was beside me, breathing hard. "I won't go. Can't you see he's hurt?"

"You want me to kill him now?" Rollie asked.

Dana looked around, her eyes wild. But there was no where to go, no where to hide.

"We'll get out of this," I whispered.

But I didn't see how.

Luther lugged the canister over to Rollie and set it down. "This it?"

Rollie looked at Ham, who nodded.

"Go and get the van, Luther," Rollie ordered.

Ham was staring at the canister, a strange light in his eyes.

Rollie joined him, taking hold of one handle, testing its weight.

Then, he bent and picked up Dr. Dave's gun. He popped the clip out, emptied it, pocketed the shells, wiped the automatic clean, and tossed it onto the floor beside me.

"Pick it up," he instructed. "Pull the trigger a couple of times. I want your prints in the right places."

When I didn't respond, he pointed his gun at Dana again. "Are you two stupid? Do it, Hemmings."

I followed his instructions.

"Good." He beckoned to Dana. "Let's go."

"No!" I tried to rise, then stumbled, dizzy and sick.

Rollie shook his head. "Stay down, kid, or I'll kill you both now."

Dana stared at me, her face stricken. "I love you."

I couldn't speak.

"We're going to leave," Rollie explained to me. "Dana will stay safe as long as you keep Hamilton and me out of your story when the agents come. Understand?"

" . . . got to be kidding," I managed.

"Time, kid. I'm just buying a little time," he said. "No one else knows the collection was ever here. Once we leave, it's your word against Ham's. Who do you think they'll believe?"

"It . . . won't work."

Rollie frowned. "You want to see your wife again? Make it work. If I were you, I'd blame Dr. Dave and Black—an old prison grudge Partone walked in on. They won't contradict you. They can't. They're dead."

It took a second to sink in. I opened my mouth but the words dissolved in a haze of pain. I shook my head trying to clear it, my right arm on fire.

"No," I whispered.

But they no longer cared what I did or said.

"Give me a hand here," Rollie grunted.

He and Ham each took one handle of the canister and lifted it.

Then the three of them walked out of the barn.

Rollie gripping the handle of the canister with one hand, his gun in the other—Dana at his side, the muzzle pressed hard against the small of her back.

51

"GOT to be strong . . ."

The room was spinning. I was hearing things. I pushed up onto my knees, fought back the urge to vomit. Dana—she needed me.

"Strong . . ."

This time it was louder, coming from the base of the hayloft ladder.

I drew a deep breath, turned my head, wondering what it meant—thinking it was no good, hearing things.

Black stood clutching the ladder with one hand, weaving slightly from side to side. The front of his shirt was soaked in blood, more frothing on his lips.

"Like steel, Ben," he whispered.

"Black," I cried, making it to my feet.

"Stop him—got to stop him."

A gun dangled in his hand, too heavy for him to lift.

"Take it," he whispered. "Two rounds—got to stop. They'll kill . . ." He groaned, unable to say more.

I stumbled to his side, my right arm useless. Taking his gun in my left hand, I grit my teeth and bit back the nausea. The room tilted, the edges rippling. Strong, I told myself. Strong as steel.

I staggered out of the barn.

They were halfway across the barnyard to the waiting

van, Dana at Rollie's side. But the canister was heavy and he no longer held the gun pressed against her back.

Somewhere sirens screamed like a pack of angry animals.

Too far away.

"Stop!" I croaked.

They didn't hear me.

Behind me, Black made a wet choking noise. What kind of strength had it taken for him to follow me out here?

I didn't look.

Bracing myself against the barn door, I steadied the gun he'd given me and drew a bead on Rollie's back. But my vision blurred and there were two of him.

Squinting, I squeezed the trigger.

The round went high.

Rollie turned, surprised. He raised his gun.

This time I closed one eye. Aimed carefully and held my breath.

Then I squeezed the trigger again.

The gun jumped, the round thwanging loudly into the top of the steel canister.

A hissing cloud of vapor exploded up and out, followed by a thick gush of liquid nitrogen under pressure—a pale soaking fire.

Rollie caught most of it, a gallon maybe more, on the left side of his body and his face. He went down screaming, writhing on the ground.

Dana had been protected by his bulk and stood rooted, watching, horrified.

The canister lay on its side, thick vapor rising as the remaining liquid nitrogen boiled off.

I dropped Black's gun and stumbled across the barnyard to Dana. She took hold of me and clung tight. Neither of us spoke. There weren't words.

Ham rolled on the ground in agony. One side of his face and his right hand covered with a frosty scrim of ice. A high-pitched wail came from deep in his throat.

But Rollie had gotten the worst of it. A solid dousing. The hand that had held the handle of the canister had frozen solid, a useless chunk of gray frozen flesh on the end of his arm. He screamed in mortal pain, clawing with his good hand at his face, trying to wipe the liquid nitrogen off. Only it was too late. It had already evaporated, but the damage was done. His eyelids had frozen solid and cracked, revealing sightless opaque orbs. Chunks of gray-white frozen flesh broke off under his groping fingers. There was a toothy hole where his lips and mouth had been. At first there wasn't much blood, but as he thrashed and rolled and bellowed and tore at his flesh, the bleeding got worse.

Dana hid her face, sobbing. It was all I could do to stand and hold her.

The sirens drew closer.

"Help's almost here," I whispered.

She nodded.

Then, Luther was out of the van. Ignoring Ham, he looked down at Rollie for a moment, his gun at his side. Then he looked at us.

"Don't, Luther," I said.

"Ain't got a choice, Hemmings." He raised the gun, the muzzle a huge round hole in the world.

Dana cried out.

I tried to think of something to say or do to stop him—I shielded Dana with my body.

"Forchet was like kin to me," Luther said. "Till this sum'bitch went and had him killed. It was my intention to take that collection and the reward for Johnny's widow. Too late now."

Luther turned the gun on Rollie and fired twice, two bullets in the center of the big man's chest, stopping the bellowing forever.

I gaped down at Rollie's still body. A gust of wind tugged at his sleeve. This was what Ham Hamilton's brilliant scam had come to . . . nothing. No winners to fill his magnificent barns. No new dynasty. Just a long, cold silence.

"Hemmings!" Luther called.

I looked up, expecting to see his gun pointed at me.

There was nowhere to go.

It was over.

"Best do something 'bout that shoulder," he said, holstering his weapon.

I stared.

He spit a thick gob of tobacco juice onto Rollie's body, then turned, climbed into the van, and sped away.

I just stood there, unable to move. The sirens were close when I remembered Black.

"Help me to the barn," I said to Dana. "Hurry. Black's alive."

He was lying in a puddle of blood just outside the barn doors, his chest rising and falling in quick shallow breaths.

"Black," I called, falling to my knees and gathering his head into my lap, my own wound a scratch compared to his. "Hang in there. Help's almost here."

He opened his eyes. "We out, ain't we?" his voice a small whisper. "Don't want to die inside—not behind no wall."

"Yeah, Black. We're out. But you're not gonna die." I wiped the blood off his face and mouth.

He smiled. "Been down too long, Ben. Want to die free."

"You are free. I swear it, you're free."

"You did good." He shuddered. "Real good."

"Fight it, Black. You have to be steel." I bit back tears.

"Feeling like I been two people," he whispered. "Livin' two lives."

He shuddered again and the smile faded from his lips. He coughed a thick bubble of blood and his eyes rolled back in his head.

I shook him. "Breathe. Goddammit, breathe, Black."

Then the sirens and the uniforms and the EMTs converged, strong hands pulling me away from my friend.

"No!" I shouted, but I was sick and dizzy again. I couldn't be sure if I thought it or spoke it.

A crowd of tall people surrounded me, lifted me onto a gurney.

Then I was in an ambulance, looking up into Dana's concerned face.

"Black?" I asked.

She didn't answer.

The sting of a needle in the crook of my arm—a small man in a blue coverall talking urgently into a radio set.

"It's over, isn't it?" I said to my beautiful wife.

She squeezed my leg, tears tracking her cheeks.

But before she could say anything, it all folded up on itself and nothing hurt and I was floating.

52

THEY kept me in the North Fulton Medical Center for three days. The actual bullet wound wasn't that bad—what they called a through-and-through. But I'd lost a hell of a lot of blood. Almost enough to have died. Once I'd been patched and transfused, an endlessly exhausting stream of investigators lined up to interview me. Federal, state, and local. They took turns.

I told them what I knew.

Then I told it to them again. And again.

The feds threatened to throw me back into prison. So I sang louder. My suspicions regarding what was in Ham's collection fell on deaf ears. But the bit about Donny Devore fascinated them.

They searched out Grace and Lexa—tried without success to find Manny Sharp. Apparently, Luther Culbertson had disappeared, deep into the hollows of the Appalachian foothills where his people had lived for generations. Reluctantly, I gave them Burke Schuster. But he'd made his own choices and I wasn't about to take another man's fall. Not again.

The FBI diligently sought out any possible corroboration to the wild story I had told them. Not to save my ass. A young, shiny-faced, button-downed agent—the antithesis of Partone—let slip that Partone's investigation had been low priority, a one-agent sideshow, a favor called in from

Washington on behalf of Ham Hamilton, one of Georgia's largest political donors. They'd tossed out a small expendable net, hoping to snag Rollie Shore. Only they'd pulled in more than they'd bargained for.

Detective Jackson from the Fulton County Police paid me a visit. But his questions were perfunctory, and I got the distinct impression that solving Ron Overton's murder was no longer anyone's priority. They'd laid it off on Rollie.

"You're a lucky man," Jackson said on his way out. "I'm through with you, and from what I hear, the feebs are dropping your case, too. You're a free man. Try and keep it that way."

It took a while to sink in. And even then, I wasn't sure I believed it.

During all of the debriefings and interrogations, the only thing I'd held back was the fact that we'd planned to play Rollie against Partone and walk with the reward. Not that it was ever much of a plan. It was irrelevant now, anyway. There would be no reward. The collection had thawed and whatever was in those precious straws no longer mattered.

Except to Ham Hamilton.

Dana and I were waiting in my room on the day I was to be released, when Ham's lawyer, a man with pale hair, a long neck, and wire-rimmed glasses, knocked on the door. He was formal and polite, asking if I would please stop by Mr. Hamilton's room before leaving the hospital. It seemed Mr. Hamilton had an important matter he'd like to discuss without delay.

Black's big sister, Annalee, had driven the girls and Rose up from Albany that morning. I was eager to get home and be with them, but I had a few questions of my own, so I agreed to see Hamilton.

He lay bandaged, IV'd and angry in the burn unit. Most of his face was swathed in thick gauze. His right hand wrapped in a cocoon of fresh white cotton. A spray of dime-size depressed dark spots on his neck and shoulder had scabbed over. I'd heard that he lost two fingers and the tip of his nose to frostbite. What was left would be scarred for life. His eyes, however, were bright and hot above the bandages.

He dismissed the lawyer, his only visitor at the moment, and came right to the point. "You have something that belongs to me. I'll pay handsomely to have it back. Two hundred thousand dollars—no questions asked."

The foregone conclusion in his voice set my teeth on edge. I was still weak, my right arm immobilized, but I thought seriously about knocking some humanity into him.

Instead, I stood at the foot of his bed and said, "You really think I'd take your money?"

"Everyone wants my money, Hemmings. Two hundred thousand will get you up on your feet again. I'll throw in a commission for a new barn."

I stared at him. "First, tell me about Overton."

"What do you want to know about him?"

"Why you killed him."

Dana was standing beside me. I could hear her sharp intake of breath.

Ham's eyes burned. "I did not kill Ron Overton."

"But you know who did, don't you?"

"Don't be stupid. I made you a generous offer. What's done is done. Why complicate things?"

"You want that breeding ledger? Tell me what you know."

He closed his eyes, calculating what, I couldn't say.

Then he looked up at me. "I may have a vague idea, but it's the broadest sort of suspicion and if it ever leaves this room, I'll deny it."

"Go ahead," I said.

"We have a deal?"

"I'll decide after I hear what you have to say."

He didn't like it, but I didn't give him much choice. "I have in my employ a certain number of people who still believe in loyalty. Maybe they're a little old-fashioned in their thinking. If they perceived that I was being threatened, even indirectly, they might react on their own to try and diminish the threat." He paused, searched my face. "If one of these men suspected that someone close to me, someone like Overton, was speaking or acting in a manner that could embarrass or hurt me . . . he might be driven to take matters into his own hands."

"Jasper!" I blurted.

Dana stiffened. "Jasper killed Ron Overton?"

Ham was quiet for a few seconds. "Your words, not mine. Jasper worked for my father before I was born. He's retired now, gone to live with distant relatives in Jamaica."

"A little sudden, this retirement," I pointed out.

"Quite," Ham acknowledged.

"Jasper did it, didn't he? How else would you know I have the ledger?" I persisted.

Ham was silent.

"He did it so Ron wouldn't slip up and talk about your goddamned breeding program. And now you're protecting him. You bastard!"

"Watch your mouth, Hemmings! I'll take only so much from you."

"You'll take whatever I choose to give you."

He stared at me, doing a quick reappraisal. "The police are convinced that your friend Rollie Shore arranged for Overton's murder. They've already closed the file."

"You and I know better. Don't we?"

He ignored the jibe. "As for my breeding program, it's been shut down."

"Then why should I sell you the ledger?"

He misunderstood. "You bargain hard, Hemmings. I'll go to three hundred thousand. Not a penny more."

I looked down at him in disgust. "I wouldn't sell you the ledger for three million dollars. I think I'll give it away."

"How about the Jockey Club?" Dana said. "They might find it interesting."

He glowered at us. "It's my property."

"Then claim it in court," I said.

"Don't be a fool!" he snarled, his voice grown shrill. "Cross me and you'll never build another thing, Hemmings. I'll ruin you. I'll crush you."

All I could do was smile. "I don't think so. You had your shot, Ham. Now it's my turn."

He cursed me, but I was through listening.

I took Dana's hand and led her out of the room without looking back.

■ ■ ■

We had one more visit to make before going home to the girls.

Black was in the ICU, wired to monitors and connected by tubes to an evil-looking assortment of fluids in clear vinyl bags. He looked up and grinned weakly when we walked into his glassed-in room.

"You're lookin' fecund," I said.

He laughed, then grimaced. "No jokes. They cracked open my ribs—hurts to laugh."

"You're lucky to be alive," I said.

"Thank God you were there," Dana added, looking misty. "For what you did—I don't know how to put it into words. It was . . ."

"It was no big thing." he said, attempting to shrug her gratitude away.

"No big thing, my ass," I said looking for a place to sit. A big picnic basket occupied the only chair. "What's that?"

"Annalee brought me up a care package. But they won't let me eat it—no solid foods."

"Too bad. You know how to swing a hammer?" I asked, opening the top of the basket, rummaging inside.

"'Course I can swing a hammer. Question is, can *you* swing a hammer? 'Cause you don't look so hot."

"Me? I'm fine. I've been worrying about you."

"Shit! Ain't nothin' but a little flesh wound. Been meaning to tell you that was a fine shot. Quick thinkin', takin' out that canister. I shouldn't have left it so close to the radiator, huh?"

"I was trying to hit Rollie," I said, nonchalantly.

His eyebrows shot up. "Get the hell outta here!"

"I missed. Hitting the canister was luck. Blind luck. Thank God you hid it next to the radiator."

Dana groaned. "I wish you hadn't told me."

Black shook his head. "Blind luck . . . well, it put ol' Rollie's ass on ice—for good. Lotta people gonna sleep better with him gone."

Including me. "Listen, Black, I though maybe we'd go into business together. We can use what's left of Rollie's cash for seed money."

"Building barns?" he asked.

I shrugged and thought about Edwina Cooper. "Maybe . . . but we'll probably have to start with decks—renovations. Remodel a few bathrooms and closets—work our way up to bigger stuff."

"Decks? Bathrooms? You're talking nickels and dimes."

"Gotta start somewhere."

He looked up at the ceiling. "What are we gonna call this business?"

"Been calling it Hemmings Construction. You got something better in mind?"

"You know what the prettiest word in the English language is?"

I shook my head. "Tell me."

"*Freedom.* How 'bout Freedom Construction?"

"I don't know—sounds a little fancy to me."

"It sounds a helluva lot better than Hemmings Construction."

I raised my eyebrows. "I kind of like the name."

He shook his head. "Too whitebread. Could name it after both of us I guess—Black and Hemmings Construction."

"Why should your name be first? Hemmings and Glessing sounds better."

"Nobody calls me Glessing."

"Better than Black and Hemmings." I dug a biscuit and some country bacon out of Annalee's care package and started chewing.

Black frowned at me. "There you go with the damn pork again. I'm tellin' you, it'll kill ya."

We looked at each other.

Then I started laughing.

Black started laughing, too. In spite of the pain, he laughed so hard he cried. He held up his hand and I clasped it.

"Partners, man. Doesn't matter what we call it."

"Partners," I agreed.

■ ■ ■

We were alone on the elevator.

Dana took my hand and looked into my eyes. "We have some work to do."

I nodded. "Whatever you think will help. A therapist . . . counseling . . ."

"A therapist?" She shook her head. "I don't want therapy. I want the radiators fixed. The upstairs hall painted. We have listening devices planted in the living room!"

I drew her to me.

She tilted her head up and kissed me.

Her lips were soft and warm and I felt that pulling deep inside me, the tightening.

She pushed away and looked at me. "What's this? What are you carrying in your pocket?"

"That's not my pocket."

"Yeah . . . I know."

Laughing, she hit the emergency stop button, ignoring the alarm bell.

And I knew I was finally home.

About the Author

David Ramus is the critically acclaimed author of *Thief of Light* and *The Gravity of Shadows. On Ice* is his third novel. Ramus lives with his wife and four daughters in Florida.